Praise for Jeannie Lin

"Lin combines wit, seduction, skill and intelligence
in a tantalizing take on *My Fair Lady*."
—*Publishers Weekly*, starred review,
on *My Fair Concubine*

"Lin has a gift for bringing the wondrous
and colorful world of ancient China to readers….
Those yearning for new worlds and age-old adventures
will savor Lin's novel."
—*RT Book Reviews* on *My Fair Concubine*

"Drawing on a lushly depicted, exotic backdrop, Lin
creates an intriguing romance between well-drawn
characters whose secrets lure readers deep into the story."
—*RT Book Reviews* on *The Dragon and the Pearl*

"Beautifully written, deliciously sensual, and rich with
Tang Dynasty historical and political detail…exquisitely
crafted, danger-filled, and intriguing… Exceptional."
—*Library Journal, Romance Reviews*
on *The Dragon and the Pearl*

"If *Crouching Tiger, Hidden Dragon* merged with
A Knight's Tale, you'd have the power and romance
of Lin's dynamic debut."
—*RT Book Reviews* on *Butterfly Swords*

"Exciting debut…especially vibrant writing…"
—*Publishers Weekly,* starred review, on *Butterfly Swords*

"If you are looking for a rich, radiant story slightly
different than your standard fare, look no further….
A wonderful tale that leaves one
hungering for more by this author."
—*All About Romance* "Desert Isle Keeper" review
on *Butterfly Swords*

the Lotus Palace

JEANNIE LIN

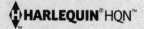

Recycling programs
for this product may
not exist in your area.

ISBN-13: 978-0-373-77773-0

THE LOTUS PALACE

Printed in U.S.A.

Dear Reader,

I first fell in love with the colorful culture of the infamous Pingkang li, also known as the North Hamlet, while writing the novella *Capturing the Silken Thief.* This entertainment district has a unique place in history, bringing about a literary culture that revolved around the specially trained women who served as companions, hostesses and fellow poets to the scholars and officials who frequented the quarter for business and pleasure. To simply call them "prostitutes" would be incorrect. To call them "courtesans" seems insufficient. The Western world occasionally refers to them as "Chinese geisha," a term that ignores the fact that China developed a rich and distinctive courtesan culture that predated the geisha culture in Japan. Chinese scholars have written numerous lines of poetry attempting to capture the complicated and multilayered nature of these clever, talented, elegant and fiery women.

At the same time, the Pingkang li was a place of contradictions. While scholar-gentlemen professed to be enthralled by the courtesans, ultimately these women were slaves. Despite their elevated status and illusion of independence, they were bought and sold as commodities.

The Lotus Palace explores the juxtaposition of this intricate social dance and the art of love versus the challenges of finding true romantic fulfillment. There is a reason so many classic Chinese love stories end in tragedy!

The Pingkang li, with its dual persona of sensual decadence and refinement, became the perfect place for me to explore the many roles that women took on in society, to investigate a murder most foul and to find true love.

To find out more about the drama and romance of ancient China, you can find me online at www.jeannielin.com. I love hearing from readers!

Sincerely,

Jeannie Lin

Acknowledgments

The Lotus Palace would not have been possible
without the help and guidance of
Bria Quinlan, Inez Kelley and Kate Pearce,
who are generous friends and talented authors.
As always, a special thanks to my editor, Anna Boatman,
for always pushing me to make the romance deeper and
more fulfilling. And to my agent, Gail Fortune.
I never thought we'd get this far,
but she has always believed.

the
Lotus Palace

CHAPTER ONE

Tang Dynasty China, 847 AD

AN UNSEEN FORCE threw Yue-ying from her pallet. The entire building shook around her and the rafters groaned until she was certain the Lotus Palace was going to be torn apart. Too startled to move, she crouched low with her hands over her head. They were all going to die.

Suddenly the shaking stopped. With her heart thudding against her ribs, Yue-ying gradually came back to herself. It was dark and she was on the floor in her sleeping area. The walls of the pavilion creaked around her as they settled.

Before she could catch her breath, the shaking started again. A cry of alarm came from outside the chamber.

It was Mingyu. Mingyu needed her.

Yue-ying struggled onto her hands and knees, while a sea of silk tangled around her. Mingyu's entire wardrobe had been tossed onto the floor. Yue-ying shoved the material aside and stumbled to the doorway, clinging on to it for balance.

There was no door between the two compartments. A gray light filtered in through the windows of the sitting area and Mingyu was standing at the center of it, her long hair wild about her face. She was dressed in her sleeping garment and the pale cloth coupled with elegant lines made her appear otherworldly. She looked more like a ghost than a woman.

Yue-ying started to go to her, but the building lurched again and she was thrown to her knees. Mingyu fell to the ground as well and they scrambled toward one another. In an uncustomary display of emotion, Mingyu embraced her, clutching her close while the walls shuddered around them. At any moment, the roof would come crashing down to bury them.

It was an eternity before the shaking stopped. Afterward there was absolute quiet; a funereal silence as the inhabitants of the Lotus Palace held their collective breath, waiting. She and Mingyu remained on the floor, holding on to one another and too afraid to move. Then the hum of voices began.

Mingyu let go of her abruptly and straightened, smoothing her hands over her shift. Her chin lifted with a regal air and she was the elite courtesan again.

Yue-ying tried not to feel discarded. She should be accustomed to Mingyu's changing moods after serving as her personal attendant for the past four years. Mingyu could be warm and engaging, affecting a smile that lit the room brighter than any lantern. When she was not surrounded by admirers, she would often become distant, lost in some inner world of her own making.

"Heaven must be displeased," Mingyu declared.

She peered out the window with a thoughtful and disturbingly serene expression. Mingyu had perfected that look. Even Yue-ying found it difficult to read her thoughts through it.

"That's only superstition," Yue-ying replied.

The ground wavered once more, as if in argument. Yue-ying pressed a hand to the wall to steady herself, while Mingyu stood tall and still, a fixed point amid the turmoil.

EARTHQUAKES WERE NOT uncommon in the capital city, though this was the most violent one Yue-ying had yet to experience. Everything that could fall had fallen. The dressing room where she slept was a disaster: silk robes were strewn all over the floor and the powder table had overturned, spilling pots and jars everywhere. She was lucky it hadn't fallen on top of her.

Madame Sun set the other girls to work clearing the parlors and banquet room downstairs. The Lotus Palace was one of the larger establishments in the pleasure quarter of the North Hamlet, also known as the Pingkang li. There were seven ladies, courtesans or courtesans-in-training, along with Old Auntie and Yue-ying.

The courtesans all called Madame Sun "Mother" and did whatever she told them. Even Mingyu, who was the most successful and thus most favored of the "sisters", never disobeyed her. Yue-ying had heard that Madame Sun could be a demonness with her bamboo switch, though she had yet to witness it.

Unlike the others, Yue-ying had no one to answer to but Mingyu. Also unlike the other girls, she possessed no literary or musical skills to elevate herself in status. Her fate had been decided from birth by a bright red birthmark that curved along her left cheek. The stain rendered her unsuitable for the pleasure houses, for who wished to invest time and money to train a courtesan with a ruined face? A prostitute required no such training.

She was a maidservant now, but up until four years ago she had been nothing but a warm body. The Lotus was indeed a palace compared to the brothel where she'd once lived and she no longer hid her face behind a thick layer of powder. No one cared if a servant was ugly, and no one paid any attention to her when Mingyu was present.

Yue-ying focused on setting their quarters back in order, righting the dressing table and picking the robes off the floor. She selected a light one that was suitable for the warm summer weather before shoving an armful of clothing into the wardrobe. Then she sorted through the cosmetics, salvaging what she could.

Later, as she was fixing Mingyu's hair, another tremor rocked the pavilion. The force of it was slight in comparison to that morning's quake, but she inadvertently jabbed Mingyu's scalp with the long pin she was holding.

"Forgive me," Yue-ying murmured after regaining her balance.

Mingyu remained seated calmly at the dressing table. "There is nothing to forgive."

Carefully, Yue-ying inserted the pin into a coil of dark hair to keep it in place. She worked in silence, mentally going over the ever-growing list of tasks she needed to accomplish that day.

"What if something happened to me?" Mingyu asked out of nowhere.

The phrasing of the question sounded decidedly odd. "No one was hurt. We were all very fortunate."

The courtesan was insistent. "I do not mean just this morning. What if something should happen in the future? Earthquakes often occur one after another. What if the next one brings the building down? Or if the ground opens up?"

"You were not afraid of earthquakes yesterday," Yue-ying reminded her gently.

Mingyu sniffed. "You know I am not speaking only of earthquakes."

Yue-ying could see Mingyu's eyebrows arch sharply

in the bronze mirror. Even agitated, she was still beautiful.

"Nothing has happened. Nothing will happen. There is no need to go searching for tragedy."

Mingyu said nothing more while Yue-ying finished dressing her in a robe of jade-green embroidered with a floral design. The courtesan resembled the paintings of immortals with her luminous skin and eyes that were mysterious and dark. The silk swirled around her as she strode from the dressing room. Her expression was tranquil, but her movements were anything but.

Yue-ying moved with purpose once Mingyu was gone; sweeping the parlor and making it presentable, propping up the broken screen that covered the bedchamber entrance as best she could. The inner rooms she left to be sorted out later.

She was right to move quickly. It wasn't long before one of Mingyu's patrons came to call, even though it was only the middle of the morning. Apparently, the earthquake had woken up the city and everyone was eager to gossip.

Taizhu, an appointed court historian, was an occasional visitor to the Lotus, though he had been coming to speak with Mingyu quite often lately. There was a touch of gray to his beard and his face was creased with more laughter lines than frown lines. For an academic, he was an ox of a man with thick shoulders and arms. The indigo color of his robe spoke of his elevated status as a member of the Hanlin Academy.

Yue-ying went to set a clay pot onto the tea stove in the inner chamber. It took her a moment to light the charcoal inside it. When she returned, the elderly scholar was already standing beside the wall with ink brush in hand.

Taizhu wielded his brush like a swordsman, writing onto the wooden panels in black ink. Afterward, he stood back to admire his handiwork and read aloud:

> *"A new Son of Heaven takes the throne. Who is it now?*
> *Hard to say, when each one seems like the last.*
> *But this time the Earth has chosen to pay homage.*
> *Should we all fall to our knees?"*

With a coy look, Mingyu took the brush from the historian's hands. She presented an elegant contrast to Taizhu's warrior pose, with one hand holding her sleeve, her brush flowing in small, graceful movements. The old scholar generously read her addition once she had finished.

> *"This humble servant thanks the kind gentleman for precious words.*
> *From a revered talent who has studied the Four Books and Five Classics.*
> *But the tea has not yet been poured,*
> *Is common courtesy no longer taught in the Hanlin Academy?"*

He burst out laughing. "Lady Mingyu thinks I'm a grumbling old man."

It was a common game in the Pingkang li, the dueling of words back and forth. Yue-ying slipped past them and headed back to the inner chambers to see to the tea. She had little grasp of the sort of language the scholars enjoyed.

The water was ready. Yue-ying measured out tea leaves into two cups and set the pot beside them on the tray. Another guest arrived as she returned to the parlor and she nearly ran into him, tea and all.

Bai Huang was a well-known fixture of the entertainment district. He was a night owl, a flirt, a spendthrift and an eternal student, having failed the imperial exams three times. He was dressed in an opulent blue robe and his topknot was fixed with a silver pin.

"My lord—" She started to mumble out an apology while trying to keep from spilling the tea.

She was met with easy laughter as the young aristocrat reached out to steady the tray. His hand closed over hers and her pulse did a little leap, despite itself.

The corners of his mouth lifted, gracing her with a sly smile, before turning to the others. "Only tea?" he asked with disappointment. "Where's the wine?"

Taizhu waved him over. "Ah, the young Lord Bai is always good for a few laughs."

Bai Huang carried the tray over to the party himself, forcing Yue-ying to follow him in an attempt to retrieve it. Her ears were burning by the time she managed to wrest the tray from him, but the nobleman was oblivious.

"When I was awoken this morning by the earthquake, my immediate thoughts went to you, Lady Mingyu," he said. "I worried for your safety and could not be consoled until I saw with my own eyes that you were unharmed."

Taizhu snorted. "Your poor suffering heart."

Mingyu placed a warning hand on Taizhu's sleeve, but Bai Huang merely accepted the remark with a chuckle. He remained deaf and blind to insult, like a contented frog in a well.

Lord Bai had taken to openly courting Mingyu over the past few months, composing effusive poetry about his loneliness, his sorrow, his aches and his pains, which he would publicly dedicate to Mingyu, reciting verses whenever present company allowed.

If he never had to speak, then Bai Huang and Mingyu would have been perfectly suited. He was the picture of masculine beauty with prominent cheekbones and a strong, chiseled jawline. His eyes were black and always able to catch the light, highlighting the perpetual quirk of amusement on his lips. He bore the high forehead that was considered a sign of cleverness, but anyone who had come across Bai Huang knew better.

Yue-ying made her own effort to keep the peace by pouring hot water over the leaves and setting out the cups. There was no better reminder to be civil than tea. She had to fetch another cup for Lord Bai. After preparing his drink, she glanced up to catch him watching her. The look was there for only a moment before he took his tea.

"Up so early, you scoundrel?" the old scholar taunted. "After last night, I thought you would still be pickled in rice wine at this hour."

"Your concern touches me deeply, Lord Bai," Mingyu interrupted in a soothing tone.

He looked obliviously pleased. Taizhu shook his head, fingers pinched to the bridge of his nose. Yue-ying went downstairs to fetch a plate of red bean cakes from the kitchen as it seemed the men would stay awhile. When she returned, the old historian had turned the conversation back to the imperial court.

"This is an opportunity to advise the Emperor that he must change course. Heaven has given us a sign. Earthquakes and floods have been known to topple dynasties," the historian pointed out sagely.

Bai Huang was already shaking his head. "A sign of

what? It sounds more like superstitious doomsaying," he said with a bored look.

"What does it matter if it's superstition or not? If such a disaster gains the Emperor's attention, then it can be used as a means to an end," Taizhu argued.

"This morning's disaster serves as a better excuse for a couple of friends to complain over tea," Bai Huang contended, lifting his cup. He attempted to drink, then frowned and peered into it, finding it empty.

As Yue-ying bent to fill the empty cup, Bai Huang startled her once again, halting her movement.

"What do you think, Little Moon?" he asked.

Mingyu's mouth pressed tight at the casual endearment. Yue-ying glanced at Bai Huang. Dark eyebrows framed his face, giving him a serious expression that was contrary to his usual carefree manner. The nobleman had never spoken directly to her in such company before.

"Has the earthquake provided you with any signs?" he persisted.

The room fell silent. Old Taizhu affected a shallow cough and sipped his tea in silence. Bai Huang was the only one unperturbed. He continued to look at her, smiling crookedly as he waited for an answer. His gaze on her was insistent, but not unkind. Yue-ying looked nervously to Mingyu before answering.

"I was frightened at first," Yue-ying admitted. "But sometimes rain falls and sometimes the earth moves. That was all it seemed to me."

"Yue-ying." The courtesan's command was soft, yet somehow sharp. "There is no need for you to remain here. You are free to continue with your other duties."

Yue-ying immediately set the pot down without refilling Lord Bai's cup and retreated toward the door.

Mingyu regained control of the conversation quickly. "Old Taizhu, have you considered that the earthquake might have been a warning to those bickering factions in court rather than our gracious Emperor?"

Bai Huang would find himself cut out of the conversation for the next hour, perhaps for the whole afternoon if Mingyu decided he deserved it. They continued on to more pleasant topics: the upcoming festival on the double fifth and the number of candidates who had passed the exams that spring.

Was Lord Bai deliberately trying to provoke Mingyu? Or had he simply forgotten that the courtesan was very strict about anyone being so familiar with her attendant?

As Yue-ying reached the door she turned to see Lord Bai staring at his still-empty cup. After an expectant pause, he reached over to pour for himself since Mingyu wasn't being amenable. As he sat back, the young nobleman directed his gaze across the room and caught her watching him. He raised the cup to her in salute, eyebrows lifted.

Her heartbeat quickened and she swallowed past the dryness in her throat. Yue-ying might have been unaffected by his beauty, but she wasn't completely indifferent. Any other woman would have been flattered by his show of interest, but she merely turned, head held high, and exited the parlor.

Lord Bai knew exactly what he was doing.

BY THE TIME Yue-ying went downstairs, the public gong had sounded eight times in the distance to signal the Goat Hour. At a brisk pace, she was able to reach the walls of the East Market within the next half hour. The merchants went about their business as usual, though apprehension hung over the stalls and shops.

Yue-ying moved through the rows ruthlessly, gathering the things that Mingyu needed as well as requests from the other girls. The courtesans didn't have the leisure of being able to browse the markets. They were often entertaining late into the night so their days were better spent resting up.

Despite this small measure of freedom, Yue-ying didn't believe in dawdling. A craftsman had visited the Lotus once, showing off a fountain that served wine. The contraption was tall, built in the shape of a mountain, and had a mechanism to draw wine out of a built-in well without the use of hands and pour it into a waiting cup. He had opened the encasing for her, revealing the wheel and levers inside. It was an illusion that everything operated so smoothly on the outside, while on the inside there was constant turning and toil. She was that wheel.

By the time the market gong sounded the start of the Monkey Hour, her basket was full and she'd finished her rounds through the shops. Her last visit was to the local temple. Mingyu was convinced that the earthquake was an ill omen and wanted Yue-ying to give an offering on her behalf.

The temple courtyard was crowded that afternoon, almost as if it were a festival day. Perhaps Mingyu wasn't the only one who felt that the angry heavens needed to be appeased.

Yue-ying went to the fish pond at the center of the courtyard to pay her respects to the tortoise who lived among the rocks. This would be her one indulgence in her busy day. The ancient creature lifted his head high as if to examine what all the commotion was about. His skin was rough and dusty and there were wrinkled folds on his neck.

"Old Man Tortoise," she called softly and considered it a good omen when his eyes flickered languidly toward her.

The whorled patterns on his shell resembled the octagonal pattern of the Taoist *bagua* symbol. Yue-ying had heard it told that the tortoise was over a hundred years old. He had come from a faraway land, across the ocean. Those black eyes had seen more than she ever would.

She had enough on her mind today without Lord Bai trying to complicate things for his own amusement. Mingyu had been agitated for days and nothing Yue-ying said or did could soothe her.

"Why is Mingyu never happy?" she asked the ancient creature.

The tortoise had no answer and Yue-ying's moment of rest was over. She left him to his afternoon sun and continued on to the main altar room. As she paused outside to remove her slippers someone ran into her, toppling her basket.

Gasping, Yue-ying scrambled to salvage her goods. The lychees she'd bought were delicate and very expensive. The round fruit was scattered all over the bamboo mat and she hurried to pick them up before they were trampled.

"Watch yourself."

She recognized who it was even before looking up. Huilan was another of the famed beauties of the quarter. Her voice was often compared to the trill of a song thrush, but she didn't sound so pleasant now.

The courtesan stood like an empress over her. "Oh, it's you."

Yue-ying kept her temper under control. "Perhaps we can all show a little more care."

Huilan's hair was an unusual shade of brown with hints of red, giving her an exotic quality that she had become known for. She knelt in a graceful sweep, but, rather than helping, she merely picked up a rough-skinned lychee between two fingers and straightened. "Are these in season now?"

With a sigh, Yue-ying packed everything back into her basket while continuing to kneel at Huilan's feet. Finally she stood.

"They were at the front of the farmer's quadrant in the East Market. There were only two baskets of them and the price was very steep," she reported, carefully maintaining a cordial tone.

Huilan made a sound of acknowledgment and let the lychee drop into the basket. "How is Mingyu, anyway?"

For a moment, her tone sharpened. A strange look crossed her face, but then it was gone. The so-called Four Beauties of the North Hamlet weren't necessarily in competition with one another, but they were mentioned and compared so often that a subtle rivalry had emerged. Though Huilan was outwardly sweet-voiced and sweet-faced, she was as shrewd as Mingyu when it came to maintaining her elevated position.

"She is well."

"Hmm…good to hear it."

Huilan turned away, concluding their exchange with no further attempt at politeness. She glided across the courtyard in a cloud of yellow silk and disappeared through the gate.

Yue-ying nudged off her slippers and entered the shrine. A spicy, camphor-laced scent filled the room from the incense smoldering on the altar. Setting her basket aside, she took three sticks of incense from the holder at the altar and held the ends to the candle flame until they ignited, releasing the fragrant oil in the coating.

Clasping the incense between her palms, she bowed her head as the smoke curled a lazy spiral around her. She tried to form a coherent prayer, but all she could think of was the angry rumble of the earth that morning and Mingyu's pale and frightened expression. So she asked the goddess Guan Yin to look over and protect them, in any way she might see fit.

When she was done, Yue-ying dropped several coins into the alms bowl and paid one final visit to the old tortoise before leaving the temple. She saw that Huilan hadn't gone far. The courtesan was standing at the foot of the nearest bridge. The sun caught the reddish streaks in her hair as a young man in scholar's robes approached her.

Yue-ying ducked her head and kept on walking to give Huilan her privacy. The temple was known as a place where scholars and candidates congregated, and it was a popular place to meet and gain new admirers.

As she traveled along the outer edge of the market to return home her way was blocked by a sizable crowd that had gathered along the canal. Although she was expected back at the Lotus, Mingyu might be pleased to have some gossip at hand to spark conversation with her visitors. Yue-ying ducked and elbowed her way through to the front to see what was going on.

Down below, a man stood beside a boat that had been pulled out of the water. He wore the uniform and headdress of a constable and towered over the other men. She was close enough to see his face, which was unfamiliar to her. He had an austere and unpleasant look about him. Not a man one wanted to see angry.

Whoever this was, he was new to the ward. Perhaps

brought in by Magistrate Li, who had been appointed just before the new Emperor took the throne. The constable gestured to the other men in uniform, who moved quickly to follow his command. She was so eager for information about the tall stranger that it took her a moment to realize why the magistrate's enforcers were gathered in the waterway.

There was a body lying in the boat at the edge of the water. An arm poked out from the length of canvas draped over the vessel and the skin covering it was black and rotted.

CHAPTER TWO

THE DUANWU FESTIVAL took place on the fifth day of the fifth month. An hour after sunrise, the dragonboats were already moving into position for the traditional race down the Grand Canal. Bai Huang stood at the keel of one of the colorful vessels as it floated toward the starting dock. He enjoyed the warm breeze over his face and the marsh and mud scent of the water, which he always associated with this city.

It was summer, the banquet season, and he was finally back in the capital of Changan, surrounded by all its grandeur. Twenty-five pairs of rowers lined the boat, operating the oars in unison. They pulled at a leisurely pace to conserve their strength. Huang stood where the drummer would be seated. He enjoyed the quiet of the morning as the crowds began to gather on either side of the river.

As they neared the dock Huang spied a figure moving among the tethered boats. Yue-ying, the industrious little maidservant. She did manage to show up everywhere, didn't she? Unlike the courtesans of the quarter, she didn't seem confined to her house. He had seen her dodging carts in the market, running to wine shops, even hauling drunken patrons of the Lotus Palace onto sedan chairs after a particularly long night.

She'd done so once for him last autumn. He'd attempted to flirt with her even though she was only a servant because he figured it was expected of him. The fool Bai Huang lacked shame or manners, but he made up for it with good looks and money, so he was tolerated.

The girl had treated him like a sack of potatoes that night. After that, Huang had made a point of trying to catch her eye, but she couldn't be charmed. She couldn't be bribed. He was fascinated.

Today she wore a pale green robe, the color almost nonexistent and only there to keep the dress from being white. She tried so very hard to be nondescript, to disappear, but her face was likely the most recognizable one in the quarter.

The birthmark over her left cheek was a swirl of dark red. It ran down her face and along the line of her jaw, stopping just short of her chin. Her complexion otherwise was fair, highlighting the stain even more. It was as if an artist painting her had started to form the shape of her mouth when he'd inadvertently splashed red ink over the paper. He then left it there, finding the stain created a spark of drama beyond mere prettiness. Like finding a bloodred peony among the snow.

"Little Moon!" he called out. The rowers kept up their rhythm, moving him closer to the dock and to her. "Little Moon, over here."

By the third time he called, he was certain Yue-ying had heard him, but was making a concerted effort not to turn a single eyelash in his direction. She continued speaking to the drummer of the yellow vessel while her hand rested on the carved dragon's head. She straightened her fingers momentarily, issuing a silent signal for him to go away. Stubborn girl. It had been over a week since his social misstep of speaking directly to her in Mingyu's company. Surely he should be forgiven by now?

"Yue-ying, don't be angry," he pleaded, laughter in his tone. The boat glided slowly past her and he had to walk down the length of it toward the tail just to keep her within shouting distance. "Come and let me apologize properly."

She turned. The look on her face was pure exasperation, but it didn't matter. He'd won a small victory.

The sweep steered the boat toward its assigned spot on the dock and the rowers lifted their oars and let momentum carry them the last stretch. A dozen boats were laid out along the canal, each one carved and painted like a celestial dragon from head to tail. By the next double hour, the officials would assemble to start the race.

Yue-ying stood on the dock, looking down at him. A vermilion sash circled her slender waist, in contrast to the muted colors in the rest of her dress. Her hair was arranged to fall over one shoulder, leaving one side of her face and neck exposed. The unmarked half, he noted with interest.

He remained in the boat while the crew disembarked to stretch their legs and rest before the starting gong. Yue-ying stepped aside to let them pass, watching them go before returning her gaze to him.

"What are you doing out here so early, Little Moon?"

"Please do not call me that."

"It's just an endearment. Between friends." The first character of her name was "moon". He thought it nominally creative of him.

Her eyes narrowed on him. "If you insist on making trouble for me, I will have to leave. Lord Bai."

The honorific was clearly added only as an afterthought. She was getting quite bold for the servant of a servant, he thought with amusement.

"Miss Yue-ying," he corrected obligingly. "Please forgive me."

She appeared to accept his humble offering. "I'm getting an accounting of the dragonboats for Lady Mingyu. In case anyone wants to discuss which one she thinks will win."

"Very clever! Your mistress sent you out here to do that?"

"I thought it might come up. How is your crew feeling today, might I ask?" She looked the boat over from head to tail as she spoke.

"Strong as the west wind," he boasted.

"Will you be rowing as well?"

His chest might have puffed out a little. He smirked as she tried to assess his physique, the calculations clicking in place inside her head. Yue-ying had been completely indifferent to his appearance before then. Did she judge him a strength or a handicap in terms of the rowing?

"Ah, I would be nothing but added weight. I'll be placing a few of my own wagers and watching from a comfortable place away from the sun," he admitted.

"Well." She angled a sly side-glance to her left. "Definitely bet against the orange dragon, then."

"Oh?" he asked, intrigued.

"And Chancellor Li's boat, the blue dragon, was just constructed last month. He wanted to have the most magnificent vessel in the water, and he will, but that dragon head looks awfully heavy."

"And who will win?"

"Green," she said without hesitation. "And perhaps gold."

"Why those two?"

She shrugged. "I like the colors."

Her eyes were alight with mischief. Huang had the sudden urge to take hold of the trailing end of that red ribbon around her waist and reel her in close.

"Have you ever been on a dragonboat?" he asked instead. He held out an inviting hand to her, but she shook her head.

"Thank you for the kind offer, Lord Bai, but my mistress is waiting." The momentary playfulness he'd glimpsed in her had been firmly banished to the frontier.

"Come, for just a moment. To make up for my behavior the other day," he coaxed.

"I prefer to stay on land." She looked nervously over the water. "Someone recently drowned not too far from here."

He hadn't heard any news of that, but there were waterways throughout the city. It couldn't be too uncommon.

"You'll be safe in here. I'll see to it myself," he assured her, flashing her a grin.

Yue-ying sighed, long and loud so he could hear. "Is there a letter or some trinket you wish me to bring to Mingyu?"

It was true he had asked her to pass along little tokens in the past. Mingyu probably expected something by way of an apology after he'd broken the unspoken rule of paying attention to anyone other than her. As if having to sit through an evening while the beautifully cold courtesan either ignored him or verbally eviscerated him weren't punishment enough.

Yue-ying looked back to the street again and he realized sadly she had only been talking to him because she was required to do so out of courtesy. She was humoring him like everyone else in the North Hamlet. This was exactly the reaction he'd deliberately cultivated, but he sometimes regretted it was so.

"How fortunate that you've reminded me." He pasted on his cheerful, witless expression. "I must bring Lady Mingyu a gift tonight at the banquet. Do you have any suggestions?"

"Whatever you see fit, Lord Bai."

Yue-ying wasn't interested in prolonging the conversation any longer. She bowed and turned away. The flutter of the red sash allowed him to track her movements long after she'd become another head in the crowd.

Huang didn't know what he would have done if she'd stepped onto the dragonboat with him. Nothing too scandalous. She was Mingyu's attendant, after all, and he couldn't afford to be shut out of the courtesan's circle. It was just that he genuinely liked Yue-ying. She was clever, engaging, imperfect and intriguing. It was unfortunate he had to deceive her the way he did.

By MIDMORNING, the crowds were layered thick along the Grand Canal. Awnings fashioned from canvas and bamboo had been set up. Beneath the shade, the ladies could be seen fanning themselves as they waited for the race to begin.

"Lord Bai!"

He turned to see Zhou Dan weaving through the crowd. Huang and the cook's son had grown up in separate sections of the same household, with a year separating them. Huang was the older of the two. Though they were the same height, Huang was broader at the shoulders while Zhou was lean, giving him the illusion of appearing slightly taller.

"You weren't at your quarters," Zhou Dan said, out

of breath. He handed Huang a parcel wrapped in paper. "From your father."

As far as he knew, Father was still at his post in the mountains of Fujian. A quick inspection revealed a sealed letter along with a stack of cash notes, so-called "flying money" sent from afar.

"Try not to lose so quickly this time, *little* Lord Bai." Zhou Dan flashed a grin with too many teeth.

"Is it any better to lose slowly, bit by bit?"

The servant laughed. "Just as long as you don't have to flee to the provinces again."

"Send my regards to my mother and sister," Huang said dryly.

Zhou waved as he disappeared into the crowd, off to enjoy the festival.

The Duanwu Festival signaled the start of the summer. The sight of peach blossoms along the main avenues had faded to be replaced with branches laden with fruit. The names of scholars who had passed the imperial exams had been announced with great ceremony at the end of spring, beginning a period of celebration for the few who had triumphed. For unsuccessful candidates, there were also a number of consolation parties. Pass or fail, everyone drank.

The candidates who had been granted the official rank of scholar would be petitioning the Ministry of Personnel for appointments and then they would wait. And wait. During the wait, they would frequent the taverns and pleasure houses of the Pingkang quarter, trying to catch the eye of someone with influence. Many court officials frequented those very same banquets and gatherings. It provided Huang with an opportunity to mingle among the officials and hopefuls, though he wasn't looking to gain influence or secure an official position.

The late Emperor Wuzong had become unpredictable during the last years of his reign, developing an unstable temperament after ingesting too many potions in his quest for immortality. Multiple factions had developed within the imperial court and they spent more effort warring with each other than administering the empire. The former Emperor had added to the feud by banishing the more levelheaded officials to the far corners of the empire.

Though his father had been sent away from the capital, Huang was able to stay close. His past reputation as a wastrel made it easy for him to be deemed as harmless and his willingness to toss cash about made him a favored guest at every pleasure house. He simply exaggerated the persona into the Bai Huang that everyone in the North Hamlet now recognized.

He dressed in overembellished silks in the brightest colors. He laughed at everyone's jokes, even and especially when they were directed at him. He was the beloved fool. The flower prince of the Pingkang li.

Several scholars called out to him as he passed by. A group of young ladies from one of the pleasure houses waved their scarves to get his attention. He gave them a smile, but passed on.

The East Market Commissioner had cornered a place near the ending point of the race. His entourage was set up beneath a large tent beside the canal. Huang searched among the party for Lady Huilan, the famous courtesan.

He found her seated on a pillow in the center of the tent. Huilan had been named one of the Four Beauties of the Pingkang li after a highly celebrated contest during the banquet season last summer. Her features were slightly elongated and her hair was the color of rosewood. Verses dedicated to Huilan mentioned her highly prized moon-pale complexion set against eyes like the sun. They called her the Precious Orchid of Silla. According to local fable, she'd learned how to sing as a child in that faraway kingdom before being brought to Changan.

Huilan sang lyrics from a popular poem about two dueling dragons while plucking out an accompanying melody on the pipa. Her silk and smoke voice carried through the crowd. Huang caught her eye and then turned to the waterway as if to watch for the dragonboats. Drums began to beat downstream at the start of the hour. The race had begun.

Eventually, Huilan freed herself and stepped away from the tent. Casually, Huang wandered toward the food stands at the same time, stopping before one that sold pickled and preserved plums.

A moment later, Huilan was beside him. "Two," she said to the vendor, keeping her gaze directed forward.

He paid for the plums, pushing a folded paper across the stand along with his copper. The vendor smoothly took the coins while the paper disappeared into Huilan's sleeve. The festival atmosphere provided opportunity for young men and women to mingle. To anyone watching, they were just another couple exchanging a love letter.

"What information did you have for me?" he asked.

"You'll get it tomorrow." Outwardly, her expression remained pleasant.

Several days ago, she had asked for his help to leave the quarter. She had been cryptic about it, offering information that she promised he'd find valuable. It hadn't sounded like the usual courtesan's plea to redeem her from a cruel foster mother. Huilan had acted genuinely frightened.

She showed none of that fear now. She was eerily

calm as she took the skewers of plums from the vendor. "I must go. The commissioner paid for a musician for the hour. I don't want him complaining to Mother."

"Can you not speak here? Is there a better place for us to meet?"

Huilan shook her head and smiled mysteriously at him. As she turned to go she paused to touch a hand to his sleeve, just over his wrist. "Thank you for your concern, Lord Bai. You are very kind."

With that, she floated back toward the minister's awning, a vision in red silk.

He remained nearby for a while longer, in case Huilan had a change of heart, but when she made no further attempt to communicate with him, he continued upstream along the canal. A group of exam candidates called him over to share wine. None of them had passed this round of examinations. Some of them would return to their homes; others would stay on to make another attempt. The setback was treated like a well-worn battle scar. They were young and invincible.

These young men were the same set who sought sport at the gambling houses and courted the young, lesser-known beauties of the Pingkang li. Huang had once taken on the city with the same exuberance, but he'd become much wiser and more reserved. Some might say he'd been taught a lesson he'd never forget.

A gasp of excitement rose from the crowd as the dragonboats came into full view. There were over fifteen in the race. They presented a dramatic sight side by side, all painted in different colors like a rainbow flying over the water. The rowers in each vessel pulled in unison while the beating of the drums set out a steady rhythm.

Out of the corner of his eye, Huang caught sight of a vermilion sash set against a leaf-green robe. Yue-ying stood beside her mistress now, holding a bamboo parasol to shade her from the sun. Lady Mingyu was carrying on a conversation with several scholar-gentlemen who appeared completely enraptured by her words while Yue-ying remained quiet in the background.

What would she be like when freed from beneath the hand of her dictatorial mistress? He wanted very much to speak to her alone again and find out.

He looked back to the racing dragons. As Yue-ying had predicted, the blue dragon was trailing and the orange was in the middle of the fleet, with little chance of pulling ahead. Her two choices for favorites were in the lead; green and gold. He doubted those were merely her favorite colors as she claimed. Yue-ying had shown herself to be neither whimsical nor impulsive.

First Huilan had sought him out with her veiled promises. Then a clever little maidservant had him completely beguiled. That was the problem when dealing with the ladies of the North Hamlet. Every look and word had two meanings. They did it deliberately to taunt young, impressionable scholars. As if women weren't enough of a mystery already.

CHAPTER THREE

THE DAYTIME ACTIVITIES of the festival centered on the Grand Canal and dragonboat races, but once the sun went down the pleasure houses competed for the evening crowd. The Lotus Palace benefited from being one of the most recognizable establishments in the Pingkang li.

The building itself was two stories high and contained a number of parlors and a banquet hall suitable for entertaining, but the topmost tier was what gave the Lotus Palace its name. The deck was open on all sides, providing a view of the night sky. An octagon of painted beams supported the eaves, which curved upward to resemble the petals of a lotus flower. It was the perfect setting during the spring and summer for gazing at the moon and composing poetry over cups of warmed wine.

In addition to their usual patrons, the new county magistrate was hosting a banquet there—his first public gathering since taking office. Magistrate Li Yen had the disadvantage of not only being young for a man in his position, but appearing youthful as well. He was twenty-five years of age and it was widely believed he was only given his position due to family connections.

Yue-ying wondered whether the magistrate and his constables had discovered what had happened to the body in the river. The boat had been docked somewhere upstream and was dislodged by the earthquake, carrying the corpse down the waterway. There was little talk of it in the Pingkang li other than a few murmurings that he was likely a laborer who had been attacked by a street thief.

With the coming of the festival, the story was forgotten in favor of happier news. Tonight, Madame took the responsibility of greeting every guest and all of the courtesans were busy entertaining. That left Old Auntie and Yue-ying to make sure there was enough food and drink to keep things lively.

An area had been set up on the top floor for the banquet. Mingyu would serve as hostess while two of her courtesan-sisters attended to provide music and pour wine. Yue-ying was busy lighting and hanging lanterns onto the eaves.

"The Xifeng wine," Mingyu reminded her as the time neared. Down below, they could already see the festival crowd beginning to gather.

Yue-ying headed for the stairs. The parlors on the second and first floors were filling quickly and the chants of a drinking game rang out. She passed by Auntie, who was balancing two trays of food.

The passage to the cellar was through the kitchen. It was a small area down a set of steps. She hung her lantern onto a hook on the wall as she went to the corner where the quality wines were kept. The jug was packed in straw and Yue-ying had started to dig it out when she heard a voice from behind. She spun around, pulse jumping.

"Is it the tremor of the earth, or the sight of you that unsettles me?"

Bai Huang had a shoulder against the doorframe. The lantern light revealed his characteristic grin.

"Lord Bai." She breathed deep to steady herself. "The banquet is upstairs. You should join it."

"I saw you coming down here and wanted to know your opinion," he said.

Despite his pleasant tone, every muscle within her tensed. Yue-ying had long considered Bai Huang to be harmless. He was well mannered and carefree, nothing more than a bored aristocrat seeking diversion. His improprieties bordered on the ridiculous rather than the sinister, but noblemen did not follow maidservants into dark cellars with good intentions.

"Do you like the verse I recited?" he asked. "I composed it after our last meeting."

"Your poetry is very dull, as always."

He straightened a little, eyes wide with surprise. She regretted her bluntness immediately. Someone like her was never allowed to insult a man like Lord Bai, but her heart was beating too fast to think clearly. She needed to make it clear that she wasn't Mingyu. She wasn't a part of his games of courtship and seduction.

Back in the brothel, the men didn't come to her for conversation. Though the customers were often merchants and tradesmen rather than gentlemen, scholars didn't by any means find whorehouses beneath them. Men of rank might exercise good manners in public, but they experienced the full force of lust like any other man. Alone here, without Mingyu's protection, Yue-ying was as helpless as she had once been, lying beneath men who weren't looking for talent or beauty.

Keeping her shoulders squared, she started toward the exit. She wouldn't show any weakness. She would show no emotion at all and he would see there was no sport to be had here.

Bai Huang remained at the doorway, his expression now more contemplative than flirtatious. She would have to get past him. She held her breath. *Don't slow down*, she told herself. *Keep moving.*

At the last moment, he shifted his weight to block her path. "You didn't get your wine," he remarked softly.

She stilled like a hare under a falcon's gaze. His beauty made him seem suddenly more villainous. He wouldn't even have to use force. Lord Bai likely thought he could lure any manner of woman into his arms and they should be grateful for it.

"Move aside," she said, her mouth pressed tight. Then she wondered if he was the sort of man who thrived on the conquest. She'd known those as well. She softened her tone. "If you please, Mingyu will be wondering where I am, Lord Bai."

She added the honorific as an afterthought, hoping not to anger him. And then she'd mentioned her mistress's name in desperation. If he'd merely forgotten himself for a moment, then he could remember himself now. She hoped Bai Huang was the sort who would be willing to laugh away a misunderstanding if she didn't make him lose face.

"So my poetry is dull, you say?" His tone was curious, thoughtful and with a hint of interest. "Why are you the only one who has ever told me that?"

"This humble servant misspoke. I beg your pardon."

She considered once again hurrying past him, back into the light and the crowd upstairs, but he was keeping his distance and his posture was relaxed. His hands were lowered by his sides and he was doing nothing more than watching her, waiting for an answer.

"Why are you the only one who doesn't laugh at me along with the others?"

"I wouldn't dare—"

"I don't believe that's the reason."

Bai Huang smiled, his expression warm. He even made as if to step aside. Like a fool, she relaxed her guard and started for the stairs only to be pulled roughly against him. She braced both hands flat against his chest, but that didn't stop him from pressing his lips to hers.

Yue-ying twisted in his grasp. The moment his hold loosened, she struck him across the face as hard as she could.

The sound of that slap resounded through the cellar, followed by an ugly silence. He stared at her, stunned. She was equally frozen, not quite believing what she had just done. Only the sting of her palm confirmed it.

Her heart pounded as she waited for him to retaliate. She'd hit a nobleman. A man so high above her, she'd surely be beaten for the insult. But Lord Bai merely straightened, dropping his hand slowly from his cheek. His eyes remained on her the entire time. He looked startled, almost boyishly contrite. His lips parted with the beginnings of a question.

Leaving the lantern, she rushed past him and stumbled up the stairs in the dark. She hurried through the kitchen, expecting to hear him charging after her at any moment. At the main hall, she stopped and bent, pressing a hand to her ribcage as she tried to catch her breath.

"Yue-ying?" Ziyi, one of the younger girls, stopped to check on her. "Are you all right?"

She glanced once more over her shoulder. Though the nobleman was nowhere to be seen, her heart was still beating fast and she willed herself to calm down. "I just need to get back," she lied.

With a deep breath, she climbed the stairs to return to the banquet on the upper floor where she was met by the cool night air and the glow of lanterns. She stood there, blinking and lost as if the Lotus had suddenly become a foreign land.

The guests were seated on pillows arranged around several low tables and the celebration was already under way. Mingyu caught her eye from the center of the gathering. Though Mingyu was in midconversation with Magistrate Li and the old historian Taizhu, she stopped and started to rise.

"What happened?" Mingyu demanded as Yue-ying came to her.

"It's nothing," she whispered.

It really was nothing to speak of. She was unharmed and it was better for everyone if she didn't make trouble.

Lord Bai appeared at the top of the stairs. He paused for a moment to scan through the banquet and it wasn't long before his gaze centered on them. With a wide grin, he sauntered over.

"Any room here?" he inquired casually, as if he weren't addressing the county magistrate and an official of the Hanlin Academy.

"Young Lord Bai," the magistrate greeted. "This banquet is to thank Lady Mingyu for an introduction to the quarter. Any friend of hers is certainly welcome."

"Lord Bai, if you please." Mingyu held out her hand in invitation, but her mouth formed a hard line.

Magistrate Li graciously offered the seat beside him and Yue-ying edged away as Bai Huang came near. He didn't even glance her way as he sat down. To Yue-ying's relief, Mingyu asked one of the girls to retrieve the wine and took it upon herself to pour. Yue-ying retreated back a few steps.

It was just a kiss, she scolded herself. It was over and done with and the nobleman didn't seem intent on exacting revenge for her slap. The best thing to do was to forget about it.

"What happened there?" Magistrate Li asked, gesturing toward his face.

Bai Huang placed his fingertips beneath his eye and felt along the reddened scratch beneath it. She hadn't realized she'd left a mark.

He seemed as surprised as she was. "This? I received this on the way over here. Made the mistake of cornering an alley cat." His eyes flicked momentarily to her. "A well-deserved punishment."

Heat rushed to her cheeks. Was he playing with her still? Despite his advances being unwelcome, she was left scandalized. It was as if she'd stolen away deliberately to meet him, as if they now shared a secret. She wanted no part of it.

The nobleman had returned to his usual tricks. He complimented Mingyu effusively, likening her to a peach blossom.

"But peach blossoms are known for being so delicate and their season is quite brief," Mingyu replied coolly.

Bai Huang blinked at her, befuddled. "A lily, then?" he offered.

The party laughed at the exchange and he continued to look bewildered for a moment before breaking out into a grin, pleased that he must have said something witty to evoke the response.

Out in the open, he hardly presented an intimidating figure. His robe was overly flamboyant, his posture laid-back. He drank too much and threw money around. He enjoyed his special place as the beloved fool of the Pingkang li, but Yue-ying had never found him amusing. His humor always seemed too forced to her. His efforts lacked spontaneity.

Magistrate Li picked up the conversation, perhaps feeling obligated as the banquet's sponsor. "Lord Bai, your love for verses must be in your blood. I hear that you are related to the poet Bai Juyi. His passing was a great loss."

"A distant relation," the nobleman replied. "Though proud of the association, I would be ashamed to boast of it. Blood matters little next to merit, wouldn't you say?"

Mingyu glanced up from her conversation with Taizhu. The two listened with mild interest.

"No one would disagree with that," Li said amiably.

"Now, the magistrate has something to boast about. What's this? Attaining the rank of *jinshi* at only nineteen years of age? I must drink to you."

The magistrate laughed and denied any special status. When not in his official robe, he could certainly be mistaken for one of the many students in the quarter with his pleasant manner and youthful face.

"He's too humble," Taizhu said. "Not only did he pass the palace exams, Li Yen earned the rank of selective talent, third overall in his class."

Bai Huang insisted on raising his cup to drink to Li's accomplishment. "I should ask the magistrate for advice," he said boisterously. "What tricks did the magistrate employ to score so well?"

Magistrate Li's ears flushed red at the tips, though that might have been from the drink. "No trick really."

"This humble student can't seem to pass no matter who he bribes."

Bai Huang's jest was met with nervous laughter from Li Yen as well as the other attendees. Taizhu scowled at him. Again he played the fool, or did he? His self-effacing smile was a bit hard at the edges.

Yue-ying was never part of such conversation. She

was to remain silent and wait to be useful, always watching and always listening. It gave her an opportunity to scrutinize Lord Bai's seemingly senseless questions and his overflowing enthusiasm. He wasn't a know-nothing who was trying too hard to impress. He was trying very deliberately to provoke a response. But why?

She would have continued to dismiss him as well, until that horrible mockery of a kiss. Her view of him was forever changed.

"Now I wonder why there are no imperial exams for women?" Mingyu chimed in, filling the tense silence.

Her suggestion was met with equal parts chuckling and enthusiastic support.

"A new exam would need to be designed. With a different set of questions," Taizhu proposed.

"Why should the process be any different for a woman? I would welcome the privilege of being able to fail the imperial exams." She gave Bai Huang a sly look and he beamed.

"Let us enforce a new rule." Mingyu held up her hand dramatically and everyone quieted to listen. In this social gathering, she was official hostess and acting magistrate. "This is a festival night. Anyone who mentions exams or appointments or politics—" she cast Taizhu a pointed look, which he accepted with good humor "—must take a penalty drink and be subjected to a punishment of the group's choosing."

Everyone raised their cups to make the decree official and, with that, peace was restored. Yue-ying was moving around the table to refill cups when another arrival stepped onto the pavilion deck. Mingyu stared at the man in the dark robe without recognition.

"Wu Kaifeng, the head constable," Yue-ying informed her.

She had mentioned the body found in the river, but Mingyu hadn't been particularly interested in the crime or the presence of a new constable. It was bad luck to speak of death, so the Pingkang li went on as if a corpse hadn't recently drifted ashore practically at their gate.

Constable Wu came directly to them. His gaze passed over the gathering and he managed a stiff bow. Afterward, he straightened and stood rigidly, uncomfortable with the surroundings. Though he held an appointed position, he was still a working man, subservient to nearly everyone present. He addressed the magistrate.

"Sir, there is a matter that needs your attention." His austere countenance cast gloom over the banquet just as it had by the river.

"Please excuse us." Li Yen stood and the two men moved to stand beside one of the columns.

After a brief exchange, the magistrate returned. "My apologies for leaving so early. Lady Mingyu." He bowed once to her, before turning to Bai Huang. "Lord Bai, I am happy to have met you, but regret that we didn't get to converse at any length. Perhaps you would like to walk with me?"

Bai Huang tilted his head in surprise. A confused smile touched his lips, but he stood and took his leave as well, leaving behind more than one set of raised eyebrows.

THE EVENING WAS warm and all the lanterns of the North Hamlet were aglow, prolonging the festival atmosphere of the day. It would have been a good night for walking, except it was difficult to feel comfortable with Li Yen beside him and his dark and brooding servant trailing behind.

It was well-known that the Li and Bai clans supported

different factions in the imperial court, with Chancellor Li Deyu dominating the court for the reign of the last two emperors. A distant relation, the magistrate would insist.

"This was my first Duanwu in the capital," Magistrate Li remarked as they continued down the lane. "I found the festival very enjoyable."

"A good day indeed," Huang concurred. "My dragonboat won today so I have a heavy purse to show for it. Are we headed to the center of the Three Lanes?"

"My apologies for this delay. Has Lord Bai ever been to the House of a Hundred Songs?"

The hairs on the back of Huang's neck rose. "The Hundred Songs boasts a few of the most talented courtesans in the district...outside of Lady Mingyu, of course."

"I promised to make an appearance there tonight," Li said smoothly. "If you don't mind accompanying me?"

Li turned onto the central lane and Huang followed dutifully, keeping his guard up. The magistrate's soft-spoken manner hid a well of ambition.

The Hundred Songs was always a cheerful place. Huang was known there as well. The house wasn't nearly as grand in style or reputation as the Lotus Palace, but pink lanterns and carved phoenixes gave it a romantic look. The atmosphere inside was busy, but more muted than the revelry they had left behind. The hostess greeted them with some reserve.

"Why so quiet this evening, Little Plum?" Huang asked with a smile.

Mei ducked her head and beckoned them to follow her. Music floated throughout the halls, a harmonious blend of the rain-song sound of the pipa and the trill of a flute. The three of them followed the courtesan to the second floor. Huang became more aware of Constable

Wu's heavy step behind him. Just ahead of him, Magistrate Li was chattering about music.

"Our household employed an old musician who played the pipa," Li was saying. "He tried to teach me once, but I had no talent for it."

The magistrate was filling the silence with nonsense—this from a man known for being very skilled with words. They halted at a door midway down the hall and Mei met his eyes briefly, before lowering her gaze and stepping aside.

As he followed Magistrate Li into the chamber, Huang was very much aware they had gone directly to the quarters without any question or introduction. He also knew who typically entertained in these rooms. The sitting area was empty, but the curtain to the inner chamber was open.

Huilan was lying on the bed, her head thrown back.

Huang went to her. Her name caught in his throat, his head pounding while he struggled to make sense of what he was seeing. A faint hope flickered in him as he took hold of her wrist, but he already knew. He had known the moment he'd seen her. Huilan's complexion was no longer moon-pale and luminous. It was colorless. The stillness about her went beyond sleep. There was no way to describe it, but he recognized the aberration of it immediately.

He sank down to his knees on the floor, unable to take his eyes off her. Her throat was bruised. Someone had ruined it forever. She would never sing again.

"She's dead," he said heavily, a part of him feeling dead as well. He'd just seen her that morning.

"You knew her?" Magistrate Li asked.

"Everyone knew Huilan," he replied sharply. "She was one of the Four Beauties."

The other two men were watching impassively by the door. Huang clenched his fists as anger heated his veins. They had known Huilan was dead and brought him there to watch his reaction. She'd been left alone all this time.

A knot formed in his chest. He was confused and horrified and at a loss for anything intelligent to say.

"Perhaps you should come out here," Magistrate Li suggested quietly.

Huang nodded. He took one final look at Huilan. She was the youngest of the Beauties. Her cheeks were gently rounded, which evoked a fresh-faced innocence. The violence was all the worse for that.

"DID YOU SPEAK with Huilan earlier today?" Magistrate Li asked.

They were in the sitting room just outside the courtesan's chamber. Huang looked up from his tea, which had gone cold. "At the Grand Canal during the race."

Li nodded gravely. "She was so full of youth and beauty. Such a tragedy. Do you come to the Hundred Songs often?"

"Once in a while. Huilan sang the last time I was here."

Huang ran a hand over his face. Huilan had been evasive that morning, but he should have insisted she explain herself. He should have never let her leave alone. He should have remembered the look of fear in her eyes when they'd first spoken.

"Were you her lover?" Li continued.

So this was an interrogation, then.

Huang straightened and met Magistrate Li eye to eye. "No, I wasn't."

"Well acquainted, then."

Li was grasping at something. The constable came forward from his station in the corner and held out a folded paper. Magistrate Li looked it over before placing it onto the table between them.

"This was found lying beside Lady Huilan's bed." His finger rested over the red seal stamped onto the paper. "Is this your family's mark?"

Huang knew what it was without looking. The paper he'd given Huilan was an official permit used to travel outside the gated wards after curfew.

"Did she use this to go to you at night?"

"I told you, we were not lovers," he said evenly.

Magistrate Li stared him down. "How did Lady Huilan come to possess this pass?"

"She must have taken it from me."

"Without your knowledge?"

His lips lifted sardonically. "I often drink too much."

Huilan had asked for his help to leave the quarter. He often moved freely through the wards at night, one of the privileges of the aristocracy, and he'd assumed that was why she'd gone to him.

"Madame Lui can speak to the extent of my association with Lady Huilan," Huang said. "The life of a courtesan isn't very private."

At that moment, the headmistress entered with Mei and a younger girl, two of Huilan's courtesan-sisters. There were tears in the older woman's eyes.

"Madame Lui."

She clasped her hands around his. "You find who did this. She was like a daughter to me!"

Madame Lui had been a great beauty herself in her youth and remained a handsome woman now, despite the redness around her eyes. She sniffed into a handkerchief.

Magistrate Li came over from the sitting area and

addressed Mei. "I understand that you were the first to find her."

The young courtesan nodded. "We were entertaining a large party in the banquet room. Huilan was acting as hostess while I was there to assist her. Everyone was in a happy mood and drinking wine for the festival. After an hour, Huilan complained of a headache. She told me to play a song and keep the party occupied while she went upstairs to rest for a little while, but she was gone for so long I finally went up to check on her. The moment I opened the door, I knew she wasn't sleeping." Mei's voice cracked and she buried her face in her hands.

Magistrate Li gave her a moment before continuing. "Miss, who was in the banquet room?"

"Commissioner Ma and a few of his friends. I…I don't remember everyone's name." She looked helplessly to Madame Lui.

"They are all regular patrons who have come here many times," the headmistress told them.

Huang wondered why the second girl had been brought in, but Magistrate Li didn't question her the same way he had spoken to Mei. Instead, the constable went to her. Towering a full head and shoulders over the younger girl, he spoke to her in a quiet tone. She looked over at Huang and shook her head.

Li turned back to him. "I apologize for intruding, Lord Bai. You understand such questions must be asked. We must continue our conversation at another time."

He bowed in kind. "Of course, Magistrate Li."

If it weren't for his lineage, Huang was certain he would have been dragged to the prison house. He started toward the door, trying to remember everything Huilan had told him. As he passed an end table he noticed a writing box lying open behind the vase. The brush had been set over the top of the case and the ink appeared fresh.

Li Yen's voice rang after him. "Before you go, Lord Bai."

He turned to see both men watching him.

"I should ask you where you were earlier this evening—as a matter of procedure, of course," Li assured him.

"At the Lotus Palace," he replied easily. "Conversing with the magistrate himself."

"Yes, but I do recall you were a bit late arriving."

"I had forgotten." Huang faced him without flinching. "I was delightfully delayed downstairs. A conversation with a charming young lady."

He had followed Yue-ying into the wine cellar hoping for a private moment away from the parlors and banquets. The plan was to be charming, to humble himself, make her laugh. But he had been mistaken about how he'd be received. Apparently, he was mistaken about many things lately.

"Ah, your alley cat?" Li recalled.

"Yes." Now was not the time to play the fool. "The very same creature."

CHAPTER FOUR

IT WAS AN obsessed patron who had done it.

It was a thief who was interrupted while trying to steal her jewels.

It was the ghost of a scholar who had killed himself out of love for her.

Or maybe it was a jealous rival, who saw how the young and talented Huilan was rising in popularity in the North Hamlet.

"Nonsense!" Mingyu snorted when Yue-ying recounted all the theories she'd heard.

"About the ghost or—"

"The gossipmongers always have to infuse rivalry into everything. As if we're filled with envy and ready to tear at each other just because we're women. I'm devastated by Huilan's death. She was so sweet-natured to everyone."

Mingyu appeared genuinely distraught as Yue-ying finished pinning her hair. She chose an understated look for Mingyu today, foregoing ornaments and jewels in her hair and only using a light trace of color on her lips and cheeks. They had found out the day before about Huilan's death and the entire quarter was in mourning.

"The worst of it is there is a murderer in the Ping-kang li and we don't know who it is. How can any of us feel safe?"

Yue-ying sighed. For all her worldliness, Mingyu was

so sheltered. "The stranger in the canal was also murdered, yet no one seemed to be alarmed then."

"I thought that was an accidental drowning."

"One does not accidentally drown and then climb back into a boat," Yue-ying pointed out.

"Oh," Mingyu said, dismissing the loss of that life with a single word. She glanced once at herself in the bronze mirror, decided what she saw was satisfactory and stood. Mingyu spent very little time preening or fixating on her appearance. "Well, I hope that Magistrate Li will find whoever did this quickly so Huilan's spirit can be at rest."

Mingyu left the dressing area while Yue-ying stayed behind to straighten the combs and pins and makeup pots. She had heard little about the mysterious body in the boat while she was certain the North Hamlet would be talking about Huilan long and loud. There would be a flood of verses lamenting her early passing, the silencing of her song, her tragic beauty.

She felt sadness over Huilan as well. How could she not? Huilan had been close to Yue-ying in age and so full of life. The rumors said Huilan had been strangled to death. She had died struggling and afraid, her final breath forced out of her. For that to be the last thing one felt on this Earth—

Yue-ying wiped away the tear that fell unexpectedly down her cheek. Strange to feel so deeply over someone she barely knew, someone she rarely spoke to. The last time Yue-ying had seen Huilan, they had engaged in a silly, meaningless conversation about the availability of lychees. So much of the banter of the tearooms, the pleasure houses and banquet halls was without any true meaning or purpose.

But how could she have known to say something

meaningful to Huilan that morning? That it would be her last chance to do so?

Mingyu was calling her from the parlor. Yue-ying straightened to go to her, wondering if she should tell Mingyu how beautiful she was, how naive she could be, how much Mingyu's distant nature sometimes hurt her and how much Yue-ying cared for her.

THE HUNDRED SONGS was a short walk from the Lotus. The colorful banners in front had been replaced with white drapery, signifying that the house was in mourning. The sound of chanting and the hollow tap of the prayer drum could be heard from the street. She and Mingyu had just reached the front door when a dark figure at the street corner caught her eye. Constable Wu started toward her, looming larger with every step until she was hidden in his shadow.

"Miss Yue-ying, if I may speak with you."

She glanced over her shoulder, but Mingyu had already disappeared into the Hundred Songs to join the other mourners.

To her relief, Wu Kaifeng directed her to the nearest teahouse rather than the magistrate's yamen, but it was difficult to relax with his iron gaze fixed on her. His height was exaggerated by his build, which was long and lean. His facial features were elongated as well, with an eagle's nose and high cheekbones that tapered down to a sharp chin. He wasn't an attractive man. He wasn't entirely ugly either, but if she had to choose—she would say his face fit his position. It was an intimidating face, not one that evoked pleasant thoughts.

The server brought two bowls of the house tea and Wu gave her a chance to take a sip before speaking.

"I have questions about Lord Bai Huang. I understand you are familiar with him."

It wasn't posed as a question, but she nodded anyway. "Yes, sir."

"He is close to your mistress as well?"

That raised her defenses. "Lord Bai and Lady Mingyu are no closer than the moon to the stars."

"But he's been courting her."

"That's what scholar-gentlemen do as a pastime. They ride horses, they compose poetry and they court beautiful ladies."

Wu raised his eyebrows. They were black and as intimidating as the rest of his face.

She didn't know why she'd spoken so cynically. It was possible Bai Huang was genuinely taken with Mingyu. She was exquisitely beautiful, with a dancer's grace and a poet's wit, and she made a livelihood out of captivating men.

"Why do you ask about Lord Bai?" she inquired.

"Our investigation into the death of Lady Huilan is hindered by one unfortunate fact: we suspect an aristocrat from a well-respected and powerful family."

All the air rushed out of her. "But Lord Bai doesn't seem to be the sort," she gasped.

"Do you know many killers, Miss Yue-ying?" Wu asked pointedly, and it was a sharp, finely honed point at that.

She fell silent, but her mind was not at all quiet. Surely an affair between Bai Huang and Huilan couldn't have escaped notice, but everyone had their secrets in the Pingkang li. His association with the House of a Hundred Songs could be more intimate than anyone realized.

"Bai Huang is the son of Bai Zheng-jian, a high-ranking official in the Ministry of Defense," Wu said.

Yue-ying nodded. This was all commonly known in the quarter.

"Though the elder Lord Bai is assigned to a military post in Fujian province, the family maintains a household in the capital. I hear it told that Bai Huang only recently returned to the city, not even a year ago."

He finished his report and looked to her expectantly.

"All I know is there was some trouble a few years ago and he was sent away," she offered. "Something about gambling debts. I was new to the Pingkang li then."

"Interesting. Anything else?"

The constable's constant gaze unnerved her. She swore he had the eyes of a snake, never blinking.

She thought back to the previous days. So much had happened that month with the earthquake and then the dragonboat festival the week after.

"Huilan met with someone on the first day of the new moon," she recalled. "A young man. He was on the bridge near the temple."

His eyebrows lifted. "Did you recognize him?"

She shook her head. "I was too far away to see."

He paused to consider the information, prolonging the silence for so long that she began to fidget. That day had been the first time she had seen Constable Wu as well.

"I didn't pay much attention to Lord Bai's exploits in the past," she continued, feeling the need to say something. It was unsettling to have Wu staring at her. "He used to have a bad reputation, a reputation for being reckless, but when he returned, his reputation transformed into something more—" She struggled for a word. Wu Kaifeng waited. "Impulsive. Ridiculous."

She felt bad speaking poorly of Lord Bai to a stranger. Constable Wu took a long drink of his tea and glanced downward at the remaining leaves, as if scrying for an answer.

"Miss Yue-ying, I am letting you into my confidence and you must consider this information very carefully. A young man who could not be identified was seen at the Hundred Songs the night of the murder. Lord Bai met with the courtesan earlier that same day. An item that belonged to him was later found in her chamber beside the body."

A shiver ran up her spine. "But he was at the Lotus Palace that night."

"That brings up another interesting point. Magistrate Li recalls that Lord Bai arrived late and uninvited to the banquet."

"He wasn't as late as it seemed. I saw him earlier. Downstairs." She blushed, realizing how it would look to the constable. "And when he came up to the banquet, he sat directly next to Magistrate Li and started a conversation. What criminal would do that?"

"A bold one, for certain," Wu said thoughtfully. "One who believes he is above suspicion. There was a scratch on his face that night. I saw it myself."

"That was my doing. We had a…a disagreement."

"That is not quite how Lord Bai told it."

His tone told her enough about Bai Huang's side of the story. She could feel her cheeks heating under the constable's scrutiny.

Wu pressed on, "Are you certain he didn't have that scratch when he arrived?"

"I'm certain. I struck him hard across the face."

But she had hit him in the darkness of the cellar. She

hadn't been able to see his face clearly. Doubt began to creep in like a festering wound.

"I commend you for that." He didn't smile, but his eyes were unusually bright. "An aristocrat of Lord Bai's stature isn't easy to accuse. His father's connections within the imperial bureaucracy are very powerful and Magistrate Li has warned me that we must step carefully," he said with a touch of ire. "In the meantime, be wary of him, Miss Yue-ying. I know when a man is hiding something."

CHAPTER FIVE

THE DEALER LIFTED the clay tumbler over his head and shook it while he chanted in a singsong: "Here, here, bet high, bet low."

The final wagers were placed onto the table as the dice rattled around inside the tumbler. With a flourish, the dealer set the dish down, paused dramatically, then lifted the lid to reveal the numbers. The result was met with a few cheers, more groans, some curses.

Huang swiped a hand over his forehead and stared at the candle flickering on the table behind the dealer. It was an oven in here tonight and he was having a tough time of it. A runner came by offering a cup filled with what would have been called water if not for the few flecks of tea floating in it. He waved the boy away in irritation.

"It must be a lucky night for you, Lord Bai."

Wu Kaifeng came up alongside him just as the dealer shoved a pile of coins in front of him. Huang stared at the cash warily before pushing it all back onto the table beside the character for "Low".

He pasted on a smile before turning to the constable. "So it seems. Let's see if it continues."

Occasionally someone he knew from the Pingkang li would come into the gambling den, but he had no desire to hold up appearances tonight. He glanced once again at the candle. There was only a stub left.

Sometimes he lost quickly and would simply get up and leave. Those were the rules. But sometimes he won, and those were the hardest nights of all.

"Do you play, Constable?"

Though Wu stood at the table, he had yet to take out any money. He looked over the painted characters on the table, each representing a wager, and then over to the three dice inside the clay bowl. The dealer shrank back as Wu's gaze raked over him.

"No," he replied after an uncomfortably long delay.

It was rare to meet someone with such a disconnected sense of social politeness. Though his words and gestures were not incorrect, they always came a touch too late or off-rhythm, as if he had to think of things others took as natural.

"It's quite easy," Huang said. "You put your coins down on the table and they take them away."

"All bets in!"

The dealer set the bowl down and lifted the tumbler to a general outcry. The total was high this time and Huang's wager disappeared. Another round started promptly after.

"I could never see the appeal of gambling," Wu said. "Too much uncertainty."

The problem was Huang liked the unpredictability. He liked the guessing and wagering and not knowing. No, it was incorrect to say he *liked* any of it. That implied there was some enjoyment or pleasure involved. He supposed there had been, at one time. Now he knew that he didn't just like the risk, he needed it. It was never about the money.

Tonight, the battle had been especially hard. With a new Emperor on the throne and Huilan's recent death, there was too much cluttering his mind. A night of diversion at the tables was very tempting. Unfortunately, Huang knew it was impossible to play only a few rounds to take his mind off things. He always followed a strict, unbending regimen he'd set for himself.

Wu looked around the dimly lit room. "So this is where you go on nights you don't spend drinking."

Obviously, the constable had come here to investigate him and couldn't be bothered with subtlety.

Huang affected a grin. "I'll drink tonight as well."

Wu was not amused. "You play the third night of every week."

His smile faltered a little. "A good night for it."

"And always from the eleventh hour to the twelfth," Wu continued. "Always this table. Exactly a thousand copper coins."

The dealer cast a glance toward Wu before he began hawking out the next round.

Huang shrugged, though the room seemed to have gotten hotter. A trickle of sweat ran down his neck. "Gamblers and their superstitions, you know."

Wu nodded, but there was very little in the way of camaraderie in it. "It must be working tonight. You look to have nearly three times that in front of you."

"More wagers? Bet now!" the dealer crowed.

The candle had melted down to a pool of wax.

Huang pushed the entire stack of coins over the square marked "Triple".

Wu's eyes narrowed on him. "I may not be knowledgeable about this game, but I would assume that is a highly unlikely outcome."

At least he'd managed to surprise the demon. "If the dice are with me, I'll be a wealthy man," Huang replied with a grin.

"You are already wealthy, Lord Bai."

They listened to the rattle of the dice. As the tumbler was set on the table, Huang felt that familiar rush, the boiling of his blood as he waited to see the result. Exquisite anticipation. Nothing else in the world felt as good as this. Not good wine, good food. Not even a beautiful woman. At moments like this, he knew he would never be free of this urge.

The dealer lifted the top off the bowl and Huang's heart almost stopped. Two fives and a three. He didn't want to think what he would have done if that last die had landed another five instead of the three.

There was nothing left but the wick on the candle. He turned as the dealer raked back all of his winnings of the past hour, leaving Constable Wu at the table to form whatever conclusions he chose.

YUE-YING SPENT THE next few days preparing Mingyu for an upcoming journey. General Deng was Mingyu's most prestigious patron. He had held a position in the capital before being transferred to Guangdong province where he currently served as military governor. Whenever he returned to Changan, Mingyu pushed all other engagements aside to see to him.

"The general will be sending an escort for me," Mingyu had told her. "We will be traveling to the nearby hot springs. There is no need for you to accompany me."

Yue-ying ignored the abrupt dismissal and started packing a trunk with all the necessary clothing and personal items Mingyu would need. She made sure to include all the jewels and trinkets the military governor had gifted to Mingyu.

This wasn't the first time Mingyu had left her for such an assignation. It was publicly known that she and

General Deng were lovers. Yue-ying could understand why Mingyu desired privacy during their time together. Perhaps Mingyu held deeper feelings for the governor than she admitted.

Once Mingyu was gone, Yue-ying was left with more idle time than she was accustomed to and no one to pass it with. Over the years, she had become friendly with the other courtesans in the pleasure house, but none of them were close. Mingyu was the only courtesan who had a personal attendant, which put Yue-ying in a unique position at the Lotus Palace. It also kept her apart from the others.

To remain busy, she set about sorting the rest of the clothing and accessories, bringing out the lighter garments from storage in preparation for the hottest part of the summer season. A pile was started for items that needed mending or other repairs. When she was arranging Mingyu's slippers, she found a pair tossed in the bottom of a trunk. The embroidered pattern had been splattered with mud.

With a sigh, she took a damp rag to it. Mingyu was so careless sometimes. Such beautiful and luxurious items held little value to her.

A knock came from the outer chamber, interrupting her task.

"Miss Yue-ying?" a familiar voice called out.

She shot to her feet. Lord Bai stepped into the parlor just as she poked her head out from the dressing room. The slipper was still clutched in her hand.

"That's not to throw at me, is it?" he asked, his lips quirking.

Bai Huang was a suspect in Huilan's murder, but Constable Wu didn't have any strong evidence. Wu had also warned her Bai Huang was hiding something, but he wasn't a violent man...yet when he'd cornered her in the cellar, he'd certainly appeared menacing.

She had been staring at him for too long while she weighed the arguments. "Lady Mingyu is not here."

"I know. I came here to see you."

For a moment, she considered telling him to go away and shouting for help if he refused, but Madame would think she had gone mad. Bai Huang was a frequent and generous customer.

"Were you at the Hundred Songs the night of the festival?" she asked, edging closer to a ceramic vase on an end table.

"I was here. Don't you remember?"

"*Before* you came to the Lotus."

She glared at him, her irritation rising. She supposed it benefited him somehow to adopt the persona of the fool, otherwise why would he do it so often and with so much enthusiasm?

"I wasn't at the Hundred Songs. I swear on my grave."

"Why did you tell Magistrate Li you were with me?" she demanded

He looked confused. "Because I *was* with you?"

"Not in the way you implied."

"I said that I was delightfully delayed by—" he paused to recall the exact words "—a charming young lady."

"Delayed?" she asked through her teeth. "Delight-fully?"

The dog. She dropped the slipper and took hold of the vase.

A light dawned in his eyes. "You think I murdered Huilan?" he asked incredulously. "Do you truly believe I'm capable of doing such a horrible thing? And to someone as gentle and kind as Huilan. She wouldn't hurt a fly."

"I don't believe you killed her." She kept the vase between them. "But I don't think you've been completely truthful."

"I am trying to find whoever did this and bring him to justice," he insisted. "I came here to ask your help on that very matter."

"Why would you need my help?"

He eyed the vase in her grasp. "Shall we discuss this over tea?"

She was overanxious. Constable Wu might be right that she didn't know many killers, but she had known men who were capable of it. She remembered a brothel owner who had beaten one girl to death and was only forced to pay a fine for the crime, the ruling being that he hadn't intended to kill her. She knew in her gut Bai Huang wasn't like that.

She set the would-be weapon down and went to light the tea stove. He sat out in the parlor as she worked. Peering out from the screen, she saw him running his hands back and forth over his knees, standing, then sitting again and looking around as if to search for some possible inspiration to start a conversation. It was disarming to see him like this, so uncertain.

Lord Bai Huang probably expected tea to miraculously appear when he asked for it, with no extra effort or delay. Once she had the fire started in the stove, she ladled water into the pot and set it on top. With nothing to do but wait, she returned to the parlor and seated herself. It was unusual to be sitting across from a gentleman, eye to eye.

"Why do you need my help?" she asked again.

"You're familiar with the quarter. People know you

and trust you." He paused, looking at her intently. "And you have a good heart."

She fidgeted. "I don't understand why you can't let the magistrate handle things."

By now, she was certain Bai Huang wasn't half the fool he presented in public, but she still didn't think he was more qualified than Magistrate Li and his constables.

"First, the pompous Li Yen and the evil-eyed Wu Kaifeng are new to the city. People don't trust them. They won't be able to act as quickly as you and I. Second, Magistrate Li has his own agenda. *I* don't trust him. And third—"

He paused for a long while on the last point. His dark eyebrows folded into a frown.

"Third, I swore to Huilan I would help her. I owe this debt to her."

He looked away. Yue-ying stood and returned to the stove to allow him his privacy. Had he been in love with Huilan? She was the sort of woman that would inspire such devotion in a man. And Bai Huang had shown himself to be the romantic sort.

She scooped tea leaves into two cups and poured the hot water over them, covering the cups with a lid to let the tea steep. Bai Huang sat wordlessly as she set his cup before him. They took a few sips and he seemed to relax, though she remained anxious. It wasn't her place to have tea with gentlemen. Suddenly she was aware of her posture and the placement of her hands and feet, knowing everything must be all wrong.

Their eyes met and an odd sensation traveled up her spine. They both spoke at once.

"About the other night—"

"We don't need to speak of it—"

Silence. Again a look between them that left her so confused, more so than his kiss had done. That kiss was forced upon her and there had been no finesse to it. Not even the barest attempt to seduce her into enjoying it. She absolutely would not apologize for the scratch that still marred his perfect face. He deserved it. But the Bai Huang she was looking at now seemed an entirely different man.

He smiled crookedly at her. "I know I'm a scoundrel sometimes."

His tone was unexpectedly intimate. Heat rose up her neck until her face burned hot.

"What exactly did you need me to do?" she asked, noting to herself that she hadn't yet agreed to help.

"Madame Lui gave me a list of everyone who was at the Hundred Songs that night. Also any patron who has come calling on Huilan. She spoke to the magistrate as well, but I believe she wasn't nearly as forthcoming with him."

With a smug look, Bai Huang pulled out a paper from beneath the fold of his hanfu robe and held it out to her. Yue-ying hesitated before taking it from him. She could only read a little, having memorized the few characters needed for her daily activities. She could write her own name and some basic numbers and read the signboards in the market, but little else.

The characters swam before her eyes, but she was too ashamed to admit that she couldn't make any sense of them. "What do you intend to do with these names?"

"We go through them and look for anyone suspicious. You know everyone in the North Hamlet."

"Only the people who come to the Lotus Palace," she protested. "And not much more than their names and faces."

He made an impatient sound. "You're just being humble because etiquette demands it. Between you and me, I would wager we can account for every name here."

Bai Huang took the paper from her and asked for a writing brush. As she went back into Mingyu's chamber to retrieve the case from her desk, he recounted what he knew about that night, speaking loud enough to be heard from the parlor.

"The Hundred Songs hosted a banquet for prestigious patrons. The guest of honor was an imperial scholar who just received an appointment to the Ministry of Revenue. Huilan was there to receive the visitors and entertain them with song. Just before the eleventh hour, she retired momentarily to her room. That was the last time anyone saw her."

The fine hairs along her arms rose upon hearing the story. The events were still so recent in memory. Yueying returned to the parlor and set the wooden writing box before him along with a sheet of paper.

"If it was like the banquet here at the Lotus Palace, people would have been coming and going all night. It would be impossible to track where everyone was at all times," she told him.

"We have to consider everyone a suspect, then."

Bai Huang folded back the drape of his sleeve in two crisp movements, exposing forearms that appeared surprisingly strong. She watched with fascination as he opened the case and prepared the ink as if it were a ritual he had done a thousand times. He selected the smallest brush and dipped it into the ink. Then he started reading names off the list, copying each one onto the fresh sheet with a practiced, steady hand.

There was something compelling about seeing Bai Huang so focused. His brow was creased with concen-

tration and the lines of his profile hardened with determination. He looked nothing like the pleasure-seeking
flower prince they all so loved to chuckle about.

"Fa Zhenggang. I don't know him," he said.

"He's a painter who lives to the south of the market."

"Ah." Bai Huang looked satisfied as he marked down
the detail.

They continued methodically down the list, which
had nearly twenty names on it.

"Ma Jun. That name sounds familiar. He's the head of
the East Market Commission office," Bai Huang noted.

"It's also well-known that Huilan was a favorite of
his," she pointed out.

"Is that so?"

She nodded. "Well-known to the quarter, at least."

He looked down at the columns of names and sucked
in a deep breath. Each name held its own web of connections and secrets. Suddenly the task appeared daunting.

"Let's continue." He took a moment to shrug out the
stiffness in his shoulders before dipping his brush again.

She wasn't yet certain Bai Huang's plan was the best
approach, but she was touched someone like him would
be concerned with the misfortunes of one lone courtesan
within the North Hamlet. She had assumed the women
of the Pingkang li were nothing but diversions to men
like him, their names and graces interchangeable. This
one was a graceful flower or a precious gem, noted for
playing the pipa or being an elegant dancer.

"Lord Bai?"

He looked up with the brush still poised over the
paper.

"Were you and Huilan…" she took a breath as she
searched for a word that wasn't too improper "…close?"

"Close?"

He was making this deliberately difficult for her.

"Intimate," she amended.

He regarded her for a moment before answering. His look was one of complete seriousness. "No."

Yue-ying didn't realize she had been holding her breath. There was so much she didn't know about him. "Magistrate Li and Constable Wu suspect that you were."

"I know this."

"I told Constable Wu that I saw Huilan meeting a young man on the day of the earthquake. They were on the bridge by the temple. From where I was, he could have been anyone."

"It wasn't me," he insisted, seeing the look in her eye. "I've only ever spoken to Huilan in public or at the Hundred Songs."

She tried hard to recall more clearly. The man's robe had been blue-gray in color without any additional accents. It was the robe of a scholar. Certainly she'd never seen Bai Huang dressed so simply.

"I apologize for my boldness, Lord Bai," she told him. "I didn't mean to sound so—"

"Intimate?" he finished for her, eyes dancing.

She didn't realize her face could heat so quickly. Best to stop talking. She tucked her hair behind her ear, thought about it, then untucked it in the next moment.

It wasn't as if she'd asked if they were involved out of jealousy. She had nothing to be jealous about. Even though he had attempted to kiss her—and it was really nothing more than an awkward attempt—this was Lord Bai, who spouted bland poetry about eyes and lips and graceful willowy figures. She wondered what comparison he would conjure were he to compose poetry about her.

What had come over her? The boundaries of this

conversation had completely slipped away from her. She wasn't seeking a lover and, if she were, Lord Bai would be the least likely of suitors.

Thankfully, Bai Huang turned back to the list, with her adding small touches based on what was known in the North Hamlet. By the end of the next hour, they had three sheets of paper spread out on the table.

"It could be any of these men." He sighed.

"Or it could be none of them."

He glanced up at her, irritated because she'd spoken the truth. Then he looked back at the sheets, lifting them into the air to dry while he studied the characters. Carefully, he folded up the pages and tucked them into his robe.

"You said Huilan was acting oddly at the temple," he said. "Let's start there."

THE TEMPLE COURTYARD was empty that morning and the old tortoise was out of his lair once more, asleep beneath the shade of a rock. The altar room was open for worshippers to come and go as they wished with the ever-present curl of incense smoke being the only sign that any shadow of a soul was about. The two of them loitered about until a middle-aged nun in gray robes came to greet them.

Yue-ying pressed her palms together and bowed respectfully. "Elder Sister."

Bai Huang stood apart from them as she asked the nun about Huilan. Afterward, she bowed once again as thank-you and farewell before returning to Bai Huang.

"The nuns say that Huilan came every month, always on the first," Yue-ying reported. "The earthquake happened on the first as well."

They left the temple and walked together to the

nearby bridge and looked down into the water. Bai Huang gripped the wooden rail, his hand placed inadvertently close to hers, while she held her breath, uncertain of whether she should move away or not. He was always testing the boundaries between them; inviting familiarity.

"Her young man probably met her here every month," he said.

"Huilan must have used the temple visits to get permission to leave the Hundred Songs," she surmised.

Most of the courtesans were bonded servants or slaves to their den mothers. Their personal time was carefully guarded.

"I wonder if he knows that she won't ever return." The water reflected a ripple of light over his face and his expression looked distant. "On the first day of next month, he'll wait here for her, anxious and lonely."

Bai Huang had a scholar's heart, all full of drama and tragic longing. But such romantic ideals were a luxury of the upper class.

They had passed a peasant woman sitting beside a basket at the bridge's entrance. Yue-ying broke away from Bai Huang to go to her.

"Scallion cakes, miss!" The woman repeated her hawker's cry.

Yue-ying recalled that same cry when she'd been passing by after the earthquake. "Are you here every day, Auntie?" she asked.

"Every day from sunup to sundown," the graying woman said. Her gaze shifted behind Yue-ying. "Unless it's raining. Scallion cakes, sir?"

"Are they delicious?" Bai Huang came up to stand behind Yue-ying.

"The best, my lord." The woman lifted the lid of her basket to show off the flat, yellow pancakes.

"I'll have two."

"Why not make it four?" the woman urged, taking in Bai Huang's fine robe. "You'll wish you had more as soon as you're done."

Yue-ying could hear the smile in his tone as he answered, "Four, then."

"Do you recall seeing a young woman, about the same age as me?" Yue-ying asked as Bai Huang handed over his coin. "Pale-skinned, brown hair. Very pretty. She came here at the beginning of every month."

"I know who you're speaking of. Skin white as snow. Every month, without fail."

"Was there ever anyone with her?"

"Ah, yes! A young fellow."

Yue-ying glanced at Bai Huang. "Similar in look to him?"

"Oh, no. My lord here is much taller. And much more handsome. This man was round of face. His clothes were plain."

They left with their scallion cakes and a description which, unfortunately, could fit any number of men in the ward.

Bai Huang pointed a finger at her. "You didn't believe that it wasn't me meeting Huilan," he accused.

"Not true. I was just using you as a point of comparison."

He snorted.

"And the woman charged you extra for the scallion cakes," Yue-ying said out of the corner of her mouth.

"She-demon."

He split the cakes with her and took a hearty bite.

Yue-ying nibbled at hers and wondered whether the she-demon he referred to was her or the peasant woman.

"So Huilan had a secret lover," he concluded.

"Someone without means. Otherwise he could have courted her openly at the Hundred Songs. He might have been frustrated, unable to have the woman he desired. That could push a man to commit murder."

Bai Huang regarded her silently. "This sort of behavior is something you've experienced yourself?"

"Not directly."

But she'd witnessed it. Such things were inevitable when women were bought and sold as property. When commerce was confused with sex and emotion. To pleasure seekers, the North Hamlet was supposed to be a place of beauty, poetry and music. All of the courtesans worked to perpetuate that illusion, but Yue-ying was no courtesan.

"The sadness of it is, such deaths are usually at the hands of angry patrons or lovers." Her mouth twisted cynically. "Some men mistake it for passion."

CHAPTER SIX

HUANG WALKED YUE-YING to the front doors of the Lotus Palace, at which time she bowed, called him Lord Bai and disappeared abruptly through the curtains. He was left wondering whether she'd only accompanied him because he was noble-born and wealthy enough that she was obligated to defer to him. He hoped it wasn't true. He was growing rather fond of her honesty.

He was so used to lies that his time with Yue-ying seemed like the only real conversation he'd had for months. If only he hadn't muddied the waters with that failed kiss in the darkness of the Lotus Palace cellar.

Before returning to his rented quarters, he stopped by the Hundred Songs to present a gift of silver. The house was still in mourning and would remain so for the traditional forty-nine-day period. During that time, the Hundred Songs would have to rely on the generosity of their patrons to keep everyone fed.

"Lord Bai! How good of you to come." Madame Lui approached dressed in her white mourning robe. She clasped both of his hands in hers. "We were all so frightened last night."

"Frightened? Why was that, Madame?"

"Sit and have some tea and I'll tell you."

It would be rude to simply come by, leave his gift, then go, so Huang sat down in the main parlor with Madame Lui while the girls brought tea and a small plate of rice flour cakes.

"What happened last night?" he asked again once the formalities had been settled.

"We heard footsteps upstairs." Madame Lui leaned closer and lowered her voice, not to keep any secret, but to impress upon him the seriousness of what she was describing. "In Huilan's bedchamber."

He remained skeptical. "Did you go to see who it was?"

"It was in the middle of the night. Everyone was asleep except for two of the girls who remained awake for the vigil. They were so scared, they couldn't move. And then, you won't believe what happened next."

"What happened?" he prompted.

"One of the candles on the altar split its wick."

"That *is* strange." Huang injected more wonder into his tone than he truly felt. "How long did the footsteps move about in Huilan's room?"

"The girls said the footsteps walked about ten steps and then halted. They ran to wake me up and at that point, I heard them as well, rushing down the hall. Huilan has come back! Her spirit is very strong."

Madame Lui's fears weren't so far-flung. For seven days after death, Huilan's spirit was believed to fly free while loved ones kept a vigil night and day over her earthly body. It was believed that sometime during that period, the spirit would return home. A murdered soul tended to linger, clinging to the life that had been ended before its time.

He preferred to find a rational explanation for what had occurred. "Madame, may I ask permission to go into Huilan's chamber?"

"Of course! She won't be upset—you were a friend."

Not good enough of a friend. He should have stayed by her side or taken her somewhere safe.

After he finished his tea, Madame Lui led him up to the apartments. Though she opened the door for him, she remained outside in the hall, daring to only peek in. Huang was careful to scan the room before stepping inside.

From the outer parlor, nothing appeared to have changed since the tragic night. The magistrate and the constable had searched the chambers, but he doubted anyone had come into the room since.

"What did the footsteps sound like?" he asked, peering into the bedchamber. Ghost or no ghost, he felt a shudder run down his spine at the sight of the bed. He couldn't forget the image of Huilan stretched lifelessly across it.

"They were muffled," Madame Lui called out. She was still hovering outside the door. "They moved quickly and then suddenly stopped."

Huang paused at the window. The shutters were closed and he took the trouble of opening them to peer down into the lane below. He pulled them shut before returning to Madame Lui.

"I have a request. I know it may be too much to ask."

"Anything," Madame Lui insisted. "Lord Bai has been so kind to us."

"May I stay here tonight?"

The headmistress looked startled. "Of course, my lord, but—"

She must have thought better of whatever question she wanted to ask. It was an odd request, but not too outrageous. And he was known for indulging in whimsical pursuits.

He shared the evening meal with Madame Lui downstairs. They were joined by the lovely Mei, who was the leading lady of the Hundred Songs now that her courtesan-sister was gone. Though the mourning period was hardly a time for flirtation, Mei took pains to be charmingly attentive while Madame Lui prodded her to refill his wine cup and place choice morsels onto his plate.

Quite early in the evening, Huang excused himself, claiming he'd had a tiring day. The entire household gathered to watch him go up the stairs. It was eerie; all the ladies dressed in white mourning robes, their dark eyes wide and fixed onto him.

He took only a single lantern with him. Once inside, he closed the doors and looked about the parlor. It remained a mausoleum to Huilan. Her writing was still on the walls alongside verses from her admirers.

Moving to the inner chamber, Huang looked briefly through what was left of Huilan's personal belongings for any hint to what had happened to her. He found only womanly things: hairpins, jars of cosmetics and articles of clothing packed away in a dresser.

There was one change from the last time he'd been in the room. Her writing box lay on top of the desk now instead of out in the sitting room and the brush had been cleaned. A few sheets of colored paper remained inside. The brush had been damp with ink the night of Huilan's death. She must have been writing a letter of some sort, but all of the papers in the box were blank. Anything of interest had probably been confiscated by the constable during his investigation.

With his brief search completed, Huang extinguished the lantern and lay back on the bed to wait. The room was left in darkness, without even the glimmer of the moon to accompany him. In the stillness, he could indeed sense Huilan's spirit. Not her ghost. Not the chill of the air or any pale, wispy visions. Rather, he felt the brief and tenuous way she'd affected him. His resolve strengthened as he lay in the same place where she took her last breath. As eerie as it was, it grounded him.

Yue-ying and likely the entire Pingkang li now suspected him of being Huilan's lover, but he'd only spoken with her a few times. She had asked for his help, but had been reluctant to give him details. She didn't yet know if she could trust him. When someone went looking for someone to rely on, they certainly didn't think of Bai Huang.

"I'll find who did this to you," he said to the darkness. "I swear it."

The moment he finished speaking, he heard the scraping sound of nails against wood. He wasn't one to be afraid of ghosts, but his heart hurtled against his chest and he shot up into a sitting position.

The sound came from outside. The shutters creaked as they swung open and a sliver of moonlight spilled into the chamber. He held himself still, holding his breath, as a hand appeared, then an arm. Soon the entire silhouette of a person stepped from the window onto the floor.

He launched himself at the black figure, colliding with arms and legs and something very definitely corporeal.

"On my mother!" the intruder cried before Huang clamped a hand over his mouth.

The man was slight of build. Huang pinned him facedown to the floor with his knee lodged between the man's shoulder blades. The sound of footsteps rushed toward them out in the hallway.

"Lord Bai!" Madame Lui's voice trembled with alarm from the other side of the chamber door.

"It's nothing," he called out, affecting a laugh while

keeping a lock on the intruder's arm. "I fell down in the dark. Quite embarrassing."

"Do you…do you need anything?" Propriety and the fear of ghosts kept the ladies from entering.

"I'm fine. Back in bed now. My apologies for startling you." He gave the intruder a warning shove, pressing his face against the floorboards when the man started to struggle.

Once the footsteps receded, he let go of the man's head, allowing him to raise it from the floor.

"Who are you?" the stranger demanded.

"Who am *I*? I should be asking you that question."

The man didn't answer. Huang had noted the tree just outside of Huilan's window and figured out how the "ghost" had gotten inside. The first time the women had heard footsteps, the intruder must have made it to the hallway, before being startled by Madame Lui, after which he ran back to the room and out the window again.

"Did you not hear me?" Huang shook him roughly. "Who are you and what business do you have here?"

"I'm not a thief. I came because—" His voice broke and the next part came out rough with emotion. "Because I wanted to see Huilan one last time."

HUANG LIT THE LANTERN. He even managed to procure a flask of wine and some cups from a cabinet in the parlor. Then he poured the wine and let the heartbroken stranger do most of the talking. His name was Wen Tse-kang. From his robe, he appeared to be a student. From the roundness in his cheeks, he appeared to be from one of the younger classes.

"I loved her." Tse-kang let his tears fall down his face without shame. "We loved each other."

"You know what happened to her," Huang said, keeping his tone neutral.

"I heard of the news the morning after. Some of my colleagues were whispering about a beautiful courtesan who had been tragically killed. I ran all the way here, praying it wasn't Huilan, telling myself that in no way could it be her. But it was." He covered his face as his features twisted with grief.

Huang's instinct told him this student wasn't the murderer. His grief and confusion were genuine. But at the same time, he remembered Yue-ying's warning about lovers being capable of violence. All it took was one moment of blind passion. They couldn't be so quick to dismiss anyone from the list of suspects.

"When was the last time you saw her?"

Tse-kang looked up, as if just seeing Huang for the first time. "Are you one of her patrons? I don't care if you have me arrested and beaten. I still don't regret coming here."

Definitely a youthful and impassioned scholar.

"I'm not one of her patrons, but I do have some influence in the North Hamlet," he lied. "I'm not going to have you arrested as long as you tell me everything I want to know."

"The last time I saw her was at the dragonboat races by the canal. I had only a moment to speak to her. She looked beautiful that day. She always looked so beautiful." The young scholar stared down at his hands. "I don't know why she ever looked at me twice."

"What did you say to her?"

Tse-kang looked directly at him as if he had nothing left in the world to fear. "I told her the preparations were ready. That we could go that night. That was our plan—

her plan. She was going to leave this place and we would go together. Get married." His chin lifted defiantly. "We were supposed to meet at the bridge by the temple, but she never came. I thought she had changed her mind."

The plan sounded plausible. There was more freedom to move about at night during festivals. Huilan had the pass that he had provided in order to get through the ward gates, but there was still the vastness of the city to contend with and then the open road beyond that.

"When did she start talking about leaving the capital?"

Tse-kang thought back. "Maybe a month ago. The first time she brought it up briefly when we met at the bridge. I protested that my studies weren't finished. What could I have to offer a woman like her as a failed student?"

Huang shifted in his seat, being the quintessential failed student himself, but said nothing.

"Huilan brushed the suggestion aside so quickly that I assumed she had been daydreaming. But the next time we met, she had thought of the details. She would sell her jewels and find a boat going east. She would hire a bodyguard if she had to. It sounded so dangerous, I knew I couldn't let her go alone. So we started planning to leave together."

Huilan would have needed a considerable amount of money, much more than she could have collected from pawning a few jewels or silken robes, yet she hadn't asked him for any silver when they had struck their bargain.

"Did Huilan tell you why she had to leave so quickly?"

"I just thought she wanted a new life." Tse-kang wiped his face with a sleeve. "She wanted to be free."

"ANOTHER POOR SCHOLAR fantasizes about a beautiful courtesan falling hopelessly in love with him," Yue-ying pronounced the next day with a roll of her eyes. "You know those romantic tales are all written by men."

Huang smiled. "Poor scholars need something to aspire to."

They were sitting on the second floor of a busy teahouse in the East Market. Yue-ying had insisted they meet there rather than at the Lotus or in the three lanes of the Pingkang li.

"There are certainly women who want to leave the North Hamlet and certainly many of them dream of becoming a wealthy man's wife or concubine." She tucked her hair behind her ear as she spoke. "But an elite courtesan doesn't dream of running away with a humble scholar blindly out of love. Huilan had many admirers. She had a level of security and comfort and a reputation within the Pingkang li which she had rightfully earned."

No matter how much Huang thought he knew the courtesans of the North Hamlet, no matter what their public personas might reveal, they kept part of themselves guarded away. That was why he needed Yue-ying's insight.

"So something happened a month ago," he continued. "Something that worried her. She needed to leave here fairly quickly."

"Madame Lui would have a record of all of Huilan's engagements and visitors." She paused to think. "There was a banquet around midspring. I remember this gathering because Huilan forgot the words to a song. She was very upset by it."

Huang frowned. "It was about that time when she first approached me."

He had been drinking at the Hundred Songs with a

couple of midlevel bureaucrats and Huilan had appeared through the curtain like a goddess through the clouds.

"I tried to think of something suitably impressive to say," he recalled. "She was known as the Orchid of Silla so I attempted to tell her she was beautiful in the language of Silla."

Yue-ying was taken aback. "You speak Sillan?"

Too late he realized his mistake. The know-nothing Bai Huang wouldn't have such a command of languages. "I once encountered some dignitaries visiting from the Kingdom of Silla in a drinking house. I learned a few choice phrases over wine—though most of them weren't exactly respectable."

She seemed satisfied with his explanation, or rather annoyed with it. Which meant she believed him. For some reason, he wasn't at all relieved.

"Huilan wasn't really from the Kingdom of Silla," she said impatiently. "It's merely a story that Madame Lui conjured up to lend an air of exoticism to her prize courtesan."

"Well, Huilan did reply in Sillan," he noted. "We exchanged a few pleasantries, before speaking in Han again. At first there was nothing unusual about the conversation. She inquired about my family and my travels outside of Changan. Then she asked about leaving the ward."

"Could she have been looking for you to redeem her?" Yue-ying asked, sipping her tea.

"I thought so at first, but she had wealthy protectors already."

"It's quite a different thing for an admirer to visit a courtesan in the entertainment district as opposed to bringing her home as a concubine," she pointed out. "As far as I know, no one had made a bid for her."

"Do you ever think of it?"

"Of what?"

"Of leaving the Pingkang li."

"I don't spend time dreaming, Lord Bai." She smoothed her hair down over the side of her face, her fingers just grazing over her birthmark. "Besides, I have a good life here. What did you want to know about the gathering?"

He could see why she was overlooked in the shadow of her famous mistress. Not because of her appearance. Mingyu had a softly curved and sultry beauty whereas Yue-ying was thinner in the face, fine-boned with a restrained sensuality that intrigued him. But Yue-ying was constantly hiding herself, trying to make herself small. Even in conversation, she couldn't stand to speak of herself for more than a few words at a time.

That brief moment when their lips had touched in the wine cellar continued to torment him. His heart had been pounding, every muscle in his body tense with anticipation before she had soundly put him in his place with a slap across the face. He had thought he was finally getting close to Yue-ying, when he was never further away.

"Who was there at the banquet?" he asked, forcing himself back to the matter at hand.

"The banquet was sponsored by an official from the Ministry of Commerce. There were merchants and wealthy businessmen in attendance." Yue-ying rubbed a hand over her temples. "Will you add those to the names from the Hundred Songs? The list keeps growing."

They both sipped their tea, temporarily at a standstill. It was possible Huilan had seen or heard something important. Influence was traded at such gatherings. Secrets were exchanged. It was one of the reasons Huang spent so much time wandering happily from parlor to parlor. If only Huilan had seen fit to confide in him. If only everyone in the North Hamlet didn't speak in such cursed riddles all the time.

"Let us concentrate on this gathering for now. Tell me everything you can remember about Huilan that night."

He'd seen how carefully Yue-ying observed everyone and everything around her. If something significant had occurred, she would have made note of it; he was confident of that.

Yue-ying placed her palms together and propped her chin on top of them, eyes closed. He watched with fascination as the thoughts flitted across her face.

"The event was located on a pleasure boat docked in a waterway to the north of the East Market. I didn't recognize most of the guests. Some of them were from foreign lands." When she opened her eyes, her expression appeared troubled. Her fingers traced a restless pattern over the wood, back and forth. "I left early that night. I had forgotten about that."

"You said Huilan was upset," he prodded.

His question snapped her back to attention. "It was strange. Huilan was playing the pipa and she stopped midsong. Something had distracted her. She finally managed to finish the song, but she was very flustered afterward. Mingyu tried to calm her. I think that was when Mingyu decided she had too many problems to worry about and sent me home."

"Problems?"

"I'm afraid of boats," she confessed. She moved on quickly. "Mingyu returned later that night, but didn't say anything. She was exhausted because it was so late."

"Did you notice anything at the banquet that might have made Huilan nervous?"

"Not particularly. Maybe someone said something

untoward to her. Merchants can be a crude lot. Many of them are too uncultured to know the difference between a courtesan and a prostitute."

Once again, her hand strayed to her cheek. He had watched over the past half hour while she absently tucked, untucked and rearranged her hair, inadvertently drawing attention to the part of her she most wanted to obscure. The bloodred mark that made her so unique. She was always fidgeting and trying to cover her face or angle herself away. Unable to ignore it any longer, he reached out and pressed his hand gently over hers to stop her.

Huang knew he'd made a mistake when her fingers stiffened beneath his touch and she pulled away entirely, sitting as far back in her chair as she could, shoulders straight. "I should be getting back."

He paid for the tea and had to make an extra effort to follow her as she deftly wove around the tables and moved down the stairs. He caught up to her, but remained silent as he matched her pace down the street.

"If people see us together in the North Hamlet, there will be talk," she said, keeping her focus straight ahead.

He was forced to direct his statement to her unmovable, unwavering profile. "You don't have to worry about your reputation with me."

There was a pause before she pulled ahead. He caught only the trailing end of her reply.

"I am more concerned with what people will think of you, Lord Bai."

CHAPTER SEVEN

HUANG WENT TO the gambling den on a different night this week. Let the unpleasant Constable Wu ponder about that.

He still lit a candle and set it behind the dealer before taking his seat. He also had his usual sacrifice of a thousand coins, held together by strings of a hundred. There was additional silver in his purse tonight and he could feel it weighing on him. It was a dangerous temptation for him to bring so much money near a dice table, but he needed information.

The dealer greeted him with a toothy smile. Huang tossed a string of coins onto the square marked "High", not bothering to untie it to parcel out a smaller bet. He gave another string to the dealer.

"Gao," he requested, using the single name that his associate went by. The dealer nodded and made a signal to the doorman.

Play continued after that with the clatter of the dice, the call for more bets, the scattering of coins over the table. He lost the first string and losing made him want to lay down even more money. There was a time years ago when he had watched the cycle repeat until the black characters on the table blended together. He had finally emerged from the den to find that the sun was out and two days had passed.

He laid down his bets a little slower after the first

one. Sometimes it took Gao a while to appear and once his thousand coins were gone, he would have to leave. He couldn't risk staying with that extra silver on him.

Huang needn't have worried. After only three rounds, a wiry, hawkish man appeared. He walked through the den with the ease of familiarity before coming to stand at the dice table.

"Lord Bai."

"Lord Gao."

They both mocked one another. One corner of Gao's mouth perpetually drooped downward, but the rest of his face was smiling.

Gao carried a knife and worked for a money-lender, but operated on his own as well. He was knowledge-able about the world of crime bosses, gambling dens and other illegal, but tolerated activities within the city. Without question, Gao was an unsavory character, but Huang figured it was better to continue on with the one cutthroat he knew rather than venture out and make con-nections with additional cutthroats.

"I think he's doing something to the dice," Huang muttered, eyeing the dealer as he shook the tumbler.

"Are they speaking to you tonight?" Gao asked.

They weren't friends, but Gao knew his mind in a way no one else did. The dice had just rolled three, four and five. He hadn't bet that combination, but those num-bers had always pleased him in a nonsensical way. That sort of strange connection with the dice and the num-bers and even the sound of coins kept him coming back.

"A courtesan was killed in the Pingkang li," Huang began.

"I heard."

"I want to know who did it."

Gao turned to him, still smiling. "It wasn't me."

Huang looked back to the table to place another bet. "You're insufferable."

Their association went back several years, back to the time when Huang had been a hapless scholar seeking a good time.

"I could have aimed a little to the left that night, you know. Gone a little deeper," Gao said mildly.

"Do you want me to thank you?"

"No, I want your silver."

They lowered their voices, but didn't move away from the table. All of the gamblers were intent on the game anyway. It really was the safest place for him to meet with someone like Gao.

Huang passed him a tael of silver, cast into the traditional boat shape. Gao turned it around once to inspect the markings before tucking it away.

"I think Huilan heard or saw something she wasn't supposed to," Huang told him. "I want to know if someone was hired to kill her."

"She was important to you."

The quiet tone of Gao's remark made him pause. "I wouldn't be asking if she wasn't."

He'd learned to admit as little as possible to Gao. He'd also learned not to be blinded by the other man's outward friendliness.

"I also need to know more about these men. Have they been corrupted? Are they taking bribes?" He provided the names of the Market Commissioner and the official from the Ministry of Commerce. The two bureaucrats who had been at the merchant banquet when Huilan had faltered in her singing.

"Those are a lot of questions for one silver ingot."

Huang slipped him another boat without argument.

"Come back in a week," Gao said.

"I always do."

Gao responded with a laugh. "That's good. You be careful walking around with all that silver, my friend."

He most certainly would be careful. He never came here anymore without carrying at least a knife. In the three years since he'd become the target of a ruthless money-lender, he'd even learned how to use it.

THE MARKET WASN'T too busy that morning. Yue-ying was nearly done with all her purchases when she heard footsteps quickening behind her. They hit a near run before slowing down at her side.

"What a pleasant coincidence this is, seeing you here like this," Huang remarked, only a little out of breath.

"Lord Bai." She greeted him with an air of coolness, switching her basket to her other arm and setting it conspicuously between them, though she could feel her skin warming. He was certainly persistent.

He fell into step with her. "What did you mean the other day?"

"What conversation was this?"

Yue-ying turned her attention to a nearby fruit stand and started picking through a basket of plums. A day had passed since their last meeting. Mingyu had not yet returned from her assignation with General Deng at the hot springs, but that was no excuse to remain idle.

"You know what I'm talking about," Huang admonished.

She listened with only half an ear as she selected out an assortment of plums and peaches.

"That's twice the amount it was yesterday!" she protested when she heard the tally.

The produce vendor was unwilling to budge. His shrewd gaze flickered momentarily to Bai Huang, who reached into his sash and fished out a few coins. He handed them over without a second glance.

"Why would you be worried about my reputation if we're seen together?" he asked again.

She walked on, headed a few stalls down. "Because I have no reputation to speak of."

"That's not true."

"I know who you are, Lord Bai. And you know who I am." She told herself she wasn't ashamed of her past, yet she couldn't bear to look at him.

"You're Lady Mingyu's maidservant."

With an impatient sound, she stopped in the middle of the lane and turned on him. "Perhaps there is some benefit for you to behave the way you do. Maybe it allows you to avoid responsibility for your actions, but people will only overlook so much. And even you are not so thick-skulled."

He looked startled by her strong words. Startled, and oddly pleased. "Assume I am so thick-skulled," he said. "Why can't we be seen together? I've seen you many a time."

"At the Lotus Palace," she pointed out. "In Mingyu's parlor."

"So…"

"There are many reasons for a gentleman to come calling on a courtesan like Mingyu. There is only one reason a man such as yourself would seek out someone like me." He continued to stare blankly at her, waiting to be convinced. She sighed. "Associating with a talented woman who can compose poetry and quote literature enhances a scholar's reputation. An aristocrat engaging in relations with a servant is nothing but an embarrassment, to himself and his family."

Bai Huang must have known she was formerly a prostitute. It was no secret, yet he didn't appear embarrassed to be seen with her.

"Don't you see what people will make of it? Mingyu refused you so you settled on her lowly maidservant. Everyone will assume I've swindled you. You'll be ridiculed."

His smile was directed inward. "I'm already ridiculed."

Maybe Bai Huang wasn't thick-skulled. He acted as if he was impervious. As if he were truly beyond shame or reproach.

"I think maybe you are too worried what others will think," he countered. "In particular, I think you're worried what your mistress will think. Mingyu can't tolerate anyone receiving more attention than her."

His comment made her ears burn.

"Why are you so afraid of her?" he persisted.

"I'm not afraid—"

"Are you afraid Mingyu will have you put out on the streets?"

Instead of answering, she turned to leave the market area. "I can't get a decent price on anything while you're hovering about," she muttered.

"Miss Yue-ying, wait." He took hold of her arm and she had no choice but to stop. "What about our investigation?"

She exhaled forcefully as she turned to him. "I think you should go to Magistrate Li."

His gaze narrowed on her. "When did you decide this?"

"Last night. I thought of all we had discussed and how we'll never be able to seek out the answers the way Magistrate Li and his constables can. It's their duty to investigate this crime."

He pulled her aside into an alleyway. His expression hardened and the look in his eyes was keen, as sharp as she'd ever seen him. "Is it the case that you think we should go to Magistrate Li? Or is it that you've already gone to him?"

Once again, she was alone with Bai Huang. In the shock of Huilan's death, she'd overlooked the incident in the cellar, but it suddenly came back to her. His mouth pressing to hers followed by the crack of her palm over his cheek.

But they weren't truly alone here. His back was to the busy street. She could yell for help if she needed it, but she wasn't afraid of him in that way. She had stayed up half the night, thinking of him and the way he had looked at her in the teahouse. He had gazed upon her without flinching, without looking away in embarrassment, as if he wanted to know her deepest secrets. Her inner thoughts were her own; she didn't want him there.

"Why wouldn't you want to tell the magistrate about Huilan's lover?" she asked. "It would remove you from suspicion."

"Consider this." He held up one finger. A tiny crease appeared between his eyes. "Why didn't Huilan go to Magistrate Li if she was in danger? She didn't go to any of her patrons or protectors either. Why did she go to a couple of no-names like her young scholar and myself?"

When he was like this, so focused, Bai Huang was difficult to resist. His features, which were smoothly handsome on the surface, took on depth and mystery. She wanted to protest that he was far from having no name. His name was rather important, yet he didn't rely on it when speaking to her.

He didn't need to reason with a maidservant to get

what he wanted. Any other aristocrat would command or threaten or simply assume she would obey.

"Maybe she didn't realize it was a life-or-death situation until too late," Yue-ying guessed, her heart pounding at his directness, at her own boldness.

"She must have known. She was desperate to flee the city. If Magistrate Li couldn't help her then, he can't help her now. She needs us."

"Us?"

Bai Huang was trouble. Constable Wu was right; he was hiding something. She had noticed that about him from the beginning. There was careful deliberation behind his every act. And when no one was watching, a calculating expression would flit across his face, transforming his careless beauty into something honed and dangerous.

Over time, Yue-ying had let herself be assuaged by his antics. He had a way of wearing away at one's defenses with his awkward attempts at charm and humor. But she'd never completely let her guard down with him. And she was right not to do so.

"I can't help you any further," she insisted.

"I understand," he replied too easily.

She paused. "You do?"

"Yes, but I need one last favor."

Before she could protest, he had taken her arm and was leading her out into the street and then beyond the Three Lanes.

"Where are we going?" she asked through her teeth, determined not to make a scene.

"To the canal. I want you to show me where the banquet was hosted."

Her slippers dragged as he pulled her along. "Enough!

I can walk. You're like a persistent housefly," she snapped.

Laughing, he loosened his grip. "Come now, Miss Yue-ying. This is an adventure."

"You've never shown yourself to be dedicated to anything before this. Why now?"

"I promised Huilan," Bai Huang said soberly.

Something in his tone made her relent. Even though they weren't close, Huilan was still one of the women of the North Hamlet. There were rivalries and jealousies among them, but they all shared a history of being uprooted and sold into the life they were forced to lead.

A series of transport canals and waterways cut through the city, feeding the artificial lakes and wells. They walked along the bank to the point where a major artery met up with the Grand Canal. The larger river barges were docked near the juncture of the two waterways.

The steps leading down the embankment were cut roughly and Bai Huang offered his hand to help steady her, a gentleman at heart. His touch was warm on her arm and the trace of it remained long after he let go. As they neared the docks the swampy, stagnant smell of water rose around them.

"The banquet was during the evening," she reminded him. "It was dark outside and there were lanterns lighting the walkway. I might not be able to find this pleasure boat."

"I know. Just try to look."

"It may not even be here anymore. Ships sail in and out of the city every day."

She set foot onto the wooden plank of the dock that stretched along the waterway. The port was clogged with every sort of vessel, large and small. Yue-ying searched among them.

"It might have been this one."

They came to a stop before a massive vessel that rose out of the water. It was a pleasure barge fitted with painted columns supporting two tiers. A dragon's head graced the bow and elaborate carvings curled along the eaves. Red lanterns hung along the length of the boat. Passengers were meant to enjoy the view of the water through the open panels, but Yue-ying had been so nervous when she was on it, all she could remember was that she had wanted to get off.

After a brief scan, Bai Huang directed her along the dock at a leisurely pace, as if they were a young couple enjoying a stroll.

"You said that the guests at the banquet were mostly merchants and traders."

"Yes."

"Do those sorts of men typically hire out registered courtesans?"

"It's not too uncommon," she replied. "Though if all one wants is some music and a few pretty faces, they could go to the less reputable houses in the upper lane or hire song girls who aren't registered. It would be less expensive."

The aristocracy generally looked down upon the merchant class as being greedy and common, but to the pleasure house madams money was money.

"The Market Commissioner was trying to make a good impression," Bai Huang reasoned. "He had an association with Huilan, so he invited her to attend, but she met someone or saw something that frightened her there."

"Nothing unusual happened while I was there. I can ask Mingyu if she remembers anything once she returns from the hot springs."

The words left her lips before she realized that he had drawn her back into the investigation with hardly any effort at all. The scoundrel.

"What about you?" he asked.

"Me?"

He stopped and turned. "Why were you afraid that night?"

"I don't like the water."

He leaned a touch closer, lowering his voice as if to keep from frightening her. "We're close to water now."

They were beside the canal and a slight breeze rippled over the surface. His gaze was intent on her. A strand of hair fell from his topknot to whip about his face as clouds gathered overhead.

She looked to the darkening sky. "It's going to rain."

"You haven't given me an answer," he said gently.

She sighed. "I already told you, I don't like boats. I've never liked them. The motion makes me feel dizzy."

"Is that all?" he pressed.

A boat had brought her to Changan after she was taken away from her family.

"It really is going to rain," she said instead.

Brushing past him, she moved back toward the street. His footsteps sounded behind her and she quickened her step, using the coming rain as an excuse to escape. What did it matter to Lord Bai whether she liked boats or his bad poetry? Why did she matter to him at all?

She didn't matter, she reminded herself. He just needed her help to solve the mystery of Huilan's murder.

A drop of water fell against her hand. And then another against the bridge of her nose. Within moments, a few drops had become a thousand. She hadn't brought a parasol since she'd assumed she would only be making a small trip to the market, not wandering outside the quarter.

Yue-ying searched about for shelter as rainfall filled her vision, making it hard to see. Suddenly Bai Huang was beside her, tucking her against his shoulder.

"Come on!" he shouted. He had to shout because water was roaring from the heavens now.

He draped an arm overhead to try to cover her. The act was more chivalrous than practical. By the time they found a small park and ran beneath a wooden pavilion, her hair was drenched. He had managed to shield her robe from getting soaked through.

She swiped a hand over her face to clear the water from her eyes. He did the same and then they stared out at the falling curtain of water. Next they looked to the single bench, big enough for two. Yue-ying decided she'd rather remain standing. It was summer and it was Changan. The rain could be gone within moments and she didn't care to invite intimacy in the meantime.

She leaned her elbows onto the wooden rail that surrounded the pavilion and looked out into the park. All she could see was a smudge of green mixed in with gray. A heartbeat later, Bai Huang perched himself beside her, his posture mirroring hers.

"I should tell you, I wasn't drunk that night."

There wasn't any need to specify which night he was talking about.

"I know." She didn't turn toward him, but she could sense his gaze on her all the same. "With your lips stumbling all over, I would have easily caught the scent of it."

Bai Huang laughed. It was the easy laugh he was so well-known for, the one that showed he was above insult, without a care in the world. She envied him the ability to be able to laugh like that.

"Was it so bad, then?" he asked.

She did look at him then, meeting his eyes squarely. "It was."

His unwavering confidence could mean only two things. Either he was deluded about his own abilities, or his clumsiness had been intentional.

"Why did you do it?" she asked him.

His gaze flicked away briefly, then came back to her. He had strong, distinctive features; eyes that were set deep and a nose that was well-defined. His mouth was full and perfectly shaped. A face like that could truly get away with anything.

"I suppose I wanted to see what would happen," he said quietly.

"That's the problem with men like you. This sort of thing is a game, as if you had a right to everything in the world for your amusement."

"I didn't mean—"

"You only meant to tease. You have the privilege of turning everything into a jest when I've never had the privilege to even refuse such an act."

She hadn't intended to become so aggravated. Bai Huang was silent beside her while she tried to calm herself.

"I didn't consider it that way," he said finally.

She didn't acknowledge his words. If it was an apology, and it didn't sound like one, she wouldn't accept it.

"Have you never—?" To his credit, he continued past her cold stare. "Have you never had a kiss that you actually wanted?"

"Why would I ever want such a thing?" she replied sharply.

Any man who had ever touched her had held something over her. Money or status and usually both. And always the threat of his physical strength. They hadn't all been brutes or drunks. A few were even kind, in their own way. Most were indifferent. In many ways, a kiss was more of an invasion than a body pressing over her. It was the touching of mouths, the exchange of breath. Too much was woven into a kiss; all the senses of touch, taste and sound. There was no way for her to explain how she had been overwhelmed by it all.

"I've been a bastard of the worst kind," Bai Huang conceded.

She made a noncommittal sound and looked out once again to the rain. Such afternoon downpours were unpredictable and usually brief, but this one conspired against her and continued relentlessly.

"You won't let me apologize, will you?"

She sighed. "Let us talk about something else."

More rain. More silence.

"Perhaps there is a way I can set things right between us."

Now it was her turn to laugh. A ringing melody poured out of her, cutting through the patter of the water.

"Miss Yue-ying." For the first time, he appeared a bit put out by her reaction.

"Shall I guess *how* you want to set things right?" she asked, her eyebrows lifting skeptically.

Bai Huang wasn't a bad fellow, she'd decided. And he wasn't at all like the face he insisted on presenting to the world. But he was still drearily predictable.

"Here," he continued undaunted. He turned around, placing his hands behind him to grip the railing as he leaned back into it. "I won't subject you to another kiss since you find my technique…somewhat objectionable." His smirk was directed at himself as much as at her. "My hands will remain right here. I'll be a statue. I'll even close my eyes…if that's what you want."

"It's not that I'm *afraid* of you," she said, rolling her eyes. "And a man accepting a kiss as 'punishment' has to be the most overplayed parlor trick since the time of the First Emperor. Next to accepting a drink as punishment. Oh, the torture of it!"

"I didn't say I wouldn't enjoy it. This is merely a chance for you to know what it is to have a kiss you were in complete control of."

"It's hardly the same. You're still allowing me this liberty, as if it were a gift you were bestowing."

"Miss Yue-ying," he sighed. "Show some mercy."

At least he understood what he offered wasn't in any way equal. It was just another game, another tease. He was still holding on to the rail, looking eagerly on like a pale-faced scholar as he regarded her. She stepped back and crossed her arms over her chest, narrowing her gaze on him.

He scowled. "Well, I'm feeling more and more ridiculous the longer you refuse. Surely my embarrassment can provide you with some sense of retribution."

She knew she was being harsh, holding this one moment over him. She'd already hit him after he'd stolen that first kiss. The scratch on his cheek was finally fading. She could only detect it when she looked closely at him, as she was doing now.

Bai Huang, the most beautiful man in the Pingkang li, was watching her and asking her with his eyes to kiss him. It wasn't that she was afraid. Or so cold and broken inside that the mere thought of men horrified her. Bai Huang didn't horrify her. Most of the girls in the North Hamlet even found him somewhat charming.

Straightening her spine, she approached him in even

strides. She told herself she would do it without any sign of hesitation. She would do it callously, as if it meant nothing more than the parlor games he indulged in.

Bai Huang's gaze didn't leave her as she neared. He swallowed forcibly, the knot in his throat lifting. She could see that his breathing had quickened. Though he had promised not to move, an exhalation parted his lips and her hand trembled as she braced it onto the rail beside him.

She had never done this before, she realized a moment before she pressed her lips onto his.

His mouth was warm and yielded only a little as she moved closer. She parted her lips to test the texture of his lips and, with the smallest touch of her tongue, the taste of the kiss. She could sense the shudder that traveled through him. It made her breath catch and her stomach flutter with excitement.

This was a gift indeed, but not one that he gave to her. It was a gift that she took for herself.

CHAPTER EIGHT

IN THE THREE steps it took Yue-ying to reach him, Huang dreamed a hundred dreams about how her lips would feel against him. Would she be soft and timid? Would she be passionate, burning like fire? Or both? Timid one moment, and full of desire and passion the next. He hoped it was both.

Yue-ying was right. His thoughtless gesture in the wine cellar had prevented them from discovering these truths together, but they could correct that now.

She was beside him, the rain and the pavilion blurring around her as his field of vision narrowed down to only her. Even though he was leaning against the rail, she still had to raise herself onto her toes to reach him. And then his breath stopped as her soft mouth pressed against his.

He had kissed many women and been kissed in return. This first touch with Yue-ying was the sweetest of them all, and he couldn't even say why. She was neither timid, nor bold. She was just as she was, single-minded and relentless when she wanted to know something.

Her mouth was warm, sensual, perfect and…gone.

Huang was left blinking and at a loss. It took a moment for his breath to return and for him to realize that she had left the shelter of the pavilion. Straightening, he turned to see Yue-ying walking away, but she wasn't fleeing. Her step was as unrushed as her kiss had been.

She stopped to raise her face to the rain, eyes closed, triumphant. She had driven him mad and now she was done with him. At that moment, he would have wrestled tigers to have her.

He pressed a hand to his chest, looking on in wonder as she disappeared.

Huang was still smiling a while later, despite the rain, despite the grayness of the skies, as he crossed the wide avenue that separated the scholars' area from the Pingkang li. His robe was soaked through by the time he reached his rented quarters. As soon as he entered, the downpour ceased.

It was poetic.

The modestly sized house was arranged around a courtyard. His landlady was an old widow who kept to a room at the back of the residence while he was left with a study and bedchamber at the front. A familiar figure was hunched beneath the overhang outside the study.

"How long have you been waiting here?"

Zhou Dan straightened as he approached. "An hour. The elder Lord Bai has just returned. He's waiting for you at the house."

"My father? Here?"

Huang pushed into his chamber to change, his thoughts awhirl. What was his father doing back at the capital? Pleasant memories of Yue-ying had to be set aside for now until he could find out.

Zhou Dan remained by the door while he watched Huang unwrapping himself from his damp robe.

"You need an attendant," the servant suggested. "And a bodyguard as well. To protect you from all the beautiful ladies of the pleasure district."

Huang snorted. "You're no match for them."

He finished undressing and pulled on dry trousers

and a new robe. A much more understated and serious outfit this time, suited for appearing before his family. No need for a display of extravagance in their own home.

The carriage was hitched at the side of the house and Zhou Dan took the reins as Bai Huang seated himself. The family mansion was located in the northeastern corner of the city, in the exclusive quadrant between the administration section and the imperial palace. By carriage, it was over an hour away. For the work that he was doing, it had been necessary for Huang to take rooms much closer to the North Hamlet.

The lanes were muddy, but relatively empty. The carts and pedestrians hadn't yet reclaimed the streets since the break in the rainfall. The carriage took them to the front gate of the mansion.

Their house was a spacious compound, organized around a double-courtyard layout with wide bays along the perimeter that housed the living areas. Father's studio was located in the second courtyard, built in a location with good light and a view of the garden.

Father was seated behind his desk while Wei-wei, Huang's younger sister, sat across from him. They were discussing the contents of a scroll that lay open between them.

"Very good," Father said to Wei-wei before glancing up at him. "Huang, come inside."

He entered and bowed to Father. Wei-wei immediately stood to greet him.

"Elder brother, you look well."

"As do you, sister."

It was all very proper.

Father rolled up the scroll. "Your younger brother's commentary on the Classic of Filial Piety," he explained.

"Wei-wei reports that he is progressing well in his studies. This makes me very happy."

Huang caught the proud gleam in his sister's eye before she bowed to their father and retreated.

He and Wei-wei were more relaxed around one another when it was just the two of them, but before their parents they treated one another with respectful formality, the very same way that Father acted with Mother.

Huang shut the studio door before seating himself. "I didn't expect Father's return so soon."

His father had dark shadows beneath his eyes, as if he'd traveled long days with little sleep. "As you are aware, the mourning period has ended for the late emperor. Emperor Xuanzong has summoned a number of officials to the capital."

"This could be good," Huang ventured.

"Or it could be bad."

Father was as he always was. He made no assumptions, revealed nothing and was prepared for any outcome. It left them both to wonder how Father had raised a son who was both impulsive and reckless. But Huang was finally learning how to exercise discipline. He was trying to show himself worthy of his name.

"What news do you have?" Father asked.

Huang had been assigned the task of reporting on the activities of several key officials who Father thought might threaten the balance of power in the imperial court.

"General Deng has returned to the capital as well," he began.

Father frowned. "Our informants were not aware of that."

"He is supposedly visiting the hot springs with his favorite courtesan."

"I will have that looked into immediately. Good work."

At one time, both his father and Deng had been influential officials within the capital. Father had feared for many years now that General Deng was plotting against the empire. It became much harder to watch over the general when he was promoted to military governor and sent to the south, but Deng continued to maintain contacts within the capital—one of them being Lady Mingyu, his favored courtesan and lover.

"And the new magistrate?" Father continued.

"Li Yen is soft-spoken, careful with his words. Hard to read."

"Does he seem like an honest official?"

"He seems dedicated to his duties." Huang considered holding back about Huilan's murder and how the magistrate was targeting him in the investigation, but he had to tell his father the truth. He explained the matter briefly. "Lady Huilan claimed to have some information I would be interested to know," he concluded.

At the time he had wondered why Huilan would offer him information. As far as everyone knew, the fool Bai Huang only cared about having a good time.

"Huang." Father shook his head. "You must take care. Our family name has suffered enough."

"I know."

"And don't become too involved with the pleasure quarter. Too many scholars become caught by its trap."

"I understand."

After all he had cost his family with his debt, after all the anguish they had gone through on his behalf, it would have been disrespectful to do anything but acknowledge his culpability.

To Father, the North Hamlet was a place of dubious

morality and untold danger—a world to be kept strictly apart from home and family. Huang had fallen to its temptations before, but it was the dice that had caught him, not the women.

"Is there anything else, Huang?"

"No, Father."

He purposefully left out his vow to find the killer. That was a personal matter and a local crime was of little interest. His father's main concern was the defense of the empire.

"Your mother will expect us for the evening meal shortly. I have several matters to take care of before then."

Huang bowed to take his leave. Before he exited the studio, his father was already reading through a stack of notices.

Dinner was a long, drawn-out ordeal. Mother and Father sat at the table along with Huang, Wei-wei and their younger brother, Chang-min. The dishes were brought out silently by the servants and set before them, one course after another.

Mother asked brief questions about how Father was getting along in the house in Fujian province. Was he well taken care of? Seeing to his health and not working too hard? She chose her words carefully so as not to appear prying or interfering. Huang and Wei-wei answered the occasional question when asked. Chang-min, who was only sixteen, did not have a word to say the entire meal.

Both Father and Mother talked in circles around *her*, that woman, the concubine whom Father had brought with him to Fujian province. Huang had met Lady Shang during his time of exile from the capital. He couldn't say much about Father's concubine other than that she was respectful, quiet and cultured. She was also much younger than Mother.

He wondered whether Chang-min even realized that this woman who was not mentioned was his actual birth mother. His younger brother had been only four years old when he was brought to the family mansion to be raised and educated.

The evening was full of heavy silences and endless pauses. Whenever the entire family came together, it seemed they spoke more in pauses than words. It made him long for the wine and music of the Pingkang li, dubious morality and all.

CHAPTER NINE

ONE DAY BACK in the city and Mingyu's parlor was already well attended. Huang noted that Taizhu, the old historian, was there as usual. There were also several notable scholars, one who had passed the exams in the highest rank, but who was still vying for an appointment. The center of the gathering was a secretary from the Ministry of Personnel. Not a position of any true authority, but he had the ability to mention a name to someone with a bigger name. Appointments were procured in such varied and sundry ways.

There was no talk of appointments at the moment. Mingyu had instigated a drinking game around couplets from popular poems. The party turned to greet him and Huang inserted himself into the gathering with a couple of wrong guesses.

"Penalty drink!" the secretary proclaimed.

Huang took his punishment in good spirit, searching the room as he drank. Yue-ying hovered in the corner of the parlor. She met his gaze only briefly before disappearing behind the screen into the inner chamber. That one look alone set his pulse racing.

After a few more rounds, he'd finished enough wine that Yue-ying finally appeared to bring more. It tormented him not to be able to look at her or even touch her sleeve. Instead, he kept his focus on Mingyu, who was watching him like a hawk.

"Your absence left such an emptiness in the North Hamlet," he told the courtesan. "The days you were gone were filled with rain."

"Oh, but surely you exaggerate, Lord Bai. You must have been breaking hearts all over the quarter while I was away," Mingyu countered readily.

"More like having my heart broken."

He raised his cup in tribute to Mingyu. She met his gesture with a cool nod that accentuated the graceful arch of her neck. The courtesan was the essence of cultivation and beauty, yet he was more transfixed by the dark shape behind the screen in the corner. Yue-ying had retreated behind it, but he could just make out her silhouette out of the corner of his eye.

"If you could provide the next couplet," Mingyu prompted.

"With pleasure."

He selected a couplet from a famous poem by Li Bai, which the secretary was able to match with ease. Huang downed another cup, feeling his blood warm.

It became a maddening game; sipping wine and throwing out careless banter, while each flicker of the shadow behind the screen made his heart pound and his stomach knot with anticipation. One candle burned down to a stub and then another. Each one marked an additional string of cash to be paid to the pleasure house. It was well past midnight when the party disbanded, leaving him alone in the parlor. He propped his head onto his fist to keep it up.

"Lord Bai." Mingyu returned from seeing the other guests off and slid into the seat closest to him. "I must say, something seems to have gotten into your blood tonight."

"Only you," he quipped dutifully.

The courtesan smiled, but like his response it was only perfunctory. "You are certainly persistent."

Throughout his very public courtship of her, he had never found himself alone with Mingyu. It was time for him to be tactfully dismissed, otherwise he would start to get the wrong impression. Mingyu knew this. He knew this.

"Sometimes I tire of all this rhetoric," she drawled. "All the effort. All the *cleverness*."

Her arm dangled over the corner of her chair and she flexed her fingers carelessly as she spoke. As her shapely eyes narrowed on him he felt like a rat being cornered by a cat. A cat who had all the time in the world to play with its prey before ripping out its throat.

He cleared his own throat. "It is because every one of us longs to catch—"

She cut off his rambling reply with her hand against the crook of his arm. "There is something to be said for the simple pleasure of youth and beauty, wouldn't you agree, Lord Bai?"

His gaze started to wander to the painted screen in the corner, but Mingyu caught his chin between her thumb and forefinger to drag his eyes back to her. It was an impetuous gesture, overtly flirtatious and unmistakably aggressive.

There could be only one explanation. She must have noticed his attention was elsewhere that evening.

"Lady Mingyu, youth and beauty are only two of your many qualities," he effused.

She laughed. "Lord Bai, I certainly wasn't speaking of myself."

On the surface, she really was everything that was feminine and desirable in a woman. Aside from her beauty, she was also sophisticated and intelligent, and most important of all, highly celebrated. Everything a scholar hoping to elevate his own reputation would want in a companion. Yet Huang was unmoved.

Mingyu could be clever, sharp-witted and sharp-tongued. She could even be playful, but she was never warm. He had spied too many moments, like this one, when all her actions spoke of seduction, while her eyes were dead.

She released his chin and let her fingers trail up along his cheek. "You must think me cruel," she said softly.

"Never." He swallowed and not entirely for show. What sort of scheme was she plotting?

"What if I told you, my dear Lord Bai, that my indifference all this time has been a ploy?"

He eyed her warily. "Lady Mingyu—"

She was leaning toward him and her red lips parted as she smiled. Damn it, she was provoking him and Yue-ying was behind the screen, listening to every word. What would Bai Huang the fool do? Quote bad poetry—except that none came to mind.

He leaned toward her as if to catch her in a clumsy embrace, swinging his arm wide enough to knock over the flask of wine. Stammering out an apology, he reached out to right the vessel only to fumble with cups and plates in the process.

In a heartbeat, Yue-ying was beside him, nudging him aside as she wiped at the spilled drink.

"We must be in the Hour of the Ox," he declared. "I seem to have turned into one."

His laughter rang out a little too loudly. Yue-ying kept her head bowed as she focused on her task. She had pulled her hair over one shoulder, exposing the line of her neck. The sight of it, so vulnerable and exposed, was enough to make his throat go dry with desire.

It was only a neck, he chided himself. There was little more than a hand span of skin showing, pale against the cascade of black hair.

Mingyu stood over them like the goddess of the night. "Yue-ying, if you would fetch a sedan for Lord Bai." Her tone was smooth. "We don't want him to meet any misfortune in his current state."

Yue-ying set the rag aside and stood to do her mistress's bidding without a glance in his direction. He watched her slender figure disappear through the curtain before rising to his feet.

"Lady Mingyu," he said with a bow.

"Lord Bai. Take care."

He thought he detected a devious lift of her eyebrow, but otherwise her expression was serene, as if nothing out of the ordinary had occurred.

Outside, the lanterns of the North Hamlet were still burning. Yue-ying stood out in the side alley, pointedly not looking at him as he came up beside her.

His grin spread a bit wider than he intended. "Little Moon—"

He didn't think it was possible, but her spine straightened further.

"Miss Yue-ying," he corrected himself. "I've waited all night for this moment."

"Oh?"

That was it. One single utterance. Her pearl earring bobbed as she looked impatiently to the corner, presumably for the sedan.

"I thought of you," he said softly, watching for any reaction in the stiffness of her profile. "Every day."

"Say that when you are not drunk," she retorted.

He wasn't, though she would hardly believe it. He had always been able to handle his drink a little bit better than those around him, which was handy for gathering information.

"She was only doing that to make you angry. Apparently, Mingyu is a jealous woman."

"You don't know what you're saying. What does Mingyu have to be jealous of?"

More bobbing of the earring. What he could see of her mouth was pressed into a tight line. He wanted to believe a woman couldn't be so agitated with him if she didn't at least care for him a little bit.

"She's jealous of anyone who takes any attention away from her," he said. "She can't stand to have anyone speak to even her maidservant in her presence. Don't look, but I would wager she is watching us from her window."

He remained standing beside Yue-ying, his eyes focused ahead. He was regretting not kissing her to his heart's content when he'd had the chance in the pavilion, but he had promised her the kiss was for her, not for him. Yet he hadn't been able to forget the sweet restraint in her touch since.

But she was hardly sweet now. "Don't anger Mingyu. It would only make things more difficult for me."

"That wasn't my intention."

The carrier had arrived to set the sedan chair down before him.

"When can I see you?" he asked.

"This isn't a liaison between us, Lord Bai."

If the courtesan truly was watching over them from on high, he couldn't delay much longer. "Tomorrow morning at the teahouse? I have information regarding our investigation."

Instead of answering, Yue-ying turned in a flurry of silk to march back into the Lotus Palace.

"WHAT INFORMATION?"

Yue-ying remained standing as she watched that too-familiar grin spreading over Bai Huang's face. It was a smile that could charm tigers. Youth and beauty indeed.

"Please sit, Miss Yue-ying. I took care to order your favorite tea."

"I have no favorite." When would he stop treating her as if she were another of the puppet goddesses of the pleasure quarter? "Tea is tea."

"You're being difficult on purpose," he pointed out lightly, still smiling.

He stood and gestured toward the empty stool. She hesitated before seating herself. She had debated all night whether or not to come that day, changing her mind several times even within the past hour. Bai Huang poured the tea while she sat and tried not to fidget. The brew was fragrant and rich with layer upon layer of flavor. Such quality, his regard, and all this attention was beyond her. She didn't know what to do with it.

"The Market Commissioner Ma Jun is taking bribes," he began.

She was unimpressed. "What official doesn't take bribes?"

"But if Huilan found out about his associations and he didn't want the authorities to know, then he might have killed her to keep her silent."

The investigation wasn't the only reason Yue-ying had come. She knew it and he must have known it as well. He had chosen a place in the corner where they could talk with some privacy and his gaze was warm on her as they spoke.

But favored sons of noblemen did not meet with lowly

servants in the normal course of events. So they forged on with the discussion to maintain the illusion.

"How did you find out about the bribes?" she asked as she considered his theory.

"Apparently it's common knowledge among the merchants and traders in the city…" His voice trailed away.

"So many people already knew?"

He continued with less confidence. "Commissioner Ma's position is a low-level one, only able to grant small favors. In return, he seems to thrive off many small bribes."

"He's likely paying up to his superior who's paying up to his superior."

Bai Huang looked downtrodden. Like most aristocrats, he cared nothing for the details of trade and commerce. The merchant class and anything having to do with them were beneath him.

"It certainly indicates that Ma Jun is an untrustworthy character," she soothed, like pouring balm over a wounded creature.

"I paid good money for that information," he grumbled.

"It's useful information. The commissioner must have been showing off his status by hosting a lavish banquet. So everyone could see how wealthy and influential he was with beautiful courtesans on his arm."

He sighed. "You don't need to make me feel better."

"He was Huilan's lover. And now we've discovered that she had another lover. It can be as simple as that."

"She was killed because Ma Jun was merely jealous? That doesn't seem fitting."

"There's no need to look for conspiracy. Emotions become easily confused in the Pingkang li." Her own emotions were in a tangle after their kiss in the park.

Yue-ying tapped the rim of her teacup restlessly. "Last night you said Mingyu was jealous of me."

"She is." A fire burned in his eyes. "Anyone can see it."

"You're mistaken," she said. "Mingyu is just worried about me."

Bai Huang waited for her to elaborate, but she refused to say more. What she and Mingyu had between them was a private matter.

"She has nothing to worry about," he assured her, the corner of his mouth lifting seductively. "Does she?"

His pupils grew dark and her pulse quickened in response. "If there's nothing else, I must return," she said, deliberately avoiding the question.

He considered her for a long, drawn-out moment, as if daring her to look away. She didn't.

"I'll walk with you," he offered.

The journey back to the quarter should have been a short one. She was keenly aware of Bai Huang's presence beside her every step of the way, knew exactly what was happening the moment he turned toward the public park instead of the Three Lanes. Without a word, he slipped beneath the shadow of a bridge and reeled her gently to him, like a dragonfly on a thread.

Yue-ying was no innocent. She had no reason to be coy, so she followed him into the darkness and closed her eyes as he pressed her back against the stone foundation. Then he kissed her until she had no breath left in her.

"We're all the same to you. Any one of us will do," she accused, breathing hard while she held on to him. His arms were strong and his shoulders surprisingly broad beneath the embroidered silk robe.

His tongue traced her lips intimately, urging her to

allow him inside. He invaded her mouth, tasting of tea and dark, sensual secrets.

"Not the same," he whispered a little later against her ear. His hands rounded her hips as she shuddered and her knees grew weak. "There is no one else like you. Do you want me to tell you all the ways in which you are only you?"

For all her life, she had been separated out and denied because she was different. She'd been condemned for it.

"No," she said, pulling him closer. "Don't say anything."

THEY PARTED WAYS outside of the park, Bai Huang going north and she headed south. Her heart was still pounding and her lips were wonderfully, pleasantly flushed. If she looked over her shoulder, the moment would shatter, so she didn't look back.

Oh, she knew who Lord Bai was. He was the sort who found all women beautiful in some way, who liked to play his games of courtship on any willing recipient.

Yue-ying had no reputation to protect and her virtue was long gone. And she had given up so much more to men who had meant so much less to her. Why not someone who was well mannered and well-spoken? Who was handsome and strong and who she was growing fond of?

On some tomorrow, she would be old. Bai Huang would be just a name and a memory. Mingyu had so many admirers, yet she cared little for them. Yue-ying, the girl once cruelly called Half-Moon because of her ruined face, had no such admirers.

So let me have this one, she thought with an air of defiance as she returned to the Lotus Palace. *Even if it is just a game to him.*

But as she reached the North Hamlet the clouds before her eyes began to thin until they were nothing more than wisps easily swept away. She was late, unaccountably late. Yue-ying was short of breath by the time she reached the Lotus Palace.

"Did you forget the time?" Mingyu asked as she entered the parlor.

The question was unnecessary and they both knew it. Yue-ying was never forgetful. She was never careless. She said nothing as she set about preparing Mingyu for the evening. Mingyu said little in response, but a chill was evident in the dressing room.

Unfortunately, an hour before they were to leave for the evening's engagement, Mingyu insisted on having a bodyguard.

"This banquet is far outside the North Hamlet. After what happened to Huilan, one can never know what dangers lay out there," she said.

Madame Sun was livid. "Stupid girl! What are you afraid of? Ghosts?"

"I won't set foot outside the door without protection."

Madame proceeded to plead and then threaten, but Mingyu would not hear it. She was the most celebrated of the Lotus Palace courtesans, commanding two and sometimes even three times the price of her sisters. It was impossible to send another girl to replace her.

Unlike Madame, Yue-ying didn't bother trying to convince Mingyu. The truth of the matter was that Mingyu was upset and, as a result, everyone around her had to suffer. Yue-ying left the two women arguing and hurried out to seek out a possible bodyguard. She could choose a laborer and pay him a few coins, but the prospect of entrusting themselves to a stranger struck her as being more dangerous than traveling alone.

On a whim, she ventured toward the magistrate's yamen and sought out the head constable.

"Constable Wu," she greeted.

"Miss Yue-ying."

"If any of your constables are not on duty, may we hire him for the night?"

His expression was severe. "It would be inappropriate for an appointed constable to take payment. It could be seen as a bribe."

"I apologize. I didn't mean any insult." She sighed wearily. "You see, a situation has come up—"

"Are you in danger?"

"No," she said quickly, seeing how his frown deepened. "But my mistress refuses to go out tonight without protection. She seems to have been deeply affected by Huilan—by the incident at the Hundred Songs."

"Then the magistrate's yamen holds some responsibility for that," Wu said. "The murderer still has not been caught and it is our duty to do so in a timely manner. I will send someone over to assist you in an hour."

"Thank you, sir."

She bowed and left the administrative compound to hurry back to the Lotus. Madame Sun was in the main parlor having tea. She was visibly agitated.

"Everything is taken care of," Yue-ying told her.

Madame sniffed, but nodded. "Good."

Mingyu was up in her chamber, seated on a pillow with her zither placed before her on a low table. Her fingers plucked ceaselessly at the strings. The tune was a strident one in the martial style that was meant to evoke battle and warfare. There were times when she was subtle in her moods. This was not one of them.

Mingyu had started training in music, dance and calligraphy immediately after Madame Sun had taken her in. She had been twelve years old at the time, older than when many of the other courtesans began their rigorous education. Yue-ying had received no such instruction. Whereas Mingyu was considered *ji*, an artist and entertainer, Yue-ying had been *chang*, nothing more than a vessel, a whore.

"The head constable said he would send someone," Yue-ying said when there was a break in the music.

Mingyu paused for a moment, then resumed playing. "Why Lord Bai?" she asked over the sigh of the strings.

There was no denying where Yue-ying had spent the morning and she didn't want to deny it.

Over the past few years together, she and Mingyu had learned each other's moods to every frown and flutter of an eyelash. The demand for a bodyguard and the entire tantrum with Madame was Mingyu's way of showing her displeasure with Bai Huang. And Yue-ying had scrambled to accommodate her, driven by her own guilt.

Mingyu was still waiting for an answer.

"Lord Bai is a gentleman" was all Yue-ying could say. He didn't treat her like a whore. He treated her as someone desirable, someone worthy of being pursued and courted.

"Is it his wealth? His status?" The courtesan's hands continued to move over the strings.

"It's not any of that."

"Then it's worse than I thought. You're lured by his beauty and by his promises."

The melody took on a hint of tension beneath the notes.

"Bai Huang is a young man and idealistic," Mingyu continued. "He might even fancy himself in love with you, but you can never be more than a servant to him. Outside of the pleasure quarter, you're nothing to him."

Mingyu never allowed herself to be attracted to a patron. They courted her with poetry and gifts and she outwardly appeared flattered, but that was part of the illusion of the Pingkang li.

The music stopped abruptly. "He'll only use you."

Yue-ying's pulse pounded. "He won't." Her throat was tight. "I won't let him."

Mingyu swung around to face her. "I knew."

Yue-ying remained in the corner, her hands clasped in front of her. To anyone observing them, she was a servant awaiting orders. When Mingyu became like this, it was better to let the storm roll over rather than fight against it.

"I knew from the first time he came to the Lotus and he saw you," Mingyu said through her teeth.

"You're making things up now. No one sees me. They only see you."

"Lord Bai certainly noticed you. I could see it in his eyes. He flatters me because he is expected to, but he was seeking your attention the entire time. I thought you would be indifferent to his charms. That you wouldn't be seduced so easily."

Yue-ying remained outwardly calm, though her stomach fluttered with a perverse thrill. Perhaps Bai Huang had indeed noticed her right from the beginning. "I have not been seduced by him."

"But you want to be," Mingyu accused.

Maybe she did. Being desired and seduced was better than being bought and sold.

Mingyu stood and went to her. "You have to be careful, Yue-ying. Everyone has two faces in the North Hamlet. Everyone wants more from you than what they ask."

Bai Huang had claimed Mingyu was jealous of anyone taking attention away from her, but the truth was much more complicated. Mingyu had always been protective of her.

"Tomorrow he will be chasing someone else. This is sport for young aristocrats like him. Their one chance to behave like scoundrels with no consequences. I see it every year—different faces, but the same poems, the same gossip, the same games of courtship."

"I know this," Yue-ying said harshly. It was rare that she ever raised her voice against her supposed mistress, but Mingyu's words stung with the pain of truth. Hadn't Bai Huang all but admitted it? *I wanted to see what would happen.*

"I know this," she repeated, her tone subdued and brittle now. "I know a great many other things as well."

Yue-ying could have conceded this battle, like so many other sacrifices she'd made all her life, but something inside her refused. She wasn't defending Bai Huang. She was fighting for herself, for the small pleasure of being kissed beneath a bridge by someone who was to her liking. Even if Bai Huang had known a hundred other bridges and a hundred other girls.

"You warn me about the dangers of being seduced by a man as if I'm an innocent maiden when you know that I am far from innocent," Yue-ying challenged. "You just choose to ignore that."

For a moment, Mingyu looked worried. She looked vulnerable. She looked as she had once looked a long time ago.

"I am still here with you," Yue-ying said gently. "I'll be here tomorrow and tomorrow after that."

"Don't be taken in by him. By his sweet words or that handsome face," Mingyu warned, building the walls back up around her. "He'll hurt you."

Maybe Yue-ying wanted him to. It would mean that she could still feel something.

MADAME SUN HAD to send someone up twice before they heeded her summons. The air between them was stretched to the breaking point as they descended the stairs. Mingyu walked with her spine stiff and her head tilted at a haughty angle. The pearl ornament in her hair swung restlessly with each step. Yue-ying followed a few steps behind, obediently carrying Mingyu's stringed pipa. It was a smaller instrument and easier to transport than the zither.

"You're going to be late," Madame scolded.

Being punctual was not something Mingyu ever worried about. Banquets were notoriously laconic when it came to starting and more particularly ending hours—a habit that Madame usually profited from.

So Mingyu breezed past Madame with only a cursory nod. It was the tall figure at the front door that brought her up short.

"Lady Mingyu." Wu Kaifeng bowed lower than was required. It was an awkward, exaggerated motion that, given his height, seemed almost like mockery.

"Constable Wu." Mingyu's bow was considerably less pronounced to the point of being nonexistent. "Yue-ying did not tell me the head constable would see to this task himself."

"I hope the lady finds this servant acceptable."

"More than acceptable." She continued past him.

The carriage was waiting in the street. Yue-ying quickened her pace to come up beside the constable.

"I didn't mean for you to go to all this trouble," she whispered.

"No trouble," he said in a tone that wasn't exactly

unpleasant. Every exchange with him was a battle. He gave away nothing in his voice or expression.

She went ahead to Mingyu, who had already seated herself. The awning had been taken down for the evening and Yue-ying could see the orange-purple sky peeking through the buildings as the sun set. Constable Wu remained in the street to accompany them on foot, his hand resting casually near his sword.

"Come up here with us," Mingyu invited. "It's a long way and I would want you to save your strength to fight off any bandits and wrongdoers that might accost us."

Yue-ying sighed in irritation. Mingyu was the one who had insisted on an escort, but now she was treating it like some sort of joke.

With his long legs, Wu climbed up into the carriage without need of the step stool and positioned himself immediately behind the driver in the seat opposite them. Mingyu remained silent, looking out into the street. Defiantly, Yue-ying did the same. She turned her head to watch the rows of shops flow by.

All the warmth and euphoria she had felt beneath the bridge had faded away. Mingyu drew the entire world around her like stars circling the Earth. If she was upset, then no one else was allowed their happiness.

At least Wu's presence assured their earlier argument would not resurface. Hopefully the discussion about Bai Huang would die away, to become yet another topic they avoided speaking of. Some things were meant to go unspoken, even among the closest of people.

The first part of the journey was dreadful. There was a lantern hanging on the carriage to provide light. Wu Kaifeng kept his hands on his knees, his glance occasionally flickering to one side of the carriage and then the other. Anyone who happened to approach them was likely to get his hand sliced off.

"You are from Suzhou," Mingyu said to him after the long pause.

"I am."

"I hear the women are beautiful there."

"Not more or less so than anywhere."

Mingyu laughed. "He speaks only when required and not one word more."

Yue-ying didn't answer. She didn't think she was supposed to.

"Tell us about all the dangerous outlaws you've arrested in the North Hamlet," she taunted.

Yue-ying wanted to pinch her; Mingyu was being combative on purpose.

"Not many at all."

"Oh, we must be quite safe, then."

"Very secretive, more like," the constable replied. "The citizens of this ward would rather a crime go unpunished than upset the peace by reporting it."

"Well, Magistrate Li speaks highly of you," Mingyu said, now trying to smooth over the rough edges of the conversation.

"He brought me here because there were a high number of questionable cases in the area," he said.

"Questionable?"

"Take the case of the body that was found in the river. The man was drowned before being dragged back into a boat. Then whoever did it took time to hide the body, which is unusual for street thieves. He was dead for a week before the earthquake shook the boat loose from wherever it had been lodged. The body had begun to decay, becoming black and putrid, yet no one reported anyone as missing during this time."

They were both staring at him in shock. Talk of death and tragedy was taboo. Maybe it was a good thing that Constable Wu didn't speak very often.

Mingyu looked a little pale by the time the carriage stopped for inspection at the ward gate. They had been issued a pass to allow them through after curfew. The city streets outside the ward were wide and empty aside from foot patrols at this time of night. The carriage rolled northward toward the lavish residences located near the imperial palace.

"Well, this has certainly been an interesting ride," Mingyu remarked sarcastically as they arrived at the banquet.

Yue-ying bit her tongue. Mingyu had demanded protection, not entertaining conversation.

The mansion was practically a palace itself. There were several courtyards within the surrounding wall. The spacious garden had been set up with banquet tables, and courtesans moved between them, pouring wine and providing stories. Lanterns were hung throughout the gathering, casting a warm glow over the guests. The darkness of night was no deterrent for celebrating such an occasion. The party was hosted by Duke Chou of Taiyuan, who had been newly promoted to chancellor, one of the highest positions in the imperial court.

Mingyu introduced herself to the steward and flowed into the banquet as if she'd been born to nobility. She was brought to the head table to be introduced to the Duke and his inner circle. Yue-ying drifted to the corner of the garden, preparing to become invisible.

"There is something I did not bring up in the carriage, Miss Yue-ying."

She started at the gravel of Wu's voice. She'd heard no warning footsteps or the clearing of a throat. The head constable materialized beside her like a granite statue, dark and imposing.

He stood with his back to the wall and raked his gaze slowly over the gathering. He made her nervous, as if he were the judge of the underworld there to demand retribution for old, undiscovered transgressions.

"About the body in the canal—a puncture wound was found at the juncture of his neck and shoulder." He tapped the spot at the base of his neck. "Upon further investigation, I found this embedded in him."

He reached into the fold of his robe and pulled out a bundle of cloth. She unwrapped it to find a broad silver pin the length of her third finger.

"I considered it might be a weapon, going so far as to check the wound for traces of poison. There was none," he assured her.

Poison? What sort of crimes did the constable typically encounter?

She picked up the pin very carefully with two fingers, turning it over and holding it close to inspect the surface. "This is from a lady's hair ornament."

The long, pointed tip, which was meant to be fixed into a coil of hair or a bun, was intact, but the topmost edge was jagged. The ornament had been snapped off.

"At first I assumed the drowned man was a vagrant or some unfortunate who had stumbled upon thieves in the middle of the night," Wu said. "The presence of this, an expensive piece of jewelry, changes everything. This was stabbed into him with enough force to break it in two. There was a struggle before he drowned."

A shiver ran down her spine. Whoever had worn the ornament was involved with murder.

"The pin is made of pure silver. Very expensive. Considering where the body was found, this ornament likely belonged to a courtesan. One who was successful enough to afford such extravagance," Wu concluded.

Mingyu glanced over at them with a curious look. Yue-ying quickly wrapped the pin back up and returned it to the constable. "Why are you telling me this now?"

"I know very little about women's jewelry. I was hoping you could help me."

When Wu spoke, his eyes didn't liven his face or emphasize his words. They remained fixed upon her. Yue-ying finally recognized that it wasn't merely a quirk of his character. Everything he said was indeed part of an interrogation. All that strange talk during the carriage ride about the dead body found in the canal—he was watching closely to see how they would react to it. Surely he didn't suspect her or Mingyu?

Then she realized he suspected everyone.

"There are hundreds of these in the quarter," she replied. "There's no way to tell who this belonged to."

"One murder shortly after another in the Pingkang li. It makes one wonder if there is some connection."

The killing would have happened around the same time as the banquet on the pleasure boat. Just weeks before Huilan's death.

"Maybe this man attempted to grab some woman and do unspeakable things to her," Yue-ying said. "She had to defend herself."

"Then why not report it to the magistrate?" the constable asked.

She looked over to where Mingyu was entertaining. The Pingkang was its own world and the constable was an outsider. Bai Huang had said as much.

"Because we're afraid," she said evenly. "We're all afraid."

The earthquake had dredged up all the hidden secrets

of the quarter. Two murders, occurring so close together. One was a stranger who meant nothing to anyone except the grim-faced constable who was ruthlessly dedicated to his duties. But Huilan was well-known and beloved. Or at least she had been.

"Miss?" A maidservant approached them. "Our steward needs to speak with you. Some issue with the banquet fee."

"The fee?" Payment was always handled between the host and Madame Sun.

Yue-ying excused herself from Constable Wu and followed the maidservant into the interior of the mansion. The entrance hall was similarly lit with lanterns, though all of the guests had congregated outside in the garden. She was asked to wait in a sitting room and was in the midst of studying a scroll depicting a flock of cranes on one wall when an arm wrapped around her waist.

With a gasp, she dug her elbow back, colliding against solid bone and muscle.

"It's me," Bai Huang said with a laugh. He loosened his hold on her as she twisted around.

"You scared me!" She shoved at him. Her heart was pounding uncontrollably. All this talk of murder and stabbings. Still, the sight of him stole her breath. "What are you doing here?"

"Don't you know that the new chancellor and I share the same surname? The Duke of Taiyuan is a distant relative—a cousin of cousins. I have an impressive lineage."

She sniffed. He grinned.

"I have to get back," she said. "I can't be away for long, especially when Mingyu sees that you're here."

"Oh, so you've been prohibited from seeing me." He

leaned in close and lowered his voice. "No more kissing beneath bridges?"

Her face heated. She turned to go only to have him catch her sleeve. It was a risk, having such long sleeves.

"Why don't we both stay back here? No one will miss us and you're the most interesting part of the banquet anyway."

"Shameless," she scolded.

But there was no denying the flutter in her stomach or the skip of her pulse. She liked the way he teased her. She even liked the look of regret that passed over his face when he released her.

"What is that brute Wu Kaifeng doing here? I heard he accompanied you."

"He's here for our protection."

"Protection?"

"Mingyu insisted she didn't feel safe." She frowned. "Her reasons are sometimes a mystery to all but herself. Whatever her mood was today, she refused to leave the Lotus without a bodyguard."

"Wu is like a great black spider. His presence would dampen the mood of any gathering."

"Black spider? Now that's hardly fair," she chided. "I really must go."

"Wait—" He caught her sleeve again, this time letting his fingers trail down to hook onto hers. "When can I see you again?"

His proposal made her heart leap. They weren't conducting an affair. It was nothing more than the touch of fingertips and the exchange of looks. One brief kiss in the rain. Another prolonged, passionate kiss beneath a bridge. She strung their moments together one by one like jewels on a necklace.

Mingyu was right; she was allowing herself to be

seduced. Not by Bai Huang, but by the thought a gentleman such as him could be attracted to someone like her. Of course it wasn't anything more than a moment's infatuation.

"We shouldn't be seen together unless you happen to be at the Lotus," she replied firmly.

"But you won't speak to me at the Lotus," he protested.

Yue-ying wanted very much to be reckless and stay with him, if only for a few stolen moments, but she couldn't endanger her relationship with Mingyu. Their bond was tenuous enough as it was. With her heart full of regret, she left Bai Huang standing in the parlor.

She had been so distracted by his teasing that she hadn't thought to tell him about the broken hairpin and the stranger in the canal. Perhaps it was best that she kept her suspicions, as vague as they were, to herself. Huilan could have left the pleasure boat that night and returned along the waterway.

The problem was that Mingyu had been with her.

CHAPTER TEN

THE LAYOUT OF the pleasure quarter was easy to navigate. There were three main lanes. The more expensive establishments such as the Lotus Palace and the House of a Hundred Songs were located in the central and southern lanes. The lesser houses congregated along the northern lane.

These courtesans were not as highly skilled and their patrons were the younger candidates or poorer merchants who could not afford the exorbitant banquet fees of the larger houses.

Given his reputation for being indiscriminate, it wasn't implausible for Huang to stumble into one of the houses of the northern lane. The headmistress took a look at the expensive material of his robe, recognized his name and his reputation for throwing money around, and immediately he found a lovely young lady at his arm leading him to a seat. Her perfume had a sweet, pleasant scent.

"What is your name?" he asked as he reclined back onto the pillows.

"Lin Li."

He rewarded her with a smile. "Very pretty."

Lin Li ducked her head shyly as she poured the wine. She wore little makeup and her face had a fresh, innocent appeal with dimples in both cheeks and a soft pink mouth. The house had only a single parlor for entertaining and three courtesans in addition to the headmistress. His attention was divided between the lovely Lin Li and Ma Jun, who was sitting at the center of the room with two men he didn't recognize.

"I haven't seen you here before, my lord," Lin Li said.

"Then I've been neglectful," he teased.

Huang didn't want the commissioner thinking he was the sole reason for the visit, so he continued his banter with the courtesan while keeping an eye on Ma Jun.

Lin Li offered wine to him. He complained about having to drink alone. She demurred and sipped along with him. They spoke about themselves. The courtesan had a way of speaking so softly that he had to lean in close to hear her. She called him handsome with a bashful flutter of her lashes. That was still pleasing to hear, he had to admit.

By the time Lin Li was getting a little bolder in her flirtation, Ma Jun's two guests had disappeared into the back, presumably to private rooms. Huang made eye contact with the commissioner for the third time that evening, each time frowning as if trying to recall where they'd met.

"Commissioner Ma?" he finally asked.

The man regarded him with a similar frown of almost recognition while Lin Li murmured in disappointment. She was attempting to lay her head on Huang's shoulder when he rose to approach the commissioner.

"It is you!" Huang shook his finger at him. "We met at the chancellor's banquet the other night. Commissioner Ma Jun, the man who knows everyone. Allow me to introduce myself. My name is Huang, family name of Bai."

"Of course, Lord Bai. I know that name very well. Please sit."

Lin Li smoothly glided over as well, pouring wine for the both of them.

"I haven't been here before." Huang looked about the room. "It's very comfortable, isn't it?"

"Well, you should come more often. It's so much more relaxing than some of the larger establishments. Good for conversation. And the ladies are just as lovely and talented."

He laughed, agreeing wholeheartedly, and gave Lin Li a sly smile. Then he insisted on buying more wine for the commissioner and after a few cups they were becoming fast friends. Such was the open atmosphere of the Pingkang li.

"Haven't I also seen you at the House of a Hundred Songs?" Huang asked, refilling Ma Jun's cup himself.

"It's likely. I've been known to visit."

"A tragedy, what happened to that poor girl there."

"Lady Huilan," Ma Jun said, sighing long and loud. "She was a rare flower."

They raised their cups and drank. After Huang finished his wine, he pressed on. "Were you close to her?"

"She served as hostess for our gatherings every so often. A great talent."

"Gatherings such as these?" Huang indicated the two seats that had been recently vacated by the unfamiliar men.

"Traders from Guangzhou," Ma Jun answered easily. "As head of the East Market Commission, I deal with many different merchants. It's always easier to discuss business over wine and music."

"It must be difficult to go back to the Hundred Songs now that Huilan is gone. It just won't be the same without her," Huang remarked, shaking his head.

Ma Jun nodded. He rubbed a hand over his beard and

looked genuinely sad. Huang was disappointed at how pleasant and accommodating the commissioner was. Ma was keeping his distance and not admitting that he and Huilan had been intimate in any way, but those sorts of things were not discussed among gentlemen, and most certainly not after her tragic end. Huang was hoping for a shifty gaze, sudden anger or a tremor in the other man's hands, which might indicate guilt.

"I hear that her ghost haunts the Hundred Songs," Huang ventured.

He knew he was reaching, but some men, even the strong, stalwart sort, would tremble at the mere mention of ghosts. As it was, Ma Jun only looked at him oddly as if he'd had too much to drink. Poor Lin Li, however, did turn pale.

"Just a rumor I had heard." He shrugged, quickly downing more wine.

Commissioner Ma was less forthcoming after that. Likely because he thought Lord Bai Huang might be a raving madman. They moved on to more neutral topics.

"There are so many considerations to keep the market running peacefully," the commissioner said. "There are regulations on quality and price. Which merchants and goods are allowed to be sold inside the walls of the East Market."

It was Lin Li who saved him from utter boredom. The courtesan detected Huang's feigned interest as the conversation veered toward types of wood and shipping from the southern provinces.

"Come with me, my lord," she whispered, her breath warm against his ear.

He did so gladly.

Lin Li took him by the hand and led him down a dark hallway into a chamber. The bed was arranged against one wall and there was a painting of sparrows and plum blossoms hung above it. He could tell from the brushwork and calligraphy that it was of low quality.

As soon as they were inside Lin Li drew a curtain across the doorway and flowed into his arms. Her perfume once again floated over him. The scent was as delicate and undemanding as she was. Large, luminous eyes fixed on him, the pupils darkening slightly. She liked what she saw. His pulse beat faster.

She ran her hands over his shoulders and down to the front of his robe while his entire body tensed. Huang laid his hand over hers with a firm grip, halting the touch.

The courtesan's smile didn't waver. "You're in love with someone."

He shook his head, though his mouth curved faintly.

Her lashes fluttered. "You can forget her for a while, if you want…or not."

"I had a suspicion you were not as shy as you appeared."

Lin Li's smile widened at that, flashing both dimples. She was quite lovely. On top of that, she was pleasant, soft-spoken and undemanding. They could spend an hour secluded together and he would leave relaxed and invigorated. But it wasn't his intention for coming here and, even worse than that, he found himself imagining what Yue-ying would say to him, or rather not say to him, if she could see him right now. He pictured the exact look on her face.

When had Yue-ying inserted herself into his head?

"Let us talk instead," he said.

Without argument, Lin Li rolled onto her side with her cheek resting on her palm. If she showed any sign of disappointment, he'd certainly missed it.

He settled in at the edge of the bed. "Does Commissioner Ma come here often?"

Her answer came without hesitation. "Once or twice a week. More often since the tragedy at the Hundred Songs."

"Does he always bring associates with him?"

"Always. He tries very much to appear more impressive than he is. Unlike you."

Huang laughed. "I'm completely unimpressive."

"He would come to us with the ones he considered unrefined," she said. "Foreign merchants or the less wealthy ones. Here, one can listen to a song girl, have wine poured and even come back for a few moments in the bedchamber. I've heard the commissioner saying all this to Mother. All the same pleasantries of the central and southern lanes, but for only a portion of the expense. Most of the outsiders don't know the difference between one courtesan or another."

The dear girl showed no signs of being upset that she was being compared to a commodity in the market and an inferior one at that. Huang shifted uncomfortably. Lin Li's words echoed what Yue-ying had accused him of once: that he thought of all the women of the Pingkang li as interchangeable.

It was easy to see how Ma Jun traded access to the market in exchange for bribes, but, other than being somewhat unscrupulous, Huang hadn't found anything that pointed to his propensity to commit murder.

"The courtesan, the one who died, she was a favorite of his, wasn't she?" Lin Li asked.

"I've heard it said so."

"And he was there the night she was strangled?" She saw his look of surprise and shrugged. "One hears things."

"If you hear anything else from the commissioner, I would like to know about it," he said.

"How do I find you?"

"I usually drink at the Lotus."

"You must be quite wealthy. I let you get away too easily."

She really was quite charming. If only it wasn't an act. In truth, it was an act and it wasn't. Just as he was a scoundrel and he wasn't.

"I enjoyed our conversation, Lin Li," he said, standing to take his leave.

Rather than bowing, she reached out to touch his arm. "Farewell, Lord Bai."

Before departing, he paid the headmistress for the wine and Lin Li's attentions, as chaste as they were. As he exited the pleasure house the evening had just begun. He wandered back toward the more refined establishments along the southern lane.

The lanterns were lit in the rooftop of the Lotus Palace and all the windows were aglow. He could hear the sound of laughter from within. None of the laughter would belong to Yue-ying. She was always the quietest person in the room. Did she ever laugh? Other than to mock him, that was?

His body was still flushed, desire uncomfortably awakened. His various activities lately had left him little time for falling into bed with courtesans, but he hadn't abstained from female company since returning to the city.

If he went inside, he would have to pretend to court Mingyu while hoping to catch the attention of her maidservant. Yue-ying would have to watch him fumble and fawn over another woman. And then if he happened to catch a moment alone with her, she would smell the perfume on his clothes and be convinced he was a good-for-nothing. Well, maybe he didn't amount to much right now, but he could be a little better than that for her.

Huang kept on walking and the sounds of the Lotus Palace faded into the night.

CHAPTER ELEVEN

THE MIDDLE OF the month brought the full moon and another visit to the temple. Yue-ying held up a parasol to shield Mingyu from the midday sun as they entered the courtyard where they were greeted by an unexpected sight. Whereas the other templegoers were strolling about the garden, Wu Kaifeng stood at the steps leading to the hall of worship, watching all who came in or out.

Mingyu leaned in close. "That constable certainly is everywhere. I've seen statues of the demon Mara that looked more inviting."

"Shh!" Yue-ying hushed, suppressing a snort of laughter.

"Are you trying to catch the interest of any particular lady, Constable Wu?" Mingyu teased as they approached.

"Madame Lui of the Hundred Songs said that Lady Huilan would come here every month." His gaze swept the courtyard, taking in the scholars and ladies who were present. "This place seems to be popular."

"You are still trying to find Huilan's killer," Mingyu remarked in a more somber tone. "I do hope you find him soon."

"Or her," Wu amended. "Women have been known to commit crimes the same as men."

Mingyu gave him an odd look. "Your dedication is commendable," she said after some consideration. There was apparently no polite and appropriate response when it came to Constable Wu.

Mingyu bowed and started to move past him with Yue-ying close behind, but Wu stopped them. "There is something I wanted to ask you, Lady Mingyu. In private."

Yue-ying looked to Mingyu with a question in her eyes. Despite the crowd gathered in the courtyard, she didn't want to leave Mingyu with the constable.

"I am sure it will only be a moment," Mingyu said to her.

She handed her mistress the parasol and watched as the two of them retreated beneath the shade of the pear tree in the corner. Wu stood head and shoulders over Mingyu and Yue-ying could clearly see his expression, which meant she could clearly see that it was blank while he questioned Mingyu. The courtesan's face was hidden mostly behind the parasol.

Yue-ying wandered to the pond to visit the venerable tortoise while she waited. Her old friend was outside on the rocks again, looking dusty and wrinkled. That was three visits she'd been able to see him. Usually he hid inside his cavern, and she might only catch the glimpse of his shell from beneath the rock.

She was pondering whimsically whether this was a good or bad omen, when the oddity of it struck her. The tortoise had been outside right after the earthquake. She had assumed the tremors had jostled him out of hiding.

"Yue-ying," Mingyu called out across the courtyard. She was obviously in a mood. "Our head constable wishes to interrogate you now to see if he can catch me lying."

She heard Mingyu with only half an ear. Ducking down, Yue-ying tried to peer beneath the rocks. Mingyu and Constable Wu came toward her just as she began to climb over the pond, hoisting up the edge of her skirt so it wouldn't fall into the water.

"What are you doing?" Mingyu gasped.

Yue-ying knelt on her hands and knees before the tortoise. His black eyes flicked at her, but he otherwise let her be as she crouched and reached her hand into the crevice. There was something loose inside, the surface of it smooth and even. Her fingers closed around it and drew the object out into the light.

It was a silver ingot, molded into a tablet and stamped with a flower. She reached in again and pulled out another then another. She looked up to see Mingyu and Wu Kaifeng staring at her hands, which were overflowing with silver.

"There is no way to be certain that the sliver belonged to Huilan," Mingyu protested.

She cast her shawl haplessly aside as she stepped into her parlor. Yue-ying followed obediently in her wake, retrieving the length of green gauze and then Mingyu's slippers, which she had discarded, one just inside the door and another by the sitting area.

"The stash was wrapped inside an embroidered shawl, one that certainly belonged to a lady of the quarter," Yue-ying argued. "Huilan had said she would sell her jewels and she was planning to leave. Who else would have hidden the money there?"

"Thieves. A greedy widow hiding an inheritance. A corrupt abbot." Mingyu's imagination was endless. "Besides, I can't imagine any courtesan possessing so much silver, even if she sold her entire wardrobe."

Constable Wu had searched farther beneath the rocks. He retrieved an expensive length of silk wrapped around a cache of coins and ingots. Despite Mingyu's talk of corrupt abbots, no one at the temple claimed the silver and Wu had promptly confiscated it.

"If Huilan had intended to run away from her foster mother, she would have needed to hide her money outside of the Hundred Songs," Yue-ying reasoned. "Even Constable Wu believes it belonged to her."

"What did that man speak to you about? He was horrible to me. No manners at all."

"He asked about that banquet. The one on the pleasure boat both you and Huilan attended at the end of last month."

Mingyu touched a finger to a point behind her ear and rubbed at the spot absently. "What did you tell him?"

Yue-ying knew that gesture very well. Mingyu did it out of habit when something agitated her. "There was nothing to tell. I left early that night, remember?"

"Oh, yes. That was the night."

Mingyu slipped back into the dressing room and Yue-ying followed her. Yue-ying opened the dresser and knelt to place the discarded slippers inside. As she did so her hand brushed over another pair that had been recently cleaned.

Yue-ying straightened abruptly. Mingyu was at her dressing table, looking into the mirror. She removed a comb from her hair to smooth out a few wayward strands. The disinterest she affected was too calm, her mask too perfect.

"I found a pair of slippers covered in mud while you were away." Yue-ying attempted a light tone though her voice sounded shrill to her ears. "I couldn't get them completely clean."

Mingyu waved her hand dismissively. "Throw them away, then."

The slippers had been hidden at the back of the wardrobe. And hadn't Mingyu been distant since the end of last month, right before the earthquake had shaken up the city?

Yue-ying felt sick to her stomach. There was mud all along the waterway leading from the docks and Mingyu and Huilan had been together the night of the banquet. A man had been killed around the same time and in the same vicinity. Only a short period later, Huilan was lying dead in her chamber.

Her heart pounded as she moved to help smooth out Mingyu's hair. A case full of combs and glittering hair ornaments lay open on the dressing table, many of them gifts from admirers. Yue-ying couldn't banish the feeling that one hairpin might be missing from among the jewelry.

Oh, she was being overly dramatic! A little mud on a slipper could mean a hundred things and Mingyu's moods were always unpredictable. It was obvious Mingyu was having difficulties with her patron, General Deng. She had returned from her trip to the hot springs in a poor mood. The general had recently considered taking Mingyu as his concubine, but the situation had somehow fallen apart. Mingyu kept to herself about it.

There were enough tales of intrigue and danger in the Pingkang li. Yue-ying didn't need to go making up more of her own.

As soon as Mingyu was perfect once more, Yue-ying went downstairs to see if Madame Sun had any particular instructions. According to the headmistress, there were no events to attend and Magistrate Li had said he would call that evening. Yue-ying hoped it wasn't for yet another interrogation. Both Magistrate Li and Constable Wu had been to every house making inquiries, though the magistrate's methods were considerably more restrained than his constable's.

She was moving toward the kitchen to see if Old Auntie needed any help, when a knock came at the door. The messenger handed her a small parcel wrapped in silk, which she assumed was a gift for one of the courtesans until she saw the two characters inked onto the ribbon tied around it. It was her name.

Yue-ying snatched up the bundle and stuffed it into her sleeve. A tingle of anticipation ran up her spine as she darted into the main parlor and hid behind the bamboo screen. No one ever sent her gifts. Her pulse raced as she unwrapped the parcel. She knew immediately whom it was from.

Inside was a long silver hairpin. An ornament dangled from the top. It was set with a pale stone that glowed with an inner light. As she turned it this way and that, tiny fragments of color reflected from within the gem like a broken rainbow.

The pin was simple, yet eye-catching. It wasn't merely pretty; it was intriguing. She hugged it to her chest and imagined Bai Huang searching for this pin, finding this one stone among all the sea of pearls and jade. Her heart felt as if it would burst.

Then a pang of disappointment struck her. How could she ever wear it? A maidservant had no use for something so frivolous. Jeweled ornaments were supposed to draw attention. A gift like this was intended to go to a lover.

She bundled the pin up and shoved it back into her sleeve. In the language of courtship, accepting such a gift meant something. She and Bai Huang were engaged in a flirtation, nothing more. That was all it could be. She would have to give the pin back.

For the rest of the morning, she went about her chores, tending to Mingyu, checking with the other courtesans to see if they needed anything in the market. Between tasks, she would hide away and take out the ornament once more, turning it to catch the light.

She realized the stone's glow was like moonlight. A little moon. Her heart ached every time she saw it. She didn't even dare to place it into her hair to give herself one glance of how the stone would look on her.

When she finally was able to get away, she moved swiftly through the market stalls to allow herself extra time to seek out Bai Huang. She didn't have the coin to spend on hiring a sedan, so she walked past the Three Lanes to the quarter just north of the Pingkang li, the area where students often took residence while preparing for the exams. It took another half an hour searching through the winding alleyways before she found the right gate. By then, her feet were sore.

The residence was a humble, modestly sized space. The entrance courtyard could be spanned in twenty paces and there were several rooms surrounding it. She wondered whether there were other students living there along with Bai Huang, but the enclosure was quiet.

The shutters were open on the first room. She peeked inside to see Bai Huang seated at a desk. He held a book roll in his hands. According to reputation, he was supposed to be dozing at this time of day, yet here he was, reading from a scroll that was as thick as her arm. A deep line cut between his eyebrows. He was so focused that she took three steps into the study before he looked up.

"Yue-ying!" He started in astonishment. Then hastily stood. "What are you doing here? How did you know where to find me?"

"I spoke with the sedan carrier who took you home the other night."

He folded the scroll closed and fumbled a drawer open. "I wasn't expecting you."

"Why are you so nervous?" She craned her neck to peer over the top of the desk.

"I'm not nervous," he denied stiffly.

She wanted to laugh. "What is that? A pillow book?"

He dropped the scroll inside and pushed the drawer shut, his movements lacking their usual laconic grace. He was dressed in an understated house robe, dark brown edged in black. Nothing as flamboyant as what she usually saw him in, but as soon as he smoothed a hand over the front a transformation came over him.

"Miss Yue-ying, are you here to spy on me?" he drawled.

That wasn't her intention, but now she was certainly curious. "What was that you were concentrating on so intently?"

"If you must know, I was searching for lines of poetry I could steal to impress young ladies. I've been told my own words are dreadfully boring."

His eyes had recaptured their playful glint. Rather than charming her, it made her uneasy. What was he really like beneath the flower-prince persona that he wore like a second skin?

"I came to return this," she said hastily.

She retrieved the hairpin, which she'd tucked beneath her sash, and laid it on the desk. Bai Huang's gaze dropped to the ornament before returning to her face. His smile faded.

"Thank you, Lord Bai. It's very pretty, but—"

Her pulse quickened as he came toward her. As he neared her breath caught in her throat, but he moved past her to the door. He lifted his hand, palm flat, and pushed it shut. The quiet rasp of wood against the frame was like the crash of thunder. She jumped at the sound.

Flustered, she tried to continue. "It's too expensive. And when would I ever wear it?"

He was behind her now, very close, and she was afraid to turn to look at him. Yue-ying fixed her gaze back on the desk to the harmless piece of silver that had given her reason to come here and invade his privacy. A mix of emotions churned inside her.

"I saw this gem in the market yesterday and thought of you," he said, his tone quiet.

"You shouldn't be giving gifts like that to someone like me. It's not—it's not proper."

Defeat crept into her. It was true. For an aristocrat to openly court a maidservant—everyone would think the worst of both of them. The literati of the North Hamlet laughed at Bai Huang's mishaps, but no one treated him with scorn. And she, they simply ignored. She didn't exist and she didn't want to, in that way.

"I don't mean any offense," she insisted, though she felt she added on more insult with those words. Why couldn't she have Mingyu's talent for deflecting a man's attention without causing him to lose face? And it *was* a talent; she could see that now.

Bai Huang moved past her again, his shoulder just skimming her arm as he returned to the desk. She felt the coldness of the near miss more acutely than any touch.

He lifted the hairpin, revealing only his profile as he looked it over. "I've never seen anything like this. Just like I've never known anyone like you." He turned it this way and that to catch the light, the same way she had done. "I thought you might like it, that was all."

With that, he opened the same drawer where he'd hidden the scroll and dropped the pin inside. Suddenly, unreasonably, she wanted it back. She clasped her hands behind her back to keep from reaching for it.

The silence that remained was uncomfortable. She turned to look over the shelves against the wall. "I've never seen so many books."

"My family has aspirations of me leaving my wind-and-wine days behind me and passing the palace exams," he said from behind her. "I suppose I should start reading them someday."

He was lying. There was dust gathered at the edge of the shelf, but not on the books or scrolls themselves. She wanted to reach out and run her hands over the pages, as if these writings held the answer to who Bai Huang really was.

When she turned back around, he was staring at her with a look that she could only describe as longing. It was there and then gone in the next moment.

"Now was that the only reason you came to see me?" He leaned back against the desk, once again the beloved fool, the failed-scholar, the do-nothing.

She took a breath and told him about the stash of silver that she had discovered and Constable Wu had confiscated. Once again, the investigation was serving as an excuse to seek him out. It was shameless of her.

"You've made better progress than I." He in turn recounted how he had spent the past few days investigating Ma Jun. "It was a waste of time. I was certain he must be hiding something, but, other than taking small bribes, he doesn't appear to be guilty of a crime. He was at the Hundred Songs the night of Huilan's death, but the other courtesans are confident that he was downstairs in the banquet room the entire time."

"What if we've been mistaken all along?" she said slowly.

He raised an eyebrow at that. "Why do you say that?"

"We've been assuming that something happened at that banquet that upset Huilan, but what if the incident occurred afterward? A lady's hairpin was found in the body from the river and Constable Wu believes the stranger was drowned near the end of the month. Right around the same time as the banquet."

Wu Kaifeng knew about Huilan's visits to the temple as well as the banquet. Yue-ying needed to uncover what had happened before Constable Wu did. It was the only way to protect Mingyu.

"Wu seems to be confiding in you quite a bit," he remarked dryly.

She was taken aback by the bite in his tone. "He confides in me for the same reasons you do. He trusts in my knowledge of the North Hamlet."

Bai Huang sighed loudly. He closed his hands over her shoulders and directed her into the chair beside the desk before taking his seat behind it. "I confide in you because, not only are you perceptive, but I can't stop thinking of you."

A thrill went through her. The warmth of his touch stayed with her even though his hands were now folded in front of him. He regarded her with a stern expression. She found his look of concentration so much more compelling than all of the smiles and flirtatious glances.

"A lady's hairpin was found?" he prompted, as if he hadn't just confessed that she was in his thoughts or that he was irrationally jealous of Wu Kaifeng.

She gathered the thoughts in her head together and tried to form a coherent picture. "The stranger in the boat could have been someone dangerous, a smuggler or a bandit. That was where all the silver could have come from. Huilan either quarreled with him or fought with him and he was drowned. Frightened, she hid the silver and planned to escape."

"But his associates found her and took revenge?" Bai Huang finished for her.

"It's possible."

He was already shaking his head. "Your story answers some questions, but raises too many others. How did Huilan come to be involved with an outlaw in the first place?"

"It may not have been a previous association. He could have attacked her on the docks and she had to defend herself."

"Then why not go to the magistrate?"

"Because of the silver. And because she was afraid." Her answer to Bai Huang was the same as it had been to Constable Wu. "Men can't understand how hard it is for us to trust anyone. Several years ago, a courtesan and her foster mother were both executed for killing a man. They claimed that he was robbing them, but the magistrate was unsympathetic because they had hidden the body. To Huilan, so much silver had to seem like freedom."

"She had asked me for help," he said soberly. "But she didn't trust me enough to confide in me. Perhaps she would have if I didn't have a reputation for being so useless."

"Lord Bai." Yue-ying could see how the memory pained him. "No one thinks you're useless."

"Not that it matters now." He shrugged, but she could still see the dark cloud over him. "If the stranger is the answer, we should search out the boats along the section of canal between where the pleasure boat was docked and the North Hamlet."

Hopefully Yue-ying was right and the dead man was indeed some bandit or smuggler. She believed in her heart that Mingyu and Huilan weren't capable of murder, even for the promise of so much silver.

"I should go now," she said. "It's getting late."

"You always say that."

"It's always true."

Like a gentleman, Bai Huang accompanied her out into the courtyard. He came to a stop at the gate. "Is your mistress the reason why you won't accept my gifts?" he pressed. "Why you won't be seen with me?"

He was standing very close to her. She could smell the faint scent of cedarwood on his skin and was aware of his every breath as he waited for an answer.

"She doesn't like that I spend time with you," she admitted.

"Has she forbidden this?" He reached up to tuck a strand of hair behind her ear, his fingers continuing the caress along her cheek.

A shudder traveled down her spine and every part of her warmed all at once. Though it was difficult, she forced herself to meet his gaze. "Mingyu doesn't need to forbid me. I make my own choices."

Her face was unsettling to most. It wasn't as if she were scarred or disfigured, but the red stain was odd enough to cause people to avert their eyes. They pretended they hadn't been staring. As a result, she was easily noticed, but often ignored. Yet Bai Huang always looked directly at her, or, at times like this, he seemed to look into her. It left her feeling worse than naked.

"I owe her everything," she tried to explain. "You don't know how it is to have your well-being, your hap-

piness or your sorrow tied to another person so absolutely."

"I know what it means to have to answer to others,"
he said darkly.

Ever since that first stolen kiss in the wine cellar,
Bai Huang always waited for her to lean toward him.
To give him some signal with her eyes or her lips to invite him to her. As much as she wanted him to kiss her
at that moment, she pulled away.

Obligingly, he opened the gate for her. Out on the
street, he waved down a sedan for her and handed a
coin to the carrier once she was seated.

"It's always been you sending me home before." The
corner of his mouth twitched. "Usually drunk."

She bit back her smile, but Bai Huang still caught it.
His eyes didn't leave her as the sedan pulled forward.
When she glanced back, he was still standing there in
the street, watching her leave.

CHAPTER TWELVE

HUANG PUT ON his plainest robe and had Zhou Dan meet him at his quarters midmorning. For the past few days, Zhou Dan had explored the docks with a few of his cronies to gather information.

They were going that day to meet Ouyang Yi, the owner of the most successful shipping fleet in those waters. He also happened to be the owner of the pleasure boat where the Market Commissioner's banquet had been hosted.

The headquarters of the shipping operation was a building on the waterway with its own private port. Boatmen and laborers swarmed over the dock, loading and unloading crates and baskets.

Huang moved past the boats with Zhou Dan following dutifully behind him, carrying a bundle beneath one arm. The swampy scent of the canal surrounded them as they headed for the office. A clerk sat at the front. After a courteous introduction under an assumed name, Huang asked to see the shipping baron himself.

"Mr. Yuan." The clerk nodded. "Mr. Ouyang is expecting you."

Huang was posing as a merchant from Henan looking for transport services. He and Zhou Dan entered the inner office and Ouyang Yi stood to greet him. He was a middle-aged businessman, robust in appearance. His beard was neatly trimmed and his robe expensive, but not extravagant.

"Your fleet is very impressive, sir," Huang began once he was seated. "You must have more ships than the imperial navy."

"Not so great as that!" Ouyang laughed. "But times have been good."

They continued with a few more pleasantries before the business discussion began. "What is it that you're looking for, my friend?"

"Monthly shipments of cargo to our associates in the capital. I hear your prices are reasonable. And your connections are good," Huang added, keeping his expression controlled.

Ouyang was equally placid. "What sort of goods are you looking to transport?"

"Silk, of course."

Zhou Dan stepped forward and placed the bundle he'd been carrying onto the shipping merchant's desk. Ouyang pulled back the hemp wrapper to inspect the bolts of silk inside. "This is quite a small shipment."

"There is more to arrive by wagon," Huang explained smoothly. "Once the details are arranged."

The silk wasn't the cargo. It was what was required for Ouyang Yi's boatmen not to inspect or inquire about what was being transported.

"Henan province," the trader said thoughtfully. "That would fall under the domain of my business partner."

"Partner?"

"We have had to add more vessels due to increased demand in the past few years. Taking on a partner was much faster than building new ships and recruiting laborers to run them."

Huang nodded. "That sounds reasonable. How do I make arrangements with your...associate?"

"He is away, but will be back in a few days. I'm certain he can find space in his holds for your shipment."

Huang had not only discovered the trader's vessels shipped all forms of goods, but there were certain boats and routes that were known to reliably be overlooked for inspection. For all Ouyang Yi knew, they all contained bolts of silk.

They spoke around a few other particulars: the size of the shipment, how many ships might be required and, interestingly, any special care the silk might require. Ouyang Yi chose his words very cautiously. This arrangement with his other half, if such a person even existed, apparently provided separation from the shadier activities that went on in his fleet.

At the end of the discussion, they arranged another meeting in a few days' time. Afterward, Huang stood and thanked the trader for his time, leaving the bolts of silk behind as a goodwill gift.

"He's certainly not on the straight and narrow," Zhou Dan declared, once they were far from the docks. "Can't you go to the magistrate and have him arrested?"

"Our goal isn't to arrest every crooked trader in the city. We're trying to catch a murderer. Lady Huilan may have happened upon illicit activity along the canal."

"Or she was involved in it," Zhou Dan suggested.

"That's possible as well."

He had considered many different angles. Perhaps he was putting too much trust in Yue-ying's instincts. She had left out important parts of the picture in her explanation; most obviously that Huilan would not have been walking alone from the banquet, no matter how familiar she was with the area. Mingyu was also on the pleasure boat and she had mysteriously sent Yue-ying home early that night. Yue-ying was protecting her mistress; he had no doubt of it.

"We need to know what activities occur along that stretch of the canal after dark," he directed.

Zhou Dan grinned. "More interesting than scrubbing pots back home."

At the next crossroad, he and Zhou Dan parted ways. Posing as a crooked merchant was only one of his tasks for the day.

Father had sent him a message the night before to request a meeting. Huang followed his father's instructions and arrived at the designated place near the Ministry of Defense. The teahouse was three stories high and every table appeared full. With some effort, they were able to procure a place beside a window in the corner.

"General Deng was not in Changan," Father said before the tea was even brought out. "Our informants report that he never left his post."

Huang frowned. "I received this information from the courtesans of the Lotus Palace."

Mingyu's supposed assignation with Deng at the hot springs was the reason Yue-ying had been free to roam the quarter with him. He had rather pleasant memories of those few days.

The memories faded beneath Father's stern look. This was the man who'd had him thrown onto a naval ship when he couldn't control his gambling impulses. His father didn't look lightly upon distractions.

"I must have been mistaken," Huang said. "I apologize." Where had Mingyu been and with whom, if not with General Deng?

"No matter," Father said. "But be careful who you trust."

The tea came and gave them a short respite to speak of Father's promotion. He'd been elevated in rank though he was still to be stationed in Fujian. "Too much unrest brewing along the coast," he recounted. "The Sillan admiral whose fleet patrolled the area was assassinated several months ago. We must be vigilant or the pirates and raiders will take over once more."

"The empire is in danger of being overrun by outlaws from all ten sides," Huang muttered. "Even appointed officials are expected to be corrupt. It's a fight that cannot be won."

"Worrying accomplishes nothing. Emperor Xuanzong is dedicated to reform. All we need is more good men dedicated to the fight." Father gestured at him with teacup in hand. "The Emperor is opening up candidacy for the imperial exams at the end of this year to recruit new talent."

"Yes, Father."

The implication was clear. There was only so much Huang could do until he passed the exams. Father didn't need to point out—though he certainly had many times in the past—that every generation of their family had passed the exams and served in office. He, the eldest son of the Bai family, was currently a black mark in a long illustrious line.

THAT NIGHT, THE DICE were a blessing. Huang stood at the table and watched the numbers roll in meaningless combinations: Two, five and one. Six, three and four. Three, three and five. It took his mind away—at least it would until the candle burned out. He needed this tonight.

While the dice rolled, he sipped the weak, tepid tea the runners brought and tried to sort out his thoughts.

Huilan had been involved in something treacherous

and had been killed for it. Somehow he had become caught in it as well. He didn't understand why solving this murder had become so important to him. He only knew that he needed to do it. Other scholar-gentlemen were moved to write poetry about these women, but verses were a thin tribute to pay. Maybe he was moved to do more.

Lady Mingyu, the courtesan he had been openly courting since he'd returned to the capital, was proving to be a fox-demon. She was lying to everyone, even those closest to her. The courtesans of the North Hamlet weren't delicate flowers begging to be rescued. They held their secrets close, and they were dangerous secrets.

And no matter how many times he'd read over the Four Books and Five Classics, he couldn't seem to vanquish that bastard of an imperial exam.

To add to all that, Yue-ying didn't want his gift and had thrown it back in his face.

So his thoughts weren't exactly orderly.

He'd had certain aspirations for that hairpin he'd given her. Seeing her wearing it. Removing it carefully and laying it by the bedside while he unpinned the rest of her hair, letting it fall down around her shoulders.

Now he had to think of a different gift. A better one that would put a light in her eyes and make her smile. Maybe earn him another kiss. She was so deadly serious all the time. Couldn't she just accept a small sign of affection from him and be happy? But her life was controlled by her mistress. Yue-ying didn't dare breathe if Mingyu didn't let her.

He couldn't imagine what it would be like to be indentured to someone like that.

The dice rattled and rattled before the dealer set the tumbler down. Three fives. Hmm...he'd wagered triples that round. Happiness surged through him, as if he'd had anything to do with that triumph.

A thin man dressed in the robes of a tradesman had moved into the spot beside him at the table. Rather than placing a bet, he huddled there and stared at the numbers with a surly air. Huang spared him only a glance before placing his next bet. As the dice clattered away in the dealer's hands the man mumbled something.

"Pardon, sir?"

"Be careful," the stranger muttered. He was still staring at the table.

Huang made a face, bemused. "Be careful with my money, you mean?"

"With your life."

Huang straightened, his muscles pulling tight. The gambling den wasn't particularly crowded, but there were gamblers at every table. A quick glance showed the burly enforcer was standing near the door to the back room.

"And watch over that half-moon whore of yours."

With that, the stranger stood and wove around the tables toward the door. Fists clenched, Bai Huang started after him.

"My lord, your money!"

The dealer's shout brought him back to his senses. What was he doing chasing after some vagabond? Damn reckless of him. He returned to the table, but blood was still rushing in his ears. That bastard had threatened him and, worse, had also threatened Yue-ying.

The candle was still burning, but his desire to play had staled. He shoved the money forward, losing it all in a short, brutal run. It only put him in a worse mood. When he stepped out into the street, his gut was churning with anger.

The night was warm and the streets quiet. He took his lantern and started toward the Pingkang li, watching each corner warily. He had been prying in quite a few places, stirring the pot, and someone had taken offense. Someone who knew him well enough to connect him to Yue-ying. He needed to go to her right now and see that she was safe.

He heard the footsteps behind him, too out of rhythm to be an echo. Huang drew the knife he kept strapped beneath his sleeve and turned slowly and deliberately.

"Who's there?" He lifted the lantern with one hand. His other hand gripped his knife.

To whoever was following him, he wanted to appear steady. Confident. In his time away from the capital, he'd learned how much a fight was determined in the first moments: when the assailant made the decision whether or not you were worth the trouble.

A whip-thin figure emerged from the shadows. The crooked, angular features were unmistakable, even in dimness of the lantern light.

"Gao."

Gao held up his hands, palms out. "I mean you no harm."

That was not reassuring.

Before Huang could reply, Gao's wolf-eyes flicked just behind him. A knife materialized from nowhere, taking flight past Huang's ear to embed itself into something solid. He swung around in time to see the gang of cutthroats emerge from the alleyways and unlit pockets along the street. One staggered to the ground, a knife protruding from his neck. There were four more—too close and getting closer.

Huang threw the lantern at the lead man's head, catching the dull glint of a blade in his hand before the light shifted. The cutthroat shoved the lantern aside and Huang moved in. He went for the weapon arm, hitting at the wrist before locking the arm at the elbow.

He didn't pause to celebrate. Instead he struck the assailant square in the face, feeling the crack of the nose beneath his fist. A broken nose wasn't a serious injury, but it didn't take much pressure to bring tears to an opponent's eyes, blurring his vision.

Gao sent another knife flying. Huang didn't have time to see where it struck; he only knew that it did from the answering grunt of pain.

"Come on!" Gao turned and fled.

The hardened killer was running, so Huang figured he'd better do the same. The remaining thugs gave chase. One of them was gaining. Huang could hear him. Then he felt the impact of something striking against his side, tearing through cloth.

Damned fool. He'd escaped death before near this very spot. He put everything he had into it; heart pounding, muscles straining. Soon his chest felt as if it would burst, but there were no more footsteps behind him. That last lunge must have set the attackers back.

Gao slowed, but did not halt until they were back in the open streets. The lanterns of a nighttime patrol bobbed on the other side of the square. Huang stopped beside him and doubled over, gasping.

"I see you learned a few tricks, Lord Bai. You better hide that," Gao said between ragged breaths. At least he was winded as well.

Huang's knife was still clutched in his fist. He slipped it back into the sheath strapped to his arm, then straightened. He pressed a hand to his side, feeling along the gash in his robe with his fingers.

He hadn't felt any pain when the knife had sliced into

his clothing, but the shock of a wound could push the pain back in his mind so it didn't emerge until later. He knew this from experience.

Huang held out his hand. It was clean of any blood. "There's some use to wearing so many layers of silk."

Gao snorted.

Though Huang hadn't been wounded this time, he was still in shock. Gao had saved his life. Twice. Well, not quite. The first time three years ago, Gao had just deliberately failed to kill him.

"Who wants you dead now?" the cutthroat asked curiously.

"I don't know."

Gao flashed him a smile with too many teeth. "I can find out—unless you've gambled away your fortune again."

What strange company he kept lately.

CHAPTER THIRTEEN

BAI HUANG HAD stopped coming by. Yue-ying hadn't seen or heard from him since she had refused his gift. She didn't mean for him to disappear out of her life and the thought that she had seriously offended him left her heartsick.

There was one night when she'd thought she had seen him. She was high above, looking down from the upper floor of the Lotus. It had been late, long past midnight. She couldn't be certain it was Bai Huang, but the visitor was of similar height and build. His silhouette had been so familiar it had filled her with longing, but the visitor had only come to the entrance before turning to leave. The next morning, Yue-ying asked the other girls about him, but no one had an answer for her.

Without him, she continued with her daily tasks; all the while she wondered whether Bai Huang was still searching for Huilan's killer. She hadn't realized how her days would feel a little lonelier without him. At night, she lay awake for too long, thinking about what had happened. What she had done.

She had made it known to Bai Huang that she didn't want his attentions. There was no use mourning for something she'd never had, she insisted to herself as she pressed her fist against the growing ache in her chest.

A week went by and she was convinced Bai Huang

would never come back. How could he when she'd caused him to lose face?

A few mornings later, Yue-ying had just returned from the market when she passed by the main parlor. Madame Sun was having tea with Mingyu, but the headmistress looked up and waved Yue-ying over excitedly.

"Come! Sit with us."

Yue-ying stepped tentatively into the parlor and took a seat beside Mingyu on the settee. Madame never asked for her to join them. Most of the time, the headmistress simply acknowledged Yue-ying's presence with the barest of nods. Today she wore a sly grin and leaned forward, her eyes narrowing with mischief.

"You'll never guess who I spoke with this morning."

Yue-ying glanced to Mingyu, who was staring intently into her tea.

"A letter had come yesterday and I didn't know what to make of it. But first thing this morning, a carriage arrived—"

"Mother, you're stalling on purpose," Mingyu scolded, irritated.

Madame was undeterred. "He greeted me very politely and we sat for tea. I hadn't seen him here in a while and started scolding him about that, but he had more important matters in mind."

"Who?" Yue-ying asked finally with an impatient exhalation.

Madame Sun grinned in triumph, having properly baited her audience. Yue-ying could see the sort of tone she had set in her days as a courtesan and banquet master.

"Lord Bai Huang."

Madame enunciated each syllable for effect and then

sat back to await a response. Mingyu's grip tightened on her cup.

Yue-ying found it hard to breathe. It wasn't fair that just the mention of his name could do this to her. "What did he have to say?"

Madame laughed. "He wanted to redeem you, of all things."

Bai Huang wanted to buy her freedom?

"That's not possible," Yue-ying gasped.

"Foolish romantic scholar," Madame Sun agreed. "Not even considering how it will look to his family. And not yet married either! What chance does he have of finding a suitable wife once he's taken a woman of the brothels as a concubine?"

"Mother." Only Mingyu could admonish the head-mistress in such a way. She then turned to Yue-ying. "He did not mention this to you?"

Yue-ying couldn't form a reply. She could only shake her head.

"Well, I told Lord Bai we would need to consider it carefully," Madame said with a wave of her hand. "He looked quite stricken, if you ask me. Choosing his words so carefully, so nervous. And so handsome too. Ah, youth." Madame Sun seemed delighted to be in the middle of a choice bit of gossip. "I was so afraid he was seeking a contract with Mingyu," she said bluntly. "I would have had to figure out how to refuse him without angering him. You would never leave me, would you, Mingyu? What would the Lotus Palace ever do without you?"

"I am perfectly content here," Mingyu said without emotion. "Why would I ever want to leave?"

Yue-ying waited for a lull in the conversation to excuse herself. Mingyu didn't look at her as she rose from her seat and hurried up the stairs. Back in the safety of their chambers, she tried to occupy herself by dusting the sitting area, though she had just completed that chore the day before. It wasn't long before she heard the door open behind her, followed by the silken whisper of Mingyu's robe.

"It's your decision," Mingyu said quietly.

"You know that's not true. There is no decision to make."

A wealthy patron occasionally offered to pay off a courtesan's debts to her foster mother. But Yue-ying was already free, or as free as a woman without family or means could be. Mingyu had bought her debt from the brothel to bring her here, something that a nobleman like Bai Huang would never have considered.

"Maybe you should go to Lord Bai," Mingyu said.

"But you've warned me away from him again and again," Yue-ying replied, puzzled.

"That was before…before he showed his feelings to be of a more serious nature." Mingyu looked out the window, avoiding her gaze. "I won't be here forever. I may leave one day, go somewhere far away."

It was only a fantasy. Mingyu was too deeply indebted to the Lotus Palace to leave Madame Sun. Still, she knew Mingyu stored away money in hopes of one day being free.

"This place will take our souls if we stay too long," Mingyu went on solemnly. "The Pingkang li never changes. The same girls are brought here, over and over. We have different faces, but we're all the same. We'll grow old and new ones will replace us. A hundred years ago, there must have been another Mingyu in a house just like this one."

"I'm staying here with you," Yue-ying said firmly.

"This is all a game to Lord Bai. He only wants me when the mood strikes him and he has plenty of money to throw around. He and I haven't spoken in over a week."

Mingyu looked stricken. A pained expression crossed her face along with something Yue-ying had never seen before: guilt.

"He hasn't been ignoring you. I sent him away. I refused to let him into the house, but even then he tried to write to you." Mingyu went to her desk and pulled out several squares of paper, dyed in the vibrant colors that scholars favored for gifting poems of love. "I thought for certain he would lose interest and go away. That he would be done with it."

Yue-ying's throat went dry at the sight of the papers. "Done with me is what you mean," she said through her teeth.

Mingyu's eyes were full of regret. "I was trying to protect you. There are so many things you don't know, Yue-ying."

She faltered and there was an awful silence between them. Yue-ying took in a deep breath, surprised to find that she was trembling. She had assumed Bai Huang had forgotten her, but Mingyu's deception wasn't the worst of it. After all of her meddling, Mingyu was now pushing her away. Did Mingyu want her to stay or not? Her changing moods were infuriating.

Yue-ying could have lashed out, but all she could summon was a cold and quiet anger that sank through her skin and into her bones. It was as if she had been thrown into a pool of black water and her very clothes were keeping her under. Any struggle only pulled her down further.

Mingyu held out the stack of letters and Yue-ying

took them without a word. What had Bai Huang tried to say? The black lines meant nothing to her.

"The choice is yours," Mingyu said softly. "I won't interfere any longer."

THE MEETING WITH Madame Sun hadn't gone as Huang had planned. He had expected her to be shrewd, to claim a sudden motherly fondness for Yue-ying and name a price that was two or three times her bond. Then he had expected she would be smug. She would smile at him with a superior air, knowing he had been snared. He was prepared for all of those reactions, as long as he was able to get Yue-ying away from the Lotus Palace. She was nothing but a slave there. But the mistress of the Lotus Palace had simply smiled that secret woman's smile and told him he would have to wait for an answer.

His other endeavor that day was also a failure. Zhou Dan had reported there were ships being secretly loaded and unloaded at night, but Huang had camped along the docks for hours, staring at the empty canal while a sudden downfall of rain kept him company.

It was late when Huang finally gave in and returned to his residence. As he neared the gate, he spied a figure huddled beneath the overhang. He stopped, muscles tensing in preparation for a fight. The attack outside the gambling den was still fresh in his mind.

"It's me."

He raised his lantern and his pulse jumped at the sight of Yue-ying peering back at him. "What are you doing here alone in the dark?"

Her arms were wrapped around herself and her hair hung damp around her face. "It was late and the ward gates were closed," she said in a small voice, as if that explained everything.

"Why didn't you come inside?"

He loosened the tie on his cloak and settled it around her shoulders. With one hand, he pushed the gate open while his other arm curved around her shoulders. The rain had come and gone, as summer rains were in the habit of doing, and the evening wasn't particularly cold, but it was Yue-ying. She was waiting for him and maybe his arms did miss her more than a little.

"I asked for you earlier, but you weren't home. The old woman said she didn't know when you would be back," she rambled. "I didn't want to intrude and she was looking askance at me as if I were—"

He hushed her, leading her through the courtyard and into his study. Once inside, he lit the oil lamps using the flame from the lantern before extinguishing it. There wasn't any other place to properly greet guests in this modest-sized house.

"I was going to say a beggar." Yue-ying was babbling and he could sense the nervous tension all along her spine and rumbling through her like a kettle about to boil. "I considered going back, but I had walked all the way here and then the rain started and it was already getting dark."

Yue-ying in the rain would always be irresistible to him. She pushed her damp hair away from her face. Her eyes were large and striking and so much emotion flickered behind them that she was impossible to read. He had missed her.

They had just started warming to each other and then she had begun playing these games, keeping him at arm's length. At first he'd been irritated. He'd tried telling himself she was just a servant while he was noble-born. Maybe it was all a ploy and Yue-ying was aiming high for her station. But he knew in his heart that wasn't the truth. Yue-ying was different. He'd watched her for so long. She was his and only his.

Of course, every lovesick scholar felt this way about his particular Pingkang beauty. And Yue-ying wasn't his. But he wanted very much for her to be.

"Tea?" he asked, finding it a struggle to keep his tone casual.

"No, Lord Bai." She seemed equally nervous. "I wouldn't want you to trouble yourself."

"No trouble," he muttered, heading for the kitchen.

He stoked the fire beneath the stove as a flood of anticipation roared through him. Yue-ying was here. She had to know what he had discussed with Madame Sun. It was a breach of etiquette for Yue-ying to come herself, when financial matters hadn't yet been settled, but she was here. Damned if his palms weren't sweating.

She was still standing in the same place when he returned with the tray. He set it down on the desk and motioned for her to sit while he poured the tea. She did so, though with some reluctance.

He realized they hadn't had a chance to speak since the attack on him. "You need to be careful traveling alone."

"I can't be your concubine," she blurted out.

"Ah." He had been wondering how he would broach that subject. He was too startled by her directness to come up with anything more eloquent.

She stared at him, wincing as she struggled on. "Please don't take any offense. Your proposal was quite generous—"

"I didn't offer it to be *generous*," he interrupted, setting down the teapot.

What a ridiculous night this was turning out to be.

It would have been ungentlemanly of him to mention his family's class and noble status in comparison to hers, but the truth was he was a little offended to be dismissed so easily. Mostly he was just confused.

"Why—?" She paused to swallow. "Why did you offer to redeem me?"

He approached her, watching every emotion that flickered over her face. Color rose to her cheeks as he neared.

"Why can't you be my concubine?"

She gave a sharp laugh. "Isn't it obvious? Look at you and look at me."

He caught her gaze and held it. "I'm looking."

Yue-ying tilted her chin upward in challenge. Not only to him, but to everyone who had ever stared at her. "Why would anyone pay for a concubine whose face was ruined like this?"

"This face isn't ruined."

He cupped her face in his hands and she flinched. He could see the tremor in her lower lip and how hard she fought to maintain her composure. She wanted to look away and hide herself, but she didn't. And he fell a little bit more for her because of it.

"This isn't the tale of 'Master Zheng and the Sing-song girl'," she said bitterly. "Someone like Mingyu would be more suitable for an aristocrat, and even then barely so."

"Mingyu again. Her beauty is worthless to me," he said harshly. "It's worthless to anyone. Beneath her skin, that woman is a fox-demon—"

"Madame Sun does not own me," Yue-ying interrupted. A spark of anger ignited in her eyes as she twisted out of his grasp. "I own myself. You can't redeem me because Mingyu has already redeemed me."

That certainly stopped his tongue. Why would a

courtesan buy a servant when she rarely could earn enough to buy her own freedom?

He had Yue-ying's face in his hands only a moment ago. The fine bone structure, the gracefully shaped nose and cheekbones were not identical, but certainly reminiscent—

"She's your sister," he murmured.

Yue-ying smiled a hard, cold little smile and he could see the resemblance even more clearly. "Our faces are actually quite similar, if anyone cared to look."

He must have been blind. All the pieces fit into place now: Yue-ying's fierce loyalty, Mingyu's overprotectiveness.

She reached across him to pour the tea. Her hands were steady and her demeanor utterly calm as she handed him his cup.

"Do you know they used to call me Half-Moon? Only half of my face was worth looking at. It was Mingyu who changed it to Yue-ying. She is really quite clever."

She poured herself a cup as well, still speaking as if she were a thousand *li* away.

"A stranger came to our village. He saw Mingyu and how beautiful she was and told our father and mother that he was searching for a bride for a wealthy merchant. I thought Father must have been fooled by the man. He must have believed Mingyu would go to a good family, but then Father told the stranger he had a younger daughter as well. One he had little hope of marrying off. They knew." She looked away as she sipped the tea. "Our father and mother knew what was happening. They were poor and had two daughters and one son. Perhaps if they didn't have a son to pour all their hopes into, they wouldn't have sold us. I thought I remembered Mother crying when the stranger took us away, but Mingyu insists that she didn't."

Another sip of tea. Huang's cup remained gripped in his hands. He was stunned into silence. There was some whispered conversation about her past in the Pingkang li, but it was very different to hear such words aloud. These were things not to be spoken of out of politeness. Yue-ying left all politeness behind.

"When we were first brought here, the procurers looked at my face and shook their heads. I was sent to the poorer areas where the lower-class brothels operated. If even they would take me, the trader said. He had paid a bride price for me and had little hope of recovering his cost. I understood that, even as a child of eight."

"That is all in the past," he said softly.

"But it's not. I've heard my face described as flawed, ruined, unfortunate. A bad omen. People avert their gazes and move away from me as if it's a disease they might catch. But after being separated for so many years, my sister was only able to find me because my face was so recognizable. The red-faced whore." A tear slid down her cheek, but she ignored it. "So you see I don't consider it unfortunate at all. You can also see why I don't wish to be owned ever again."

More tears fell, though she made no sound. She didn't bother to wipe them away. It was as though she didn't acknowledge them, then they didn't exist. He took the tea from her hands and set it aside. They were already close, but he pulled her closer.

"I'm going to kiss you now," he warned.

Yue-ying blinked up at him. Her lashes were damp, her nose red. She didn't say yes, but she didn't say no, so he did, folding his arms around her and pressing his mouth to hers until the tension finally drained from her shoulders. Until he could feel her lips softening and warming against him. Until they found each other once again in the kiss.

"When I first came to the Pingkang li, it was like a dream," Bai Huang said.

They were standing in his study. At some point, they had stopped kissing, but he still did not let go of her. He brushed away her tears and she let her head sink against his chest. She could feel the rise and fall of his breathing and his voice resonated wonderfully beneath her ear.

"Night and day were one and the same. Wine flowed like rivers. I took beautiful women to bed and gambled away all my money. It was as if the world was there for my pleasure and I could never get enough."

She ran her fingers along the front of his robe, tracing the intricate embroidered pattern there. His outward appearance spoke of luxury and excess, but she had sensed for a long time now that there was something more beneath it.

"What changed?" she asked.

"I went away. Or rather I was forced to leave the city. When I returned, everything looked like an illusion. All that was so beautiful before was no more than a layer of lacquer and paint. Except for you."

Her chest squeezed tight. An unrecognizable emotion rushed through her, seizing her limbs. The closest thing she knew to it was fear.

"I should go." Her heart was pounding too fast.

"But—" His arms tightened around her waist. "It's very late," he said mildly. "And the ward gates are closed."

Their gazes locked and once again she felt as if he was not only seeing her, but into her. And for once she wanted to be seen. She wanted to see herself the way he saw her.

There was nothing to do but kiss him again. She raised herself onto her toes and pressed her mouth against his, welcoming the thrill that traveled down her spine and curled wonderfully through her limbs. His hands flattened at the small of her back to fit her against the hard planes of his body. She wanted to close her eyes and melt into him.

He bent until his lips brushed her ear. "Will you stay?"

Such a gentleman, asking like that.

Why shouldn't she? She had only lain beneath strangers before. At least she liked Bai Huang. At least his hands were gentle and he knew how to hold her so she felt like a woman instead of a piece of warm flesh.

She needed to stop thinking like that. She pulled him close and kissed him harder, letting that be her answer. Her tongue stroked against his and a low rumble sounded at the back of his throat. He tasted of black tea.

His muscles grew taut beneath all that expensive silk. The hard shape of his organ pushed against her with quiet urgency and she was flooded with unwanted memories. The sensations were imprinted onto her skin: sweating shapes merging into the shadows, a man's weight pinning her, the inevitable intrusion of another body into hers.

She let him lead her to the bedchamber while her pulse skipped frantically. This was Bai Huang, not some stranger. He took a moment to light the oil lamp and the halo of light revealed a plain bed and a few simple furnishings. Suddenly an unbidden image of her pallet in the brothel came back to her and she couldn't move.

"Yue-ying?"

Bai Huang's voice was gentle, soothing, with a husky undertone of desire that sent her pulse racing. She was glad he was no longer holding her hand because her palms were sweating. Desire and fear felt the same inside.

She fought past the ghosts to go to him. Her first touch was to the edge of his robe. She skimmed the border of it, not yet touching skin, then pressed her palm flat to his chest. It felt good to touch him like this. It felt good to choose to touch him. His heart pounded beneath her hand.

It was a common saying in the brothel that every man was the same in the dark. It would be different with Bai Huang. That was why she could barely breathe. That must be why.

He reached for her and she thought he would undress her, yet he didn't. Instead, he pulled the wooden pin from her hair and brushed his long fingers through the length of it. His breathing deepened as it fell about her shoulders. Then he lowered her onto the bed, still clothed. Rather than lying on top of her, he angled himself alongside her, shoulder to hip, anchoring her without trapping her.

Yue-ying closed her eyes and breathed in the scent of his skin, the faint hint of cedarwood and spice. When she opened them again, he was looking down at her. There was that faint, familiar smile on his lips.

"You're always trying to hide this."

He stroked her cheek with his thumb and she fought hard not to flinch. People always asked if it hurt. *No, it doesn't*, she'd answer. But yes. Yes, it did.

"Do you know it was at times fashionable for court ladies to paint their faces with red marks just like this?"

"That's nonsense," she snorted. "You made that up."

"No, it's true. Sometimes they drew a slash high across the cheekbone." He demonstrated with the soft brush of his thumb. "Or a sunburst design that curved all along the jawline. It was meant to draw attention and accent their features."

"That's the stupidest thing I've ever heard."

He chuckled softly and the sound was both sensual and comforting. He bent to touch her again, but this time it was with his lips.

"This is not a flaw to me." He feathered a trail of kisses along the side of her face, grazing her ear and neck. Each one sent a tingle through her. "This is a part of you, like your eyes, your lips, your hands. This mark has kept unworthy men away so that I could find you."

But men hadn't stayed away. Coldness poured into her. Bai Huang had meant to court her with his words, but they only opened old wounds. Poetry was wasted on her.

Yue-ying took his hand. His gaze darkened as she guided him into the opening of her robe and settled his palm over her breast. Then she held her breath.

At first he remained unmoving, still watching her. The lamplight danced off his eyes as he followed the slope and curve of her breasts with his hand. She wore the simplest of bodices beneath the robe, just a sheath of cloth that wrapped around her bosom. He stroked her through it, his breathing growing deeper with each passing moment.

She tried to relax and accept his touch. She had always shut her eyes in the past, so she kept them open now. Bai Huang must have seen something of her struggle in the look on her face.

"You're thinking too much," he chided. He kissed the

spot between her eyes, as if to smooth out the crease there.

He continued touching her, soft touches, slow touches. He untied her sash and stroked along her shoulders, her breasts, her stomach. The sensations felt detached from her, as if she were watching Bai Huang treating someone else with such care.

He tried to woo her with his words and the gentleness of his tone, but the more he spoke, the more her ears deafened. She tried to recapture the rush of emotion she'd always felt when they kissed. In the rain and beneath the bridge, while she dug her fingers into his shoulders and her body pressed against him in hunger.

There was none of that same heat or desire now. Finally, she had to close her eyes to block out the room, the bed. Even the sight of Bai Huang leaning over her. It felt like surrender, as if she had lost a battle with herself when she did it.

With her eyes shut, she tried to focus on Bai Huang's touch on her, but it was no use. He slipped her robe from her shoulders and her mind receded. She had no sense of time or self as he loosened the bodice and peeled away all the layers of her robe.

Once again, he surprised her. Instead of running his hands over her body, he reached for her hand. Her fingers were curled tight as he held them up to his lips. Once more, her eyes flickered open.

His dark brows drew together. "Are you afraid?"

"No," she said, puzzled. "Are you?"

He laughed at that and the laughter echoed in the hollowness within her, momentarily lifting her spirits. He bent to kiss her lips and she made an effort to wrap her arms around him and return the kiss.

Remotely, she felt his palm curving over her breast

once more, but now the bodice was gone and he stroked against naked skin. Her flesh pulled tight beneath his touch, her nipple peaking. Though her blood warmed, her mind remained cold. The two halves of her couldn't find one another.

She stared at the ceiling when Bai Huang rose to remove his clothing. When he returned to her side, he was completely bared and she quickly fixed her gaze on his face. She saw a question in his eyes that she didn't have an answer to, so she closed her eyes again.

For a moment, she imagined herself watching from the corner, peeking out from behind the dressing screen.

There were books that gentlemen studied, Mingyu had told her. Books that provided lovemaking instructions for the bedchamber. Yue-ying wondered if Bai Huang had read such pillow books. His attention was painstaking. She found herself clutching at his shoulders, wrapping her legs around him to urge him on—but not because she was burning for him.

Because she wanted to be done with it.

The horror of the thought struck her, leaving her hollow inside. She wanted to be done with this act as soon as possible.

Bai Huang guided himself to her gently. Or as gentle as one could be when one's body intruded upon another's. He was patient. The care he took threatened to bring tears to her eyes, so she kept them squeezed shut.

"Yue-ying?" His voice was low, urgent, barely restrained as he held himself still within her. "Is this...? Am I...?"

"Don't say anything," she hushed.

Keeping her eyes shut, she held on to him. He began to move slowly in and out of her. Her muscles remained lax, her flesh yielding to him. His slow thrusts gave way to harder, longer movements. The rhythm was disturbingly familiar, no matter how much she tried to forget it.

At the critical moment, he pulled himself out of her and turned away, preventing his seed from spilling into her. The act also shielded her from seeing him in this most vulnerable state, with his face twisted in passion. This union was not for the purpose of procreation or the joining of essences, the meeting of the clouds and the rain. It was sex. A vulgar pleasure.

When Bai Huang turned back to her, his eyes were heavy and lidded. Languidly he planted a kiss against her shoulder. Another one at the base of her throat. Then he fell away to settle heavily beside her.

"Little Moon," he murmured, his voice thick like honey.

She didn't reply. Only then did she realize that she didn't know what to say in these moments after.

Bai Huang's breathing gradually deepened. The lamplight sputtered as the small flame ate up the last of its oil. Yue-ying turned her head so she could see him. His eyes were closed and his expression relaxed in sleep. Dark brows framed his features and his lashes were fine and long. His cheekbones cut high. He really was handsome. Beautiful even.

She reached out to him as the light faded, resting her arm lightly over his shoulder. He didn't awaken. He didn't move or appear to sense her presence in any way. She closed her eyes as sadness washed over her.

It was true, as those wise and weary sisters in the brothel had said. There was no difference between one man or another in the dark.

CHAPTER FOURTEEN

YUE-YING MADE A POINT of waking before Bai Huang did. Before the sun was up, she had already dressed and repinned her hair. Then she sat on a stool beneath the window and waited.

Eventually sunlight started to seep in through the window. Bai Huang had rolled onto his stomach at some point during the night. His face was hidden and one arm dangled over the side of the bed. She spent a long time inspecting the play of light and shadow along the muscles of his back.

Finally, she couldn't bear it any longer. "Lord Bai," she whispered.

He stirred, his arm reaching across the empty spot beside him. Groggily, he lifted his chin from the pallet. It took a moment for his gaze to focus and fix onto her. "Yue-ying?" His voice sounded throaty and heavy with sleep.

"The ward gates will be open soon."

He squinted toward the window, gauging the light. Then he lay back down, head propped up on the crook of his arm. He regarded her with one visible eye.

"What are you doing?" she asked.

"Considering how I might persuade you to come back to bed."

His tone was unmistakably sensual. She felt a soft flutter in her belly. He was completely naked, a portrait of bare skin and muscle. His hair was untied and fell over his face. She had hardly touched him while he was bedding her. Everything that had happened between them in the night had rolled forward in an inevitable chain. She wanted to touch him now, when he wasn't caught in the heat of passion. When it would be touching, just touching.

"But you won't be persuaded, will you?"

She managed a smile and shook her head. With a sigh of surrender, he sat up, rubbing a hand over his eyes.

His movements were unhurried, marked with a laconic grace, and he seemed unperturbed that she was fully clothed while he was naked. She supposed last night should have taken down whatever barriers were left between them. Instead they were left in this odd state of intimacy and nonintimacy.

"You don't need to rise." She looked uncertainly toward the door. "I can go on my own."

"No, you shouldn't. It could be dangerous."

His robe was just beyond his reach and she moved to help him. Their eyes met momentarily before she lowered her gaze. She caught a glimpse of the scar beneath his ribs. It was a faint line, the width of her second knuckle, where the skin was smooth and pale. She hadn't noticed it at all when they had been skin to skin. She considered asking about it, but instead moved away, leaving him his privacy as he dressed.

The courtyard was quiet with only a few sounds coming in from the street. She wandered into the study, rinsed her mouth with a bit of cold tea left over from last night and then glanced over Bai Huang's shelf. With a careful hand, she eased a slim volume out from the collection. It appeared less intimidating than the others.

The cover was bound with blue cloth. When she

opened the book, the pleated pages unfolded in one long sheet filled with column after column of characters. Though they meant nothing to her, the order and flow of the brushstrokes held a power of their own.

Folding the pages back in, she closed the book and wandered back to the desk. Unlike the humble furnishings in the bedchamber, the writing desk was extravagant. It was crafted from a dark, perfumed wood, the scent of which reminded her of Bai Huang. The subtle fragrance was imbued in his clothing and on his skin. She inhaled and he flooded her awareness, bringing a flush to her cheeks. She wondered how the thought of him captured her so completely, yet their actual physical joining had paled in comparison.

Bai Huang would realize now that they were not meant to be lovers or—she felt a sharp pang in her chest—or perhaps he had fulfilled his urges and was satisfied. One night was all he needed from a woman like her.

Servants were not allowed such pride, so she swallowed it. If she simply did not acknowledge it, did not permit herself to feel these emotions, they would have to go away.

She turned her attention back to the desk. The chair had been fashioned from the same dark wood and the backing was decorated by an elaborate carving of a somewhat ugly image. The figure was hunchbacked and appeared to have horns on his head. He balanced on one foot over a great sea turtle. She ran a fingertip along the spiral grooves in the turtle's shell, entranced by the detail.

"That's Kui Xing, the god of examinations."

Bai Huang was at the door, his hair neatly combed

and tied back. His silk robe was dark blue with black accents; not extravagant, yet still recognizably expensive.

"He looks like some sort of demon," she remarked.

She straightened as he came around the desk. His face had been scrubbed clean and there were no traces of the disheveled and shamelessly naked man she had woken up to, though she had knowledge now that he was there beneath the silk. Waiting.

"Demon might be appropriate," he said with a laugh. Standing very close, he bent to brush his fingers over the same part of the carving she had been admiring. "Kui Xing is standing on top of Ao, the mythical turtle of the south sea. There's a statue of Ao on the steps where they announce the scholars who have passed the examinations."

A wistful look crossed his face, but then it was gone, to be replaced with one that was characteristically mischievous.

"Here, sit." He guided her into a chair, with a hand gently at her arm, her elbow. Light touches that demonstrated a familiarity that wasn't there the day before. "My father commissioned this for me when I began formally studying for the imperial exams at fifteen. I must have spent every waking moment for the next four years sitting here."

Yue-ying closed her hands over the arms of the chair. The wood surrounded her with the musky fragrance of the natural oils within it. It was the most opulent piece of furniture she'd ever touched. She surveyed the desk as well. It was neatly organized. A paper had been laid out with more cryptic writing on it. The study contained a thousand mysteries that she could not penetrate.

"A shipping contract," Bai Huang explained, leaning

over the back of the chair. "I was a little disappointed to receive this."

When she turned, she had a sharp view of his profile. "Why?"

"I was hoping Ouyang Yi was engaged in shady, criminal undertakings. A written agreement seems so legitimate."

He went over his efforts from the past week, finding out information about Commissioner Ma Jun as well as the wealthy shipping merchant who worked out of the docks beside the East Market.

"You've been very busy," she said, impressed.

He turned and they were face-to-face. "We shouldn't spend so much time apart."

His mouth was excruciatingly close and her pulse quickened. "It's been little more than a week."

"A lifetime, an era, an eternity," he returned dramatically.

She laughed and he smiled along with her. Bai Huang was so good at mocking himself.

"I didn't get your letters," she confessed.

"I wondered about that."

"But even if I had, I couldn't read them. I have no learning to speak of."

"I could teach you."

Her heart stopped. "Wouldn't that take years?"

"I don't mind."

His voice was thoughtful. Quiet. He straightened and turned around, setting his weight against the desk. She was captured between the arms of the chair and by the intensity of his gaze.

"When my letters went unanswered, I was certain Mingyu and Madame Sun were conspiring to keep you from me. I was determined to free you from their tyranny."

"How honorable of you," she teased.

"Not really. I wanted you and someone else had you. Or so I thought." He smiled crookedly. It was a jagged little weapon and the point was aimed at himself. "I'm a self-important, entitled nobleman, after all."

Bai Huang posed as a dissolute aristocrat, but it was apparent from this room and the grandeur of the desk that an imperial degree was not merely some distant goal. His study was a hall of worship, the chair a throne. Books and scrolls and poems were his religion, a legacy from his family.

They were already night and day from the moment he sauntered into the Lotus Palace, but now they were even further apart. The Earth and moon.

Her throat tightened. "I should go now."

As soon as she stood his arm circled her waist. Though she put her hands up to brace against his chest, her body flushed warm as he pulled her up against him, so quick that she had no defense for it. The intimacy of his hands on her and the way she responded, body and mind, left no doubt. She had accepted another person into her for the first time. Everything was different between them. She just wasn't certain how.

He touched his forehead to hers, exhaling slowly. "I expected a different sort of morning entirely. Last night—" He paused then, as if a stone were lodged in his throat. "Did I hurt you, Yue-ying?"

She shook her head. He drew her closer and held on to her, not knowing what questions to ask. It didn't matter because she didn't have the answers for him. Her heart ached when she thought of how careful he had tried to be with her.

"You said when you returned to the city, the Ping-kang li seemed like a dream," she began. "Last night was a part of that same dream. It was a pleasant dream, but I really must go now."

"Will you come back to me?"

He dropped his voice so low that it was merely a vibration of sound against her skin. When she didn't answer, his tone hardened only a touch, but it was enough to cause her to tense. "Is it Mingyu again?"

"She's my sister. She needs me."

They needed each other. Yue-ying had meant what she said about no longer being owned. A concubine could be bought and sold. She could be thrown out of the house based on her master's whim or the will of his family if they disapproved of her.

Most of the women in the Pingkang li had been cast aside by their families. They had no freedom to choose for themselves, but Yue-ying was different. She was still a peasant and poor, but Mingyu had sacrificed so Yue-ying had some choice over her future. And right now, she chose to go home.

"I was angry with her when I left. She'll be worried."

Bai Huang regarded her for a long time, his thumb stroking a half circle into the small of her back. He was asking her when he could have just as easily made demands with his wealth and status.

"I'll fetch a carriage for you, then," he said with some regret as he released her.

"I would rather walk," she insisted.

She left the study and hurried through the courtyard. For a moment, she thought she was free and started to breathe a sigh of relief, but she heard the gate close behind her followed by the sound of his voice trailing after her.

"I'll accompany you." In two strides, he was beside her. "A walk will allow us more time together, in any case."

HUANG TOOK SOME comfort that Yue-ying was walking at a leisurely pace beside him. At least she wasn't hurrying back to the Pingkang li to be rid of him sooner. The streets were still quiet as they wound through the smaller lanes and her gaze was directed downward.

What was she thinking? His own thoughts were rather predictable. He was thinking of how soft her skin was. The spot on her neck just above the shoulder. How good it felt the moment their bodies joined together. How absolutely right it felt.

He had tried to meet her eyes as he caressed her last night, and again when he'd entered into her before the grip of pleasure had taken hold of him. She had evaded his gaze both times. But he was too blinded by desire to do anything about it. Or to stop. Yue-ying had given only her body to him last night. Her mind was still locked away and he didn't know how to reach her.

Perhaps if the lovemaking had been more—he searched for a good word, one that didn't make him seem somewhat inadequate. If the lovemaking had been more of an enticement, this morning's conversation would have been very different. For one, it would have started while she was still disrobed and in his bed rather than in a hurry to leave it. She might have also tried to call him by something more endearing than "Lord Bai".

"We enjoy each other's company," he said finally, breaking the long silence.

He thought he saw Yue-ying nod once.

"I'm from a good family," he continued. "And you are well mannered and of a pleasant disposition."

"Are you discussing a match between us?" Her tone was incredulous.

"I am. Since you are not quite convinced."

Her only reply was to shake her head in disbelief.

"You don't mean to discard me ruthlessly after only one night, do you?" he asked, attempting a light tone.

The part that he could see of her mouth was smiling, but her gaze was still fixed ahead. In addition to that, it wasn't the pleasant smile of someone who had been successfully charmed. It was that secret, knowing smile women used.

"Women do not discard men, Lord Bai."

"My wounded heart disagrees."

"In order for a woman to discard a man, she would need to possess him and have some power over him. A situation which is unlikely unless she is your mother."

"But you do have power over me," he countered, fully expecting her snort.

"Laments of torture and cruelty and suffering hearts are all made up by scholars and poets. You know I have no power over anyone, let alone you, Lord Bai. It's nonsense to pretend that I do."

The discussion was a troubling one. He had thought all courtesans longed to be redeemed.

"I wanted to offer you a better life," he said.

"That is generous," she replied. "But may I ask, have you consulted your family about taking a concubine into the household?"

"Not as of yet—"

"I suspected so. A favored son, such as yourself—" she gave him a pointed look, which he accepted "—rarely needs to bother with practicalities, so it's likely you wouldn't even think of such things."

So he had offered for her on impulse. Surely such

"practicalities" as she mentioned would work themselves out.

"Two years ago, a young gentleman wanted to marry one of the girls at the Lotus Palace," she went on. "He had been appointed to a low-level position and had some income to his name. He was young, which is always something to take as a warning, but Ziyi was in love, so she was hopeful. They made their promises to each other, we drank to them at the Lotus, and then he left for his home to arrange it with the family. When he didn't return, Ziyi insisted he had suffered some tragedy, which delayed him. She was very much in love. But there was no tragedy. We found out that he was back in Changan, working as a scribe in the Ministry of Rites, and simply chose to avoid the Lotus Palace. The belief is when he couldn't get permission to marry, he was too afraid to return."

He frowned. "I think you're making this up to taunt me."

"I'm not. This happened exactly as I recounted," she said curtly. She returned her gaze directly ahead. "The Pingkang li is filled with discarded women."

His romantic declarations seemed as thin as paper suddenly.

"My intentions toward you were sincere," he said soberly. "They still are."

She graced him with a faint smile, but her eyes were sad. "I believe you, Lord Bai. And I was very touched by the gesture."

Touched enough to offer herself for one night in his bed. On his grave, this was not going well at all.

They had reached the edge of the wide lane that separated the scholars' quarter from the North Hamlet.

"Thank you, Lord Bai. I can go the rest of the way on my own."

She started to bow politely by way of dismissal, which made him scowl. He was in too foul of a mood to engage in the proper rounds of refusals and protests.

"I'm going with you. You shouldn't be walking around alone everywhere," he muttered, starting off across the avenue. Yue-ying followed after a moment's pause.

This was all a mess. He had attempted to do the honorable thing by paying off Yue-ying's debt to the Lotus Palace. So he hadn't thought of what would happen next, but he was fond of her. He liked her. He cared about her—and she was being stubborn about it, but she cared about him too. At least a little.

Perhaps this was too much to conquer at the moment. He was trying to find a killer, catch a general in the act of treason, possibly, and pass the palace exams all at once, but once those obstacles were overcome he would figure out a way for them to be together. It couldn't be so difficult. His family had forgiven him for much greater wrongs.

"It could be dangerous."

He snapped out of his ruminations to see that Yue-ying had stepped in front of him as she spoke. They were back in the pleasure quarter, though without the glowing lanterns and lovely ladies in the windows it looked like any other neighborhood.

"You said it could be dangerous for me to walk alone," she repeated. "When you told me that this morning, I thought you were just being a gentleman or making an excuse to draw out our time together."

"You are right on both counts," he admitted.

"But you made another remark just now about how I shouldn't be walking alone. Why is that?"

"There was an incident," he began. "I was threatened in the street the other night by men with knives."

She gasped. "Were you hurt?"

"I escaped and went directly to the Lotus after it happened to make sure you were safe. Madame Sun said you were fine, but refused to let me in to see you."

"Because of Mingyu," she muttered. "So it *was* you I saw that night. You could have let me know."

"I had someone watch over the Lotus. I wanted to know you were safe until…well, until I redeemed you." He rubbed the back of his neck sheepishly.

She started walking again, choosing not to address his failed attempt to buy her freedom. "Who were these men? What did they want?"

"I'm not sure. Before the attack, a stranger threatened me. He called you—" He hesitated to repeat such ugly words, but Yue-ying had probably endured worse. "He called you a half-moon whore. I had never heard that phrase before you mentioned it, but I could guess what he meant. Someone knows we've been searching around."

Frowning, Yue-ying rubbed a knuckle along her eyebrow, a gesture she used when something perplexed her. He found it endearing.

"It's not a common phrase," she said, looking away. "That name was only well-known in the brothels. No one has called me that in a long time."

They continued the rest of the way in silence. He felt as if he'd intruded on something unassailably private: a memory that had been locked away. When they reached the Lotus Palace, she stopped once again.

"Perhaps you should go now. If we're seen entering together, there will be talk."

"They already know and there's already talk. It'll be worse for you if you go alone."

Surprisingly, she didn't fight him. As soon as they were through the doors, Madame Sun swept toward them like a typhoon wind.

"She isn't with you?" she demanded, looking the two of them over. Her gaze paused only briefly on him.

"Who?" Yue-ying asked.

"Mingyu. She left shortly after you did and she's been gone all night."

Yue-ying turned to him. Her expression was both troubled and agitated. "Lord Bai, thank you for accompanying me. There is a private matter that I need to attend to."

"I can help," he offered.

She lowered her voice. "Mingyu and I didn't part on good terms. She's probably still upset. She behaves like this sometimes."

He wasn't sure Yue-ying believed her own explanation. The other ladies of the Lotus gathered near the entrance hall to listen in. He could see the worry on all of their faces. In times of tragedy, the houses tended to close up to outsiders as they turned to each other. The same thing had happened at the Hundred Songs the night that Huilan was killed.

"I'll try to find where Mingyu could have gone," he told her.

"I don't want to start any rumors needlessly."

"The people I go to for information are not likely to gossip." He wondered if there was a way to reach Gao during the day. "But you need to stay here until I return. Promise me."

She nodded solemnly.

With one courtesan dead and another missing, the warning he'd received in the gambling den was taking on dire weight. He was not going to let Yue-ying be the next person to disappear from the Pingkang li.

CHAPTER FIFTEEN

ONCE BAI HUANG was gone, Yue-ying turned to Madame Sun.

"Did Mingyu say anything before she left?"

"Nothing. Not a word." Her brow creased with concern. Of all of her courtesan-daughters, Mingyu was her favorite.

"She will be back sooner or later," Yue-ying assured her.

Mingyu was known as one of the most elegant ladies of the Pingkang li, but she could be as willful as any child when she didn't get her own way. Yesterday was the first time they had ever truly quarreled and Mingyu was probably brooding in dramatic fashion.

She left Madame to go up to Mingyu's quarters. The rooms appeared the same, but somehow not the same. Every object was in perfect place, but there was a haunting stillness about it. After spending the night with Bai Huang, she felt like a visitor upon returning.

Mingyu was the Earth and Yue-ying was nothing but a lone star that revolved around her, along with everyone else. Maybe Bai Huang was right. Mingyu was jealous, not of her, but of him. Of anyone that drew attention away from her.

As soon as Mingyu came back, Yue-ying would tell her that the affair with Bai Huang was over. It would be as it was before: just the two of them. Sisters. Family.

Yue-ying spent the first hour straightening things that didn't need to be straightened, but Mingyu still hadn't returned. After that, she stretched the boundaries of her promise to stay at the Lotus by questioning the porters and carriage drivers in the street. None of them had taken Mingyu anywhere last night. She appeared to have left on foot and alone.

The only time Mingyu ever was away from the Lotus was when she was hosting a banquet or with one of her patrons like General Deng. In any event, it was always with Madame Sun's full knowledge. Mingyu's time commanded a high price.

By the afternoon, Yue-ying had taken to pacing. She paused at the sitting-room wall where many a scholar had been inspired to leave verses of poetry. Mingyu's elegant hand was easily recognizable among the other characters. Yue-ying touched her fingertips to the most recent poem as if she could reach her sister through the brushstrokes.

There was a knock and the door opened before she could go to it.

"Miss Yue-ying." Bai Huang filled the doorway with a concerned look on his face.

"Lord Bai."

He came to stand beside her and she could feel the heat rising up the back of her neck. Everything had become serious. It was no longer about careless and stolen kisses in parks and beneath bridges.

"The moon appears so often," she said absently as she glanced over the collection of verses. "Moon" was one of the few characters she knew.

"All of the poems in the Pingkang li sound the same. The light of the moon, perfumed clouds, jade flutes."

She bit back a smile. "All the bad poetry you compose, you've been mocking everyone all this time!"

He grinned at her and some of the weight lifted from her chest, but it didn't last long.

Bai Huang saw how her smile faded. "Madame Sun told me Mingyu hasn't returned yet. A friend of mine said he would scour the streets for any word of her. She is unlikely to go unnoticed, as well-known as she is."

"And remarkably beautiful," she added, feeling a sadness sweep through her. "I checked her belongings. She didn't take anything with her, wherever she went. I even checked her store of cash and jewels. It's all here, untouched."

Yue-ying pressed the back of her hand to her mouth, her throat constricting. At her mention of money, something so practical, the reality of the situation finally descended on her. Mingyu kept a hidden stash of silver and gifts from wealthy patrons in a box at the bottom of the wardrobe. Only the two of them knew about it. If Mingyu had planned to run away, she would have taken it.

Bai Huang took hold of her hand. He did it only to comfort her, but even so she felt guilty. She'd chosen him over her sister, if only for one night, and now this was her punishment.

"We always talk about leaving this place." Her eyes stung, but she blinked back the tears. "She told me yesterday that I should go with you and she wouldn't interfere, but I thought she was just angry. Because of you. I was angry too about how she'd kept you away from me. So I went."

"Yue-ying. Love. Everything will be fine."

His deep voice flowed over her and she wanted to lay

her head against his shoulder. He was so close, his presence embracing her even if his arms weren't.

"What if the same thing that happened to Huilan—?"

She couldn't finish. Mingyu was the one who had expressed fear that there was a murderer in the North Hamlet. She had demanded protection when they were traveling outside the ward, but Yue-ying had assumed Mingyu was being temperamental.

"Don't worry yourself needlessly." Bai Huang tightened his grip on her hand, but he was also frowning. "I can make more public inquiries in the guise of being lovesick. Everyone already believes I'm taken with her and I'm known for being indiscreet."

It was the first time Bai Huang had admitted that his courtship of Mingyu was little more than a ruse, but why so much effort? He'd become famous for it, or rather infamous.

She couldn't ask him about his reasons now. She was too grateful for his help. "If you can inquire with some of her patrons. General Deng had wanted to make her his concubine at one point. She might have gone to him."

"Deng." Bai Huang paused and his look darkened. "You know she wasn't at the hot springs with the general a few weeks ago."

"What do you mean?"

"You were mistaken about that. Everyone was mistaken. General Deng never left his command. Whoever Mingyu was with when she was away, it wasn't him."

A frantic knocking on the door made her jump.

"Yue-ying! Come quickly!"

She looked to Bai Huang, who appeared equally puzzled. They disengaged, her hand slipping away from his, and went to the door. Whoever had come to call them had already gone downstairs. They hurried down the steps to where the courtesans were gathered.

Madame's voice rang from inside the main parlor. "What is this? What's happened?"

"It's about Mingyu," one of the girls whispered.

A fist closed around Yue-ying's chest. She pushed her way into the sitting room where Wu Kaifeng stood like an ill omen all in black. Another constable stood beside him holding a set of iron chains.

"It will be worse for everyone here if you refuse us," Wu said tonelessly. "Where is Lady Mingyu?"

"We don't know where she is." Madame Sun stretched to her full height before them. Constable Wu still towered head and shoulders above her. "You can search every corner of the Lotus and she still won't appear."

Wu's eyes glinted dangerously.

"She's telling the truth." Yue-ying came forward to stand beside the headmistress. Despite her instinct to shrink back, she squared her shoulders. "She left yesterday evening. We've been looking for her ourselves."

"Do not lie to me," Wu warned her. "Wherever your mistress is, it is very important she come with me."

"What is this regarding?" Bai Huang demanded.

All heads turned to him. The Bai family name held considerable weight, whereas the protests and demands of a house of women could be easily denied.

Wu affected a slight bow. "Lady Mingyu is wanted for questioning before the tribunal. I meant to bring her in quietly to avoid any unnecessary scandal."

Yue-ying eyed the assistant constable with his iron manacles. The seeds of scandal were already sown.

Bai Huang wasn't satisfied by Wu's answer. "What is the charge, Constable? Her foster mother should be fully informed about her daughter's plight, wouldn't you agree?"

Charge? Surely there was no accusation here. Magistrate Li and Mingyu were on good terms. They were friends. Li must have had a few questions to ask Mingyu about some case or another, that was all. Yue-ying's heart thudded as she waited for an answer.

Wu Kaifeng stared at Bai Huang for several long seconds. When Bai Huang didn't flinch, the constable turned his gaze to her. She wasn't nearly as strong.

"An arrest warrant has been issued for Lady Mingyu," Wu reported. "She is to be brought in on suspicion of murder."

BAI HUANG INSISTED on accompanying her to see Magistrate Li Yen. Yue-ying was certain Constable Wu wouldn't have been as cordial if she had gone there alone. With Bai Huang at her side, they were escorted directly to the inner office. It was half an hour before Magistrate Li was finished with the day's schedule of cases and petitions.

Finally, Li appeared with Constable Wu by his side like a mismatched shadow. Yue-ying straightened and bowed low. She had never been so formal when Magistrate Li came calling at the Lotus, but she was in his domain now.

"Lord Bai." Li acknowledged Bai Huang with a bow of his own, though much shorter than hers. "It appears we have an unfortunate situation."

Li seated himself behind his desk, which was raised upon a dais. Yue-ying wasn't forced to kneel as she would have in the tribunal, but the magistrate still looked down at them from on high.

"When the honorable magistrate first arrived in

Changan to take this position, Lady Mingyu was of great help to him," she pleaded. "The magistrate must know that Mingyu is honest and upstanding—"

Li raised his hand to stop her. "Any past friendship holds no weight here. The law is the law."

Her stomach sank. Magistrate Li gestured toward the constable and Yue-ying could see that all of the gatherings and banquets, all of the pleasant conversations he'd held with Mingyu, meant nothing. If Mingyu were here, perhaps she could sway his judgment, but to Yue-ying he was a cold, efficient bureaucrat bent on his appointed duty.

Constable Wu handed the magistrate a small parcel wrapped in cloth, which he unwrapped and placed on the desk. "This was found yesterday on a dock. The same dock where a boat was reported missing after the recent earthquake."

Yue-ying was allowed to approach. The wind rushed out of her as she stared at the magistrate's desk. A hair ornament decorated with pearls and a jade butterfly carving lay there, the sort of trinket designed to swing and catch the eye as one walked. The attached pin had been snapped off.

"Did this belong to your mistress?" Li asked.

It would be useless to deny it. General Deng had gifted it to Mingyu, who had worn it during the Lantern Festival while she stood by his side. Everyone had seen her that day. The sight of Mingyu was, regrettably, unforgettable.

"I—I'm not certain," she stammered, earning a deep frown from the magistrate.

It was a lie and a poor one, but she couldn't bring herself to speak out against her own sister. She sensed

Bai Huang coming up behind her. He didn't touch her, but his closeness lent her strength.

"The ornament matches the broken pin found on the body of a man who had been forcibly drowned," Magistrate Li went on, his voice filling the chamber. He was often described as soft-spoken, but no longer. "The owner of this pin used it as a weapon, attacking the victim before he was killed. It is highly probable she was also present while the murder was committed."

"Or she committed the crime herself," Constable Wu interjected.

Magistrate Li paused to stare at his constable before nodding soberly.

Though her instincts had insisted something was amiss, it was a very different matter to be confronted with harsh evidence. Yue-ying stared at the two halves of the silver ornament. It had been rendered in two by an act of violence.

Her mind was in turmoil, unable to focus on any thought other than that Mingyu was in danger. But what had happened? And why had her own sister hidden the truth from her?

The magistrate was watching and weighing every emotion that flickered across her face. "You must tell us anything you know about where your mistress may be."

She forced herself to remain calm. "No one knows where Lady Mingyu has gone. She left yesterday without telling anyone."

"And where were you, miss? You have always been faithfully by her side."

"I was—" She felt the back of her neck burning.

"She was away," Bai Huang answered for her. "Miss Yue-ying is telling the truth. She knows nothing about her mistress's whereabouts."

The possessiveness of his tone beat back any question the magistrate and the constable might have. Even though she had refused him, Bai Huang was still offering her his protection. Without it, she was little more than dust before these men.

"Well, then, with Lord Bai's assurance—"

Wu made a scoffing noise in the back of his throat, which Magistrate Li ignored.

"Constable Wu will continue our search for Lady Mingyu so this case may be resolved quickly." The magistrate rose to his feet. "We trust that you will inform us should she return."

Her last image before she left the office wasn't of Magistrate Li, but of Constable Wu's dark stare. As much as Yue-ying wanted to know where Mingyu was, it made her blood run cold to think of the ruthless constable hunting her sister down.

They were far away from the magistrate's office and almost back to the Pingkang li before Bai Huang spoke. "You need to tell me everything you know."

"I spoke the truth. I don't know where Mingyu has gone."

"But there's more. I could tell from the look in your eyes as you were answering the magistrate's questions."

She looked over her shoulder to make sure there was no one else around. Then she pulled Bai Huang beneath the shade of a banyan tree that lined the lane before speaking.

"I think Mingyu may have known she would have to leave. She told me I should accept your proposal." She looked away from the intensity of his gaze. "In case she could no longer be with me."

Bai Huang always appeared as if he was trying to see inside of her, to the depths of what she was thinking and feeling. To that part of her that was locked away from everyone, even from herself.

Her stomach knotted. "Something frightened her and she had to go quickly. She was afraid the way Huilan was afraid."

Bai Huang lifted a hand to his temple, rubbing at it as he tried to concentrate. Finally he lowered his hand, having come to a decision.

"You can't remain at the Lotus."

She started to protest, but he cut her off. "Something happened that night after the banquet and both Huilan and Mingyu started behaving strangely afterward. Then I was chased down the street by men with knives, one of whom mentioned you in a way I did not like at all." His expression hardened. "You'll come and stay with me. It's safer."

"Wouldn't I be safer in the Three Lanes, among familiar faces?" She was thinking it was Bai Huang who needed to be careful, wandering into all sorts of dangerous areas while looking like such an easy target in his expensive clothes.

"Huilan was strangled while the Hundred Songs was *full* of guests," Bai Huang pointed out. He lowered his voice. "If this is about last night—"

"It isn't."

Yet everything seemed to be about last night right now.

"Have you considered that without Mingyu, you have no protector within the Pingkang li? Do you believe Madame Sun will house you out of kindness?"

He was right. Madame only tolerated her presence because of Mingyu.

"I expect nothing from you in return," he promised. "We started this together. It's even more important now that we find Mingyu and discover the truth of what happened that night of the banquet. Unless you want Wu to hunt her down and bring her in."

Weakly, she shook her head. She had no choice but to trust him.

They returned to the Lotus Palace and Bai Huang waited downstairs while she went to pack a few belongings. Madame Sun saw her arrival and swooped in like an eagle.

"What has happened?" Madame Sun demanded once they were alone in Mingyu's chambers.

"The magistrate wants to question Mingyu. I don't know anything more," she lied.

There was a small hope that Magistrate Li and his constable Wu would remain discreet. In the event they did, Yue-ying didn't want to add to any of the rumors that must already be taking root.

Madame Sun stared as she retrieved a plain robe from her corner of the dresser along with a wooden comb. "Where are you going?"

"Lord Bai wishes me to stay with him."

Madame's eyebrows lifted. "Is that how it is between the two of you now, hmm?"

Yue-ying turned away from the headmistress's smug expression. If the entire quarter didn't already assume she was Bai Huang's mistress, they certainly would after she had left with him. If Bai Huang wasn't concerned about it, then she didn't have the mind to be upset either. There were more important things to worry about.

Besides, there was some truth to it, wasn't there? They had been lovers for a night. Her reputation wouldn't suffer from being Bai Huang's discarded mistress because she had no reputation to speak of. Not that any of that mattered as long as Mingyu came back to her unharmed.

"You know you don't have to leave, child." Madame

Sun set herself down at Mingyu's dressing table and watched as Yue-ying retrieved a few other personal items. "Mingyu will be back and will want to know where you've gone."

She bundled her few possessions into a square of cloth and tied off the corners. Everything else belonged to Mingyu and she didn't feel right taking them.

"I won't be far," Yue-ying said. "Just north of here in the scholars' quarter. When Mingyu returns, she'll know how to find me."

They spoke as if Mingyu hadn't disappeared, as if she'd gone on a visit to the local temple. Otherwise, they would go mad with worry.

"Swear to me you don't know where Mingyu has gone," Madame said. "She hasn't left me, has she?"

Yue-ying was taken aback. "No. She didn't say anything like that."

"The moment you know anything, you tell me."

"I will."

The awkwardness was palpable and even Madame Sun's earlier attempt at kindness felt oddly misplaced. Bai Huang had spoken the truth when he'd pointed out that she had no place at the Lotus Palace or even in the Pingkang li without Mingyu.

How could Mingyu leave now? They were sisters. Wherever Mingyu had gone, whatever the reasons, they should have gone together. She had been hiding something for weeks, but Yue-ying hadn't been able to find the words to confront her about it while Mingyu hadn't trusted Yue-ying enough to confide in her. Not even after the past four years together.

Yue-ying was lost and she hated it. She had believed that she was free, but all she had done was attach herself to her sister, clinging on to her to stay afloat.

CHAPTER SIXTEEN

HUANG TOOK OVER the arrangements before Yue-ying could think to protest. She waited on the bench in the courtyard while he finished preparing the rooms. Her belongings, what humble few they were, rested in a bundle in her lap. She spent an inordinate amount of time inspecting every leaf on the lone peony tree. Absently, she reached out to touch a finger to a snow-white blossom.

Finally he returned to her, taking the edge of the bench. "What's the matter?"

"This is an unusual arrangement." Yue-ying picked at her pack nervously. "Your landlady was giving me the eye."

"Did she say anything impolite to you?"

She studied the peony blossoms again. "She didn't need to."

"What does it matter what she thinks? She's merely a servant."

Yue-ying looked back to him with a faint smile on her lips. "*I'm* merely a servant."

"Not to me," he said firmly. "Your room should be ready if you wish for some privacy. You'll be staying in the bedchamber. I've set up a sleeping pallet for myself in the study."

"I should protest."

"I'll only persist."

"If you do that, then I have no choice."

"You always have a choice."

Yue-ying had been bold enough to refuse the attentions of a wealthy and handsome young aristocrat, hadn't she?

"Thank you," she said softly.

He shrugged. "I tend to spend half the night with my books anyway."

A faint smile touched her lips. "The eternal scholar."

He wanted so much to kiss her right then, but she'd become distant again. A worry line appeared between her eyes.

"We'll find Mingyu," he promised, adding it to the list of vows he had made that had yet to be fulfilled. "Let's think this over. We now know Mingyu was on that dock. She couldn't have overpowered a man by herself, but, if it was indeed the night of the banquet and if Huilan was with her, the two of them could have done it."

"You talk as if you're already certain she's guilty."

"We won't know the exact circumstances until we find her, but we can't disregard the possibility," he insisted. "The stranger who was killed could have been someone she knew. Perhaps someone close?"

"Like a lover?" she returned acidly. "The public notice described his clothing as plain, like that of a laborer. I doubt he was Mingyu's lover or Huilan's either."

"Then let us assume they happened upon some illegal activity on the docks," he suggested. "The stranger pursues them. Mingyu and Huilan fight back and manage to kill him. Whoever his associates are, they either don't report him missing because they either don't care or want to avoid any attention from the authorities. Instead, they hunt down the women themselves. Why?"

"Perhaps to keep them quiet." Yue-ying frowned, her

expression troubled. "Both Huilan and Mingyu were acting strangely, refusing to confide in anyone."

"Or maybe they wanted to retrieve the money that was stolen from them."

"I'm not certain that's the answer." Tension ran along her jaw and the red mark along her cheek lent her a fierceness he hadn't noticed before. "It was a good amount of silver, but not enough to die for. They got caught in something very dangerous, so dangerous that Huilan had to die for it."

"We need to discover who was on the docks that night," he said. "That stretch of waterway is rumored to be a center of illicit activity."

"Then the dead man could have been an outlaw."

He nodded. "I might have enough information to get those ships detained and searched." He attempted to lay out the plan in his head. "I'll need to enlist the authorities."

She stared at him in awe. "You can do all that?"

"Well, I need to ask a personal favor from someone I'm already indebted to." He let out a deep breath, already dreading the conversation. "It's my father."

Father considered matters of commerce beneath him. He would probably dismiss the case as a distraction involving a couple of notorious courtesans who were women of questionable reputation to begin with. They were only useful for the knowledge they might possess; a means to an end.

But the women of the Pingkang li had become important to Huang. He'd spent time in their company, knew their names, learned about their lives. His failure to save Huilan continued to hang over him. He was too deeply involved to turn his back on such injustice.

BAI HUANG WAS gone all day and still hadn't returned by nightfall.

Meanwhile, Yue-ying was anxious for news. Where had her sister gone? Mingyu should have known Yue-ying would be frightened, yet she'd left without a word. It was thoughtless of her, but Mingyu was notoriously single-minded when some idea took hold of her. Maybe that was all this was. Mingyu off on some whim.

Focusing on her anger didn't chase away her fears, but at least it distracted her. Yue-ying searched for other distractions and was cleaning away the dust on the bookshelves in Bai Huang's study when he returned late in the evening.

"You don't need to do that," he said.

She turned around, dust rag still in hand. What little propriety there was between them was gone now that they were living in such close quarters. Yue-ying was very much aware of how her presence intruded on his privacy.

"Is there any word of Mingyu?" she asked anxiously.

"Not yet."

He approached her and gently took hold of her wrist. Prying the rag from her fingers, he tossed it aside. The gesture spoke not of flirtation, but of familiarity; a sentiment that was more intimate than even a kiss.

He was so close that she had to tilt her head upward to meet his eyes. "I needed to do something. Anything," she said.

"I understand. If Mingyu doesn't return—"

She held up her hand. "Please don't speak of it."

Yue-ying knew all the dire possibilities. She had spent night and day going over them until she was sick inside.

"Have you eaten?" he asked instead.

"I'm not hungry."

It was apparently not an acceptable answer.

Bai Huang took her out to an area of the scholars' quarter where a thriving ghost market had emerged.

"The market started as a few food stands operating only late at night outside the regulated hours," he explained as they walked toward the glow of lanterns. "More vendors joined in. Soon pawnbrokers and moneylenders also set up shop. At first, everything needed to be put up and taken down quickly should the city guards come by, but now the ward officials are no longer intent on shutting the night market down. Many of the guardsmen even stop by for refreshment after a long patrol."

Lanterns were hung up on bamboo poles to light the area and there were tables and benches set up along the lane. Both sides of the street were lined with different vendors.

They found a table at a stand serving bowls of noodles in a bone broth. Bai Huang grabbed a flask of rice wine from an adjoining stand and set it on the table along with two cups before seating himself. Using a soupspoon, she lifted the noodles to her mouth along with the fragrant broth. The soup was rich and salty and the noodles had been freshly made. Roasted chilies added a dose of spiciness. After a few spoonfuls, she glanced up to see Bai Huang watching her.

He had his wine cup in hand once more. "This is pleasant."

His gaze stayed on her a moment longer before he looked away, apparently focused on the meal. "I let my father know about the plan. He has connections with the garrison commander and officials within the Ministry of Works. It's said that the merchant Ouyang Yi owns a secondary fleet of ships that are routinely bypassed for inspection. Once one is captured, we can search the cargo and interrogate the crew on board. This is certainly a gamble, but we have nothing else to go on. Hopefully we'll find Mingyu long before then."

Yue-ying picked at her food sullenly, barely tasting any of it. "Maybe it's better if she isn't found. Huilan is dead and now Mingyu is wanted by the magistrate. If she was able to flee to safety, then everything is for the best."

"But you would go mad with worry."

"That can't be helped."

Part of her wondered if Mingyu was glad to be free of her. They had never fully rediscovered their bond after Mingyu had redeemed her from the brothel. Over time, they had gradually become accustomed to one another, but even so Yue-ying continued to act as Mingyu's attendant. After being apart for so long, they didn't know how to be with one another. They occasionally shared moments of closeness broken by cold, uncomfortable silences. It was undeniable that Yue-ying was a burden.

Bai Huang was watching her with concern.

"I must thank you, Lord Bai, for all that you've done for us. For all that you continue to do."

"You know why I do it." He gave her a meaningful look she took as only part of the truth. What they had between the two of them—did she dare call it friendship? It couldn't be the only reason he had become so determined to solve this mystery.

They finished the meal and walked back to his quarters. Once there, Bai Huang excused himself to his study, though he gave her a dark look full of longing before they parted.

It had been the same the night before. The exchange of an unspoken question before retiring to separate rooms. Only two nights ago, she had lain beneath him as their bodies joined together. Now she had been given that same room while he slept a thin wall away.

She spent a while longer in the kitchen, heating a basin of water to take back to the bedchamber. Once inside, she loosened her robe and retrieved the cake of soap she'd bought earlier that day. She soaked a washcloth into the basin and rubbed the soap into it. Working her way down from her neck and shoulders, she scrubbed herself clean.

Yue-ying had to be practical about what to do if Mingyu was gone. She could return to the Lotus and beg a position from Madame Sun or offer herself as a servant in one of the many households in the quarter. Perhaps one of Mingyu's patrons would take pity on her.

If all else failed, she would have to return to the brothels. The thought left her cold. Yue-ying never wanted to feel that way again: used, worthless, dead inside. She would beg and steal before she allowed that to happen.

The truth was there was an easy path open to her. Bai Huang was interested in a liaison between them. She certainly could trade her body for security; she had done so all her life. But she hadn't wanted to with him. She didn't want to have to. It was a much more pleasant fantasy to think they could be together as lovers without any arrangement or exchange of favors between them.

Their first time together had been her decision, like the kiss in the rain, like her refusal of his gift. Games of courtship. Lovers' games.

She pulled the wooden pin from her hair and bent over the basin to wash it, careful not to drip water onto the floor. The choice wasn't difficult really. Bai Huang was kind. He was handsome. Their time together was not unpleasant. The only thing that made her hesitate was that he was a romantic. She didn't want him to think this was more than it was. She didn't want him to feel as if she had deceived him.

HIS STUDY AWAITED him with its shelf of books and scrolls, all required for the imperial exams. The ritual was a familiar one. Huang lowered a bamboo case from the shelf and opened it, pulling out a thick scroll comprising the first section of the Book of Rites. He unrolled it to the marked passage and then mixed up a plate of ink.

Then the sound of Yue-ying at her bath came from the adjacent room, sending him past desire into lust. The thought of her undressed and so close was enough to remind him of the hot slide of his flesh into hers and that irreplaceable sensation of being consumed whole: body and mind.

Swallowing with some difficulty, he stared down at the passage. Preparing for the exams was as much a matter of discipline and endurance as it was talent. Once the Classics were memorized, it was important to be knowledgeable about the prescribed commentaries by members of the Hanlin Academy as well and be able to formulate one's own intelligent responses.

It was no use. With every slosh of water, he was imagining slender, naked limbs and smooth skin.

With a sigh, he set the brush aside. The ink had dried on it and he had reread the same passage four or five times. His studies were, without a question, done for the night. He returned the scroll to its rightful place and cleaned his brushes, then removed his outer robe as well as his tunic to prepare for bed. Once he was situated on the pallet, he blew out the lamp.

The sounds on the other side of the wall had quieted. In the darkness, he touched a hand against the wood, pressing lightly as if he could reach through to the other side. To Yue-ying.

This was why there were so many stories of lonely scholars becoming infatuated with courtesans only to fall into ruin. The Four Books and Five Classics couldn't compete against such erotic imagery and reckless, all-consuming pleasure. Though his own experience with ruin had nothing to do with a beautiful woman. All he had to blame was his own youth and stupidity.

Huang lay back. Was he any wiser now? The dice no longer held the same lure for him. Instead he was fixated on a woman. A stubborn-headed, strong-willed woman who was determined to feel nothing for him but a reluctant fondness. He closed his eyes and his breathing deepened as he thought of her. Of her eyes, her lips. That neck. Long, damp, lovely. The graceful lines of it leading down to her breasts. He'd held them in his hands once and dreamed of doing so again. He drifted away happily on that thought.

At least she was in his bed—even if he wasn't there with her.

Faintly, he heard the creak of the floorboards, the opening of the door. He opened his eyes to a brief sliver of moonlight that came and went. Suddenly, Huang was no longer alone in the darkness. He started to drag himself up, his head still clouded with dreams, when firm hands pressed against his chest to pin him down.

"Yue-ying?"

She lowered her mouth to his and if he had any doubts about who was with him, the kiss swept all question away. He had only known her body for a short span of time, but he knew her kiss. She tasted of the faint sweetness of plums and the tang of rice wine. With one hand in her hair, he dragged her down, his other hand rounding her waist to hold her to him.

The shape of her molded against him and he was already hard, his body straining toward her. Yue-ying pushed up and his hands reached blindly to bring her back, to no avail. Her knees anchored themselves on either side of his hips as he heard the shift of cloth just above him.

He lifted himself, his abdominal muscles tensing as he moved to help her. Her sash was already open and his fingers collided with hers as he slid the robe from her shoulders and freed her arms. There was nothing binding her breasts, no bodice or undergarment of any form. He thanked heaven for that. As soon as she was freed, his mouth closed hungrily over her nipple.

He was rough in his eagerness, rasping over the sensitive peak with tongue and then teeth. She gasped, arching just out of his reach. He fell back onto the pallet, blissfully trapped beneath her.

Yue-ying tugged at his tunic and pulled it over his head. His chest was bare now and he wore nothing but a pair of short trousers. His heartbeat quickened against her palm and his breathing grew harsh.

"Is this what you want?" she whispered.

Yes. "No." He took hold of her wrists. "Not only this," he amended, since his initial answer was an obvious lie.

"I could see it in your eyes all night. This is inevitable, isn't it? You're a man. I'm a woman."

There was no passion in her words. They were as cutting as a knife and they cooled his desire enough for him to regain his reason.

"Yue-ying, I think you should be mine. You know I'm already yours."

"That's just bedroom talk."

"It's not."

"Huang," she admonished with a sigh.

"All right, then, it is." His hands found their way to the small of her back. "What else is more important between Heaven and Earth than this?"

"You make the joining of bodies sound like something profound."

This said while she was straddled on top of him.

"You make it sound as if it *isn't*."

For once he appreciated his scholar's propensity for words, because Yue-ying finally fell silent. Maybe she was thinking. He closed his eyes and pulled her to him, tucking her head against his chest. Maybe she would finally stop thinking.

"I know most women would be grateful," she said in the darkness.

"I don't want you to be grateful," he said harshly, then much softer, "Well, at least until I've done something to earn it."

She chuckled at that. He could feel her squirming against him and *he* was grateful. What a wonder she was. What a challenge. There were certainly easier women to engage in affairs with, but it couldn't be helped. He wanted Yue-ying and only her.

They lay nestled together chastely, his chest rising and falling as his heartbeat settled.

"Do you want me to go?" she asked into the crook of his neck.

"No."

Regardless, she pulled away and coldness crept over him in her absence. He could hear her righting her clothes in the dark and breathed with relief when she settled back beside him.

"Then I'll stay."

Though she was no longer in his arms, the feeling of closeness remained. He didn't want Yue-ying to give herself to him out of obligation or because he wanted it and she was indifferent either way.

It was clear now she hadn't truly wanted to bed him their first time together. He had already suffered the consequences of that, the selfish pleasure of the moment doused by her withdrawal afterward. He had experienced physical release, but was no closer to having the woman he truly wanted.

Yue-ying was too clever to be courted with romance and poetry, and too honest to lie to him about her intentions. But she didn't abhor his touch or his company. There had to be some way for them to meet in between. They were from two different worlds, but he wanted to understand her and no book existed that could give him the answers.

Huang breathed deep and exhaled, silently reciting the Analects to keep his desire at bay. He hoped that, with her clothes on, he would at least be able to make it through until morning.

THERE WAS A TOUCH upon her wrist and a sensation of light through her eyelids. Yue-ying fluttered them open to the sight of Bai Huang beside her on the pallet, his face so close she could see every handsome feature in detail, bathed in the orange morning.

She was lying on her stomach and her hand rested between them, palm up, as if she were reaching out to him in her sleep. He had laid his hand over her so that his knuckles caressed along the inside of her arm from wrist to elbow. A tremor slid down her spine. She held her breath, afraid to move should the moment break.

"Close your eyes, Yue-ying. You're still dreaming."

His tone was gentle and rough with sleep. She did as he asked, though his face remained imprinted before her. She could hear him getting up and tensed as he moved beside her.

It wasn't as if she were afraid of him. She wouldn't have come to him if she had been. If Bai Huang had taken what she offered last night, then their roles would be established with her as his mistress. But to her surprise, he had refused. Now she didn't know what he wanted.

She could feel his presence over her and hear the deepening of his breath. Her fingers curled reflexively over the pallet as she waited. His first touch upon her could be anywhere and her skin tingled with anticipation.

He laid the flat of his palm between her shoulder blades, pressing lightly. The weight was possessive, but reassuring. He slid it along her spine in one broad stroke.

"You can breathe, love."

There was amusement in his tone. It was the second time he'd used such an endearment with her. It was presumptuous, but the words still made her quiver. She exhaled, willing all of her fears to leave with the expelling of her breath, but that was impossible.

His fingers grazed the back of her neck as he swept her hair over her shoulder, sending another wave of sensation through her, warming her skin. Then his touch became deeper. Strong, but not overpowering. He started at her neck, caressing firmly, moving downward with the slope of her body as a guide.

Her robe remained as a barrier between them. She

could feel the pressure of his ministrations, but, other than the occasional brush against skin at her neck and again at her wrists, the touch felt removed from her body, so she wasn't so vulnerable.

It was…comfortable. She floated without a sense of place or time as if she were still dreaming. His hands were at her waist now, rounding her hips. What he was doing to her was certainly intimate, but not invasive. For once, she allowed herself to reach out a little, like the first spring bud peeking up through the moss toward the sun. Rather than hiding away, she awaited his next caress.

She had been taken many times, but so rarely touched. And never in this way. Her body before had consisted of only those few parts that seemed to interest most men. And their interest never lasted for long.

Before she realized it, she was breathing more freely. Her fingers were no longer curled tight, her muscles no longer braced against the pallet. She was filled with a lazy warmth and she never wanted this feeling to end.

When she had come here last night, there had been something unanswered within her. Though she felt no particular joy in the sex act, she still longed to be close to Bai Huang. She didn't have the words to explain what he had become to her.

It was no great sacrifice to lie in his bed, and be what he wanted her to be for a few moments while he panted over her and became like any other man. The act wasn't unpleasant with him, but she could see how he wanted more from her than just willingness. She didn't know if she could feel that way for him, but as his hands moved over her with such care she wished so very deeply that she could.

Bai Huang had reached her legs. He took hold of her

ankle and stroked gently along her instep. It tickled. She
wriggled in his grasp, kicking a little in protest, and her
eyes came open to glance over her shoulder. He was
kneeling by her feet. There was laughter lighting his
eyes, but his expression was focused.

He shifted back up alongside her, rolling her onto
her back. Yue-ying closed her eyes again as he lowered
himself over her. She could feel the weight of his hands
pushing against the pallet on either side of her and she
swallowed.

She knew this part. Some of the languid warmth that
filled her ebbed away as she prepared for what would
happen next. But Bai Huang didn't remove her clothing. He didn't position himself between her legs or push
inside. Instead, he did…nothing.

Her eyes flickered open and once again he was there,
very close. His pupils were fathomless as he touched a
hand to her cheek.

"This, you like," he murmured before bending to
kiss her.

She sighed against him, accepting the kiss, returning
it. The soft caress of his lips quickly grew hard and urgent. Though he tried to hold his weight off her, his hips
moved restlessly and she could feel how aroused he was.
Yet he did nothing more than kiss her. Yue-ying circled
her arms around Bai Huang's shoulders and arched into
him, losing herself in the simple pleasure of touch and
warmth and closeness. And of him.

CHAPTER SEVENTEEN

YUE-YING LEARNED MORE of Bai Huang in the small intimacies of the day to day. Despite his reputation for never waking before noon, he actually rose quite early. He also seemed to roll out of bed with a book in his hand, the same way he went to sleep.

Though he dressed extravagantly, he lived simply, immersing himself in studies and buying food and necessities from the nearby stalls whenever required.

After two days away, Yue-ying returned to the Ping-kang li to seek out news of Mingyu. Madame Sun complained about Constable Wu bringing in his gang to search every corner of the house, but business at the Lotus didn't appear to be suffering in Mingyu's absence. Every room was full of guests.

The historian Taizhu was there as well, wearing a somber expression. Yue-ying served the old scholar tea and tried her best to listen to his diatribe about the new Emperor's reforms. Mostly she nodded.

He lowered his voice as soon as Madame Sun left to see to other patrons. "Has Mingyu tried to reach you?"

"No, sir. I thought she might go to you."

Taizhu sighed. "I wish I could help her. Truly I do."

His broad shoulders appeared sunken and there was more gray in his hair. The last time she had seen him had been the night of the dragonboat festival, the same night Huilan was murdered. Since then, everything had changed.

He finished his tea and said his farewell to Madame Sun. Moments later, Yue-ying took her leave as well and saw that Taizhu's carriage was still in the street. The historian waved her over.

"If you ever need anything, don't hesitate to come to me," he said, handing her a bundle wrapped in cloth.

There had been some murmuring that the historian and Mingyu were lovers, though he was more than twice her age. As far as Yue-ying could see, the scholar was merely protective of her sister. Like an old uncle. Taizhu even knew that she and Mingyu were sisters. Though they didn't speak of their relationship openly, it wasn't a secret they made a special effort to keep.

She waited until the carriage rolled away before lifting the cloth. Inside was a small amount of silver, enough to get by for a little while.

Yue-ying returned by foot to Bai Huang's place and was surprised to see a young man and woman she didn't recognize in the courtyard.

"He isn't here," the man was saying.

His clothing showed him to be a servant, though one from a notably wealthy household. The woman was elegantly dressed in blue silk with long flowing sleeves. She held a parasol in her hands.

"Where could he be?" she asked. "It's too early for him to be out drinking at the pleasure houses."

The man mumbled some reply before they looked up to see Yue-ying inside the gate.

"Oh!" The woman stopped midstep and lowered her parasol. "I'm looking for my brother. I didn't realize there was anyone else here."

"Lady Bai," she greeted with an awkward bow,

acutely aware of two pairs of eyes staring at her. "I am not certain when Lord Bai will return. He's gone to the city academy."

Bai Huang hadn't spoken of a sister, but then, he hadn't spoken much of his family. They certainly weren't on that familiar of terms.

"I'll wait for him, then," his sister said breezily. "What is your name, miss?"

"I'm called Yue-ying, my lady."

"Hmm, a very good name. Like Chancellor Zhuge Liang's wife in the Record of the Three Kingdoms."

Yue-ying stared at her, confused and unable to return the compliment or courtesy in any way.

"My family calls me Wei-wei," the young lady added in a friendly tone, perhaps sensing Yue-ying's discomfort.

Bai Huang's sister was evidently a woman of considerable learning. Yue-ying invited her into the study, using courtesy and ritual to fill the awkward silence, and set about brewing tea in the kitchen. She was really as much of a guest as Lady Bai was, but she did her best to act as hostess.

Once the water was boiling, Yue-ying set the pot onto a tray and headed out into the courtyard. The manservant remained outside the door and gave her a brief nod as she passed by. Inside the study, Wei-wei had seated herself on a stool beside the desk. She was scanning the shelf of books with her posture straight and hands folded in her lap.

Yue-ying set the tea tray at the edge of the desk. After a moment of hesitation, she carefully moved Bai Huang's books and papers aside. It felt like an intrusion to touch his personal belongings.

Wei-wei waited, watching with feline curiosity as

Yue-ying poured hot water over the tea leaves. Though the two of them appeared to be of the same age, the lady had a confidence about her that made her seem older than Yue-ying. Her hair was fastened into a simple, elegant coil and she wore no makeup. She had no need of any embellishment. Bai Huang's sister shared his features: his finely shaped nose and mouth. Her ivory skin was flawless, even without the benefit of powder.

Yue-ying balanced a teacup in two hands before offering it to the lady. Then, with nowhere else to go, Yue-ying sat down behind the desk and began to pour another cup.

A knowing look danced across Wei-wei's face, but she composed herself. "Does my brother go to the academies often?"

"He leaves to study almost every morning."

"How wonderful that must be," Wei-wei remarked. "I wonder what the library must look like. So many books. Have you ever seen the academy?"

"No, my lady."

What would a woman, any woman, be doing in such a place?

"I didn't realize my elder brother spent so much time with his studies. When we were young, we would have lessons together. He would always try to make me laugh." Wei-wei spoke rapidly, crisply, as if she had a thousand things to say and time were short. "But you see, if I laughed, I would be punished and nothing would happen to him. If I was caught even smiling, Father would think I lacked the ability to concentrate."

"Lord Bai is much more focused now" was all Yue-ying could think to say.

Wei-wei drank her tea, watching Yue-ying the entire time. The silence lasted for no more than two sips.

"Are you one of the infamous courtesans of the Ping-kang li?" she asked with barely contained excitement.

"I do live in the quarter, but am in no way famous or infamous, Lady Bai," Yue-ying answered humbly.

"I hear that in the North Hamlet, women compose their own poetry and carry on battles of wit with the most distinguished scholars of the imperial court."

"The scholars are more likely to be young candidates vying for a position and a battle of wits is not so impressive when you consider everyone is drinking quite a lot of wine."

Wei-wei laughed. "You are exactly as I imagined a courtesan must be like! Outspoken and fearless."

"I'm no courtesan, Lady Bai. I'm just a maidservant."

"But you're here as a friend of my brother's," Wei-wei pointed out. "A very good friend."

Yue-ying started to protest, but Wei-wei was a step ahead of her.

"A mere servant wouldn't have taken that seat." She indicated with a tilt of her head. "Or poured herself a cup of tea and engaged in such free-flowing conversation. Which tells me that, unlike the old woman who lives in the back of the house whom I encountered earlier, my brother must hold you in very high regard."

A night in Bai Huang's bed was not enough to make her blush and giggle.

"Something unexpected has happened to my sister and Lord Bai is merely helping me," Yue-ying replied evenly.

Wei-wei seemed disappointed. "But still, you're here alone in his house with him. Such freedom! To be able to go where you please."

"But the lady is here as well."

"I had to make quite an effort to get out of the house.

And only with a trusted chaperone." She indicated the
manservant outside. "But I am so happy to have met
you, Miss Yue-ying. I've been curious about the North
Hamlet for a long time."

They sipped tea while Wei-wei asked questions about
banquets and drinking games. "Huang never tells me
anything," she complained.

Yue-ying was able to satisfy some of her own curiosity about Bai Huang as well. She learned that his family
lived in a gated ward just to the east of the Six Ministries. Bai Huang chose to stay in the scholars' quarter
to continue his studies and also be close to the circles
of influence.

"Nowadays, one has to establish a reputation even
before passing the palace exams," Wei-wei said sagely.

"Lord Bai is attempting to establish a good reputation?"

"Of course. What else would a son from a good
family want other than to distinguish himself in the
exams and secure a good appointment?" Wei-wei said.
"Though he has at times become distracted."

Yue-ying didn't think it polite to point out Bai
Huang's reputation in the Pingkang li was hardly an
exalted one or that he appeared to be doing everything
possible to ruin it. Then again, all sorts of behavior
were waved aside in the North Hamlet. Wasn't it known
as a place for young scholar-gentlemen to spend their
wild youth before the responsibilities of family and state
took over?

"How was Lord Bai distracted?" Yue-ying asked.
The question was likely too personal, but she was too
curious to stop herself.

"I misspoke." Wei-wei waved the question away and
sipped at her tea. "It's all in the past anyway."

Yue-ying let out a sigh of disappointment. Bai Huang had admitted to enjoying his share of wine and women. Perhaps there was a tale of heartbreak or unrequited love in his past. Maybe he always wooed unlikely girls like her.

That wasn't fair of her. Only now was she starting to know Bai Huang outside of his antics in the pleasure quarter. The two halves didn't fit together.

Wei-wei lingered over the last of her tea and teased out more details about banquets and poetry duels. Finally, she rose to her feet. "Well, I have to go home now. Our younger brother has lessons I must attend to. I assigned him a composition this morning that he should be done with by now."

Wei-wei stepped out into the courtyard and raised her parasol overhead. She looked about wistfully, seeing something besides the cracks in the wall and the weeds growing up between the stones. "Hopefully we can speak again soon, Miss Yue-ying."

The manservant started after his lady, but paused as he passed by.

"Give this to Lord Bai," he said, before disappearing through the gate.

She stared at the letter in her hands. It was something important, maybe even something about Mingyu, but its meaning was locked away until Bai Huang returned.

HUANG RETURNED FROM the city academy a few hours later when the sky was not yet dark. He set his writing box and notebook aside and removed his scholar's cap.

"Your sister came to visit," Yue-ying reported.

He raised an eyebrow. "Wei-wei?"

"Her manservant handed me this to give to you."

"That would be Zhou Dan. She must have grabbed

him by the ear and forced him to take her here." He opened the letter and glanced at the contents before returning his attention to her, looking her up and down. "You'll need something to wear."

She hardly had time to question him before he was back in the bedchamber, searching through his wardrobe. Though it had become her sleeping area, she couldn't really complain about his intrusion since the rooms were all his.

"You have more clothes than Mingyu," she remarked dryly.

He shot her a cross look, one hand still on the door of the wardrobe. She blinked at him innocently.

"There is a cargo ship scheduled to arrive tonight," he explained. "The city authorities are planning to capture it once it docks. I intend to be there to inspect the cargo along with a manservant."

"Zhou Dan?"

"You." He disappeared once more to hunt through the wardrobe. "This is very close to the location where Mingyu's hairpin was found. She and Huilan might have encountered a similar shipment when they came by at night. We need to pay attention to every detail, see if there's anything suspicious about."

He emerged with a garment in hand. "We might encounter some unruly characters, so it's better that you go in disguise."

She took the brown robe from him and held it up before her. "This is silk, which is hardly fitting for a servant. You're also much larger than I am. It would fall off of me. Practicalities," she reminded him.

He shot her another look, this time a heated one that said he wanted to take her clothes off himself.

Yue-ying's pulse skipped. "I will see what can be done."

She found a seamstress working from a small shop near the market area. With the exchange of a few coins, the seamstress adjusted the robe to fit her and fashioned a cap for her. She would have to rely on darkness to hide everything else.

As evening approached she and Bai Huang walked toward the canal and found a seat at a wine shop that faced the waterway. A little farther up, a string of boats housed a settlement of people who made their living through various jobs along the docks. Small cooking fires were visible now upon the vessels.

"We have a lookout watching for the cargo ship," Bai Huang said. "He'll signal once it approaches."

She looked down the stretch of dock and across the black water, but saw nothing. "You think Mingyu and Huilan might have become mixed up with these smugglers somehow?"

"It's possible. If that's not the case, then at least the crew can be interrogated for more information about who operates here. Perhaps the magistrate can get them to identify who the dead man was."

"It's hard to believe Mingyu and Huilan would have come here alone."

It was possible the two women could have passed by on their way back to the North Hamlet, but they were unlikely to have done so by coincidence. The docks were dangerous and known to be frequented by drifters. Bai Huang had insisted Yue-ying come in disguise even though he was by her side and guard patrols were nearby.

"Maybe they were lured here," he suggested, which led to questions of why and how.

Though the night was warm, a chill lifted the fine hairs on the back of her neck. Mingyu hadn't been a helpless victim. She had likely stabbed the man before he was drowned. It had happened here, not a hundred paces away.

"It would have been very late," she pointed out. "Mingyu didn't come home that night until halfway between dusk and dawn."

"The patrols will thin out after the first hour. It would make sense for any illicit activity to occur then."

Which meant they had a long time to wait. The wine shop eventually closed down, leaving them on a bench outside with a jug of wine. By the end of the twelfth hour, the jug was empty. Only the glow of the stars provided any light.

"Are you cold?" Bai Huang asked.

"No."

He reached out his hand to twine his fingers through hers. If the rice wine didn't warm her blood enough, his nearness certainly did. She sat shoulder to shoulder with him and let the balmy night air flow over her.

"Your sister was asking about your studies," she said after a while. "Lady Bai showed an interest in how you were doing."

Bai Huang snorted. "More like she wanted to use me as an excuse to explore the city."

"Excuse?"

"My sister can be deceptively manipulative. Everyone has her marked as an obedient daughter, but the truth is she does whatever she wants. Why are you laughing?"

"You sound envious of her."

"Of course I'm not!"

He sounded so offended that she wanted to laugh even harder. "She was envious of you as well."

"Wei-wei is convinced that if she had been born a man, she would already be an imperial scholar and rising through the ranks of the imperial court. She's spoiled."

"You're spoiled," she pointed out. "You do whatever you want."

"*Whatever* I want?" He grinned, reaching for her.

She stopped him, her hand pressed against his chest to keep him at bay. "I'm posing as your manservant."

"It's dark." Obligingly, his arms loosened their hold on her, but he didn't let her go.

"Your sister also said something about you being distracted at one time."

"I'm distracted now—"

She punched him lightly in the arm, the blow not moving him in the slightest. For someone who had never labored a day in his life, Bai Huang was surprisingly solid.

"I know Wei-wei is clever," he admitted begrudgingly. "She's always been more focused than I am and more dedicated as well. In the past, I didn't know anything. I made mistakes, foolish mistakes. Wei-wei may sound envious, but my success or failure reflects on her as well as on our entire family. I need to redeem myself for them."

Hearing Bai Huang speak of his sister made her think of Mingyu. They had been separated from each other when Yue-ying was so young. Yue-ying had grown up in the brothel, suffering the indignity of being bedded by strangers, having no will of her own. All the while, she dreamed of one day finding her sister again.

Then Mingyu had floated through the door like a goddess. For a long time, all they had done was stare at one another, unable to find words. They knew each other immediately, but so much time had passed. Ten years. Their birth names had been cast aside for new names given to them by their masters. The place where they had been children together was long gone.

Even when Mingyu brought her to the Lotus Palace, they remained distant. Neither of them spoke of the home they had left behind or the parents who had abandoned them. Without those memories, the only life they shared was these past few years in the Pingkang li, as they tried to become sisters again.

Bai Huang must have sensed where her thoughts had wandered because he pulled her in close. "Whatever happens, I swear you will be taken care of."

"I'm not worried for myself." She allowed herself to lean against him. "I worry about Mingyu. She was the one the procurer noticed among the dust of our village, and she has borne the scar of that all these years. It's difficult for her being the older one, the prettier one."

"But you're the stronger one," he said gently.

"I'm not. All I had to do was endure."

Yue-ying had never fought back. She never tried to flee, but she never gave up. She had watched and waited, always searching for a way out even when there was none.

Mingyu was the one who took it upon herself to bring them back together. She used her beauty to find the means to do it. Certainly Bai Huang as eldest son could understand the weight of such responsibility.

A bright flash came from the other side of the canal. It was there and gone, making her wonder if she had imagined it, but Bai Huang straightened beside her. He'd seen it as well. Another orange flash came and then another, controlled and directed. They must be using a mirror to deflect the light from a fire.

"That's the signal," Bai Huang said. "The ship is approaching."

CHAPTER EIGHTEEN

IT WAS AN efficient operation. The ship glided into the passage from the main waterway, oars extended and pulling in a steady rhythm. As it neared the dock two smaller, more agile patrol boats moved into position, blocking any exit. The foot patrol, manned with soldiers from the local garrison, rushed the dock with lanterns lit and swords drawn.

After his experience with smugglers off the eastern coast, Huang half expected a fight to erupt, but within moments the boat was secure. He approached with Yue-ying closely behind as the crew was escorted from the vessel and taken into custody for questioning.

A command had been established on the dock and Huang stepped up to identify himself to the head of the patrol as well as to the official from the commerce office.

"Interesting to see the Ministry of Defense working on a local smuggling case," the official remarked, referring to the elder Lord Bai's involvement.

"These are unusual circumstances." Huang looked to the hull of the ship. "Are we free to board?"

The man signaled to someone who signaled to someone else. The word that came back must have been a good one.

"The young lord is free to do whatever he requires.

The cargo is being unloaded and the inspectors will make their rounds shortly."

Huang thanked the official and started up the gangplank. Yue-ying's soft, careful step followed behind him.

"I didn't realize your father had such influence," she remarked.

Once they set foot on deck, he was able to get a sense of how many men had been pulled together for this scheme. He sincerely hoped something would come of it. Otherwise, Father would have to suffer the embarrassment of this mishap. The Bai family might find themselves wishing for the days when their son's exploits, though disgraceful, had been less public.

The soldiers formed a line from the cargo hold and began to transfer sacks from one man to the next, stacking them onto the deck to be transferred dockside. Huang loosened the tie on one of the sacks.

"Tea," he declared, sifting a pinch of the dried leaves through his fingers.

He headed to the cargo hold. As he started to climb down the ladder Yue-ying's hand tightened over his arm. When he looked up at her, her mouth was set in a thin line, but she said nothing. She merely raised the lantern over the passage to light the way down. A moment later, she descended the ladder to join him and remained silent as they explored below deck.

There was little space to move and the few lanterns below provided only dim lighting. The hold was filled with more sacks stacked from floor to deck. An inspector was supervising the transfer of the cargo.

They could have easily stayed topside to await the official account, but Huang was too impatient for that. Searching through the other sacks, he found more tea as well as a supply of grain. At one point, he felt a tug on his sleeve but thought nothing of it. Moments later, he looked behind him to find that Yue-ying had disappeared.

He found her up on deck, sitting with her head bent, breathing steadily. A wisp of hair had escaped from her cap and the image she presented was undeniably feminine: the delicate shape of her chin and long neck. Even the way her hand was raised to press against her brow was graceful and womanly in manner.

Everyone was too busy to notice a woman among them. Even he had been too caught up in the search to recognize the subtle signals she had relayed.

"You don't like boats," he recalled, lowering himself beside her.

"It's nothing. Just very confining down there."

Her voice was pitched too high and she still wouldn't look at him. Instead, she focused on breathing. He wanted very much to touch her then, just to run a hand along her cheek or tuck that stray hair back beneath her cap. Unfortunately, it was no longer dark and they weren't alone.

"You didn't have to go down there."

"I'm fine," she said, a note sharper.

It was so like Yue-ying to continue on without complaint, just as it was so like him to push forward without any regard to those around him. Maybe she got along with him so well because she was accustomed to attending to Mingyu, someone else who was also self-absorbed and self-important.

Now that he understood how protective the two sisters were of each other, he knew Mingyu would have had to force Yue-ying to leave the night of the banquet. Fear of being on a boat wasn't enough to chase Yue-ying away from her sister's side.

The commerce official approached them with his report. "We found tea and other common goods, my lord. The shipment will need to be weighed and recorded. The crew will be held for questioning as well. Most claim to be mere laborers hired for the job."

"Well, this is disappointing," Huang muttered. "We were looking to apprehend some vicious outlaws."

"Not a disappointment at all!" The official gestured toward the stacks surrounding them on the deck. "It could be that this shipment was brought into the city on the sly to avoid required taxes. We'll know once we check against all the required documents and manifests."

"I suppose that's something."

The man chuckled. "Thankless work, my young lord. Such is corruption, a little here and a little there. Like ridding oneself of rats. No glory in it. Nothing as dramatic as battling gangs of pirates or river bandits."

The official moved on to finish his business, which apparently involved the exciting act of looking through records and official documentation.

"I want to go back down below," Yue-ying said. She appeared a little less pale, but not too enthusiastic as she rose.

"There's no need. A ship like this would have workers unloading for hours in the middle of the night. We can interrogate the crew to see if anyone went missing recently or if any of them had seen Huilan or Mingyu on their last run."

"I just felt suffocated in that small area," she insisted, as if saying the words would make them true. "I'm not afraid."

Huang stayed close this time as they climbed back down into the hold. The men were still clearing the cargo. Yue-ying wove around them, heading to the end where most of the sacks had been removed. Bending over, she held her lantern up while running one hand along the boards.

"What are you looking for?" he asked, crouching beside her.

"I'm not certain, but we hear stories in the quarter."

She paused at one section and directed the light downward. There were small holes bored into the wood.

Together, they felt along the floor. What appeared to be a flaw in the wood was really a handle to a trapdoor. Yue-ying glanced at him anxiously before lifting it.

The area below the door was black as night. He thrust his lantern into the opening, not knowing what to expect. What he saw was a small hollow, only big enough to hold a person if they curled up knee to chest. Though the compartment was empty, a set of iron chains lay at the bottom, leaving no doubt as to what was usually smuggled inside the hidden chamber.

WAGONS WERE BROUGHT in to move the tea and Huang enlisted one of the transports to take them back to his residence. They said nothing during the ride home, but once they were inside the front gate, he could remain quiet no longer.

"Is that how you and your sister came to the capital?"

She reached the door of her bedchamber before turning to face him.

"We were sold by our parents. There was no need to be smuggled in."

The answer gave him no relief. He had known about her past in the brothels, yet he'd managed to push it aside. He had tried very hard not to think of how many men she had lain with. He had been with other courtesans and their pasts simply hadn't mattered, but with Yue-ying it did.

How much would a child be sold for? Ten bolts of silk? Enough grain to feed a family for a few months? Huang had owed several million in cash at one time, thrown away for nothing but his own pleasure. He had been utterly blind.

"I understand now why you won't be owned by anyone ever again." The words alone seemed inadequate. "I never meant to try to purchase you in that way."

Yue-ying only nodded once. She looked tired. Very tired.

He headed to his study, prepared to collapse onto his pallet, but she reached for him. She drew him into her chamber and shut the door behind them, enclosing them in darkness.

Though sightless, they found one another with no trouble. His hands rounded her waist at the same time her arms circled his neck and she pressed her mouth eagerly against his. He had told her once she was the only thing in the Pingkang li that seemed real to him. She never felt more real than tonight.

They only stopped kissing to slip off their clothes. She was wearing his robe, he recalled as he untied her sash and pulled the silk from her shoulders. She did the same for him, her hands working deftly, before she pushed him back onto the bed. Her hand paused on his abdomen, her little finger just brushing the scar beneath his ribs, before dipping lower.

He shuddered as her hand closed around him. He had been aroused for days, living so close to her, hearing her dressing and washing from the other side of the wall. Her fingers circled him and her hand ran along his entire length, stroking him until he was so hard it bordered on pain. Her grip was knowing, teasing, merciless.

Whomever he had made love to that first night wasn't Yue-ying. He hadn't known her then. She had hidden herself from him on purpose and he had made assumptions of who she was and what she wanted. The woman in bed with him tonight wanted him as much as he wanted her.

He sat up and she climbed onto his lap, straddling him. He could feel the flex of the muscles along her legs as he gripped the backs of her thighs. Without a word, she guided him into her.

"Go slow," he murmured desperately, already lost at the sensation of her flesh parting to allow him entrance.

Yue-ying did go slow, slow enough that he could feel the wet clasp of her body as she lowered herself. She rested her palms flat against his chest once she was fully seated onto him and the moment of stillness drove him mad. He wanted to thrust up into her, to seek more of that heat and the unbearable pressure of her surrounding him, but if he did it would be over quicker than it began.

Her weight shifted in his lap. She bent to kiss him on the chin. The gesture was sweet, almost innocent, but the change in position caused her muscles to tighten intimately around him.

"Yue-ying." He gritted out her name.

She had begun to move over him and he was enslaved inside her. Her voice was a seductive whisper against his throat.

"Lord Bai."

"Lord Bai?" he groaned. "Is that what you call me… in your dreams?"

He could only pant out the words. The heat, the pressure of her flesh squeezing tight around him, the sheer pleasure of their joining had taken over him and he was making no sense. Right there, at the height of the crisis, Yue-ying started laughing. It was a seductive, beautiful sound and it resonated through her into him.

He wrapped a hand around the back of her neck, needing to maintain some illusion of control as she rocked over him, driving the pleasure deeper.

"Be with me." His voice was rough, unrecognizable.

With what little focus he had left, he eased his fingers between them and reached for her center, for that pleasure point that would take a woman to the heavens. He only knew he'd found it when Yue-ying cried out. Her body drew impossibly tighter around him and her movements fractured, losing their rhythm.

The last of his control was gone. He couldn't think to pull out of her. He couldn't stop the flood of his seed into her and the dark wave of pleasure came with such force that he was blinded. He held on to Yue-ying and distantly heard her cries through his own release as he continued to stroke her. Then she was shuddering against him and clinging to him, her nails digging into his shoulder.

It was beautiful. He had no other words for it.

Perhaps seconds, perhaps an entire hour had passed when she laid her head onto his chest. He was still inside her. Though the fire in him was momentarily satisfied, he was loath to separate from her.

"Huang," she conceded sleepily.

"Much better," he murmured.

His fingers continued to stroke soft little circles over her sex. He could feel the tremors within her as her body responded faintly out of instinct. But their flesh was well sated and not yet eager to stir again. He just needed to keep on touching her.

"A concubine isn't the same as a servant," he said after a while. "She's a companion. A wife."

She lifted her head from his chest, sought out another spot and settled down again. "This is what you want to speak of now?"

"I was thinking you might be better persuaded now that you seem to like me...more."

"A concubine is far from a first wife. She's a little wife. A lesser one."

He shushed her. "Those are just names."

"To a man. There is no such thing as a lesser husband."

"Because that wouldn't make any sense," he scoffed. "A teapot may serve many cups, but you never see one cup with many teapots."

She laughed at him. "You are better at making love than at making arguments, Lord Bai."

"I am?" he asked suggestively. He pulled her up and kissed her, then they wrestled until he was on top, still kissing her.

Yue-ying was right. Things were going well. It wasn't time to argue. He had wanted to assure her she didn't need to be afraid of what would happen next. She would never have to contemplate selling herself to a brothel or wonder what her future would be. He could take care of her. He wanted to.

He wasn't good for much, but he was at least good for that.

His flesh was responding to having Yue-ying beneath him. It wasn't long before he was hard enough to enter her again. He did so slowly, listening to the catch of her breath in the dark.

"This is good between us, isn't it?" he asked, thrusting gently.

Her thighs curved around his hips to hold on to him. "Yes."

He had been holding his breath waiting for that answer. He exhaled now and eased himself deeper into her, loving the arch of her back in response. Over the past few days, he had wondered from moment to moment whether Yue-ying would ever let him into her heart as well as her body.

She let out a sigh as she wrapped her arms around him. "Despite everything that has happened, this is good."

CHAPTER NINETEEN

YUE-YING DIDN'T KNOW what time it was when they finally fell asleep. She suspected it was very close to morning because she had barely closed her eyes before there was sunlight peeking through the bamboo shutters. Bai Huang reached for her when she stirred.

"Sleep," he urged.

She obeyed without argument, closing her eyes and drifting off with the scent of his skin surrounding her. He smelled of books, of fragrant wood and morning forest. She must have been dreaming. She had never been in a forest.

When she woke again, he was gone. The room was warm, telling her it was past morning and heading well toward noon. She dressed herself and combed her hair before fixing it with a pin. Then she took a moment to set the chamber straight before venturing out into the courtyard.

The windows and door of the study were propped open. She could see Bai Huang inside. He wore a light tan-colored robe, suitable for the summer heat, with striking blue trim. The contrast between his present groomed appearance and the raw sensuality of the previous night sent a rush of emotion through her.

Bai Huang was patient. He was persistent, gently pushing against her doubts and fears without overwhelming her until suddenly she found he'd worked his way inside those barriers. He had disarmed her bit by bit and Yue-ying had never thought she would feel this way about any man. She hadn't known she was capable of it.

He was writing into a booklet and had already filled several pages with tidy columns of characters, perfectly spaced apart. He had a look of concentration on his face, the one that caused a faint crease to appear between his eyes. She knocked before entering.

"Yue-ying."

He moved his brush instinctively back over the ink stone to prevent any dripping and he greeted her with a smile that held many unspoken sentiments. Her stomach fluttered.

"Lord Bai."

He raised his eyebrows at that, but she let the honorific stand, though there was an underlying intimacy in the way she settled into the chair opposite him without invitation. Just being near him made her skin flush warm. This was very new to her. She decided she liked it.

"A commentary on the Spring and Autumn annals," he said in response to her curious look. He waved his hand dismissively toward the booklet. "Senseless rambling on my part really."

She watched as he held up the booklet to ensure the last of the ink was dry before folding the pages in.

"You don't have to do that," she said.

"Do what?"

"Act the fool."

He regarded her with a thoughtful expression. "It's not always an act," he said finally with a self-mocking smile.

Perhaps humility was a virtue, but Bai Huang habitually belittled himself. She had seen how he had taken command at the docks. He also had proven himself to be a much more serious scholar than he claimed. His behavior continued to be a puzzle.

"Last night," he began.

She stopped him. "Lord Bai."

"You're blushing."

"The day is uncustomarily warm," she returned without pause.

"Is this love?" he asked simply. His voice was low and sensual.

"Scholars and their romantic notions," she chided, though her heart was hammering inside her.

Most gentlemen who visited the pleasure quarters were looking for a temporary diversion. They enjoyed the games of courtship without having to be serious about it.

Bai Huang was at the height of his youth. It would be likely another two or three years before he was required to settle down and dedicate himself to career and family. A decent amount of time for an affair, long enough for a few good memories. Her chest constricted around the thought.

"Let us see what comes," she said.

He wasn't satisfied with her answer, but didn't press on. "I'm being selfish again. There are other things on your mind, of course."

She nodded, grateful he was providing her with an escape. "Nothing is more important than finding Mingyu. What if she and Huilan encountered a slave trader on the docks?"

It made sense. The member of the gang who had threatened Bai Huang in the gambling den had mentioned her by her old name. She had obviously been recognized from the brothels.

"Could Mingyu have killed the man out of revenge?" he asked.

Yue-ying let out a deep breath. "We were sold by our parents," she reminded him. "There's no use blaming procurers and slave traders. We might as well curse poverty, or famine, or simply misfortune."

"Mingyu might not be as forgiving. She is known to bear a grudge," he pointed out.

Yue-ying didn't have an argument for that. Mingyu could wield a barb like an assassin's knife. She'd been known to cut down many an unworthy scholar for some infraction or another and she had the ear of key public figures. Mingyu wielded just enough influence to decry a potential appointee as lacking in manners or strength of character. But such social vindictiveness didn't mean she was capable of murder.

Bai Huang continued, "I mean to inquire with the Ministry of Works today to get a full account of last night's operation. The crew is being questioned about the body in the river as well. Perhaps some new information will be revealed. And if that fails..." He hesitated. "This is the sort of information my associate may have some insight about."

She remembered how he had gone to speak to someone the day after Mingyu had disappeared. "Who is this mysterious associate you always speak of?"

"Just a friend of mine. Well, not really a friend," he corrected. "Someone I've come to know."

She frowned at that. "Is he a friend or isn't he?"

"He can be helpful, but I have to always remember that he can also be very dangerous." Bai Huang sifted aimlessly through the papers on his desk, rearranging them as he explained the situation. "There's a place just outside the Pingkang li, in the adjacent quarter. A gambling den. I only go there once in a while." He rubbed at the back of his neck as if something had just stung him. "Once a week."

Once in a while was not the same as once a week, but she refrained from pointing that out.

"In any case, if there's no information from the ministry, then I'll try to see if there's any news from the street."

"I was thinking I would speak to Constable Wu today."

He scowled. "That demon Wu again."

Bai Huang was showing the prejudices of his noble birth. Constables were working men who got their hands dirty and had the unpleasant duty of dealing with outlaws. They weren't considered much higher than the criminals they chased after.

"I regret not being more forthcoming with him from the beginning," she confessed. "Constable Wu has a reputation for being ruthless and I was afraid for Mingyu, but it's been five days now since she disappeared. It's better that Wu finds her than a gang of outlaws seeking revenge."

The thought of losing Mingyu left her numb. They had parted so unexpectedly, it was like being torn away from her sister all over again.

"I'll send for Zhou Dan to accompany you," Bai Huang said gravely. "We still don't know exactly what happened that night, but it's obvious Mingyu has become involved with something very dangerous, just as you feared."

BAI HUANG LEFT FIRST, headed toward the commerce offices. A little while later, Zhou Dan arrived driving a carriage. He wasn't alone.

"Lady Bai," Yue-ying greeted, more than a little surprised to see Bai Huang's sister sitting beneath the canopy.

"It's so rare that I have the opportunity to venture into the city, I thought I would accompany you." Wei-wei, much like her brother, was accustomed to getting her way.

Yue-ying glanced over to Zhou Dan, who shot her a helpless look. There was not much Yue-ying could do either, so she climbed up onto the carriage and took her seat without protest.

"How old are you, Miss Yue-ying?" Wei-wei asked as the carriage rolled forward.

"Twenty-two."

"I'm twenty-three. I shall call you Little Sister, then." She looked satisfied to have established such status. "And you should call me Elder Sister."

Yue-ying bit back a smile. Bai Huang's sister was a bit of a tyrant.

"May I ask a question, Little Sister?"

Yue-ying nodded, but did so warily.

"I've never known anyone like you. How is it living so freely? Here you are, with my brother, just the two of you. I sometimes wonder how it must be to be a courtesan," Wei-wei said wistfully. "To be admired for your accomplishments. To live on your own."

"Elder Sister. I would advise you not to make me into something I'm not."

"But you are from the North Hamlet, are you not? And you are my brother's—" She cast a furtive look about, as if her amah were lurking nearby with a bamboo rod in hand. "His lover?"

"I'm not certain this is something we should speak of."

Wei-wei was undeterred. "But why not? It's just the

two of us here and we're friends. At least, I would like to be friends," she added hopefully.

Her earnestness was touching. There was no hiding that Yue-ying and Bai Huang were lovers now, but that was a private matter between the two of them. Certainly not for polite conversation with his overly curious sister.

"Huang hasn't ever mentioned you," Wei-wei complained.

"I am not the sort of woman one speaks of," Yue-ying said, more amused than embarrassed. "We can be friends for the time being, but I don't exist, at least not to anyone as important as family. One day your brother will find a woman who is fit to marry him and I will disappear like smoke."

Wei-wei gave her an odd look before glancing over at the passing scenery. For once, she had nothing to say.

"Lady Bai?"

Wei-wei finally looked back to her. "My brother is already betrothed. His marriage was arranged a long time ago."

The air rushed out of her. Yue-ying struggled to recover. "Of course. She must also be from a good family."

Bai Huang could at least have told her. But then again, why should he? He was living his life in a half dream away from his family. Pouring out money as if it were water. Why ruin the illusion by mentioning things like familial obligation?

This changed nothing. She was never going to be his wife; she knew that. She was merely a lover he had taken before passing the imperial exams and starting his life. There were poems about such wistful romances floating throughout the Pingkang li on colored paper. Melancholy poems centered on the impermanence of youth and love.

"I shouldn't have said anything," Wei-wei apologized.

"It was to be expected." She shrugged and tried to appear indifferent. From Wei-wei's look of concern, she was apparently unsuccessful.

The carriage stopped before the gray walls of the magistrate's yamen. Yue-ying suggested Wei-wei stay with her servant outside. Wei-wei stared at the imposing gate with its retinue of armed guards and made no protest.

Yue-ying approached the gate with some trepidation herself. Once inside, she found a clerk and asked to see Constable Wu.

She was brought to a small room with narrow windows near the back of the compound. Wu Kaifeng was deep in conversation with two other constables. The three of them were seated on wooden benches and the room appeared to be a communal area.

She stood by the door politely and waited to be acknowledged. Wu lifted his gaze to her, his eyebrows rising in question. His discussion ended shortly after, and he came to her.

"Miss Yue-ying."

He was dressed in his usual dark uniform and his head nearly brushed the top of the doorframe.

She took a step back. "Constable Wu. I wondered if you had any news of Lady Mingyu?"

His look was flat and unwelcoming, but his look was always so. Yue-ying had become accustomed to it and stood firm.

"No news," he reported. "I would ask the same of you."

"I have not heard from Mingyu, but I've learned of something that might be helpful. This might help you find the identity of the stranger who was found dead."

She told him of the previous night's events and the smuggling boat captured at the docks.

Wu regarded her for a long time. From his reaction, he appeared to not have heard of the incident, nor was he particularly moved by it.

"Come with me," he said finally.

They passed by an enclosed and guarded corridor where she assumed the holding cells for prisoners must be located. She shuddered, imagining how frightening it must be to be locked in the darkness.

Wu led her into what appeared to be a record room. Scrolls and books were organized onto rows of shelves. On the far wall was a set of drawers, each one marked with a number. The wall resembled the medicine cabinets she would see in an herbal shop, but the drawers were much larger. The constable pulled one open near the top and removed a familiar-looking bundle wrapped in green silk.

He carried the makeshift sack to the table beneath the window. The silver inside made a solid clank as he set it down. The stash appeared intact from when she had discovered it, showing Wu to be an upstanding individual. The constable could have easily kept half the stash for himself and no one would have been any the wiser.

Wu pulled out five of the ingots, placing them beside one another in a line. "The molds used to cast taels of silver vary according to the local silversmiths and moneylenders. This one here—" he pointed to a saddle-shaped ingot inscribed with several markings "—is commonly used in Suzhou prefecture. A few of these other molds are not commonly seen in the capital. The variety of ingots found in this stash indicates that the silver came from many different origins."

Yue-ying studied the designs before her. At least the

discussion kept her mind away from what she'd just learned about Bai Huang's betrothal.

"So the silver could have come from smugglers," she speculated.

Wu shook his head.

"Why not? It's possible."

"It may be possible, but you have already decided on a conclusion and now you are fitting what information you find to that idea. That approach is inherently flawed."

After being in the hold of a smuggling ship the night before, it was easy for her to imagine dreadful scenarios involving greed and murder.

She swallowed nervously. "There is something I wanted to ask you, Constable. If someone were to have stolen from a dishonest person, are they still guilty?"

"You mean is it a crime to steal from a thief?" Wu asked, an eyebrow raised. "That's a matter for the magistrate to deliberate."

"What of a situation where someone caused the death of another person when it wasn't intended," she went on. "Surely that wouldn't be considered as great of a crime?"

Wu wrapped the silver back inside the shawl and returned the entire stash to the drawer.

"I think you should be careful of what you reveal to me," he said after some thought.

Though she was wary of him, there had always been a connection between her and Constable Wu. Like hers, his harsh features lacked beauty and symmetry. The two of them weren't even blessed with plainness. Wu's appearance was upsetting to others, just as hers was. She wanted to believe that his coldness came from this.

"I was hoping we could be of assistance to each other

so Mingyu can be found," she said. "All I ask is that all circumstances be considered when judging her."

"Such an appeal is better made to the magistrate."

Who would ignore her as a humble servant pleading on behalf of her mistress.

Wu continued, "We have been searching throughout the Pingkang li for days. Given how Lady Mingyu left no notice to even her most trusted servant, it is my belief your mistress does not want to be found. Unfortunately, that also leads me to believe that her involvement in the stranger's death was neither an accident nor a defensive act, as you tried to insinuate."

"But you'll question the smugglers?" she asked, feeling desperation set in.

"I will question everything and everyone," he assured her. "But I am not a friend, Miss Yue-ying. I will find your mistress and bring her before the tribunal, as is my duty. Lady Mingyu lost any chance for mercy when she went into hiding."

CHAPTER TWENTY

THE WARM SMELL of garlic and spices hovered in the courtyard when Huang returned at the end of the day and there was movement in the kitchen. He peered inside to see Yue-ying at the woodstove behind a haze of steam. Her hair was tied back with a scarf, but strands of it had fallen loose and hung damp around her face.

He leaned against the doorframe and waited, watching. It wasn't long before she spied him out of the corner of her eye.

"I didn't realize you knew how to cook," he said with a grin.

"I don't. Auntie Mu prepared everything." She opened a clay pot to peek inside.

"Who's Auntie Mu?"

She shot him an odd look. "Your landlady."

"Yes, of course."

He recalled the old woman's name. It was just that they tended to stay out of one another's way and spoke in polite honorifics when in conversation—what few conversations they'd had. Yue-ying was shaking her head in disbelief as she spooned some greens onto a dish.

"Let me help," he offered, moving in to transfer the clay pot to the table.

She gave him only a cursory glance before going to the back shelf to fetch the wine.

"Is there something wrong?" he asked, disconcerted

at having to call to her from across the kitchen. Though she was only ten paces away, a valley had opened up between them.

"Nothing," she said in a tone that was clipped. "Please sit."

He did so, watching her carefully the entire time. She ladled stew into a bowl for him and tilted the ewer of wine over his cup. Even when she sat down beside him, she continued to avoid his gaze. He had come to look forward to sharing the evening meal with Yue-ying where they could recount the moments of the day together, but tonight was different.

"Something has happened," he stated.

"Constable Wu," she replied. "I thought he could be reasoned with, but I was wrong."

An encounter with that demon could put anyone in a foul mood, but he knew Yue-ying well enough to see that she wasn't telling him the whole truth. Her shoulders were tense and there was no softness about her mouth or eyes.

She covered her agitation in the business of dinner, ladling stew and pouring more wine for herself. They ate at first in relative silence. Last night, Yue-ying had been full of passion and, this morning, full of warmth. Now the walls were high around her once more.

"This is very good," he said, figuring complimenting a meal was the most proven way to ingratiate oneself. The stew was made of a rich, thick broth with cuts of lamb meat heavily seasoned with spices. A simple, yet luxurious offering.

"I'll tell Auntie Mu," she said quietly. "It will make her happy."

He finished his first cup of wine a bit hastily, but understandable given the circumstances. They reached for the wine ewer at the same time, fingers colliding. He took the opportunity to try to take hold of her, but she slipped out of his grasp, like a carp in water, and picked up her spoon again to resume her meal.

He was left to pour his own wine, which he did while keeping his eyes on her. "I thought of you today."

Her lips twitched, though her expression remained frustratingly blank.

"Wherever I went, people spoke to me, but I could barely hear them. My head was full of thoughts of you."

She narrowed her eyes at him, while he grinned from ear to ear. One of the lessons he'd learned while playing the lovesick fool was how often the lovesick fool was quite effective. He also knew Yue-ying liked sweet words and flattery, though she would never admit it.

"I hope you were able to listen for at least part of the day. We were looking for more information on the smuggling ship," she replied coolly, though a few stones had crumbled from her wall.

Whatever he had done to upset her—and he was certain there was something given the painfully mild expression she wore—it certainly wasn't deliberate on his part. But given that she was a woman and he a man, he was going to have to try to make amends without ever knowing his wrongs in the first place.

"The owner incurred a heavy fine for importing goods without paying a tax, but other than that there was little that could be done," he reported. "The crew claimed to have no knowledge of the nature of the cargo and will likely be released after forfeiting a day's wages."

"So we have little more than we started with," she said sadly.

"Other than more theories, which are worth as much

as the dust beneath our feet," he concurred in all seriousness. "But tonight I hope to find out more about that gang who tried to attack me. Perhaps they are in some way connected to the ship."

She stopped eating to stare at him. "You don't plan to go roaming the streets at night, do you?"

"Of course not. Someone much more fearsome than I roams the streets on my behalf and then I pay for a report from him."

"The friend who's not a friend," she recalled.

"Yes, exactly. I plan to meet him tonight at the gambling den."

She sipped slowly at her wine while regarding him. At least she didn't seem as upset anymore, but she was still frowning. "You sent Zhou Dan with me this morning because you were worried for my safety. You should be concerned for yourself as well."

"I know this place."

Yue-ying was not convinced. "Gambling dens are frequented by scoundrels."

He certainly couldn't argue with that. "I'm very much aware of the dangers." His throat felt dry. He finished his wine to help ease the conversation along. "You may have heard I incurred a substantial debt to a moneylender three years ago. I got caught up playing the dice and started spending more time at the tables than at my studies."

He had failed the palace exams twice already, and the pressure to pass had become overwhelming. Without the *jinshi* degree, he couldn't receive an imperial appointment. Not many scholars passed the highest-level exams, but he came from a family of distinguished poets and statesmen. There was never any question of failure.

It wasn't allowed. The dice took him away from all that for a few hours.

"When I lost my monthly allowance, I borrowed from friends to scrape by. But I had a bad run and lost the next month's allowance as well. I couldn't tell my family. I was too proud—or too scared."

It was hard admitting these things aloud. He'd never done so, not even to his father, who didn't need the details to figure out what had befallen him. But Yue-ying listened to his story quietly, without judgment. He felt a weight lifting off his chest as he spoke. It was as if he were speaking of someone else's life. As if he could leave the past behind if he finally revealed everything to her. He could be rid of these ghosts.

He went on, emboldened. "I thought for sure I could recover the money. I started borrowing from a money-lender. He recognized my name and that alone was enough for him to provide me with money to seed my bets for a while. I swore I would only borrow enough to earn back my allowance as well as enough to pay off the rest of my debts. The dice surely couldn't keep rolling so foul for so long. They had to turn."

"It happens to many a young scholar," Yue-ying said gently. "They spend small fortunes on dice or women."

She did understand. He relaxed into the story, feeling they were Bai Huang and Yue-ying once again.

"I had been raised right here in the capital, so I foolishly thought I was too worldly to be lured in. I wasn't one of those poor peasants from the countryside, having never seen such pleasures.

"But I was wrong about everything. I did win some nights, but it was never enough. If the dice were rolling well, I had to stay and maybe I would double my winnings. If the dice were not rolling well, then I had to stay and cover my losses.

"Finally I owed too much and tried to stop going to the tables. It only made matters worse. The money-lender's minions started coming after me, demanding repayment. I thought I was above them. That I could forget that seedy part of the city ever existed and go on with my life. There was nothing they could do to me."

"You didn't go to your family?" she asked.

He met her eyes regretfully. "I couldn't."

Too much was at stake. Money, but more importantly face. Honor.

"But my father found out anyway," he said. "After I failed the exams yet another time, the money-lender hired men with knives to hunt me down. Father sent me away from the capital then. He used his name and reputation to keep the money-lenders quiet, but the debt was legitimate. So he paid it all. He could have disowned me, but instead he took me to his post in Fujian province and taught me everything I had forgotten about responsibility and restraint."

"I can imagine how he must have taught you."

"My father is very strict with his teachings." He managed a baleful smile. "And I deserved every bit of it."

He had left out crucial parts of the tale: that the money-lender's hirelings had done more than simply threaten him. He didn't want to subject her to such ugliness.

"You were very fortunate. I'm glad."

This time, she reached over to refill his wine cup for him. Her fingers remained curled tantalizingly close after she set the ewer down.

"But there's one thing I still don't understand," she

began slowly. "After what happened to you, why go back to the gambling den?"

"I don't want to." This was the difficult part to admit, but the more he said aloud, the more he felt the black poison was leaving his veins. "I vowed I would never gamble again, but after a month in Changan I found myself standing back at the table, staring at the dice. It's in my blood," he confessed. "It's a…a weakness. I know this now."

"If you know this—"

"I have strict rules," he went on, trying to figure out the best way to explain it. "I only go once a week, never more than that. I bet a certain amount of cash, but I never leave with any winnings."

She looked confused and he didn't blame her. It was difficult to explain how having this control, paying out a little bit at a time, made him able to resist being dragged down by greater temptation.

"Consider the money I lose as somewhat like a banquet fee in a pleasure house, a payment for time spent." He had never thought of that before. It made a lot of sense in comparison and he was feeling confident now. "There are other benefits as well. You have noticed that I try to keep up a certain reputation in the quarter with the drinking and the gambling. Many government officials, high and low, also enjoy the gambling tables. It's as good of a place to gather information as the Pingkang li."

"What sort of information do you need to gather?"

This was drifting quickly into another conversation entirely. He would have to tell her at some point, but now was not yet the time.

"It's a matter of making connections with the right people."

There. She would accept that. The activities of the

Pingkang li centered around social functions of that very nature.

"And there are people I've met who know of the black markets and other dark dealings in the city," he continued. "I discovered Commissioner Ma Jun took bribes and also how to approach the shipping merchant, Ouyang Yi. These connections have been very useful for our investigation."

Surely that explained the situation to her satisfaction.

It didn't. "But the money-lender's men threatened you. You lost so much money that they were going to kill you."

"That was all in the past. I was younger—"

"Lord Bai." Her tone sharpened. "Listen to yourself. There is no logic there. If you no longer care about winning, why play at all?"

He could feel his muscles tensing. "This keeps me from losing my way ever again."

"Like a man who drinks a little every day isn't tempted to get drunk? It doesn't make any sense."

"It does! I'm careful now. I know my limits."

"I have another suggestion for you." She was glaring at him all of a sudden. "If you want to stop gambling— *don't go*."

He was stunned into silence, but she wasn't done.

"You keep on going to a place where they've threatened you. And you keep paying out money willingly to them. As if money rains from the sky over you. Maybe it does." She grabbed her wine cup, but didn't drink. Her hand was shaking too hard. "Do you even realize how much a thousand coins is worth? People work their entire lives and don't see so much as that. People are sold for less—"

"You're making too much of this."

Her mouth twisted. "If you go there tonight, you're a fool."

All of the warmth he had once felt faded away, along with his feelings of trust in confiding his past to her. There was a heavy silence between them as the food grew cold.

"You've forgotten your place," he warned quietly.

Yue-ying met his glare without flinching. If he was cold, then she was hot, burning with a fire in her eyes. She pressed her palms flat against the table and stood.

The fire faded away until her eyes were empty of any emotion. "Forgive me, Lord Bai."

He picked up his wine and drank, not acknowledging her as she moved past him and out of the kitchen. He heard the door of her chamber—no, of *his* chamber shutting.

Huang waited in the kitchen, forcing down the rest of the wine before he strode to the study. He opened the locked chest beneath the desk and lifted out a purse containing exactly one thousand coins. Even the weight was familiar to him now. The door to the bedchamber remained closed as he left the courtyard.

Out on the street, he waved down a sedan. As they set off he leaned back and folded his arms over his chest, not watching the lanes as they flowed by. He had started the evening pleasantly and now he was unsettled.

He had confided in Yue-ying only to be scolded as if he were a child. She wasn't his wife. She wouldn't even admit to being his mistress.

Yue-ying had ridiculed him at times, which he'd found endearing, but this was going too far. He expected respect from her, at the very least. To not have his decisions questioned. Not to be scolded or challenged. He shouldn't need to explain himself. Yue-ying should just hold her tongue about matters she had no knowledge of and leave him in peace.

Like his mother did with his father.

Quiet and respectful…and cold.

The carrier had brought them into the familiar streets of the Pingkang li. His blood was still running hot. The gambling den was not much farther and his hand itched to place a bet. He wanted that rush of waiting for the dice to take his cares away.

"Stop."

The carrier at first didn't hear him. He had to repeat himself. "Stop at once."

"My lord?"

"Turn around."

By THE TIME Huang returned to his house, the sky had darkened. He lit an oil lamp from the smoldering charcoal in the stove and went first to the study to return the purse to the chest. Then he stood still, listening for sounds of movement from the adjacent chamber. There was nothing.

Yue-ying had raised her voice to him and he had put her in her place. The memory left a sick, sinking feeling in the pit of his stomach. The civil thing to do would be not to wake her, to wait until morning and they could both speak to one another calmly.

Or not speak about it at all, which was more likely to happen.

With the lamp in one hand, he went to the chamber door and tapped lightly on it. His heart thudded as he waited for an answer. When there was none, he pushed the door open a crack.

"Yue-ying."

She was curled onto her side fully dressed with her back turned to him.

He sat on the edge of the bed. "I didn't go."

When she turned to him, her face looked pale in the darkness. The red mark was like a bruise on her cheek. She blinked at him, waiting, saying nothing. Her eyes looked as if they might have been swollen, but he couldn't be certain.

"I wanted to, but I needed to come back and tell you that I'm not angry with you."

"I'm not angry either," she echoed, but he could see it was a lie.

"If you want me to leave…"

"I can hardly demand that of you. It's your chamber." She turned back to the wall. "I have no right to demand anything of you, Lord Bai."

Her tone cut into him.

"Then I'll stay."

He set the lamp aside and removed his outer robe, then lay down on the empty half of the bed. There was an invisible line drawn down the middle and he reached a hand toward it, silently willing her to turn around and close the gap between them. It wasn't as easy as that.

"Please put out the light." Her voice was tight. "I would like to sleep now."

He did as she asked before lowering himself back down. He let the darkness gather for a few moments before speaking.

"I am glad you said what you did," he said.

His heart was pounding as he spoke and his gut clenched. This wasn't the small rush of excitement he felt upon each roll of the dice. This was something much, much more frightening. The risks were so much greater.

"I needed to hear those words," he continued quietly. "Because I have been a fool. I only convinced myself otherwise."

He waited for her answer, but she said nothing. Her silence spoke for her. She wanted the matter done with. Forgotten. It was the way of servitude and humility and of keeping the peace at the sacrifice of everything else, but Huang didn't want to forget. Something was happening between them that he couldn't ignore.

"Yue-ying, say something, whatever is on your mind. Scold me, if you have to."

He knew this sort of silence could harden around you until it was as unbreakable as a wall of stone.

She shifted restlessly in the dark. "You are right, Lord Bai. I've become too familiar."

"I want us to be familiar." Just the previous night they had been wrapped around each other, naked.

"It isn't my place," she replied softly.

Something told him this wasn't just about their argument earlier. Yue-ying had been agitated from the moment he returned that day. But how to speak of things that weren't supposed to be spoken of between people like the two of them? Man and woman and unmarried, for one. Nobleman and peasant, for another. They might be separated by class, but she was here with him, in his bed. He had never trusted anyone else with the worst parts of himself.

There was no way to explain to her what he was feeling without telling her everything, starting with the part of the story that he had left out to preserve his pride.

"It wasn't just debt that chased me from the city," he began. She lay across from him in the dark, close enough to touch though he couldn't see her. "The money-lender hired someone to put a knife in me and he succeeded, leaving me bleeding out in the street for the city guards to find me. The wound wasn't deep. It was bound and I was brought back home.

"My father came to me as I lay in bed, weak from the loss of blood. Somehow he had learned of the debt, because he didn't need to ask me of it. He sat beside me and told me I was worthless, that I was a do-nothing, a good-for-nothing and that I was a disappointment as a son. The look on his face made me wish that I had died. I certainly deserved to."

Huang fell silent then to let the words sink in. Unlike their conversation earlier that evening, he had no excuses. He imagined Yue-ying must have agreed with his father at that moment. She might as well hear the rest of it as well.

"After that, Father paid off the debt without another word. As soon as I healed, he had me sent out to Fujian province and put me to work, believing that was why I had been tempted by the dice. I had no responsibilities. I was easily distracted.

"Father taught me the duties of his position. He was in charge of protecting several key river ports in the province. Stretches of the waterway had become overrun by bandits, some of the gangs numbering over a hundred men, enough to challenge the local militia. It was arduous work patrolling the ports. Father would position and provision men along the river. He would confer with garrison commanders and city officials to track down and capture the worst of the bandits. The outlaws often blended in among the villagers along the rivers, so I would pose as a merchant to lure them out."

"Such work would suit you."

He was startled to hear her finally speak.

"You're a different person when something that matters to you is at stake," she went on.

"Different? How so?"

"You become focused. Dedicated."

Was that how she saw him? He had to admit he was moved.

"At first it seemed to help," he agreed. "I wanted very much to redeem myself in my father's eyes, but apparently I hadn't had enough. As soon as Father wasn't watching over me, I started to gamble again. Just a little at first, to entertain myself. A harmless diversion—until I was once again in debt.

"One night, I was dragged away from the dice table by ruffians. They tied me up and threw me into a large crate. When I was let out, I found myself on a boat with ocean on all sides and no sign of land. It was all my father's doing. His people were following me and reporting to him. Father had left me alone to see what I would do and, once again, I failed."

"This was your punishment? Abandonment at sea?" she gasped.

"This was his way of teaching me. The sailors cut the ropes—there was no need for them when there was nowhere to escape to. At the time, I couldn't even swim. It was an imperial navy ship, patrolling the coast for pirates. Immediately I was put to work, as any other crewman on board. I had never spent a day beneath the sun in my life. I had never lifted anything heavier than a calligraphy brush. By the first day, my hands were raw from scrubbing the deck and hauling rope. I fell asleep the moment I was allowed into my bunk, too exhausted to be angry.

"Over the next months, I labored every day with the sun and wind beating down on me. I ate what everyone else ate and lifted and carried and spent long nights on watch. Slept with rats always scurrying somewhere nearby. The crew would occasionally play the dice, but the game no longer held any appeal for me."

He managed a chuckle to which Yue-ying did not respond. At the time, he was certain his father meant to leave him there to a life of forced servitude and hard labor.

"When the ship docked at port, I saw my father once again. At the time, I hated the man for being so rigid, so unyielding. There was no compromise with him. There was no warmth or humor or affection. He lived life by exacting standards and expected the same of his family. Anything less was unworthy."

The sun had been punishing that day. He remembered everything in stark brightness, with no shadows to hide behind. His clothes had been worn to threads and his skin so dark, he was unrecognizable. Father had stared at him with a hard and piercing look, a look that held no remorse.

"As much as I wanted to curse him, I was also humbled. We didn't speak of what had happened. He merely met my eyes as I came to join him and it was understood that I could no longer be the hapless fool I'd been. I had to take responsibility for my actions, for myself, but more importantly for my family.

"But when I was back in Changan once more, I still couldn't stay away from the dice. So I tried to trick myself into thinking I could scheme and plan around this temptation, as if it were an unseen enemy. But you were right—I am the fool."

"I spoke without thinking," Yue-ying said quickly. "Forgive me—"

"No, there's nothing to forgive."

He paused. He needed her to fully understand this next part.

"My father is strict. There's no warmth to him. A word of praise is as rare as finding a pearl in an oyster, but when he dragged me out of the gambling den and threw me onto that ship, it wasn't punishment. If I was no longer his son, he could have disowned me, but he did not. At first I was angry at him for being so hard, but I came to realize the truth of it. This is how he shows his love."

The silence between them was interminable. He reached out through the darkness to touch her, resting just his fingertips against her back. Yue-ying stilled beneath the touch, not moving toward him.

"You don't have to say anything," he told her, his voice deep with emotion. "I know you are not sentimental by nature. You're too stubborn and practical to ever submit to any notions of romance, but I know what it means for you to reprimand me the way you did. Only one other person has ever cared enough to do so."

CHAPTER TWENTY-ONE

BAI HUANG REGARDED her from across a bowl of tea the next morning. They continued to drink in silence, as if meditating. Her thoughts were not profound, but they were significant. They were of him and all that he had confessed to her.

Yue-ying had stayed up late into the night, listening to the chirping of the crickets, while Bai Huang lay in bed beside her. His breathing eventually grew deep and slow, but sleep still wouldn't come to her. The echo of his words kept her awake. She had no knowledge of what to do now that he had revealed his feelings so plainly.

"We have forgotten something," he said finally.

Her pulse jumped. There had been no talk of last night. There had been no talk of this morning, when they had woken up with their limbs inadvertently entwined. They had untangled themselves without a word and continued about their daily ritual, dressing, washing, sharing tea. She was hoping that they would continue as they were and act as if last night hadn't happened.

"What have we forgotten?" she asked, forcing herself to appear calm as she sipped her tea. No need to let good tea go cold while she brooded over the uncertainty of the future.

"Lady Huilan," he replied. "We've forgotten to consider her connection in all this. She and your sister were together on those docks. It was Huilan's death that brought everything to light. Who killed her?"

She regarded him closely. Bai Huang was a contradiction. His time at sea, slaving under the sun, had briefly opened his eyes, but it certainly wasn't enough to erase a lifetime—no, generations—of wealth and privilege. He threw good money away on elaborate clothing and dice games out of boredom and treated Auntie Mu as if she didn't exist. Yet at the same time he was willing to risk himself to pursue Huilan's killer when he had nothing to gain from it.

He believed in justice, even for someone who was merely a servant.

"Huilan could have been attacked by the smugglers who were seeking revenge for their comrade," she suggested. "While they were looking for their missing silver."

"Let us assume that's true. How would such rough characters get into the Hundred Songs while all those guests were there?"

"It was a festival night. A stranger could have slipped inside unnoticed."

"Or maybe he was noticed. An unnamed young man was seen there before Huilan was found dead, but afterward, he disappeared," Bai Huang reminded her. "There was also the tree outside. Her murderer could have climbed the tree to her window and entered undetected."

"But he would have had to know it was her room," she reasoned. "It could have been her scholar-lover. Maybe her death isn't part of all this."

"Don't be so hasty to abandon this path," he admonished with a pointed look. "Some truths take a while to reveal themselves."

Was he speaking of the murder, or something else entirely?

Yue-ying focused back onto what was most important. "After Huilan's death, Mingyu becomes frightened. So she runs away before the smugglers can find her to exact revenge—though it still seems that she'd be safer at the Lotus than alone on the streets as a fugitive."

"Maybe she was hiding something," Bai Huang offered. "Her own stash of silver. The two women hid the body and divided the money among them. Mingyu went to retrieve her stash and has now fled the city."

Which might explain why Mingyu had taken none of her own jewels or cash before going. It was difficult to think of her sister being so cruel and calculating, but if the dead man was a slave trader, then Mingyu and Huilan might have felt justified in their actions.

"Perhaps Mingyu is already far from the capital." She turned the bowl of tea around in her hands. "There are murderous bandits searching for her. Given the constable's lack of sympathy, maybe it's better if she's never found."

And Yue-ying would be left to wonder, once again, what had become of her sister and if they would ever see each other again. When she looked up, Bai Huang was watching her with an intent look.

"No matter what happens, you should know you'll be taken care of," he said earnestly.

She looked away from him, her face heating. "That won't be necessary."

"But I want to."

He acted as if he were free to make such promises, as if the decision weren't already out of his hands.

"You're living in a dream world," she muttered.

"What do you mean?"

"I know you're already promised to someone else."

Bai Huang fell silent. She could hear him slowly letting out a breath at the other side of the desk. When he spoke, his tone was calm and controlled. "How did you find out?"

"Your sister told me."

He waited until she looked up before speaking. His face was a mask.

"The marriage was arranged when she was only eight years old. She's sixteen now. We've never even met."

Yet this girl had more of a claim to him than she would ever have.

"You don't have to explain," she said, her voice rough.

The bell rang at the front gate, interrupting them. At first, he ignored the summons. His next words were caught on his tongue. As he struggled with them the bell clanged once more insistently.

Bai Huang met her gaze and held it before rising. His meaning was unmistakable: their conversation was not finished.

She knew that he hadn't been deliberately hiding the arranged marriage from her. It was a part of his personal life, a private matter between two families. By bringing the betrothal out into the open, she had all but accused him of wronging her. She was making demands she was not entitled to make.

This young woman, who was likely from a good family with a cultured upbringing, would become Bai Huang's wife. Yue-ying would become nothing more than a memory to fade with time. Yet he had revealed such startling sentiments to her in the dark: about his father, about his own failings and about his feelings for her. She didn't know what to make of his confession, so she drank her tea. The leaves had imparted a slightly bitter taste as the liquid cooled.

It wasn't long before Bai Huang returned. She could see the servant Zhou Dan behind him as he stood in the doorway. His expression was grim.

"There's news."

The breath rushed out of her. "About Mingyu?"

"We need to go now."

THEY SAT SIDE by side in the carriage with Zhou Dan at the reins. He navigated them quickly through the ward and out into the main avenue. The summer heat was already building toward a swelter even though it was not yet midday. A broad canopy overhead provided shade from the sun, but soon they would be roasting like ducks in an oven.

She could see that they were headed south. "Where are we going?"

"Zhou Dan received a report this morning from a servant who resides in the house adjacent to General Deng's mansion. A carriage left the general's residence late last night. He was able to bribe a location out of the driver, but little else."

"But you said the general wasn't in the city."

"Which is exactly why this is suspicious."

Mingyu had used General Deng once before as a diversion. Earlier in the month, Mingyu had claimed to be visiting the hot springs with Deng. Yue-ying had assumed it was a lovers' tryst, until Bai Huang told her differently. Mingyu had been lying to her for a long time now, and she wasn't the only one hiding the truth.

"You are still doing the same thing you were doing in Fujian, aren't you?" she asked.

Bai Huang only presented his profile when she turned

to him. He didn't answer immediately, but she could see the tension along his jaw.

"You're still working for your father, gathering information," she persisted. "You only found out about this mysterious carriage ride because you've been spying on General Deng. He's the one you've been interested in all along, not Mingyu. You only act the fool so everyone will think you harmless."

He looked downward, smoothing the edges of his sleeves over his wrists. The border was flamboyantly embroidered with gold thread. It was a costume, she realized now, part of the role he played. Though he admitted to nothing, she knew. The explanation fit him perfectly.

The journey continued in silence past the last of the gated wards. Here the roads were unpaved and traffic upon them was sparse, with a few wagons and carts here and there. Instead of the shops and residences of the northern part of the city, the southern end was all fields and plots of farmland. Irrigation ditches fed rows upon rows of crops and there were holding pens for goats and other livestock. Aside from the sections of road, they could have been out in the country.

They must have been traveling for over an hour. Yueying couldn't be certain without the sound of the market gong to mark time. Finally, they came to a stop at a wide plot of land near the eastern city wall. Bai Huang called out to one of the farmhands who were harvesting what appeared to be yams. The man wiped the dirt from his hands as he approached the side of the road.

"Is this General Deng's property?" Bai Huang asked.

"It is, my lord."

"We're looking for a woman, a famous courtesan from the northern part of the city."

The laborer looked confused.

"You would know if you saw her," Bai Huang assured him.

He enlisted the man's help, pulling him away from his task to act as their guide. They continued on foot, tracking through the fields with Yue-ying and Zhou Dan at the rear. She hadn't thought to bring a parasol and the sun was relentless without the cover of any buildings around them. Before long, her face was damp with perspiration and her slippers covered with a layer of dirt, but she continued on without complaint, trying to match the longer strides of the men.

Two thatched huts stood beside a well near the edge of the property. Bai Huang went to the first hut. Her stomach churned as she came up behind him and her palms began to sweat. A curtain covered the doorway. He stopped to call out to whoever was inside, only to be met with silence. The second hut was empty as well.

"Our foreman lives there," the farmhand explained.

"Bring him here. Tell him it's an important matter," Bai Huang instructed.

The man went to do as asked. Once he was gone, Bai Huang swept aside the curtains. Inside the hut was a single room with a stone hearth in the corner. The dirt floor had been dampened down. There were two pallets woven from hemp, a low table and a shelf of household items.

"General Deng's carriage brought someone here last night, but the driver claimed to have returned alone," Bai Huang said.

"The bowls have been washed and the floor was recently swept," Yue-ying observed. "Whoever was staying here might return if we just wait."

She circled the tiny space, trying to sense Mingyu's

presence, to gain some confirmation her sister had indeed been there, but it was no use. Yue-ying was met with nothing but a sense of desolation.

The sound of voices from outside indicated that the farmhand had returned. As Bai Huang went to meet him something on the floor caught Yue-ying's eye. She lifted the corner of one of the pallets to reveal a rag doll. Her heart squeezed tight as she ran her finger over the doll's blue robe. She recognized the pattern woven into the cloth from one of Mingyu's handkerchiefs.

The conversation outside grew louder. Hastily, she tucked the doll into her sleeve and went to see what was happening. She swept the curtain aside and froze.

Though the day was bright, a gray cloud had drifted over them. Standing beside the farmhand was the forbidding and towering figure of Constable Wu. He looked from Bai Huang over to her and his face creased into a frown.

"You have been withholding information from me," Wu said darkly.

"Funny thing is, I happened upon a curious rumor this morning," Bai Huang said with more composure than she would have been able to manage. "I thought to see if there was any truth to it before troubling the magistrate. Unfortunately, it looks like rumor was all it was."

Wu turned on the middle-aged man who Yue-ying assumed was the foreman. "Have you seen a woman? Tall, pale-skinned." After a pause he added, "Beautiful. As beautiful as a goddess."

Yue-ying was taken aback. Wu wasn't usually one for embellishment.

"A lady came last night," the foreman replied. "She and the old woman left with the child this morning."

"The child?" Wu echoed.

If Yue-ying hadn't seen the doll, she might have reacted in the same way. As it was, she was able to keep her expression neutral while the constable interrogated the foreman. An old woman and a young child had been brought to the farm several weeks earlier, supposedly on General Deng's orders.

"My wife brought them food every day. They spoke to no one, stayed inside most of the time." The man looked first to the constable and then over at Bai Huang. "We don't want any trouble, my lord. We were only doing as we were told."

It appeared that the place had served as a temporary haven and Mingyu had already fled. Constable Wu moved to search through the huts while Bai Huang and Yue-ying took the opportunity to return to the carriage.

"He must have followed us," Bai Huang said as Zhou Dan pulled away. "He has always suspected you would lead him to Mingyu."

Yue-ying scanned the area. "She must still be nearby. We have to find her."

"In all this?" Bai Huang indicated the endless plots of farmland, some owned by wealthy families within the city and others by individual farmers. "That demon is already rushing back to report to Magistrate Li as we speak. Then they'll return with fifty constables to search the area."

He directed Zhou Dan back to the northern part of the city. As the carriage rolled away from the fields a sense of the inevitable crept over her. The magistrate was going to arrest Mingyu for murder.

"We don't have much time," Yue-ying murmured.

"No, we don't," Bai Huang agreed. "You need to stop protecting Mingyu and tell me the entire truth."

"Me?" She was incredulous. "Tell *you* the truth?"

Bai Huang didn't flinch at the accusation. "Did you know about the child?"

"I found out about her at the same time you did."

He raised an eyebrow. "There was no mention that the child was a girl."

She pulled the rag doll from her sleeve and held it out to him. The doll was the height of her palm, suitable for small hands. Bai Huang ran a finger over the blue robe. No doubt he recognized the fine quality of the silk just as she had.

His brow creased into a frown. "Did General Deng father a child with Mingyu?"

Surely Mingyu would have told her about something as significant as having a child of her own. That would have made the girl family. Yue-ying took back the doll and studied its features. Someone had sewn the doll with care, painting on the face with a delicate brush.

"Mingyu didn't take a stash of silver from the smugglers," she concluded. "She took this child. That's why she's been so secretive—to protect the girl."

Because the girl was a slave. She was property and Mingyu had killed her owner and stolen her. Yue-ying felt a deep ache within her chest. She knew exactly why Mingyu had done such a thing.

"But where could she be going now?" Bai Huang asked. "It will be difficult to hide with a young child and an old woman at her side."

Yue-ying smoothed back the doll's hair with her thumb. It was black and silken, cut from a lock of real hair.

"I know where she's going." Yue-ying raised her voice so Zhou Dan could hear her from the driver's seat. "Take us to the Pingkang li."

CHAPTER TWENTY-TWO

YUE-YING STEPPED DOWN from the carriage the moment it came to a stop before the Lotus Palace. Bai Huang caught up with her as she reached the front doors, which had been propped open to welcome in the breeze.

"Yue-ying, you've returned!" Little Hong, the young courtesan-in-training, was the first to meet her in the entrance hall. Apparently she had taken on the new role of welcoming guests.

"Where's Madame Sun?"

The inquiry wasn't necessary. Madame appeared at once, resplendent in silk and jade and ready to greet the Emperor himself should he arrive.

"Dear girl, have you heard from Mingyu finally?" she asked.

A faint worry line appeared between her eyes. She was quite convincing. Until now, Yue-ying had over-looked that Madame Sun was a celebrated courtesan back in her day. She knew how to play to an audience.

"I haven't heard from Mingyu," Yue-ying replied calmly. "And you know why, Madame."

The headmistress's gaze narrowed on her before re-suming a mildly pleasant expression. "I am not certain what you mean, but we've missed you. No need to stand here by the door—come inside for tea."

Yue-ying shot a glance to Bai Huang before they fol-lowed Madame down the corridor. As with her last visit, all of the parlors appeared to be filled with patrons. Madame brought them to the back of the house into one of the smallest sitting rooms before closing the door.

"The Lotus appears quite popular in Mingyu's absence," Yue-ying remarked. "Perhaps scandal is good for business."

"Oh, enough!" Madame snapped, her civility tossed aside. She looked Bai Huang over before turning back to Yue-ying. "Mingyu isn't here. I don't know where she's gone to."

"There's no need to lie, Madame. When I saw that Mingyu hadn't taken any of her money, I suspected she hadn't gone far. What I didn't realize until now was that Mingyu never left the Lotus Palace. She has been hiding here the entire time."

Madame fell silent. She clutched her silk handkerchief and dabbed it beneath her eyes. "What nonsense is this?"

"Madame was the one who first reported Mingyu missing," Yue-ying pointed out. "You ran out practically into the street, distraught, so everyone could see. This was immediately before Constable Wu came to arrest her."

"Foolish girl, I have been searching everywhere for my darling Mingyu. She was my favorite."

"And your highest earner," Bai Huang interrupted. "But while you were wailing all over the quarter that she had run away, Magistrate Li had a warrant out for her arrest. This must have brought in many curious patrons. With five other courtesans to entertain in her absence, Mingyu's disappearance was probably quite profitable."

Bai Huang's presence was undeniably useful. With him there, she didn't appear to be challenging Madame Sun directly.

"You make it sound as if I staged her disappearance out of greed." Madame Sun sniffed at him. "Evading the constable has only made matters worse for her. And why would I risk the magistrate's wrath as well?"

"This started long before the arrest warrant. Earlier this month Mingyu claimed to have gone on an outing to the hot springs with General Deng." Yue-ying directed her explanation to Bai Huang. "Mingyu's time belongs to Madame Sun. For her to be away as long as she was, the general would have had to pay a substantial sum each day for her companionship. But there was no General Deng and no payment. Madame had to have known what Mingyu was doing and allowed it."

The headmistress sank onto the settee. "I would have told you where Mingyu was as soon as Constable Wu was no longer skulking about, but by then you were under his protection." She tilted her head toward Bai Huang. "Mingyu said it was better that way, for everyone. So I said nothing."

"Your plan worked well, for a time," he acknowledged. "But everything is unraveling. We want to see Lady Mingyu immediately. Constable Wu is the least of her concerns. A gang of bandits may also be hunting for her. We believe they also killed Huilan."

The headmistress paled. "So much death and misfortune. Mingyu has always been a good foster daughter to me. When she said she needed help, I trusted her."

"Then tell us where she is," he urged.

Madame shook her head. "I was speaking the truth. Mingyu was here, but she left yesterday and…and I don't think she's coming back."

Her lip trembled as she pressed the handkerchief to her eyes. Yue-ying and Bai Huang were left looking down at the older woman as she huddled there, trying to compose herself. Whether or not it was an act, it was a pitiful sight.

Bai Huang lowered himself beside Madame Sun until they were eye to eye. "I want to help her," he said in a steady tone meant to soothe and reassure. "Do you know where she could have taken the child?"

The sniffling stopped and Madame looked up from her handkerchief, startled. "Child? What child is this?"

"Mother!" Little Hong came flying into the room. "Come outside quickly."

The four of them hurried through the front door. A small crowd had gathered along the street and Bai Huang pushed his way through as he pulled Yue-ying alongside him.

A lone figure stood in the lane, surrounded on either side by pleasure houses and wine shops. Mingyu was wearing red, made more startling by the pale appearance of her face and hands. Black hair fell loose from its combs and pins and the effect was one of careless elegance rather than dishevelment. Without cosmetics, her lips appeared colorless and her eyes endlessly black. Pedestrians stepped aside nervously as she passed by.

Some whispered she was a vengeful ghost and scurried from her path, but it was just an effect of the afternoon shadow cast off the Lotus.

"Mingyu!" Yue-ying started to go to her, but Constable Wu appeared at the end of the lane with his sword at his belt. Two assistants flanked him.

Mingyu had chosen that red dress and had planned this dramatic appearance at the heart of the Three Lanes. She didn't want to be found crouching in some corner as a fugitive. She wanted to appear like an empress. Mingyu didn't move as the constable approached. She stood with her head held high and let Wu come to her.

Mingyu was as tall and graceful as a willow, but the constable still towered over her. She didn't tremble as she faced him though her face was bloodless.

"I hear you are looking for me, Constable Wu." Her voice carried over the murmur of the crowd.

Wu stared at the defiant set of her chin. He didn't waste any words in his answer.

"I am."

Constable Wu didn't put Mingyu in chains as he led her out of the Three Lanes. He walked beside her, a stark figure in black beside Mingyu's slender silhouette in red. A wave of whispering traveled through the crowd.

Who is she? What is happening?

She is one of the famous Four Beauties of the Pingkang li. She killed a man.

Mingyu walked facing forward, never looking right or left or back at the sullen constable who escorted her. The crowd remained in a hush until she had disappeared from sight, presumably led to the magistrate.

"I have to talk to her," Yue-ying said to Bai Huang.

With one arm settled protectively at the small of her back, he shoved his way through the crowd. Constable Wu and Mingyu disappeared into the judicial compound before they could reach them. Two armed guards immediately moved into position, spears crossed to block the entrance.

"Stand aside," Bai Huang demanded. "We have an audience with Magistrate Li Yen."

She marveled at how easily and insolently he gave commands to armed guardsmen, but they were unmoved.

"Get back."

The warning was barked not only to them, but at the crowd forming behind them, curious to know more about the beautiful and tragic woman who had dramatically given herself up to the head constable. Yue-ying was jostled from behind, leading Bai Huang to close his arm around her again.

He pulled her aside, away from the crowd. The yamen wall loomed high beside them. "I need to speak to my father."

"What can he possibly do?"

"His rank is higher than the magistrate's. There must be some way he can help." His expression was grim. "I have to try."

"You would do that?"

"Yue-ying." He sounded hurt that she would even doubt it. "Come with me. We don't have much time."

She shook her head. "I can't leave Mingyu." He hesitated, but she wouldn't waver. "You go. I'll stay and find a way inside."

He gave her hand a reassuring squeeze before hurrying away from the yamen. Yue-ying made her way back to the gates. The crowd had dissipated as there was no spectacle to keep them, but the guards remained at the front.

"My sister is in there," she told them. "Tell the magistrate I won't leave until I'm allowed to see her."

She sank to her knees dramatically before the gate, prepared to wait all day and night if she had to. One of the guards left to relay the message and she prayed. Magistrate Li had called on Mingyu in the past. He had held the banquet on the double fifth in her honor; he had to show some sign of mercy.

It was the surly Constable Wu, not the magistrate, who appeared at the gate an hour later. By then, Yue-ying's knees were sore and her legs had started to go numb. He looked down his nose at her, his height even more intimidating when she was on the ground.

"Come."

He turned away before she could struggle to her feet. Wu was already halfway across the courtyard and she rushed to catch up with his long stride. As soon as she was beside him, he spoke again.

"Lady Mingyu refuses to answer my questions."

"She'll talk to me," Yue-ying assured him, though she couldn't be certain of it.

"In Suzhou, I was known for being able to elicit a confession from the most hardened of criminals." He looked down at her once more. His nose appeared long and sharp from that angle, like a bird of prey. "I do not wish to use such techniques here."

His words chilled her blood. Wu took her down a long corridor to the back of the compound while her heart pounded harder and faster with each step.

His conduct toward Mingyu out in the street had appeared courteous, but his restrained manner had nothing to do with kindness or manners. The man was without emotion. He felt no joy or triumph in apprehending a criminal, just as he felt no pleasure in beating a confession out of Mingyu. But he would do it all the same.

The corridor led to a smaller courtyard surrounded by several smaller buildings. Armed guards were posted before each set of doors, which were locked with heavy chains. Despair took hold of Yue-ying when she realized this was the prison area. Mingyu was to be kept in one of these foreboding cells until her trial.

Wu unlocked the chain in front of one of the sets of double doors, then held the door open until Yue-ying came forward. The air inside was stagnant. There were no windows and the only light came from vents cut high toward the ceiling. It took a moment for her eyes to adjust.

Mingyu sat on a bench behind iron bars. Her hands were folded in her lap and her expression was blank. The cell was not even the size of her dressing room. There was straw laid out on the floor and a bucket in the corner.

As soon as Mingyu saw her she stood and came forward. "Yue-ying."

Yue-ying clasped her sister's hand through the bars and held on tight. The rough metal bit into her cheek as she tried to get as close as she could.

"Why did you leave me?" she whispered, angry and relieved at once. "I was so afraid."

"I had to," Mingyu said sadly. Gone was the cool, distant expression she'd worn out in the street. "I had to."

"You have to tell them everything that happened. There had to be some reason you did what you did."

Mingyu glanced behind Yue-ying. "There's nothing to tell."

Constable Wu remained at the door, making no sound. Yue-ying had almost forgotten about him. He was a black spider as Bai Huang had described, utterly still and ready to snatch up his prey in his jaws.

"Listen to me." Mingyu brought Yue-ying's attention back. "I don't regret anything. I did what had to be done."

"That banquet on the pleasure boat. You sent me away because you knew something would happen."

"Huilan was upset," Mingyu explained. "She had overheard two men talking during the banquet. The traders discussed a precious commodity being held in a boat nearby, but she knew they were not speaking of goods.

She couldn't stand by and do nothing." She paused and glanced momentarily away. "I couldn't either."

"The stranger in the canal—"

"Deserved his fate."

Yue-ying flinched at the venom in Mingyu's response. "Magistrate Li will have you tried for murder. If the man attacked you or if he was an outlaw, then the magistrate might take that into consideration. You have to tell him everything."

Mingyu shook her head. "It doesn't matter. Huilan is dead and I must bear this burden alone. It's better this way."

Yue-ying wanted to reach through the bars and shake her. Why was she being so stubborn? What was she still hiding?

"Is it because of the child?"

Immediately, Mingyu's gaze shuttered. She was distant again, retreating within herself. "Lord Bai Huang," she said finally. "I saw him beside you today, out on the street."

"Lord Bai is a good man. He's gone to his father to see if he can petition the magistrate."

Mingyu didn't hear any of it. "Go with him. You must make him fall in love with you. Find out what he wants most and use it to keep him. It's not so hard, Little Sister."

She couldn't believe it. Mingyu was trying to give her advice on how to seduce Bai Huang while her very life was in danger.

"He cares for you," Mingyu went on. "And I can't watch over you any longer. If I know you're taken care of and that the girl is safe, then I can be at peace whatever happens."

A knock on the door interrupted the conversation.

They sat on the filthy floor with the cold, hard iron between them, holding on to each other as if the demons of hell would tear them apart.

Wu came to stand over them. "Magistrate Li will be arriving shortly to question Lady Mingyu. It is time for Miss Yue-ying to leave."

Yue-ying didn't want to weep or wail in front of this man. She sensed that he had no tolerance for weakness, but strength he at least respected. "Let me stay. I can convince her to speak."

"No. You need to go," Mingyu insisted. She looked to Wu. "Take her out of here, Constable. I don't want her in this place."

He was taken aback by Mingyu's imperious tone. There was a pause before he spoke again. "Miss Yue-ying, I do not wish to use force."

He said it with the same unapologetic tone he'd used to warn her that he was not above beating a confession out of Mingyu. She squeezed Mingyu's hand one last time and pressed her lips to it. "I'll return, I promise. I'll do everything I can to get you out of here."

She stood before Wu could take hold of her. It was hard for her not to look back as he led her outside and locked the door once more. Before she left, she met Constable Wu's eyes and tried to follow Mingyu's example.

"Take care of her," she implored.

His jaw clenched and his eyes were unreadable, but she thought she saw something that might have been a nod.

CHAPTER TWENTY-THREE

HUANG SOUGHT HIS father out at the Ministry of Defense, bypassing the petitioners to be brought directly to a private office in the interior of the building. His father sat at his desk, wearing an indigo robe and silk cap, which indicated his elevated rank. He had a brush in hand and was writing a letter as Huang approached.

"Father." He bowed respectfully. "I must ask something of you. This is an urgent matter."

"Another urgent matter?" Father asked, unblinking.

His father didn't need to raise his voice or issue threats to be intimidating. Huang took in a breath and forged on. "Magistrate Li has arrested a courtesan for the death of an unidentified man, but she's innocent. The man who was killed was likely a smuggler involved in the illegal slave trade."

"I don't see what I can do in this situation. The magistrate is fully within rights to do what he sees fit."

"If Father can urge Magistrate Li for leniency or for him to hold back on his decision, then I'll have time to track down this gang of outlaws."

His father set down his brush and exhaled slowly. "Huang, I was concerned when you came to me about the cargo ship."

"But we did manage to uncover illegal activity at that port."

"The Ministry of Defense does not bother with the

capture of petty thieves. There are other offices for that." He tapped his knuckles impatiently. "I cannot interfere with the magistrate's decision. This appears to be your personal quest and I would lose face if I became involved. *We* would lose face," he emphasized, reminding Huang that his actions reflected on their entire family.

"This is a matter of justice," he insisted.

Father rubbed a hand over his beard, his frown deepening. "The only crime I see here is of the wrongful death of a laborer. This courtesan, though perhaps popular in the Pingkang li, possesses little merit to warrant a pardon."

"It would be a different matter if she was a noblewoman from a good family."

"But she is not," Father countered and there was nothing that could be said to refute it. He leaned back in his chair, hands clasped thoughtfully before him. At first Huang thought Father was reconsidering his request, but apparently he was occupied by another thought. "Does the accused have any relation to the woman who is currently living in your quarters?"

Huang stopped short. He hadn't made any effort to hide his association with Yue-ying, but he was surprised that Father would make note of it. Then again, his father had ordered him watched back in Fujian. Apparently he had continued to do so in the capital.

He squared his shoulders as if readying for battle. "Was it Wei-wei or Zhou Dan who told you?"

"I see that I am not mistaken."

"You still don't trust me, Father."

"I do trust you, Huang." Father stood from his desk, exhaling sharply. "It is not uncommon to have affairs or to take a mistress during this time in your life, but it is your responsibility to know your limits. You have become too deeply involved in the scandals of the pleasure quarter."

"As you and I had planned," Huang challenged.

Father shook his head at the spark of defiance. "You will cease this investigation and end this affair immediately."

"I apologize, Father, but I cannot do that." There was no retreating now. He might as well wager everything he had. "I want Yue-ying to be my wife."

"It is hardly appropriate for you to take a concubine at this time."

"Not a concubine. My wife."

Father paused, as if gathering strength for a counterattack, but all he said was, "You've forgotten yourself."

Picking up his brush, he made as if the conversation was finished.

"She's loyal," Huang argued, refusing to be dismissed so easily. "She's clever."

With a sigh, Father set the brush back down and regarded him calmly. "She's a prostitute."

He met his father's gaze without wavering. "We belong to one another."

Huang knew what he was proposing was unconventional, even scandalous, but whatever Yue-ying had been in the past, she was his now. He wouldn't throw her aside even at his father's command.

All of his passion was wasted. Father shook his head, refusing to engage in the debate enough to even become angry.

"Impossible." His next words were issued with the solemnity of an oath. "Huang, if you insist on doing this, you are no longer my son."

HUANG LEFT THE administrative sector in a dark mood. Even in their worst moments, Father had never threatened to disown him. He walked through the streets at a demanding pace, hoping the physical exertion would be enough to clear his head.

In the past, he had gambled himself into debt and became entangled with crooked money-lenders, but those were apparently wrongs that could be forgiven. An arranged marriage was an agreement between families. To break an arrangement would bring the entire family's honor into question. He should have known better. It wasn't done.

It was exactly as Yue-ying had foretold, and he was just as blind and idealistic as she'd accused him of being. Their affair was assumed to be a momentary infatuation, an indiscretion of his youth. But he'd engaged in liaisons before and he knew in his soul, in the very marrow of his bones, that what he felt for Yue-ying was different.

She was clever without the benefit of flowery words. Brave without the benefit of strength. Generous without the benefit of wealth. Yue-ying was true and honest, and thus could see the truth when no one else could. She had seen him, while others were distracted by his wealth and the spectacle of himself he'd deliberately created.

He spent the next half hour wandering in the direction of the Pingkang li, trying to figure out what to do about Mingyu and cursing himself for bringing the subject of Yue-ying to his father in such a clumsy fashion. Father was a man of logic. He should have spent more time composing a solid argument before trying to open a discussion.

A figure stepped into his path, and Huang snapped out of his reverie, all senses alert.

"You can stop reaching for your knife," Gao said with a half smile.

For a moment, Huang thought that his gambler's affliction had dragged him unknowingly back to the gambling dens, but they were in a residential area just outside of the East Market.

"Why are you here?" Huang demanded, keeping his knife close at hand. It was still daylight and a steady flow of traffic filled the street, but none of that meant he was safe if Gao was there to kill him.

"Don't worry, friend. I came to find you because you never returned for the information you paid for. I could have simply taken your money but—" his grin showed a row of white, even teeth "—I'm an honest businessman."

Gao fell into step beside him and assumed an outward appearance of friendship. "Those rats who were sent to bully you were hired hands, pulled off the street. They were only ordered to frighten you, not bring you any harm."

"How do you know that?"

"The money offered wasn't nearly enough to attack a favored son such as yourself."

Which reminded him of how much money Gao must have accepted to leave him bleeding in the street.

"Do you know who hired them?"

Gao shook his head. "Whoever did it was very careful. Those men weren't from the local gangs."

One of them had referred to Yue-ying as a half-moon whore, a name she had thought she'd left behind when she was taken from the brothel.

"They were from the South Market area," he guessed.

Gao looked surprised at his sudden intuition. "It's possible. How did you know?"

He shrugged. "A guess. We've uncovered some illicit activity in the quarter with smugglers and slave traders—vermin who kidnap young girls to sell them off," Huang told him.

"It's a common practice, here as well as throughout the empire. Most officials choose to overlook it."

The sideways glance that Gao shot at him clearly marked him as one of the blissfully ignorant.

"No glory in catching petty smugglers," Huang muttered bitterly beneath his breath. The upper levels of government cared nothing about this business of the streets. His father was right: this was a personal quest. He had to see it through to the end.

He turned his attention back to Gao. "There was a child who was taken from the slave traders. She's been hidden somewhere close."

"That's interesting. There was someone looking for a child quite recently."

"The kidnappers want the child back?"

Gao's mouth turned downward. "Or they want her silenced. Same as that courtesan of yours who was strangled at the Hundred Songs."

Someone didn't want to be exposed. Perhaps the city officials tended to overlook certain crimes in the city, but there was a newly appointed magistrate and head constable as well as a new Emperor on the throne. Whoever was in charge of this ring was intent on keeping things the way they had been.

"This involves someone with influence. Someone who has been profiting from this for a long time." Huilan and Mingyu must have discovered his activities, but Huilan was dead now. Huang rubbed a hand over his temple. "I need to find the missing girl. She's in danger."

"I might be able to help."

"I know." He shook his head in disgust. "For a price."

Considering the amount of money he kept paying out, no wonder Gao kept him alive. Huang supposed it was no worse than throwing his money away at the tables. Gao didn't care for the intricacies of honorable conduct or bureaucracy. He was focused simply and effectively on getting the job done, which was exactly what Huang needed at the moment. And who better to find a killer than another killer?

YUE-YING WAS SO lost in thought when she left the yamen that she didn't see Zhou Dan until he was right in front of her.

He dipped his head in a slight bow. "Miss Yue-ying."

She looked over to the carriage in the street. "Did Lord Bai ask you to wait for me?"

"He instructed me to take you safely home."

Zhou Dan helped her into the carriage before climbing into the driver's seat. There was always a mischievous glint in his eye even when he was making an effort to appear serious, as he was now. She liked him, though it felt uncomfortable to have him wait on her when they were both servants.

"Have you been with the Bai household very long?" she asked once they were on their way.

"From the day of my birth, miss," he replied over his shoulder. "My father works with the horses. Mother is in the kitchen."

"Then you and Lord Bai must have been children together." Zhou Dan looked to be about the same age as Bai Huang.

"Though we grew up in the same household, it might as well have been the sun and the moon. We all knew we weren't supposed to distract the young lord. Bai *Furen* was always strict about his education."

It was the first time she had heard of Bai Huang's mother. She imagined the wife of such a powerful man would be a formidable woman herself.

"You seem so familiar with one another. Almost like brothers," she prodded.

He laughed. "Lord Bai was always a cheerful, fun-loving sort. He would seek out all sorts of diversions, ways to escape for a few moments from his books. I was a wild sort myself, running about. I was kept outside, supposedly out of trouble, while the young Lord Bai was locked inside at his studies.

"One day, the elder Lord Bai accidentally left a long, thin case in the carriage. I was to return it to him, but became too curious. I was young and yearning for adventure and became convinced there was a sword in there. I had never held a sword before. So I stole into a corner of the garden to open the box. When I did, there was nothing but a scroll. I unrolled the entire thing and all that was written on it were five characters. I couldn't read them and was rather disappointed after all my excitement. At that point, I heard someone coming and quickly tried to roll the scroll up, but I was clumsy and the paper tore. I quickly put it back into the case and ran it to the study, hoping not to get caught. Young Lord Bai was there, so I shoved the box into his hands, saying nothing. Little did I know that scroll was worth a lot of money, more than what both my father and mother earned in a year, several years even. Imagine that, a strip of white paper with only five marks written on it!"

"How unfortunate!" she exclaimed in sympathy. "What happened then?"

"Well, young Lord Bai took the blame. We never played together, weren't even friends, but he admitted to ruining the scroll. What happened next was awful."

"Oh, my."

"His father gathered the entire household and struck him ten times with a bamboo switch before everyone. I felt like a dog the entire time while I watched, but once it started I was too afraid to admit my guilt. Afterward, I hid from his sight for days out of shame, but young Lord Bai sought me out. Do you know what he did?"

She shook her head, completely absorbed with the tale.

"He jumped on me and started punching me hard in the arm, saying, 'You scoundrel! I didn't think I was going to get beaten so badly.'"

Yue-ying erupted into laughter. "The noble hero indeed. Did you fight back?"

"Of course not! I knew I deserved it. Lord Bai took his revenge, which wasn't so bad since he hadn't been in any fights to really know how to hit hard, and we have been friends ever since."

She imagined Bai Huang as a restless boy bent over his books, but in his head always plotting escape. Even then he'd shown a sense of self-sacrifice, knowing the punishment for Zhou Dan would have been so much worse than his own.

By the time they returned to the residence, the afternoon was fading into the last slow hours before evening. Zhou Dan went to secure the horse and carriage off to the side of the house. Apparently, his instructions were to stay with her. Bai Huang was concerned for her safety, which was nearly as touching as his concern for Mingyu. He might be idealistic and caught up in notions of romance and heroism, but he was a good person at heart.

She wished she could be as blind as he was and accept his protection. He was wealthy, he was privileged and she had nothing without Mingyu. Certainly she owed him for all he had done for her. But the thought of obligation between them left her cold. She would be anyone else's servant but his. With Bai Huang, she wanted to believe she was more than she was, if only for a little while.

As Yue-ying headed to the kitchen to prepare a pot of tea for Zhou Dan she remembered that Bai Huang wasn't the only person who had offered her protection. Instead of the kitchen, she went to the bedchamber.

The past two nights had been spent there with Bai Huang, the first night in his arms and the second one pressed far to the opposite side of the bed, yet wanting him the entire time. She'd thought nothing more of the silver she'd tucked underneath.

She crouched and reached for the bundle hidden behind one of the wooden legs. It was small, fitting neatly into both of her palms, but heavy. A knot formed in her chest as she pulled the cloth aside.

When Taizhu had given the silver to her, she had been out on the street. One did not display wealth openly for fear of tempting thieves, so she had only taken a quick peek before stowing it away. And with Bai Huang's hospitality, she had little need for silver. She had hoped if things ended well, she could leave the silver for him to repay his generosity.

She knew it was a stupid gesture. Bai Huang didn't need her money and the thought of her actually paying someone like him would have made even the humorless Constable Wu laugh.

Picking up one of the silver ingots, she recalled Wu Kaifeng's explanation in the record room. There were five taels of silver in there and they were all the same. The rectangular tablets were inscribed with a flower, a design she had seen at the magistrate's yamen. She covered up the silver and tucked the stash back beneath the bed before rushing out.

Zhou Dan had just entered the courtyard when she intercepted him and bade him to turn back around. "I need you to take me somewhere else."

"But it will be dark before long."

"Then we must go quickly."

He obliged her without further argument, as if she were a well-born lady instead of a woman of the street. The poor horse was given only a moment's rest before he was untethered and hitched back onto the carriage. Soon they were once more on the road, this time traveling past the markets and farther north to the grand residences adjacent to the imperial city.

She had known of Taizhu's background, though he preferred not to speak of it. His family was involved in commerce, considered lowly by the aristocracy. They were wealthy merchants. It was possible they engaged in money-lending in Yangzhou, molding their silver into ingots stamped with the city flower.

By the time the carriage stopped before a modestly sized house, the last of the daylight had faded. The house was surrounded by a wall and there was a wooden placard over the front gate painted with what Yue-ying assumed must have been Taizhu's name and official title.

Zhou Dan stepped down from the carriage and moved to help her, holding his arm out. No one met them at the front when she rang the bell, but the gate wasn't locked. When they entered the courtyard, the house was eerily quiet around them. Yue-ying considered for a moment that it had been abandoned, but she spied a light flickering from the interior.

"Xueshi?" she called out, using the honorific reserved for academics.

"Miss Yue-ying?" Taizhu's broad-shouldered form appeared beneath the shadow of the portico. He beckoned her forward.

"Mingyu was arrested." She rarely spoke to the scholar outside of Mingyu's presence and she hoped her directness wouldn't be taken as impolite. "She's being kept in the prison house and refuses to speak in her own defense."

His head was bare of its usual scholar's cap and his gray hair was combed back and fixed with a wooden pin. He spared Zhou Dan a quick glance before returning to her.

"Let us speak inside."

His tone was grave. Zhou Dan remained by the door as the old historian led her through a beaded curtain into the parlor. Unlike the rest of the house, the room was warmly lit with yellow lanterns, which allowed her to appreciate the elegant furnishings. A painted screen separated out the sitting area and a long scroll decorated one wall, adorned with a few simple characters written in bold brushstrokes against a stark background of white. It was a room worthy of a distinguished scholar.

Taizhu seated her on the settee before bending over a tray to prepare tea. His hands moved with ease, scooping leaves into the bottom of the cups, lifting the clay pot with one hand to pour the hot water, the other hand holding back the length of his sleeve. Even his house robe was opulently cut.

"These are the finest leaves," he began. "A tribute tea from the Mengshan Mountain region, gifted by the imperial court."

He placed the two cups onto the table with lids covering them to allow the leaves to steep. His manner was polite and solicitous. It was strange enough to have such a gentleman exchanging pleasantries with her and, due to his venerable status, she found it difficult to interrupt his tea ritual even though a burning question hovered on her lips.

After a few moments had passed, he made a gesture inviting her to drink. She sipped obediently, using the lid to hold back any floating leaves.

"I understand that you and Mingyu are very close," he said.

"Yes, sir."

"You're worried about her, of course."

Taizhu seemed to be meditating over his cup. She noticed a slight tremor in his hands as he set the tea back down untouched.

"*Xueshi*, there was a banquet a little over a month ago held on a pleasure boat in the Grand Canal. Mingyu and Huilan were in attendance. You know what happened to them that night, don't you?"

His gaze lifted sharply before dropping back to his hands, which he rested over his knees. Finally, he let out a long sigh. "I feel like I must apologize. You see, I come from somewhat humble beginnings. My family line wasn't one of distinguished scholars and academicians. We are merchants, as you may know."

She nodded as an invitation for him to continue.

"Not merely merchants. What I mean to say is that we were privateers. Generations of my family became wealthy through trade, but not all of our activities were strictly sanctioned by the government. We made connections in Changan that allowed me to study in the academies of the capital and take the palace exams. I passed in the top tier the first time I took them, ranked third out of the entire class," he boasted before his expression darkened. "I worked harder than any of the aristocrats with their tutors and expensive connections, yet even now there are still insinuations that my family bought my degree. That my position in the Hanlin Academy came about through bribes."

Yue-ying cast about, uncomfortable with the impassioned nature of his confession. She hadn't seen anyone but Taizhu in the entire house.

"Where are your servants?" she asked, her shoulders tensing.

"I sent them away. It's best that they not be here to witness my shame. All of my achievements, everything I've worked for gone because of a moment's impulse. At first, I thought I could continue as if nothing had happened, but I can see now that's impossible."

An awful realization came to her as to why he was acting so strangely. She had come there thinking he'd known about what Huilan and Mingyu had done. They had confided in him and he'd given Huilan silver to help her leave the city. Now Taizhu was sounding as if he was much closer to the crime.

The words were out of her mouth before she could stop them. "Did you kill Huilan?"

"No! What gave you that impression? I killed that vermin, that slave trader. Mingyu stabbed at him and I dragged him to the water. I held him under until he stopped moving."

"But—"

"What, you don't believe me?" He was in a fervor now, puffing out his chest and thumping it loudly. "I was a fair wrestler in my day."

"You were with Mingyu and Huilan that night?"

"I killed a man with these two hands." He held them out and stared at them as if they belonged to someone else.

It was the historian who had taken the stranger's life. Her blood heated. "Mingyu kept silent to protect you? You're a man of rank and status while Mingyu is nothing, and yet you hide behind her? You have to confess."

His shoulders sank and some of the bravado drained from him. "I know what I must do, but you have to understand why it took me so long. These same hands passed the palace exams, the first ever in my family."

He slumped over his chair with a hand over his face. Despite his sharp tongue, he had always been kind and generous to Mingyu.

"You were very brave that night," she said, her tone gentle. "I know you will do the honorable thing now."

He nodded slowly, running a hand over his robe to straighten it. "Mingyu made me swear to take care of the child. She thought to turn herself over to the magistrate and protect my name so that the girl would be safe, but what man allows such a sacrifice and says nothing? I've been a coward. I must give the child over to you."

"The girl is here?"

A loud noise came from the courtyard, and then the sounds of struggle.

"Miss! Run—"

Zhou Dan's cry came from outside, cut off by a harsh grunt and the sound of something heavy hitting the ground.

Two figures burst in through the curtain, ripping through the strings of beads. Taizhu shot to his feet and threw up his arm, catching one intruder across the chest and sending him to the floor. He grappled with the second man, wrapping his arms around the man's torso and hefting him up with a startling display of strength for a gray-haired academic.

Yue-ying shrank back, too stunned to move. A blade

flashed within the struggle and Taizhu slumped over. The blow had been soundless, the consequence unfathomably quick.

The intruders turned and her instincts came to life. Yue-ying grabbed at her teacup and flung the contents into the face of the closest attacker. By now, the tea was only warm, but it was enough to startle him.

There was no time to think. She didn't dare look back as she struggled to her feet. Grabbing on to the painted screen at the edge of the room, she shoved it toward her attackers before running for the corridor. From behind her came the sound of crashing wood and the tear of silk.

Her heart pounded as she stared down the hallway. The house was a maze and she was trapped inside it. She ran away from the light in the parlor, hoping to hide in the darkness. A doorway appeared just around the corner and she ducked inside.

The chamber was dark, but she heard a sound from the far corner, almost like the whimper of a kitten. Yue-ying approached slowly and saw a small figure crouched behind a trunk.

Yue-ying knelt down beside her. "I'm a friend."

Two small arms wrapped around her neck and held on tight. From her size, the girl couldn't be more than six or seven years old.

"What's your name?"

Yue-ying had to repeat it twice in a whisper before the girl replied, "Hana."

From what Yue-ying could make of the room, there wasn't much inside. Nothing that could be used as a weapon and few places to hide. Hana trembled as footsteps echoed through the hall. Yue-ying tried to soothe her, holding the child tight though she was shaking hard herself. They were cornered and sooner or later they would be found.

"Hana, you need to try to get away and get help. Do you understand?"

There was no reply. Hana held on to her neck and murmured something unintelligible in the darkness. She had been brought here from some distant province and probably understood very little of the dialect of the capital.

Yue-ying knew why Mingyu had needed to rescue this child. Yue-ying had been only a few years older than this girl when she had been brought to the city, lost and confused and just as frightened.

Gently, she freed herself from Hana's arms and spoke slowly, hoping the girl would understand enough.

"Run," she said, pointing to the door. "Run and find the city guards."

Hana finally nodded, her hair brushing Yue-ying's cheek. Hopefully, she was small and quick. It was the only chance they had.

Yue-ying stood and led them toward the door. Her head was throbbing and blood pumped hot through her veins. The sound of footsteps outside stole her breath. Flattening herself against the wall, she positioned the girl behind her.

The door opened. Yue-ying launched herself at whoever came through and the man staggered behind her full weight.

She couldn't see whether Hana had escaped or not. All she knew was that this was the fight of her life. She turned her hands into claws to rake at the intruder's eyes and face. Strong hands grabbed her and shoved her aside, cursing and calling her a she-demon.

Yue-ying recovered and scrambled toward the door

on hands and knees. Suddenly her head was yanked back. She was hauled out into the corridor like a sack of rice. Her ankle banged against the door as she struggled to get away, but the man tightened his hold on her hair until tears gathered in her eyes. All she could do was hang on as she was dragged back to the parlor.

Her attacker dumped her onto the floor beside the broken screen. Taizhu lay unmoving near the tea table.

"It's the red-faced whore," came the sneering remark.

When Yue-ying glanced up, she stared into a pair of glittering black eyes framed by thick eyebrows. He was a stranger, but in her heart she knew he wouldn't hesitate to kill her.

"Where is the child?" he demanded.

Yue-ying feigned a look of confusion and shook her head. He crouched beside her and gripped her chin to tilt her face upward. His beard was trimmed to a sharp point and the lines along his mouth were so deep they looked as if they had been carved with a knife. The look in his eyes was predatory, piercing through her as if she were nothing.

Was this the face Huilan had looked upon as she'd breathed her last?

Two men returned to stand behind him. When she saw that they were empty-handed, hope lit in her chest, but it died quickly.

"Let us be done with this."

The leader held up his hand and his minion placed a knife in it. Yue-ying started distancing herself from what was happening, something she'd learned to do to survive in the brothel, but this time she forced herself back, away from the numbness. If this breath was to be her last, she wanted to feel everything. She thought of her sister. Of Bai Huang. Of how brief everything had been.

It will be over soon. She started to close her eyes, but caught a flicker of movement beneath the settee and the tiny shape of a hand within the shadows. Hana was attempting to wriggle out the other side.

"They know about you," she piped up, trying to keep the bandit distracted. "The constable knows you strangled Huilan. He'll come for you."

The bearded man regarded her with a look of disbelief. Then his mouth curved into a cold smile. "Who is Huilan?"

CHAPTER TWENTY-FOUR

GAO SUGGESTED THEY search in the taverns and brothels along the docks. The two of them quickly established a system; Gao asked the questions and Huang provided bribe money should it be required. After an hour, they found out who had been searching for a missing child and traced the inquiries back to the captain of a small boat.

The ship had been docked and left unmanned except for a single watch. Gao was able to persuade the look-out at knifepoint to reveal where the rest of the crew had gone and they set off toward a residential ward to the north.

The sun had set by then and the streets of the ward were relatively empty. The empty carriage in the street raised Huang's suspicions. They hurried over and Huang confirmed that it was indeed the Bao family carriage as well as their horse. The placard over the gate had been carved with Taizhu's name.

Bai Huang scanned the area around the house. "Something is wrong here."

He drew his weapon from beneath his sleeve and tried the gate. It opened to a dark and silent house, but there was movement beneath the portico.

"Who's there?" Huang gripped his knife, holding the weapon close to his body.

Zhou Dan staggered into the pale moonlight with the

side of his face dark with blood. He held up his hand to ward them off as a high-pitched shriek came from within the buildings. It was the cry of a child.

As he and Gao started toward the interior, a little girl ran past Zhou Dan into the courtyard. Huang caught her with one arm as she rushed into him. The girl was fine-boned and delicate in appearance with wide, captivating eyes. This must have been the child that Mingyu was hiding. The girl started babbling in dialect, but he couldn't make sense of her other than that she was frightened.

"The lady!" she cried finally and pointed. "The lady, the lady!"

Yue-ying. His stomach plummeted.

Zhou Dan stumbled over and Huang handed the girl to him. "Get her out of here."

Two men emerged from the house and Gao faced off against them. A quick flash of steel was met with a scream. One of the bandits staggered blindly with a hand pressed to his eye.

"Go." Gao held two knives now, one in each hand, as he faced the remaining bandit.

Huang maneuvered past them into the interior of the house. What he saw made his blood run cold.

Yue-ying was on her knees. A bearded man had her by the hair. Her head was pulled back cruelly with a knife pressed against the pale skin of her throat and the fragile veins beneath. All it would take was one swipe of his wrist.

"Stop!" Huang growled.

The man looked up and he pressed the knife tighter against Yue-ying's throat in warning. Huang had faced this sort before. The outlaw was intent on spilling blood and negotiation was pointless. He was too late.

Yue-ying's gaze flickered to him and Huang saw everything in her eyes. He felt everything in his heart. Blood surged to his muscles. Desperately, he lunged forward, forgetting his knife as he threw his full weight behind the attack.

Another figure rose from the floor to grab the bandit around the knees just before Huang crashed into him. They were all thrown into a heap while Yue-ying was knocked aside. Huang could only spare her a glance before a blade slashed at him. He twisted away, avoiding the knife, but ending with his back to the ground. The bearded man loomed over him.

Huang struck upward and felt the hard crack of bone against his knuckles. From there, it was a struggle, instinct and emotion over skill. A hand grappled for his knife. Nails raked across his face, catching his eye. The pain blinded him, but he wrestled his way on top of his opponent and started punching. Once he connected against flesh and bone, he reared back and swung again, each blow propelled by rage.

Only when he heard a loud voice calling his name did Huang realize the body beneath him had gone limp. He stared down at the slaver, whose nose was bloodied and broken. His eyes were shut, his mouth slack. It was the face of a coward. A killer of women.

Huang finally looked up to see Gao standing over him, knife in hand. The blade was dull with blood.

"I never realized what you were capable of, Lord Bai," he remarked in a tone that might have bordered on respect.

Huang looked about the room, his head turning in a daze. Taizhu was sprawled on the floor, but his eyes were open. Yue-ying was on her knees nearby with her hand clutched to her throat. Their eyes met and his heart squeezed painfully. He had almost lost her.

He crawled over and gently pulled her hand away, holding on to it as he made sure she hadn't been cut. The pulse in her throat beat wildly. He was mad with the urge to press his lips to her neck to assure himself that she was alive and unharmed. Instead, he folded his arms around her as tight as he could, so tight that nothing could get to her, and held her like that for a long time.

EVERY TIME YUE-YING tried to concern herself with anything or anyone for the rest of the night, Bai Huang hushed her.

"Taizhu is wounded," she said.

"He will be taken care of."

"Those men—"

"Constable Wu and the city guards have taken them."

"And the child? Where's Hana?"

"She is safe. Enough now."

Bai Huang led her to a carriage. Zhou Dan sat opposite them. Despite his injury, he was grinning, proud to have survived such an adventure.

As they rode through the streets Bai Huang held on to her. She pressed close, willing the warmth of his body to pour into her and bring her back to life. Soon they were back in his quarters and secured in his bedchamber.

"But what about Mingyu—?"

"She will be fine. You've done everything you needed to do."

He settled her onto the bed and looked deep into her eyes.

"What about you?" she asked finally, barely able to find her voice.

He pressed his lips against her forehead in answer. Then placed a kiss over one eye and then the other. When he reached her mouth, he lingered. There was a quiet urgency in him she'd never experienced before. His mouth was hard, but his touch soft. She wanted to weep against him as she returned the kiss, her emotions a reflection of his.

He untied her sash and took the time to remove all her clothing so that she was completely bared to him. With the lanterns still burning, he undressed until there was nothing left between them. The hard lines of his body and the old wound beneath his ribcage told a story of him completely different than the one known in the North Hamlet. Yue-ying wanted to believe it was a story that only she knew.

Beneath his expensive clothing, Bai Huang wasn't dissolute and sheltered. He was fierce when pushed to it. Protective. When he eased himself into her, it was as if he belonged there, his body fitting inside her until there was no room in her heart or mind for anything else.

He began to move, stroking deep, gradually increasing the way he had discovered she liked.

There were no preliminaries, no soft caresses or whispered words. Though sensation built within her, the act wasn't as much about pleasure as it was about possession. Even when he took her breast into his mouth as her pleasure rose, it was an attempt to claim her further. His tongue rasped against her nipple until she wept and moaned. With each thrust of his hips, he was willing her climax, her surrender to him. And she did surrender, her muscles taut and straining until she thought she would break.

He remained deep inside her as he peaked, his eyes open and watching her face while he poured every bit of himself into her. So she would know he held nothing back.

"I want you always with me," he said a moment later.

They were both breathing hard, their skin damp with sweat, their limbs entangled in one another. She never wanted to move from the spot.

"Don't answer," he said when her lips parted. He stroked her cheek with his thumb and kissed her mouth possessively. "Don't say anything until I've convinced you."

Despite all his assurances, he was still full of restless energy. He had fulfilled his vow to Huilan and Mingyu was now safe, but something was still weighing on his mind. It had driven him during their lovemaking and turned her skilled and gentle lover into a creature of passion and desperation.

Yue-ying couldn't say anything. So much had happened that night that she deserved a moment of peace. She closed her eyes and inhaled the scent of his skin. His words of the past hour wrapped around her like a blanket as she drifted off.

Everything will be taken care of. You are safe. Enough now.

YUE-YING WAS AT the yamen as soon as the gates opened with Bai Huang at her side. They were forced to wait in the courtyard while Magistrate Li deliberated. His constables had arrested the gang of bandits the night before, while Taizhu, who had confessed to drowning the slave trader, was left at his mansion under watch.

"You needn't worry. The magistrate will have to release your sister now," Bai Huang told her, seeing how she paced.

Despite his assurances, Yue-ying didn't feel any relief until Wu emerged from the prison house with Mingyu before him. Her sister stumbled upon the uneven step, but when Wu reached out a hand to steady her, she tore out of his grasp and shot him a poisonous look. The constable's expression was unreadable as he gestured with his hand to indicate she was free to go.

Yue-ying rushed to her and they embraced wordlessly in the courtyard. Mingyu felt frail in her arms.

"Hana?" Mingyu asked, the very first word from her lips.

"She's safe. She's at the Lotus Palace."

Mingyu nodded. Her complexion was pale and her eyes appeared sunken. Even so, she was still beautiful: a fragile, tenuous beauty like the last blossom on a branch. Though she had only been in prison for a night, the experience had shaken her.

Bai Huang's shadow fell over them. "I brought a carriage," he offered.

Yue-ying was grateful for his thoughtfulness. The carriage was covered, shielding them from prying eyes. She and Mingyu seated themselves on one side with Bai Huang opposite them.

"Lord Bai, what happened to your face?" Mingyu asked.

The bruises from his scuffle the night before were beginning to show and a vicious scratch raked from the bridge of his nose over his left eye. He ran a hand absently over his chin.

"Ah, this? I can see why smugglers aren't the most handsome of men," he said with an attempt at humor. "It's hard to stay pretty after a fight."

Mingyu stared at him, saying nothing. Bai Huang cleared his throat and cast about for the next thing to say. Yue-ying almost felt sorry for him. She placed her hand over Mingyu's, feeling for the moment as if she and her older sister had traded places.

"He was very brave last night," Yue-ying said quietly.

Bai Huang met her gaze and a look passed between them that transcended all words. For a heartbeat, she was alone with him once more, naked and straining in his arms.

Stories of last night's skirmish were already floating through the quarter. An old historian and a young, foolhardy aristocrat defeated a bloodthirsty gang and managed to avenge the death of the beautiful Orchid of Silla. It was a glorious ending to a tragic story. The Pingkang li devoured the tale.

"Huilan wasn't from Silla, but rather from Shandong province in the east," he explained. "The province was settled by immigrants from the Kingdom of Silla. At one time, Sillan women were so prized as slaves that pirates would raid the coastal towns, kidnapping girls to sell at a high price. The imperial court enacted a law against the practice, but it didn't stop the pirates. The trade continued on the black market and prices increased. Hana must have been taken from Shandong as well."

"And once a child is alone and isolated, she's helpless," Mingyu murmured. "If it weren't for her value as a slave, she'd be left to starve."

They all fell silent. Yue-ying reached over to touch a hand to her sister's arm.

"I must be blind to have missed the resemblance," Bai Huang said with forced brightness, looking between the two of them. "Anyone can see you're sisters. The two most beautiful women in the Pingkang li."

Yue-ying fidgeted with her sleeve and wondered why he was reverting back to his flower-prince persona. Maybe he was that nervous.

Mingyu was too exhausted to be charming in return. "Thank you for taking care of my sister," she said simply, then laid her head against the frame of the carriage and closed her eyes.

When they reached the front of the Lotus, there was an awful moment of uncertainty. Bai Huang got out to help Mingyu from the carriage and then Yue-ying and Mingyu started together toward the door. Yue-ying turned back to see him still in the street, watching her with a question in his eyes.

So much had happened between them in the past few weeks. She had become his lover and companion. What else they were to each other, she didn't know.

They had held on to each other so fiercely last night. Bai Huang had demanded her complete surrender. They hadn't spoken of what would happen when morning came, but some unspoken promise had certainly been made. But it meant little right there, in the street. Mingyu was back now. Huilan's murderer had been caught and life would return to what it had been.

Bai Huang raised his hand in farewell and she returned the gesture absently, her thoughts too dulled to think of anything better. So polite after everything that they had shared. He retreated into the carriage and all she could do was watch it drive away, her heart in her throat.

Yue-ying followed Mingyu back into the familiar walls of the Lotus. There was so much activity and commotion that it was easy for Yue-ying to fade into the background once more.

Within days, Taizhu sent a long and impassioned petition to the newly crowned Emperor pleading his case. He refused to apologize for taking the life of a man who preyed on others. The divine Emperor brought the respected scholar before the throne to issue a pardon the same day the petition was presented. Bai Huang was a hero as well, though no one was quite certain how everyone's favorite fool happened to be in the right place at the right time to rescue the historian. Call it fate.

Then there was little Hana. She was startlingly pretty, even as a child. Her mouth was perfectly shaped like a cherry and her eyes were large and mysterious, the irises so light they were golden in color. Her hair had a reddish tint to it, similar to Huilan.

With features that were prized as exotic, it was heartbreakingly easy to see why Hana had been kidnapped by the slavers. Huilan and Mingyu would have seen themselves in this girl. Both of them had been marked by the curse of being beautiful.

Hana was staying with them at the Lotus. She was still timid, never venturing far from Mingyu or Yue-ying. She slept on Mingyu's bed and was gradually learning the dialect of the capital. They didn't push her for her story lest they dredge up bad memories, but it was easy to fit the pieces together. Her family was murdered by bandits just as Huilan's family had been.

Yue-ying fell back into her duties at the Lotus attending to Mingyu. They didn't speak in much detail about the killing of the slave trader or the events surrounding Huilan's death. Yue-ying wondered if they would merely return to what they were before, with so many things left unspoken, but the next morning a soft voice woke her up.

"I had to rescue her."

Her head was still foggy and it took a moment for Yue-ying to recognize Mingyu kneeling on the floor beside the pallet. Her sister was in her sleeping garment and her hands were resting on her knees. She looked so young with her hair tied in a single tail at the back.

"I had to save someone, because I was too late to save you."

"You did save me." Yue-ying rolled onto her side and rubbed at her eyes. "You brought me here. We're together."

Mingyu fell silent. Her sister had hidden herself for so long, playing a part. It was hard for her to be close to anyone, yet Yue-ying could see she was trying.

"I don't regret what I did, but if I hadn't stabbed that man, then Huilan might still be alive."

"You can't think that way. What's past is past," Yue-ying said soothingly.

"Huilan's entire family was murdered. The pirates spared her only to sell her. When she heard of a child whose parents had been killed, all of those memories came back. There are some things one cannot forget."

Mingyu bent her head. What was she remembering? The look on their mother's face before the two of them had been dragged onto the boat? Their parents had sold them for a few coins, but at least Yue-ying could imagine them alive somewhere. And she and Mingyu still had each other. Even when they were separated, Yue-ying had known Mingyu was somewhere in the city. She had kindled a small hope inside her that they would find one another someday.

"You sent me home from the banquet to protect me."

Mingyu nodded. "Taizhu arrived later that evening and when I told him what we knew, he joined the cause. We all convinced each other we were doing the noble and righteous thing, but the truth was all three of us were very afraid.

"After we followed the traders to the docks, we hid and deliberated what to do. If we waited to report to the magistrate the next morning, the smugglers would all be gone, but then the decision was made for us. Hana was huddled behind a crate on the dock. She had managed to escape.

"She looked so small and helpless. We managed to coax her out of hiding just as one of her captors appeared, demanding that we return her to him. I don't know what demon possessed me. I stabbed him when he tried to grab her and then there was no turning back. Taizhu took hold of him and held him beneath the water. The trader struggled for a long time before he stopped moving." Her eyes looked haunted. "And then the three of us were caught in it together."

"But why didn't you tell anyone when Huilan was strangled to death?"

Mingyu closed her eyes and a look of pain crossed her face. "It was then that we knew how dangerous those smugglers were. We had killed one of them and Taizhu had blood on his hands. I had to protect Hana, but I had to protect him as well."

As courtesans, Mingyu and Huilan were already accustomed to playing their part and keeping their secrets close.

"Lord Bai noticed from the beginning that Huilan was afraid to go to any of her patrons or even to Magistrate Li. He assumed whoever she was afraid of was very powerful."

"Every man has power over us," Mingyu said.

That was the hard truth of it. The realities of birth and status. Mingyu and Huilan might be revered within the confines of the Three Lanes, but they were women who were owned and kept. Their names were celebrated by merely a few lofty poets and gentlemen over cups of wine. Even Taizhu, who had been elevated to the Hanlin Academy, had been so afraid of the implications of his low birth that he had been afraid to come forward.

"If Lord Bai hadn't been so dedicated, this crime may never have been resolved."

"And you were so brave as well. The stories always forget that," Mingyu said warmly.

Yue-ying looked away. She wasn't used to such open praise, and certainly not from her sister.

"Why are you not with Lord Bai now?"

Her heart beat faster at the mention of his name. "My place is here with you. We were supposed to grow old together, remember?"

Her humor failed to amuse. "So I can become just like Madame Sun and you can be Auntie? There is no future for us here."

"Do you know Bai Huang is already betrothed? His family arranged it many years ago. How long do you think a man like Lord Bai could remain infatuated with a woman like me?" This was the first she'd dared to speak her fears aloud. The hopelessness of it sharpened into a palpable ache. "Sometimes I would rather he be a merchant or a tradesman. Then I could be more than his concubine."

"There are greater hardships than being a wealthy man's concubine."

"Even if his emotions were to remain true, what of his family? What happens when his wife won't tolerate sharing her husband with a concubine?"

"You don't know any of these things for certain," Mingyu soothed.

Yue-ying sat up, brushing her hair from her face in agitation. Mingyu had an answer for everything and it was infuriating.

"Why didn't you become General Deng's concubine when given the chance?" she countered.

Mingyu fell silent. A concubine who had been cast out had little choice but to return to a life in the pleasure houses or brothels—if she was still young and desirable enough.

"Lord Bai is different," her sister said finally. "I watched him for months trying to make a show of courting me, when all he could look at was you. I've seen how you look at him as well. What you and he share is…is something I know nothing about."

The wistfulness in Mingyu's tone startled her. Yue-ying had always thought Mingyu to be the more practical, the more cynical of the two of them. She had been wrong.

"It won't last forever," Yue-ying said sadly.

"Nothing lasts forever."

They sat together in the dimness of the room, with Mingyu trying so hard to push her away out of love for her. And out of hope for both of them.

Mingyu reached out to touch her arm. "I don't want Hana to remain at the Lotus Palace. I didn't free her so she could be trapped here, with her life decided for her. I don't want you to be chained here to me either."

She laid her head against Mingyu's shoulder. It was a rare moment, to be allowed so close.

"Yue-ying. Little Sister." Mingyu stroked her hair softly. "Life is fleeting and we will never know what tomorrow will bring. Go to Bai Huang and be happy for as long as you can."

CHAPTER TWENTY-FIVE

HUANG SAW YUE-YING the moment he opened the gate. She was sitting on the bench beside the peony tree. It had been days since he had seen her and there she was like a cool breeze; an unexpected gift in the middle of the summer heat.

"You're here," he said.

He went to her and she made room on the bench for him to sit. "I am."

Her hand found its way into his and he was flooded with relief and happiness. He'd been holding in his breath for days and he could finally exhale.

"I'm happy to see you," Huang said.

She turned to him and graced him with a smile that was crooked and mysterious. "I'm happy as well."

She never smiled for him completely, without reservation. She always held something back and it made him even more determined to make her eyes light up and hear her laughter.

They rose and retreated to the bedchamber. Then, not caring that it was the middle of the day or that the windows were open, he slipped off her robe and made love to her. Afterward, they lay together in the languid heat of the afternoon. His fingers played with the strands of her hair as his eyes traced every inch of her face. She no longer flinched from his gaze. He couldn't hide the truth from her any longer.

"When I went to ask my father's help with Mingyu's case, we spoke about other matters as well." His throat closed around the next words. "I mentioned the two of us."

She rose to sit over him. "Us?"

"I told him that I wanted you to be my wife."

She was bare from head to toe, presenting too pretty of a view as she stared down at him in astonishment.

"You know that can't be."

"It's the truth. It's what I want here." He tapped a hand to his chest. "My father said he would disown me if I insisted on it."

His voice rasped low, grating against his throat. His father could have threatened to kill him and it would have hurt less.

"I couldn't let you do that," Yue-ying said softly.

"You wouldn't run away with me? We can find a place in the woods," he teased. "Raise chickens. Catch fish."

She managed a laugh. The sound of it was enough to lighten his heart just a little, even if she did it only for his benefit. She touched a hand to his chest.

"You've spent the past three years redeeming yourself in your father's eyes. You won't leave your family. It's not what you truly want…here." She placed her hand against his heart and it beat even faster.

His heart was selfish and entitled and greedy and he had always assumed, despite his father forbidding it and despite Yue-ying's insistence that she never wanted to be owned again, that somehow everything would fall into place for him. He'd taken a knife to his gut and had survived. Heaven smiled on him. He was privileged from birth and he was invincible.

But he wasn't invincible now. His insides were exposed; his heart lay open and beating.

He sat up so they could see one another, eye to eye. "I'm expected to marry as soon as I complete the palace exams."

Her mouth pressed tight, but that was all. "I know. I knew this when I came to you."

"I don't want to. I want this here, with you, I wish this would never end."

"It's your responsibility," she said, turning away from him. "I've always known I could never be your wife. You need to accept that and stop this romantic nonsense."

Yue-ying was right. These were the realities of his noble birth and her low status. It was cruel for him to continue to pretend otherwise.

Her back was to him and he admired the subtle curve of her spine, the span of bare skin as blank as a canvas. That view of a woman was always alluring to him. With her face turned away, it could be anyone. Only secret knowledge told him it was Yue-ying. It was the view of parting after an intimate encounter. A bittersweet image in every way.

"Yue-ying, this woman that I'm to marry…I don't even know her. I don't feel anything for her, not like what I feel for you."

He reached across the bed and pulled her to him, her back to his chest.

"I have a brother," he began. He couldn't see her face, but he pressed his cheek to her hair. The scent of jasmine enfolded him. "Of the same father, but from different mothers. When my father was reassigned to Fujian province, our family stayed here and he took his concubine with him. Though he never speaks to us of her, I know he cares for her very deeply."

How was he to explain this to Yue-ying in a way that she could believe? For one, he had to stop talking about his father, about someone else's life, and speak about his own.

He turned her around in his arms so that she could see his expression and know that he was sincere. "Will you belong to me and me alone?" He took hold of her hands. It was hard to keep his voice from shaking. "And I would belong to you and you alone. There are things I am required to do, out of honor and duty and respect. But there are the few precious things that I can choose and you are the only woman I would ever choose. You would always be with me. You would be the wife of my heart."

A faint tremor ran along her lower lip as she absorbed his words. He could see the wetness gathering at the corners of her eyes and he wanted to take her in his arms again, but he was afraid to shatter the moment. She held all the power over him, more than his family or the cursed examinations.

"But you would have another wife in truth," she said, barely above a whisper.

He kissed her, pouring all of his intention and sincerity into that kiss. Her lips parted for him. Her arms accepted him and he was filled with a rush of gratitude and elation.

"This is the only truth," he said, holding her tight.

WHEN THE END of the year approached, Bai Huang declared his candidacy for the imperial exams and threw himself into his studies in earnest. Other than Yue-ying's weekly visits to Mingyu, they spent little time in the North Hamlet. The neighborhood surrounding Bai Huang's residence became their world, enjoying small meals and snacks from the food stands that dotted the adjacent lane or purchasing charcoal from the man who came by every day with a basket full of it.

His sister, Wei-wei, came by frequently as an excuse to leave the family mansion. She would challenge Bai Huang with questions and read over his written commentaries. The depth of her knowledge was awe-inspiring. Yue-ying could see how the two of them, brother and sister, had truly spent their entire lives studying for this examination, though only one of them was allowed to take it.

One day, Wei-wei sat Yue-ying down at the desk and placed a brush in her hand. Just like that, she was taken under Wei-wei's tutelage as well. In exchange for her instruction, Yue-ying would tell colorful stories of the Pingkang li.

"You must take me there one day," Wei-wei insisted.

"No," Bai Huang replied sternly from his vantage point at the doorway.

His sister made a face at him, but Yue-ying smiled. "The North Hamlet might not be the best place for a well-bred lady," Yue-ying told her.

Even if she did learn how to read and write, Yue-ying was far from being a proper lady. She knew that the elder Lord Bai had demanded that Bai Huang end their affair. With Wei-wei's constant visits, it was no secret that Bai Huang had refused to do so, but she heard of no other protest from his family. They assumed she would go away quietly in due time as mistresses should.

The weather became colder and the two of them remained indoors most days, closed off together and away from the world. At night, they would pile on extra layers of blankets and Bai Huang would read to her from books that had nothing to do with the imperial exams: stories of fox-demons and dragon princesses and scholars who overcame insurmountable obstacles. He avoided the love stories about scholars and song girls. They were overly sentimental and tragic and she had no liking for them.

A fervor gripped the city the closer they came to spring and the impending examinations. Yue-ying had known this time to be a quiet one in the Pingkang li, but now she knew why. Throughout the scholars' quarter and in households throughout the city, candidates were at their books, only stopping to rest their eyes or sleep, dreaming of the Analects behind closed eyelids.

Bai Huang was among them, his fingers smudged with ink from writing practice essays, his eyes sunken from late nights memorizing passages from the Classics. Yue-ying brought him tea and food, urging him to eat. Rubbing his shoulders. He would reach for her hand, holding it while still reading. This was what it must feel like to be husband and wife: taking care of one another in little ways.

As the days went by she could feel the tension in his neck and shoulders intensifying.

"You have to study every line, every verse," he complained. "The examiners could choose any passage from any of the Four Books and Five Classics and remove two lines. You would be expected to produce the missing section, word for word."

"I've heard there are pamphlets with common questions and passages selected by the Hanlin Academy," she offered, trying to be helpful.

"Those are the tools of scoundrels and cheaters," he scoffed. Then a while later and much quieter, "I've studied those as well."

Laughter bubbled out of her. She pressed her hand

to her mouth to try to stop it, but it was useless. At first he frowned at her, looking offended, but soon he was laughing too. Then he was chasing after her. She let herself be caught.

His arms rounded her waist and then he let out a long sigh, bending to rest his forehead against hers. He was weary and anxious. She could feel it through the embrace. She could sense it in the air as he wielded his brush and even hear it in every turn of a page.

"What happened all the other times?" she asked. Perhaps it wasn't the right question to ask, but he had to be thinking of all his other attempts.

"The first time, I figured I was young and ill prepared. The second time I studied twice as hard and felt invincible. The third time—" He stopped himself and exhaled slowly before meeting her eyes. "The third time, I just fell into despair."

She grabbed hold of his chin and gave it a little shake. "The answer is easy, then. Don't fall into despair."

It at least earned her a smile.

On some nights, the pressure would build and become overwhelming. Yue-ying could tell by the way he would pace the courtyard or move from book to book, unable to concentrate. She would see a stack of scrolls on the desk and know it was time to come into the study.

"Come sit with me," he would implore.

She knew he wanted to gamble to take his mind away, so she would brew tea and sit with him, sewing or sometimes studying her own lessons. Time would pass and Bai Huang would regain his composure enough to continue.

There were nights when she would drag him from the study. He was tired, but too anxious to sleep, but she knew how to be persuasive. She would peel the robe from his shoulders, remove his clothes and pleasure him with her hands, her mouth. On nights when he was too exhausted to make love, he would hold her close, naked skin to naked skin, stroking her gently and then gradually quicker until she reached her climax.

"Yue-ying," he said after one of those long, slow days that started before sunrise and ended late into the night with them clinging to one another. "Dearest, I can't remember what life was like without you."

"You're going to make yourself ill if you don't sleep," she said in return as she settled into the crook of his arm.

He pressed his lips to her forehead. The examination period was only three days away. Bai Huang would succeed this time. She believed it in her heart, and once he did he would marry his betrothed as their families had intended. Whenever she looked at him, his brow furrowed in concentration, or asleep in bed with his long graceful fingers still curled around a book, she knew it would tear her heart in two to share him with another woman.

Inevitably he would turn his thoughts to family. His wife would bear him sons and share in all his joys and sorrows. A concubine, aside from the intimacies of the bedchamber, was little more than a servant to the family. But Yue-ying would at least have Bai Huang, if only in part, and she would be taken care of. She should be happy with the thought. It was selfish of her to doubt. It was greedy of her to want more.

ON THE MORNING of the imperial examinations, drums beat in rhythm throughout the city an hour before dawn. In the local wards, a gong sounded to signal to all candidates that it was time to rouse and travel to the examination hall. Carriages set out from the home of every candidate, clogging the streets with hopefuls dressed in dark robes and scholars' caps.

Huang's carriage joined the procession on the main artery that led into the administrative quarters of the imperial city. Examination day was practically a festival in and of itself and a large crowd gathered on either side of the road. The examination hall would be packed with over a thousand candidates in the next hour. Only one in ten would pass, if even that many.

It was nearly impossible to find anyone in such a throng, but just before Huang disappeared into the gates of the imperial city he sighted a vermilion sash tied onto a parasol. Yue-ying had come to see him off to battle as she'd promised. Mingyu was beside her with the old ox Taizhu towering over them both.

Yue-ying was smiling, her eyes bright with pride. She had sewn a sachet for him in the shape of a carp for good luck. It was an uncommonly sentimental gesture for her. She had only pressed it into his palm and hadn't allowed him to say anything to her about it. The charm was stuffed with cassia bark. Huang had fallen asleep with it beside his pillow and the sweet cinnamon scent had followed him into his dreams.

She lifted a hand to wave at him and his heart was ready to burst out of his chest. He felt invincible, as if he could leap over mountains. Who wouldn't want to feel this way every moment of every day?

There had to be a way, his heart insisted. There had to be a way for them to remain together.

The examinations hadn't even started and he was already distracted. Yue-ying would scold him for it if she knew. He gave her a final nod before turning back to face the dreaded palace exams for the fourth time.

CHAPTER TWENTY-SIX

IF THERE WAS anyone more nervous than Bai Huang, it was his sister. Wei-wei managed to find one excuse or another to come and visit every day that her brother spent sealed inside the examination hall. On the third day, Yue-ying was preparing a meal for his return when Wei-wei wandered into the kitchen.

"It's a very grueling process," Wei-wei explained, watching from the table as Yue-ying slipped sesame cakes into the fryer. The hot oil sizzled around the round flats of dough. "Do you know if someone dies during the process, they simply take him from his cell and throw his body over the surrounding wall? Then everyone else continues as if nothing happened."

"Wei-wei."

"Yes?" she replied anxiously.

Yue-ying leveled a gaze at her. "Lord Bai is not going to *die*. The examinations are only three days long and he's quite healthy."

She glanced back at the cakes, turning one gently with her chopsticks to make sure they were browning evenly. Throughout the fall and winter, Auntie had taught her a new recipe every day and Bai Huang joked that he was becoming round from her cooking.

A pang of longing struck her. If this was how she felt after only three days apart, how hard would it be once he passed the exams and moved on to his new life?

She started flipping the cakes over, hoping that Wei-wei hadn't seen the telltale emotion in her face.

"You're right," Wei-wei said from the other side of the kitchen. She remained far away from the stove and the crackling oil. The Classics were second nature to her, but domestic tasks were a frightful mystery. "I wonder if the questions this year will be especially difficult. The Emperor is looking to recruit talented officials, they say."

"You can interrogate your brother yourself in a few hours."

"Oh, no, that would only make him more nervous. The results are not announced until the end of the month. I just needed somewhere acceptable to go and clear my head. One can only wander to the temple so many times. I've been a poor tutor this week and Chang-min can hardly concentrate on his studies. The entire family is too anxious."

Something about the way Wei-wei had spoken sparked Yue-ying's curiosity.

"Is this the only place you're allowed to go?" she asked.

"There's the local temple or I can call on close friends of the family with Mother or…" Her voice trailed off. "There are not many places that are acceptable for an unmarried woman in public. I would think that an old maid such as myself should have at least some freedom."

The cakes were golden on both sides now. Yue-ying fished them out of the pan and set them on a cloth to cool. Maybe she was fit to become a cook in some household, she thought wryly, since she was an old maid of twenty-two herself.

She brought a cake over to Wei-wei, who held it gingerly between her two fingers before taking a small taste. She smiled wide and took another less dainty bite. "These are good. What are they called?"

"Concubine cakes." Yue-ying found that darkly humorous.

Wei-wei finished her cake and dabbed at her mouth with a handkerchief. "I should go. I've been away for nearly two hours now. Sometimes I envy you. You can go anywhere, do anything."

No. No, she could not.

"There are greater hardships than being the daughter of a wealthy family," Yue-ying replied, her tone sharper than she intended.

"Oh, I didn't mean—" Wei-wei fell silent, looking embarrassed.

Yue-ying felt a little bad for reprimanding her in such a way, but it was the truth. A truth that she was all too aware of. Yet at the same time, it wasn't as if Wei-wei didn't have any struggles of her own.

"I suppose we all yearn for what we don't have," Yue-ying said, attempting to make peace.

Wei-wei smiled faintly and nodded. "They say the moon is always rounder in the west."

THE CARRIAGE STOPPED before the gate and Huang stumbled out. His head was full of thousands of characters and his hand was stiff from holding the brush for hours upon hours. And his body ached as if he'd stayed up the entire night drinking.

Yue-ying bounded out to greet him as soon as he entered the courtyard. "Huang, how were the exams?"

He nodded, not quite an answer.

"I made your favorite dishes." Her eyes were warm as they regarded him. She was glowing, full of life and energy, while he was ready to fall asleep midstep and crash face-first into the dirt.

"It smells wonderful." He reached up to tuck a strand of hair behind her ear. His hand was heavy as if it were made of lead. "Let me change out of this robe."

Plodding to his room, he sat down on the bed. When Yue-ying found him there, he didn't know how much time had passed, but he was holding one shoe in his hand and the other was still on his foot.

"My poor, weary scholar," she murmured, gently prying the shoe from his grasp and removing the other one as well.

He sat, limbs heavy, as she removed his cap and outer robe. Her touch was knowing and firm, while he was a puppet completely at her mercy.

"We should eat," he mumbled.

She chuckled at that. He felt her arms circle around him and his head drawn down onto her breast, the softest, most comforting pillow he'd ever known. He tried to tell Yue-ying she was his goddess, his treasure, his butterfly, but instead he yawned wide and fell asleep.

A CEREMONY WAS held at the end of the fourth month before the steps of the main hall in the imperial palace. The statue of Ao, the great tortoise of myth, watched over the proceedings. There were over a thousand candidates gathered there, yet the courtyard was silent enough to hear the beat of a hummingbird's wings.

The Emperor himself was in attendance, seated on his throne at the top of the steps. This was the first set of *jinshi* degrees he would award and it was said the sovereign had read and ranked the top candidates himself.

Each name was read aloud in order with the highest rank first. When the names in the first tier had all been announced and the second tier was halfway through, Huang felt sick to his stomach. The familiar feeling of dread loomed over him. By the time they reached the third and final tier, he had broken into a sweat.

The members of the Hanlin Academy stood in their scholars' vestments upon the dais. Taizhu was among them. He and the historian had become somewhat friendly since the skirmish with the bandit gang. Huang tried to read the answer in his eyes, but the old ox was inscrutable.

There were examination periods where only a handful of degrees were awarded. Some years, there were none who were deemed qualified. Today there were over a hundred candidates lined up. Surely the list was reaching its end and Huang tried not to think of what it would be like to be studying for the exams a fifth time.

Finally he heard his name. His heart was pounding so fast, he thought he might have misheard, but it was repeated once more and then a third time as was customary. He moved through the crowd to take his place among the other scholars.

Huang closed his eyes and raised his face to the sun to let the warmth sink into him.

The entire family had been waiting for this moment. His time wandering the Pingkang li was over. He would be expected to secure an official appointment now, marry as his parents had intended, begin a family with the young bride he had never met.

This was the start of a new life, yet throughout the announcements and the celebration that followed Huang had a sense that he was breathing life into one dream at the death of another.

CHAPTER TWENTY-SEVEN

YUE-YING SAW LITTLE of Bai Huang over the following week. The examination period was over and the pleasure houses were once again alive with banquets and celebrations. Now that Bai Huang was a graduate of the palace exams, the invitations poured in. One did not bring a mistress to such affairs, but for tonight's event he insisted that she accompany him.

That evening's party was hosted by the Emperor. All of the recent graduates of the palace exams were invited along with other notable officials.

"You have to come," Bai Huang had said. "There is no one else I'd rather be with."

He had been exuberant, happier than she had seen him for a long time, and so she agreed. She had to send a message begging Mingyu for a dress, which her sister responded to promptly. By midday, a messenger arrived bearing a parcel from the Lotus Palace. Yue-ying unwrapped it to reveal an elegant robe fashioned of deep rose-colored silk.

At the bottom of the parcel, buried beneath the silk, was a bodice to be worn beneath the robe. The undergarment fit snugly around her breasts and waist to create a smooth, flattering shape without ties or loops to interrupt the lines. She was attempting to wrap the bodice around her without the benefit of an attendant when the door opened behind her.

"Let me help you." The sound of Bai Huang's voice resonated through her, warming her skin.

Before she could protest, his hands were gliding over her back, smoothing out the cloth. She gathered up her hair and lifted it away to make it easier for him.

"It closes in front."

His lips were very close to her ear. "I know."

His simple reply spoke of all sorts of illicit knowledge. His thumbs grazed the sides of her breasts as his arms circled around her. He took a long time pulling the garment in place.

"I don't believe I've seen this before," he said, his voice deepening with desire.

"It's only a piece of cloth," she said, but her throat was dry.

He chuckled. She released her hair and he swept it aside, bending his head to place his mouth over the juncture of her neck and shoulder where the skin was especially sensitive.

The position was unaccountably sensual, with him behind her where she couldn't see him, performing such an intimate yet humble act. Having Bai Huang dress her was more arousing than having him undress her.

"It's been a while," he said against her skin. He lifted his lips and found a new spot on the side of her neck to explore. A shudder ran down her spine.

"Only a week," she murmured.

"It feels longer. Like a lifetime."

It was lovers' talk, meant to be light and playful, but there was a weight hanging on every word.

"Things have been...different between us since the day of the graduate announcements," he ventured.

"We've hardly had a chance to see one another, that's all."

She was lying and doing a poor job of it. Deflection was an art that her sister had mastered, while she was a novice.

Bai Huang was no longer the eternal student. He was embarking upon a new life now. He couldn't spend every waking moment by her side and she didn't expect him to, but she missed the little moments between them. The light touches Bai Huang would bestow against her hand, the small of her back. Brushing her arm as he walked by or circling her waist just because he was close and she was there. Just a single look from him and her heart would be full once more, but they couldn't find any time even for that lately.

"Is something upsetting you?" The situation must indeed be serious for him to be asking such a direct question of her.

"Of course not." She turned around, arms crossed over her front demurely. The gesture was out of place given that they had been living in close quarters as lovers. "Now I must finish dressing."

He flashed a grin, more hopeful than seductive. "Must you?"

"Go," she commanded in a teasing manner.

He reached for her once more before he left, tracing a finger along the sensitive underside of her arm. They were making a valiant effort to be as they were, as if everything weren't changing.

She draped the outer robe over her shoulders and fixed the layers of silk in place with a pink sash wrapped about her waist. The accompanying shawl was pale yellow and so fine it was translucent. It was meant to drape and accent her figure rather than provide any warmth. The night would be warm enough.

The boldness and sensuality of the outfit was more

suited to a courtesan like Mingyu than to her. Yue-ying knew the depth of her anxiety when she considered trying to hide her birthmark. It could only be done with thick layers of paste and powder and the effect was nearly as unflattering as the stain.

Bai Huang was waiting in the courtyard when she emerged from the chamber with her hair in a simple coil and only a touch of color on her lips. His eyes darkened upon seeing her and her spirits lifted.

He was wearing a black robe with a high collar and a cap adorned with the tails that signified his status as a degreed scholar.

"Why are you grinning?" he asked.

"I'm not." She bit back her smile, though it threatened to escape.

The carriage was waiting for them in the street. As they rode beneath the darkening sky Bai Huang leaned over to her.

"Every time you look at me, you look like you can't help laughing. As much as I like it, you have to tell me what's causing this merriment."

She shook her head.

"Tell," he demanded, looking like a little boy denied.

"Look at you, then look at me."

He did. The answer still eluded him.

"A year ago, you were more likely to be wearing a robe like mine than what you have on now," she pointed out.

"I never wore anything that pretty."

She lifted her eyebrows to express a different opinion. He scowled at her. When their laughter faded, he was still looking at her as if he'd never look away.

"I like it when we're like this," he said, his eyes alight.

It was impossible to keep her heart from overflowing at the words. She liked it too, these moments when it felt as if the world were made for just the two of them. There would be fewer of those as time went by. It was inevitable.

Summer was upon them once more. The candidates who had passed the exams would petition for official positions now. All of the banquets became opportunities for the recent graduates to impress someone important.

Not that Bai Huang needed to worry. He was related to the new chancellor and his father was a high-ranking official. His great-uncle was a renowned poet. He had been born under the most favorable of stars.

The Serpentine River Park was at the very south-eastern corner of the walled city, the farthest point from the administrative halls and palaces. The river and accompanying lake had been dredged by laborers and the area created as a tranquil escape from city life. Yue-ying had never attended a banquet there, though Mingyu had spoken of it.

When they arrived, lanterns swayed from poles all along the river and the guests congregated around several grand pavilions. She could hear music floating from them. The Emperor had brought his army of court musicians and dancers to provide entertainment.

Yue-ying gasped as they came closer. There were hundreds of guests.

"Thousands," Bai Huang corrected her when she commented on it. "It is the Emperor's banquet."

They crossed the wooden bridge together and became engulfed within the festivities. It was more crowded than the New Year celebration in the Pingkang li.

"Mingyu said she would be waiting for me in the Lotus Garden," she said, almost forgetting in all the commotion.

"Old Taizhu asked to speak with me. Probably feels he hasn't insulted me in a while and needs to make up for lost time."

They parted with promises to find one another later. She certainly couldn't cling to his side the entire evening while he mingled among the elite. It would be unseemly.

The garden was located to the left of the lake and Yue-ying found her sister sitting alone on a bench near the water, gazing at the blanket of broad leaves and pink-tipped flowers floating on the surface. Her outer robe was a pale blue, almost glowing in the lantern light, and there were pearls in her hair.

Mingyu looked up as she approached, patting the spot beside her on the bench.

"Bai Huang wants me to stay with him," Yue-ying said as soon as she sat. "He wants me to be his concubine."

Mingyu touched Yue-ying's hair gently. "This is good. This is all we could have hoped for."

"Then why do you look so sad?"

"It is always a little sad when a woman marries." Mingyu ran the edge of her little finger along the corner of one eye. "She leaves her own family to join her husband's."

"But this wouldn't be a marriage," Yue-ying protested.

"For women like us, it is," Mingyu said firmly. "Do you know the procurer who took us from our village offered marriage? He saw me at the river and told our father that he was seeking a wife for a wealthy nobleman. Instead of refusing, our father offered up that he had two daughters. People sell their children for less of a promise than what Lord Bai has offered you."

"I know. I'm very grateful."

Over the past few days, she was often telling herself that she *should* be grateful and that she *should* be happy. Yet why did she herself feel so lonely inside when she should be filled with joy? She had been waiting all week to speak to Mingyu about it. There were so many times when she wanted to leave the courtyard and walk back to the Pingkang li, but something had always stopped her. She didn't know how to put her feelings into words.

"I'm afraid of what I feel for Bai Huang." Heat rose up her face until her ears burned. "I'm afraid this is what love feels like."

Mingyu didn't laugh at her. She understood. "That's unfortunate."

Yue-ying looked to where Bai Huang was standing. He and Old Taizhu were in conversation on the other side of the lake. In his flamboyant attire, he had been eye-catching, but now, in his newly earned scholars' robes, he took on a more serious, distinguished air. Strange how the extravagant clothing had actually detracted from his beauty. Without the distraction, he was star-tlingly handsome and it hurt to look at him.

From the beginning of their affair through the past year, she had felt many things. At first excitement, passion, warmth. Then she'd felt a sense of caring develop, of wanting to protect him, of pride when she saw how determined he was to succeed. Happiness when he felt happy and sadness when he was sad. But the over-whelming feeling she had now was pain. An ache had taken root in her heart and every time she looked at him, the ache only grew deeper. At times she couldn't even remember the other feelings.

"First he'll be wed," Yue-ying said, the words weigh-ing heavy on her. "And soon. It wouldn't be appropri-ate to take a concubine first before a wife. And then, of course, he must take time to be with her, to start their family. During all this, there is nothing for me to do but wait."

"You can come back to the Lotus with me," Mingyu offered. "Time will pass quickly."

"How much time? One year? Two? When he returns, will his wife already have a son? Will he even remember who I am?"

Her sister couldn't answer those questions for her, so Yue-ying made her own attempt.

"He will remember," she said, confident in Bai Huang's regard. "But what he'll remember is the Yue-ying I was before the waiting and the hoping. And he'll remember the Bai Huang he was, before the duty and the sacrifice. But still, I'm grateful."

By now, the word was bitter on her tongue. She had said it too many times. She smiled ruefully at Mingyu, who leaned toward her. Side by side, they touched their heads together, Mingyu nudging playfully. "This is why you should never love a man too much. It will drive you mad."

Bai Huang glanced over to them, his smile crooked. A ray of light broke through the haze.

"If it had been you that Lord Bai wanted, would you go with him?" Yue-ying asked.

"Of course. He's wealthy and of a tolerable disposition."

"Surely you must have received many offers of redemption."

Mingyu laughed. "Not as many as one would think, Little Sister. There are less expensive and easier concubines to manage."

It had taken the incidents of the past year to bring them close enough to speak this way.

"Why did you not become General Deng's concubine when he offered?" Yue-ying asked, hoping that Mingyu would finally answer. At first Yue-ying had assumed it was because of her, but Mingyu was crafty enough to bring her along as her maidservant if she had wanted to. She had managed to manipulate the general's household into helping her stow Hana away on his property.

"I have my own reasons," Mingyu evaded. There was a brief pause before a sly look replaced her serious one. "But it certainly wasn't because I loved him too much."

THEY CROSSED OVER the bridge to join Bai Huang and Taizhu, who were conversing beneath one of the canvas tents. Thick rugs had been laid out over the grass. The two men sat on the ground before low tables filled with food and wine.

"I would recommend you to the Hanlin Academy," Taizhu was saying. "But you would be trapped inside record rooms and libraries, bent over one edict or another. I have a sense Lord Bai is a bit too...energetic to find such work fulfilling."

"You think I lack focus, old man."

Taizhu snorted gleefully and gestured for the servers to pour more wine. The old man's disposition toward Bai Huang had improved considerably since Bai Huang saved his life.

Mingyu took over the task of serving wine and then took the seat beside the historian while Yue-ying sat beside Bai Huang. He touched his fingertips to the back of her hand beneath the table.

"This is like being back at the Lotus," Taizhu proclaimed. "With old friends."

"Yet so much has changed," Mingyu said. She glanced

across the table to Yue-ying and Bai Huang. "Most of it for the better."

She had never loved her sister more.

The greatest change was that she was now part of the conversation.

"Hana has come to live at my residence," Taizhu told her solemnly. "I intend to adopt her as my daughter."

"That is so very kind of you," Mingyu murmured. "And noble."

The old scholar and Mingyu exchanged a look between them. There had been many secret glances and hidden meanings between them last summer, now that Yue-ying thought of it. When Bai Huang pretended to woo Mingyu, Taizhu had lashed out at him out of a sense of protectiveness.

The old scholar looked pointedly at Yue-ying. "Being the old disagreeable bachelor that I am, the girl will need an amah to see to her upbringing."

"Yue-ying is too young and pretty to become an amah," Bai Huang protested before she could reply.

"The flower prince returns," Taizhu sighed, wagging his finger at him.

"Better a prince than an old goat."

"Your carefree days of wine and women are over now, my friend. Soon there will be a wife to answer to and you'll envy this goat."

The table fell silent at that. Yue-ying spent a long moment studying her wine cup. Everyone saw it as a matter of course that Bai Huang would be respectfully wed.

A year ago, there was only meaningless banter between them, made more meaningless by Bai Huang's efforts to play the fool. Now even the simplest jest took on meaning. Too much had happened since then.

"Do you remember the slaver gang that was arrested last summer?" Taizhu went on in more sober tones.

"Constable Wu and Magistrate Li acted decisively. The bandits were questioned before the tribunal and executed within days," Bai Huang replied.

At the mention of Wu Kaifeng, Mingyu's expression darkened. She had not forgotten or forgiven how he'd imprisoned her.

"Perhaps this unpleasant topic is not suitable for this gathering. This is a night of celebration," Mingyu reminded them.

"Ah, it's just the four of us here," Taizhu said. "We won't speak of it again after tonight—what do you say to that?"

This would be Yue-ying's only chance to resolve a few lingering questions she had about the whole affair.

"I was curious about something," she began. "If we are to believe that the same bandits who killed Huilan also went to your house to find Hana, what could they possibly have been trying to hide that they were willing to kill for it? They were only caught because they threatened you."

"They threatened me in public as well," Bai Huang noted.

"Miss Yue-ying is right," Taizhu said thoughtfully. "It wasn't worth the risk for the outlaws to return to try to seek revenge on Huilan or to warn Lord Bai away from his investigations. When they knelt before the tribunal, it was evident they were nothing more than common thieves. They should have considered Hana a loss and gone about their business."

"Common or not, they were enough to frighten Huilan," Yue-ying said. "Did she ever tell either of you why?"

Mingyu shook her head. "After the drowning, we hardly spoke to one another. She never mentioned any fear of retribution. It wasn't until her death I realized how dangerous those slavers truly were."

"I didn't realize Lady Huilan was trying to escape the city either," Taizhu admitted.

"But didn't you give her the silver so she could leave? I found a stash of it hidden in the temple. A portion of the silver ingots were marked the same way as the silver you gave me. That was how I knew you must have been involved somehow."

"It wasn't I," Taizhu said regretfully. "I would have helped her if I knew she needed it. The silver could have come from any merchant from Yangzhou. With the capital being a center for trade, it would be quite easy for silver to change hands."

"We may never know all the answers," Mingyu interrupted, looking around at the four of them. "But we rescued Hana and the world is free of a few bad men. Let us consider ourselves fortunate and not disturb the spirits by so much talk of tragedy."

BEFORE THE NIGHT was done, Yue-ying left once more to stroll through the park with Mingyu while Bai Huang mingled with the other scholars. In the final hour, the remaining guests converged along the river to float candles along the river in paper boats.

She finally found Bai Huang waiting for her near the bridge where they had first entered the park. He sat on the bank with his arms hooked around his knees.

He didn't turn until she was close and his face brightened up at the sight of her. There was a stack of colored paper beside him. His cap was removed and strands of hair fell over his face. He looked handsome and boyish and undeniable.

She lowered herself onto the grass and took one of the sheets, laying it onto her lap as she folded it in half, then ran her fingers along the edge to sharpen the crease. She was aware of his gaze on her, as she had been the entire night.

"How is Mingyu?" he asked.

"She is well."

"You had a lot to say to her tonight."

There was silence between them then. Unspoken things. She kept on turning and folding until a boat emerged. The candle was tiny, no bigger than her little finger. Bai Huang lit the wick using one of the hanging lanterns and they placed the candle inside the boat before setting it afloat. Kneeling beside the water, they watched their vessel join the stream of other lights floating down the river.

"Pretty," she murmured.

He reached out to her, his fingers searching for hers in the grass. Yue-ying remained still, afraid to move while she shattered into a thousand pieces inside.

"Huang," she began, her chest so tight she could barely draw breath.

"When?" he asked quietly. "When did you change your mind?"

"I don't know," she whispered. "Maybe last night. Maybe just now."

He bowed his head and exhaled sharply, but it did nothing to expel the tension that coiled through his body. Their hands were still clasped together, but there was no warmth to the touch. She withdrew and he let her go.

"Mingyu told me there were greater hardships than

being a wealthy man's concubine," she said. "And that you would take care of me when she no longer could."

"I would," he said fiercely. "I will."

There should be no question. She was a maidservant and, before that, a prostitute. She was poor and she had nothing, while Bai Huang had everything. But while Mingyu's reasoning had spoken of an arrangement of security, Bai Huang spoke only of love.

Love.

Mingyu was also speaking out of love for her. Mingyu's love was honest, refusing to ignore all the realities of their lives and circumstances. Bai Huang's love was blind. Yue-ying wanted to be blind as well. She wanted to close her eyes and sink into his arms.

"I always knew that our time together was an illusion. A dream."

"You are not an illusion," he said, his jaw hardening. "I will not accept that and I won't allow you to think that either. I once felt that way about the North Hamlet—that it was an adventurous and romantic place. But when I was sent away and thrown on a ship to work my hands raw with the sun on my back, I returned and saw the wine, the beautiful women, even the learned scholars with their meaningless poetry for what they were. Shadow puppets, performing an elaborate show. Why do you think I always noticed you? You were more real to me than anything else. Even though you were always trying to hide, I couldn't look away. I wanted to know who was this girl who dressed like a servant, but seemed to own the world. You were never intimidated by who I was."

"You're wrong," she said softly. "I was always aware of who you were. I have to be. Look at Taizhu. Even as well respected as he is, he still feared retribution because of where he came from. One never forgets. The world does not let you forget."

"This is the same argument once more," Bai Huang countered. "I'm not asking you to forget. Just allow yourself to think of a new life, a different life. We were happy together through the autumn and winter seasons. I know we were."

She nodded sadly. "We were happy, yes. But now we must think of the future. The concubine that your father keeps, you said that your family rarely speaks of her. She barely exists to you. Your family would always think of me as a servant. Or even worse, they would think of me as nothing at all."

"That isn't true. And what does it matter what they think? That's not how *I* see you."

She could see the anguish in his eyes, but she felt that same anguish for how hopeless the situation was. "How can it not matter? They are your family. Your blood. And I will never be family. You would become my husband, while I could never become your wife."

"Many men keep harmonious households with a concubine. I would strive to make you happy every day, Yue-ying. You know I would."

She wanted so much to believe him, but she shook her head. "If I give birth to a child, to our child, who would raise him?"

Bai Huang had no answer for her. After she and Mingyu had been abandoned, the thought of giving her sons over to be raised by a first wife was unbearable. But she would have to if she wanted them to be recognized as legitimate heirs by his family. For this and so many other reasons, she knew she had to remain strong.

"The Pingkang li is the capital city of mistresses and discarded women. I know in my soul what will happen if I go with you. And I want to come with you, Huang. I want to close my eyes and hold on."

"Then why not stay?"

She smiled sadly. "If I felt nothing for you, then I would say yes without a care."

He stared at her, letting her words sink in. "That's hardly fair," he growled.

"Quiet, obedient concubines can fit themselves harmoniously into a household. A jealous concubine, a possessive concubine, soon finds herself cast out onto the streets by a wife. Your wife will have claim to you, Huang, not me. And I would be envious. I would want you so much it hurts like the way it hurts now. But to stay with you, I would need to bite my tongue and become docile. I would kill these emotions until there was nothing left inside me for you to love. And I would resent you for requiring this of me."

"So you would rather tear us apart now than face the fear of what *might* happen?" he challenged.

"I know this will happen."

"I think you're afraid," he threw back at her.

Tears blurred her vision. She was afraid. She was afraid of the day when she could come to hate him and he would be cold toward her, all because of the choices they had forced one another into.

"These past few months have been the happiest time of my life. Let us not fight now."

"We should fight." Bai Huang threw a stone into the water. It didn't skip, but rather it sank and took one of the floating lights with it. He was in a vindictive mood. "We should scream and shout and wail. We should fight it so hard that there's no mistake that there is more pain in leaving than staying. Yue-ying—"

He was breathing hard. He had learned so many clever words and they were all useless on her.

She bit down hard on her lip and tried to focus on that small pain to keep the larger one at bay. "I don't want our last moments together to be angry or hurtful."

"What if you're with child?" he asked, his tone flat. It was a final desperate play.

"I already know that I'm not."

The last of the paper boats had floated by, leaving the water before them dark. In the silence, she turned to look at Bai Huang's face. He only gave her his profile as he stared out across the river. As hard as it was to do, she wanted to remember everything she could about him.

"I need to go soon," she said. There was a flutter of pale blue silk on the other side of the bridge. Mingyu knew to keep her distance.

"I don't want you to."

She leaned toward him and only then would he face her. She had never seen him look the way he did at that moment. Drained of life. He had no more fight in him.

"One last kiss," he said quietly.

"And then I'll go. No farewells. Let this be our last memory of each other."

"Am I the illusion now, Yue-ying?"

She didn't answer. Instead she kissed him, softly, as she had the first time. He accepted it without moving, as he had the first time. And then she stood to go, just as she had promised.

CHAPTER TWENTY-EIGHT

HE WROTE YUE-YING poetry on ten-colored paper, a different color every day. Actually, it wasn't poetry, but rather the first thoughts he had each morning, which had no rhythm or sense to them.

I woke up and you were not there.
I wish I could hear your voice again.
Yue-ying, I miss you.

He pursued her with the same dogged intensity with which he had pretended to court Mingyu. One night, he went to call on the Lotus Palace only to be told Yue-ying was not there and Mingyu could not see him. Madame Sun allowed him graciously to stay, which he did for hours listening to sad songs played on the pipa, hoping to catch the sight of dark, thoughtful eyes and a smooth cheek marked dramatically with red.

I rode on a boat today and thought of you.
I wish it were winter once more.

There was no way, absolutely no way, wooing a woman could be harder than passing the palace exams. Yue-ying was being difficult and stubborn. And he knew that courtship games wouldn't impress her, yet he tried them anyway.

Amid his turmoil, Mother was already consulting an astrologer to pick an auspicious date for his wedding. Father was arranging meetings for him with influential officials across the Six Ministries. He found himself avoiding the Bai mansion, if only for a few moments of freedom before duty and obligation took over.

The morning Huang was summoned home, he went obediently as always. His father and mother were seated in the garden, drinking tea and speaking of everyday things: the running of the household and his upcoming wedding.

Huang meant to approach, but stopped himself when he saw Father reaching over to place his hand onto Mother's shoulder. He would have thought nothing of the gesture, if he hadn't caught how his father's thumb moved tenderly upward to stroke his wife's neck. Mother's expression immediately softened and their eyes met. Huang stopped, realizing that he was intruding upon a moment that was private and profound.

His parents never spoke openly of love. He had never seen them touch or exchange soft looks with one another. All he had learned from them was honor and respect and duty, which were all important qualities in a marriage for certain. But that one tiny movement, so quick he had almost missed it, told him of all the things he didn't know of between his parents.

Quietly, he retreated from the garden and went to seek out Wei-wei. As usual, his sister was in the study watching over Chang-min's studies.

"Ah, the illustrious imperial scholar himself," she said, beaming.

Wei-wei had been in an unshakably good mood since he had passed the exams. His achievement was a reflection of her own success as a tutor, which he didn't begrudge her. Wei-wei had always been more focused and more dedicated than he was.

"Can we speak privately, Little Sister?"

"Follow your brother's good example," she told Chang-min as parting advice before she closed the study door.

They walked together into the parlor where he noted the furnishings had been rearranged. A prized painting as well as jade carving had been taken out for display.

"What's happening here?"

Wei-wei swatted his arm. "Don't you remember? Your wife's family is visiting today."

His family always spoke of the arranged marriage as if the ceremony had already taken place.

"Right, I remember now. I wanted to ask you about something," he said, eager to change the subject.

Wei-wei waited with her face tilted toward him expectantly. She wore a serious expression, truly having inherited all of the determination and focus that he lacked.

"Does Mother ever speak to you about Lady Shang?"

She blinked at him. "Whatever do you mean?"

"Does she—?" This was difficult. These were private matters that even family rarely intruded upon. "Is she angry that Lady Shang is Father's constant companion while she remains in the capital?"

Now Wei-wei was uncomfortable as well. "From everything I've seen, Lady Shang is always obedient and agreeable."

He rubbed at the back of his neck. "But there must have been strife when Father first brought another woman home. Even if there wasn't love between Father and Mother—"

"What makes you say there isn't love between them?" she asked.

"Well...ah..."

They were huddled in the corner and whispering as if they were children conspiring together. He certainly felt like a youth, his face heating the way it was.

"I assumed if a man was truly in love with his wife then he wouldn't feel the need to...well, since Mother had already given him a son and a daughter, what other reason...?"

This was awful. He was miserable. He could see his sister was miserable listening to him struggle.

"Huang." Thankfully, she stopped him. "Don't you know? Father didn't bring Lady Shang into our family. It was Mother."

"What do you mean?"

She sighed. "These are women's issues, Huang. Why do you need to ask such things?"

"They concern our family. I...ah...should know about them."

Wei-wei, who was usually brash enough to say anything to him, was blushing. The boundaries between parent and child and between the issues of men and women in the household were so distinct that it was difficult to even broach the subject. There was no language for it.

"I was a difficult birth," Wei-wei began. "Mother lost two unborn children after me. When she couldn't share Father's bed— Must you really hear all this?" When he didn't answer, she continued. "She sought out someone who was well mannered and respectful who would make Father happy and who would join harmoniously with the rest of the family. Is that not love?"

Suddenly, all of his memories of his parents took on

a new light. He had been a fool to think that separating his life would be so easy: honor and duty on one side, love and passion on another. He had been mistaken about everything: what it meant to raise a family, to run a household. To sacrifice. To love.

"Little Sister."

"Yes, *jinshi*?"

For someone who had attained an imperial scholar's degree, he was ignorant about a lot of things. Wei-wei had proven herself much more clever than he when it came to being an obedient daughter, yet still getting her way.

"I need your help."

NOT SINCE THE earthquake last year had there been such commotion. Excited chatter filled the Lotus Palace as the house completed its preparations. Every surface had been swept and polished and cleaned. Old Auntie stocked the pantry with the finest tea available in the marketplace and everyone was dressed in their best silk robes for the occasion.

The highly anticipated visitor that morning was not a gentleman, but a woman. Yue-ying hid behind one of the screens in the entrance hall to catch a glimpse of the illustrious visitor. She tried to remain as still as a cat as she peeked through the tiny crack between the bamboo panels.

The moment their guest arrived, a hush fell over the Lotus Palace as if the Empress herself were visiting. With jade bracelets on each wrist and strings of pearls in her hair, Madame Sun greeted the noblewoman just inside the door.

"Welcome! Welcome! Please come in." She bowed three times to the elder Lord Bai's wife.

Mingyu was beside her, speaking in that sultry, stately tone that she had cultivated.

"Bai *Furen*, what an honor to receive you here at our humble establishment."

"Lady Mingyu, I have long heard of your name spoken with great praise."

Yue-ying squinted and caught a glimpse of a surprisingly small woman. Her robe was deep green in color, embroidered with gold chrysanthemums and elegantly draped. Her hair was tucked into a high chignon, resembling summer clouds, and her high cheekbones and well-defined chin lent a strength to her features that was tempered by a delicately shaped mouth and soft, strikingly sensual eyes.

Though she was hidden, Yue-ying's palms began to sweat and her pulse skipped at the realization that she was standing no more than ten paces away from Bai Huang's mother. She had heard very little about the woman, but the *furen* of a powerful man was someone to be respected.

Lady Bai and Mingyu retreated to the parlor for tea and Yue-ying slipped out from behind the screen to sneak along the corridor, stopping just short of the doorway blocked off by a sheer curtain.

She had hardly believed the letter when it arrived. Bai Huang's mother had come to have tea and discuss matters of importance between their two families with Mingyu. The women were exchanging a few pleasantries now, though the conversation was overpowered by the pounding of Yue-ying's heart.

She leaned closer to the curtain and contemplated pulling it back just a sliver, when a low voice sounded very close to her ear.

"What underhanded deeds are you planning here?"

She spun around and was immediately caught in a pair of strong arms.

"Huang! What is going on?"

Bai Huang hushed her while his arms circled with aching familiarity around her waist. He glanced toward the curtain. "Don't interrupt. They're discussing our future in there."

A mischievous half smile was fixed on his face and the sight of it hooked deep into her. She'd missed his smile. She'd missed him, but she hadn't lost her sense of reason. Why would he bring his mother to arrange for a concubine when he was to be married soon?

"There is no future between us. What of your wife?"

He drew her closer. The smile had faded away and his look was as serious as she had ever seen him. "It's my hope that you will be my wife, Yue-ying. My first wife. My only wife."

"I don't understand. How is that possible?"

Their conversation was interrupted by a figure wandering at the other end of the hall, peering curiously into various chambers.

"Wei-wei!" Bai Huang whispered sharply.

Wei-wei kept on moving, clearly ignoring her brother as he called out to her once again. She darted into one of the smaller sitting rooms while the two of them trailed after her.

"You're supposed to be with Mother," Bai Huang admonished.

"I've never been inside a pleasure house," Wei-wei protested, her gaze sliding over every inch of the room. She paused to study a set of characters that had been written in black ink directly onto the wooden panels of the wall. It was a couplet about the beauty of the peonies in spring, a thinly veiled erotic poem brushed onto the wall at some late hour by some ardent scholar. Wei-wei stared at it as if committing it to memory.

"Why is your family here in the Pingkang li?" Yue-ying's heart had been beating too fast for too long. She was startled and confused and her head was beginning to throb.

Bai Huang opened his mouth to speak, but Wei-wei was quicker. "When our father refused to let him marry and threatened to disown him, Elder Brother was at a loss." She brushed at the front of Bai Huang's robe sympathetically. "So he asked me for my help and now we are both here to accompany our mother. She wanted to formally ask Mingyu's permission, as the head of your family, for the two of you to marry."

Yue-ying looked over at Bai Huang. "But your marriage was arranged years ago."

His eyes never left her face. "A new arrangement has been made."

"Ah, yes," Wei-wei began with pride. "I brought my younger brother to the park where I knew Huang's bride-to-be would be taking a stroll with her cousin. From there, I simply let youth and the spring air take its own course. An arranged marriage is an agreement between families, so our two families were able to…rearrange things to everyone's agreement."

Yue-ying frowned at the both of them in disbelief. "So the girl is now betrothed to…"

"My younger brother," Bai Huang finished.

"It was a minor scandal. Lovesick weeping on both sides," Wei-wei added, quite satisfied as she took hold of Yue-ying's arm conspiratorially. "Chang-min ignored his studies for three whole days. He's *never* done that. You see, Little Sister, or, rather, Elder Sister, since you will soon be married to my brother, we women cannot take the imperial exams or hold office. The only power we have is within the home—in the decisions surrounding the education of children and betrothals and marriages."

"And I am very grateful for your wisdom as a woman, Little Sister," Bai Huang said with grudging affection.

"My elder brother made the mistake of going to Father to try to break his betrothal. What our imperial scholar never realized was that the only person who could challenge Father—was Mother."

"But how could Bai *Furen* ever accept someone like me as a daughter-in-law?"

"Someone like you?" Bai Huang replied.

She narrowed her eyes at him. "You know what I mean."

"A woman who has shown herself to be clever and brave?" he challenged softly. "A woman who I could never forget even when she wanted me to?"

"More like a woman who is able to keep my brother in line," Wei-wei interrupted. "He hasn't gambled in a year and you didn't even have to throw him onto a ship. That and Mother wants grandchildren before next summer. The best chances for that are if Huang marries someone he's obviously enamored with."

They both stood blinking at Wei-wei, who regarded them with a smug look before turning back to the poem. Bai Huang's hand stole around hers.

"I am," he whispered. "Enamored with you."

She looked at him and her breath caught in her throat. When she closed her eyes, then opened them, he was still there. This was no illusion. He was solid and real beside her.

"Why do the scholars write on the walls?" Wei-wei asked, interrupting the moment.

"Because we want our thoughts to be immortalized. The entire quarter serves as a monument to our cleverness," he replied dryly.

She touched her fingers to the calligraphy. "I think it's fascinating."

"You should watch your sister closely," Yue-ying warned. "She may run away and register herself as a courtesan."

Wei-wei sniffed. "What if I did?"

There was no answer. Bai Huang had gone quiet as he stared at the characters painted onto the wall beneath his sister's hand.

"The ink was still fresh," he muttered to himself. "She had been writing something that night."

"Lord Bai?"

Wei-wei joined in, "Elder Brother?"

He looked up at them, but his gaze was far away. "Huilan told me she had information. Father was known for hunting down pirates and smugglers. Huilan came to me not because she thought I was trustworthy, but because she knew about our father."

"Why speak of this now? Huilan's spirit is at peace," Yue-ying said. It was bad luck to speak of the dead. She wasn't always so superstitious, but, with their match being such an unlikely one, she didn't want to take any chances.

"I don't think Huilan is at peace yet, but she soon will be," he said darkly. He turned to Wei-wei. "If Mother asks for me, tell her I needed to attend to an important matter and I'll be back shortly. Yue-ying as well."

"Scandalous," Wei-wei huffed beneath her breath.

Bai Huang's expression softened as he turned to her. "Come with me, Yue-ying. We started this together— let's finish this together."

Soft music floated from the windows of the House of a Hundred Songs and Madame Lui answered the door herself.

"Lord Bai, it's been too long!" she greeted warmly. Yue-ying received the barest of nods, a greeting that was considerably less warm. "So the news must be true. I must offer my best wishes for your happiness."

Despite her words, Madame Lui made no effort to hide her disappointment. She had hoped that after Huilan's unfortunate death, he would have given his attentions to another one of the courtesans in the Hundred Songs.

The headmistress started to seat them and offer tea, but Huang interrupted her. As rude as it might seem, he couldn't hold back any longer. Huilan's murderer had gone unpunished for too long as it was.

"This may be impertinent to ask, but may I see Huilan's chamber once more?" he asked.

They followed Madame up the stairs to the room at the corner. Inside, the furniture had been rearranged and the walls were covered with draperies.

"We hired a Taoist priest to come and exorcise any evil spirits that lingered," she explained. "Afterward, I offered the chamber to Mei, but she refused to sleep here, so two of the younger girls share it. They feel less afraid staying here together."

For a moment, Huang feared that all of the writing on the wall had been scrubbed away. He pulled aside one of the draperies and was relieved to see the calligraphy was still there. Starting at one end, he searched methodically beneath each curtain until he had circled the room.

"What are you looking for?" Yue-ying asked.

"When I came to Huilan's chamber the night of her death, there was an ink stone and brush set out in the sitting room. I assumed that she had written a letter the night of her death, but it had been taken or destroyed by her killer."

He scanned the characters on the wall and a chill ran down his spine. The brushstrokes were hastily executed, likely put in place by a hand that was trembling.

"Madame Lui, can you call Mei in here?" he asked, not taking his eyes from the calligraphy.

Because Bai Huang was who he was, the headmistress disappeared immediately to see to his request.

Yue-ying came to stand beside him. "What does it say?"

"These two lines are from a famous poem." He traced a finger down the two columns on the right. "But from here, it becomes nonsensical. These characters have no meaning when put together like this."

"Lord Bai, did you wish to see me?" Mei stood in the doorway with Madame Lui just behind her.

"Come in."

The courtesan hesitated as he beckoned her forward. Finally, with a fortifying breath, she stepped into the room. Her gown was yellow in color with embroidered trim that looked like peach blossoms. Her hair was swept up and pinned in a romantic style and jewels sparkled like dewdrops throughout it. With Huilan no longer there, Mei was the Hundred Songs's most celebrated courtesan and she was dressed for the part.

"It's been a while since we've spoken," Huang began.

He gestured toward one of the stools and she hesitated before sitting down. He sat down next to her and affected a smile. "Madame Lui mentioned that you refused this room. There's nothing to be afraid of, Little Mei."

Yue-ying made a coughing noise and shot him a

quick, but pointed look. He continued in a less flirtatious manner, not that the courtesan noticed his attempt at charm. She was picking at the edge of her sleeve and her eyes darted away from his.

"You're not afraid of ghosts, are you?" he asked.

"Lord Bai," Yue-ying scolded. "Don't frighten her."

Mei gave her a grateful look and relaxed a bit. "I'm not afraid. This room always feels a little cold when I pass by it, that's all."

"You and Huilan were friends, were you not?"

"Like sisters."

"After the dragonboat festival, you were both hosting a party in the banquet room. Then Huilan left to go up to her chamber, while you remained with the guests."

"Yes, my lord."

"And you never left the room."

"No…never."

The answer came after the barest of pauses.

"Not even for a moment?" he demanded.

"Maybe for just a moment. But not long at all!" she amended.

"Did you go to meet someone?" Yue-ying chimed in. "With so many guests coming and going, festivals provide plenty of opportunity for couples to meet in secret."

Mei's gaze darted to Madame Lui, then back to him. "Why are you causing trouble for me?"

"This is for Huilan's sake. She has been gone for a year now. It's time to make peace with her spirit."

"I left to meet with a friend. He came to the back door and we only spoke for a short amount of time. He was only *a friend*," Mei said fiercely.

Madame Lui was listening to the conversation with her mouth pressed tight in disapproval. As soon as they were finished, Madame Lui came and took hold of her elbow. With a sharp tug, she led her foster daughter from the room.

"That was the young man that Constable Wu assumed was you," Yue-ying realized.

Huang nodded and stood to face her. "And I don't believe Mei and her friend merely talked."

Mei's corroboration wasn't strictly necessary, but it served as another piece of a puzzle that was rapidly coming together. While the young courtesan was enjoying a tryst with her secret lover, anyone from the banquet could have slipped away and then returned.

"What does this have to do with the strange characters on the wall?"

"They aren't strange at all, actually. It's called *Idu* script," he explained. "Used by the Kingdom of Silla as well as the other two kingdoms of the Goryeo empire. The characters look just like our *hanzi* characters, but they have a different sound and meaning. An unwanted visitor came to the Hundred Songs that night and Huilan excused herself to her room, hoping to flee."

Yue-ying's eyes grew wide. "The writing on the wall—"

"Reveals the name of Huilan's murderer. She was trapped in her room and helpless, yet still she managed to expose him before joining her ancestors."

"I think you're wrong about one thing," Yue-ying said after he read the name out to her along with the accusation Huilan had inscribed. "She wasn't a helpless victim. Huilan's family had been murdered by slave traders. It wasn't enough for her to rescue the child. The silver I found in the temple was payment. She was demanding money to remain silent. That's why she said nothing. Huilan meant to bleed him dry before making her escape. And then she would have denounced him anyway." Yue-ying studied the calligraphy before them. "She wanted revenge and now she finally has it."

CHAPTER TWENTY-NINE

A SIZABLE CROWD gathered by the lone willow tree in the corner of the East Market. The sentence had been proclaimed the day before. Ma Jun, the former East Market Commissioner, was charged with corruption, smuggling, kidnapping and murder. His appointment was a lowly one without much in the way of wealth or status, but Ma had turned the East Market into his domain, growing rich by taking bribes and a cut of the illegal profits. But he'd become greedy, letting in bandits and outlaws indiscriminately until he had no choice but to become one of them to maintain order. The bandits who had been executed a year ago were Ma Jun's hirelings, sent to protect his interests by silencing Hana.

Huang waited near the front of the crowd. Beside him stood Tse-kang, Huilan's young scholar. A solemn look pulled at the corners of his mouth and eyes, aging him beyond his years.

"If only we had left the city together earlier," the young man said softly.

"Huilan sacrificed herself so that he would be brought to justice," Huang told him.

Justice sounded more honorable than bloody revenge, but either way Ma Jun would pay for his crimes. It was only fitting that Huang see this to the end since Huilan's eyes were closed forever. This case had taken on such meaning for him. It wasn't only because of how it had brought Yue-ying and him together, nor was it his new-found attachment to the inhabitants of the Pingkang li.

It was because he had experienced his own encounter with death when Gao had spared him. He didn't deserve to survive any more than Huilan had deserved to die. For that, he owed. This was atonement.

A murmur rose over the crowd. The prison wagon had appeared at the end of the street. Ma Jun was locked in a cage, the top of it closing over his shoulders to leave his head exposed. A vertical placard was attached to the iron collar around his neck, detailing his crimes in bold black characters. He had been stripped of his clothing other than a pale gray tunic that clung to his body. As the wagon proceeded he was pelted by rocks and rubbish.

Once the procession reached the square, the executioner opened the lock and positioned the prisoner onto his knees before the crowd. The charges and sentence were read aloud once more for all to hear.

Huang watched Ma Jun's face as the executioner removed the placard and tossed it in the dirt. The former official's eyes were flat and lifeless as the heavy broadsword swung downward. His head fell like a stone to the dirt while his body remained kneeling. It slumped over a moment after.

Tse-kang looked away, his hand pressed to his mouth. Huang reached out to clasp his shoulder.

"It's done," he said quietly. "Huilan's spirit is finally at peace."

BAI *FUREN* AND MINGYU had chosen a day in the late summer, after the downpour of the plum rains and past the height of the banquet season. The first part of the celebration occurred in the Pingkang li as Lord Bai came with the wedding sedan to retrieve his bride. The ladies of the quarter came out into the streets to watch as the wedding procession went by accompanied by the crash of cymbals and gongs. Was this not every singsong girl and courtesan's dream?

After a brief ceremony at the Lotus Palace, Yue-ying said farewell to Mingyu, Old Auntie, Madame Sun and the other courtesans and disappeared into the sedan to be taken to her new family.

The true celebration was at the Bai mansion where over three hundred guests had been invited. Yue-ying missed most of it as she was ushered away to the wedding chamber. The bridal bed was carved from dark wood with a canopy arching overhead and draped with red sheets. A lantern was placed on either side of it to represent their union.

She was waiting for hours before Bai Huang came to the wedding chamber, escorted by a rowdy entourage from the banquet. Once they were alone and the well-wishers had retreated, he gently removed the pins from her hair. His hand paused on the hairpin ornamented with a luminous moonstone, which he had gifted to her once more upon their engagement.

As he pulled it away her hair fell to her shoulders. It was the first time Yue-ying had truly felt naked before him. He removed the rest of her clothes without a word, with only the sound of their breathing punctuating the silence. They made love with the glow of the twin lanterns surrounding them.

Afterward she put her arms around him and pressed her lips to his throat, so filled with emotion that she was afraid to look at him. The act of coupling was different, very different, with a husband.

But the night was far from over. An hour later, Yue-ying lay on her stomach, head rested on her arms while Bai Huang traced a character onto her back.

"Do it again," she implored. "Slower this time."

He obliged her. His fingertip made a stroke across her spine, followed by two short dabs beneath it, then she lost track as his touch danced over her. She was squirming by the time he finished. It tickled.

"I can't figure it out," she confessed.

"It's the character for 'ai'."

Love.

She twisted around to face him. "Why is it so complicated?"

He smiled lazily, lowering himself beside her and propping himself up on one elbow. "Because love is complicated."

"I didn't even know that character before," she complained.

"You do now."

Her heart did a little leap as he bent and placed a kiss onto her shoulder. Then he touched a hand to her cheek, looking at her as if he never wanted to turn away.

"You're beautiful, wife."

When he said it like that, she felt beautiful. There was no need for her to flinch or avert her eyes. She didn't need to hide any longer.

"You're beautiful, husband."

At first she had thought of him only as that: a handsome face, clothed in wealth and privilege, as far removed from her world as the moon and stars. But she was here and he was here, and he was smiling at her as if she were something infinitely precious.

This was the beginning of things. She finally believed it in her heart.

"Write another one," she implored.

"With pleasure," her husband replied with a mischievous grin.

He blew out the lanterns, one and then the other, and Yue-ying laughed as his clever fingers drew a new pattern tenderly over her skin.

* * * * *

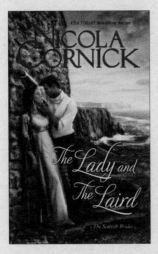

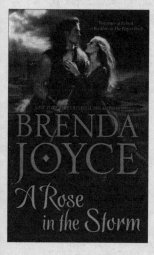

REQUEST YOUR FREE BOOKS!

2 FREE NOVELS
FROM THE ROMANCE COLLECTION
PLUS 2 FREE GIFTS!

YES! Please send me 2 FREE novels from the Romance Collection and my 2 FREE gifts (gifts are worth about $10). After receiving them, if I don't wish to receive any more books, I can return the shipping statement marked "cancel." If I don't cancel, I will receive 4 brand-new novels every month and be billed just $6.24 per book in the U.S. or $6.74 per book in Canada. That's a savings of at least 22% off the cover price. It's quite a bargain! Shipping and handling is just 50¢ per book in the U.S. and 75¢ per book in Canada.* I understand that accepting the 2 free books and gifts places me under no obligation to buy anything. I can always return a shipment and cancel at any time. Even if I never buy another book, the two free books and gifts are mine to keep forever.

194/394 MDN F4XY

Name _____ (PLEASE PRINT) _____

Address _____ Apt. # _____

City _____ State/Prov. _____ Zip/Postal Code _____

Signature (if under 18, a parent or guardian must sign)

Mail to the Harlequin® Reader Service:
IN U.S.A.: P.O. Box 1867, Buffalo, NY 14240-1867
IN CANADA: P.O. Box 609, Fort Erie, Ontario L2A 5X3

Want to try two free books from another line?
Call 1-800-873-8635 or visit www.ReaderService.com.

* Terms and prices subject to change without notice. Prices do not include applicable taxes. Sales tax applicable in N.Y. Canadian residents will be charged applicable taxes. Offer not valid in Quebec. This offer is limited to one order per household. Not valid for current subscribers to the Romance Collection or the Romance/Suspense Collection. All orders subject to credit approval. Credit or debit balances in a customer's account(s) may be offset by any other outstanding balance owed by or to the customer. Please allow 4 to 6 weeks for delivery. Offer available while quantities last.

Your Privacy—The Harlequin® Reader Service is committed to protecting your privacy. Our Privacy Policy is available online at www.ReaderService.com or upon request from the Harlequin Reader Service.

We make a portion of our mailing list available to reputable third parties that offer products we believe may interest you. If you prefer that we not exchange your name with third parties, or if you wish to clarify or modify your communication preferences, please visit us at www.ReaderService.com/consumerschoice or write to us at Harlequin Reader Service Preference Service, P.O. Box 9062, Buffalo, NY 14269. Include your complete name and address.

ROM13R

JULIETTE MILLER

In the midst of a Clan divided, two unlikely allies must confront the passion that binds them...and the treachery that may part them forever.

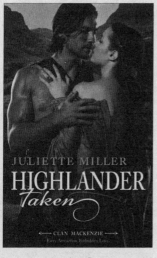

JULIETTE MILLER

HIGHLANDER
Taken

◄— CLAN MACKENZIE —►
Fiery Attraction. Forbidden Love.

To secure her family's alliance with the powerful Clan Mackenzie, Stella Morrison has no choice but to wed the notorious Kade Mackenzie. Unable to ignore the whispers that surround him, she resigns herself to a marriage in name only. Yet as the fierce warrior strips away Stella's doubt one seductive touch at a time, burgeoning desire forces her to question all she holds as truth.

Leading a rebellious army should have been Kade's greatest challenge...until conquering the heart of his reluctant bride becomes an all-consuming need. Now more than ever, he's determined to find victory both on the battlefield and in the bedchamber. But the quest for triumph unleashes a dark threat, and this time, only love may prove stronger than danger.

Available wherever books are sold!

Be sure to connect with us at:
Harlequin.com/Newsletters
Facebook.com/HarlequinBooks
Twitter.com/HarlequinBooks

HARLEQUIN® HQN™
www.Harlequin.com

PHJM767